The Cotton Flower

To Jeff and Pat
Two wonderful
friends and dance buddies
whom, of late, I've
reconnected with and
grown to love being
with. Hope you enjoy
reading about the
Cotton Flower. Cliff.

The Cotton Flower

Copyrighted Material

The Cotton Flower

Copyright © 2022 by Cliff Wilkerson.
All Rights Reserved.

No part of this publication may be reproduced, stored in a retrieval system or transmitted, in any form or by any means—electronic, mechanical, photocopying, recording, or otherwise—without prior written permission from the publisher, except for the inclusion of brief quotations in a review.

For information about this title or to order other books and/
or electronic media, contact the publisher:

Douglas C. Wilkerson, M. D.
readclif@protonmail.com

Library of Congress Control Number: 2020901949

ISBNs
978-1-7341600-2-4 (softcover)
978-1-7341600-3-1 (eBook)

Printed in the United States of America

Cover design: 1106 Design
Interior design: 1106 Design

This is a work of fiction. Names, characters, places, and incidents either are the product of the author's imagination or are used fictitiously. Any resemblances to actual person, living or dead, events, or locales are entirely coincidental.

Dedicated to:
Velma Rhodella
My mother

Contents

Chapter 1	Ruth	1
Chapter 2	Ida	18
Chapter 3	Bob	30
Chapter 4	Ruth	41
Chapter 5	Chester	50
Chapter 6	Ruth	56
Chapter 7	Ruth	71
Chapter 8	Ruth	87
Chapter 9	Ida	93
Chapter 10	Ruth	101
Chapter 11	Chester	111
Chapter 12	Bob	121
Chapter 13	Ruth	130
Chapter 14	Ida	140
Chapter 15	Chester	146
Chapter 16	Bob	152
Chapter 17	Ruth	163
Chapter 18	Bob	170
Chapter 19	Ruth	177
Chapter 20	Charlie	190
Chapter 21	Ruth	200
Chapter 22	Ruth	214

Chapter 23	Chester	224
Chapter 24	Ruth	231
Chapter 25	Ruth	246
Chapter 26	Chester	256
Chapter 27	Ruth	265
Chapter 28	Ruth	272
Chapter 29	Bob	282
Chapter 30	Chester	293
Chapter 31	Ruth	305
Chapter 32	Ruth	315
Chapter 33	Ruth	322
Chapter 34	Ida	333
Chapter 35	Chester	342
Chapter 36	Chester	349
Chapter 37	Ruth	359
Chapter 38	Chester	364
Chapter 39	Ruth	370
Chapter 40	Ida	376
Chapter 41	Bob	383
Chapter 42	Chester	390
Chapter 43	Ruth	397
Chapter 44	Ruth	403
Chapter 45	Ruth	407
Acknowledgments		419
About the Author		421

CHAPTER 1

Ruth

Distant lightning flickered, playing across clouds that hovered, dark and threatening, across the western horizon. Ruth watched from the side porch of the house, keeping one eye on the sky and another on a quilt piece she was sewing, each stitch so small it could have been done on a treadle sewing machine. Or so her mother had said. An air-and-sea battle raged on one end of the porch's cement slab, as her nine-year-old son brought up the low-pitched boom of battleship guns from deep in his throat. His nasal twang of rapid-fire machine guns peppered her nerves. A faint rumble of thunder sent shivers down Ruth's spine, and, losing concentration, she pricked her finger. "Shit fire and save the matches," she mumbled.

"What?" he demanded, interrupting the air attack on a fleet of Japanese ships.

"Nothing," she snapped. "I just stuck my finger with a needle. You just mind your own business." She tried to keep her eyes off the clouds, but another low rumble of thunder commanded her attention, and she laid the quilt piece aside. "I wish you could find something else to do than make that awful noise," she complained, fidgeting nervously with a strand of her long black hair.

"Okay," Charlie said. Then he drew back his arm and let fly one of his small paper airplanes. It sailed out into the yard, where it caught an updraft of air and glided toward the milk house. Giving a whoop of joy, he ran after the plane, his bare feet kicking up plumes of dust from an oft-traveled dirt path.

"Thank you," she called after him.

She watched the plane flutter and lose altitude; it dove into the middle of a sticker patch filled with those hard, two-pronged barbs that looked like the horns of a goat. When she was Charlie's age and running barefoot, she'd punctured the bottom of her feet more than once on the spikes lurking in the grass or dirt. Charlie came to a halt when he reached the edge of the threatening, hurtful patch and yelled, "Could you get it for me, Mama? Please?"

"Charlie Scarsdale, get your shoes on, and fetch it yourself," she yelled back but then, relenting, walked off the porch into the stickers and retrieved the downed plane.

She held it for a moment while Charlie danced from one foot to the other at the edge of the patch, yelling, "Throw it to me, Mama. Come on, throw it to me."

She drew back and sailed it straight at her son, but it turned and, as if she were the enemy, dove at her head. She ducked. The aircraft landed at her feet.

Charlie exploded into laughter. *Do it again. Do it again,*" he screamed.

She grabbed it up and ran at him, making a loud humming noise as she bore down on him.

CHAPTER I ♦ RUTH

He turned and fled. "Can't catch me. Can't catch me," he yelled back over his shoulder.

Ruth caught him and, with her free arm, encircled his waist and twirled him around and around, mimicking the whine of an airplane engine.

He squealed, "*Put me down. Put me down*," flailing his legs and arms like a four-bladed windmill.

Out of breath, she came to rest on the cement slab of the porch, holding Charlie close to her in one arm as, with the other, she gently flew the airplane in the direction of his naval ships and airplanes. It nosed its way into the fleet and sent two ships onto their sides. Then, she wrapped both arms around him and held him tight. It felt good to hold him close for a moment, to smell the little-boy sweat mixed with the odor of her papa's hayloft and the more pungent fragrance of what he'd stepped in near the chicken house. His sun-browned face was all smiles, and his intense blue eyes sparkled with fun. Thick blond strands of curly hair tickled her nose as she buried her face in his neck. Then her eyes filled with tears. She had not played like this with Charlie in weeks—hardly once since they had arrived on the farm. She'd been too tired and listless from thinking of this awful war raging across the world and of Chester, overseas somewhere in the South Pacific, being shot at by the Japs. Might even be killed before it was all over. She shuddered at the thought of being a widow, held Charlie even closer, and let a few tears escape.

"Mama! You're squeezing me too tight." Charlie wriggled in her arms, pushing at her.

Darn little wiggle-wart hadn't been still since the first time she'd felt him kick against her ribs. She tickled him under the arms and let him go, wiping her eyes with the back of her hand so he wouldn't see the tears. "Get on with you, so I can get some work done."

Now free from her arms, Charlie said, "Can I walk over and see Will and Carl? Ride back with Grandmother and Grandpa?"

"No! It's getting ready to storm."

"Aw, come on. I can get to Aunt Pearl's house before it rains."

The wind kicked up. Flashes of lightning, closer now, drew Ruth's gaze to the darkening skyline and then to the weathervane on top of Papa's barn roof that had begun spinning crazily. Deprived of the sun's light, a false dusk descended, and all the setting hens began disappearing into the henhouse. Her heartbeat raced as fear rose into her chest with the quickness of a helium balloon escaping some child's hand. "I'm afraid there's a bad storm coming. I'm going to call and see if Mama and Papa will come home right now." Her voice came out in a little-girl whine she sometimes used, but hated, though she detested even more the need for her mother nearby when it stormed. Ruth knew there would be little relief; her mother was as frightened of storms as she. Had been since Ruth was thirteen. Memory of that time during WWI always blew in with every black, lightning-scarred storm like the one now closer on the horizon.

She remembered being a skinny thirteen-year-old sitting on this very same porch with her mother, papa, and two sisters, talking about God only knows what. She'd been the first to take notice of a very small cloud blowing up from the southwest, traveling fast in a clear sky. The air became deathly still for a moment; and when she pointed at the cloud, everyone on the porch stopped talking. Then, a noise like an approaching freight train roared toward her. The train tracks were three miles away; she'd known this was no train.

Three things always stayed vivid in her memories: her mother's scream, the sight, less than a half a mile away, of the Fraziers' house exploding in all directions like a dandelion puff that she sometimes playfully blew into the air, and the snaking tail of that little cloud whipping about as it left the Frazier place and came skipping across the pasture heading right for her. Ruth firmly believed that she would have sailed out across the yard if her papa hadn't gripped her arm so tightly that it hurt as he pulled her and sister Pearl to the cellar. Mama and Joan were right behind them.

CHAPTER 1 ♦ RUTH

The storm over and her standing outside by the cellar door, it was weird to see an empty spot where the chicken house had stood, its boards scattered all across the yard and over into the pasture. Some of the laying hens lay dead while others that had survived pecked at the ground as if nothing had happened.

"Thank the good Lord the house didn't go," Mother had said.

"Amen," Papa added. "And that the barn's still standing, too."

Since then, she had always dreaded seeing black clouds appearing on the horizon. During the dust-bowl years when the billowing dust storms appeared on the horizon, she'd felt the same panic even as she knew it was silly to be afraid.

Finished musing, she looked up at Charlie staring at her, a shadow of uncertainty crossing his face.

"What's wrong, Charlie?"

"You're looking funny."

"I was just remembering something from a long time ago," she said, rising from the porch and patting him comfortingly on his rear as she passed him. "You run down and shut the henhouse door while I go inside and close all the windows. Hurry back. I want us in the cellar when the storm hits."

"What about Spot?"

"You don't have to worry about that old hound. He's probably been down in the pasture chasing jackrabbits and is hightailing it back to the yard right now to crawl under the wash house."

She took another look at the nearing thunderheads and the play of lightning across the sky before going inside and closing windows in her and Charlie's bedroom. She closed those in her papa's bedroom, and then the dining- and living-room windows. As she hurried into Mother's bedroom, thunder cracked, shaking the house. She pulled the last window down so hard that she was thankful it didn't shatter.

Back in the kitchen, she spoke harshly to Charlie, who was now sitting at the kitchen table with his paper planes and boats he'd rescued from the sharp gusts of wind that promised a coming storm. "Stay there—right there—while I ring Pearl to see if the folks will start home now." At the boxy, party-line phone, its long mouthpiece jutting out as if reaching for her words, she raised the receiver and gave two long and three short turns of the handle. Waiting a moment, she repeated the ring. Wind blowing in from the open kitchen door set the nearby curtains to dancing. Another crack of thunder was followed by a flash of lightning that seared the sky and left behind the fresh, clean smell that follows a nearby lightning strike.

Her sister Pearl finally answered, but the electrical storm set off loud crackles on the party line and interrupted Pearl's words, causing them to break up into fragments of sound. Another predatory growl of thunder drew Ruth's eyes to the window next to the phone. The darkening purplish-black clouds were turning day into night. Brilliant lightning played endlessly across the huge front moving in.

Panic, stark and beyond reason, now tore at her chest, and she hung up the phone, cutting off Pearl's garbled words. Grabbing a newspaper and matches, she rushed to the door, yelling, "Charlie, get to the cellar. Right now." Slamming the door behind her, she rushed around the house right on the heels of Charlie. The temperature dropped, and a brisk, cold wind pushed clouds of dust swirling across the yard.

She and Charlie made it to the door of the cellar as the first drops of rain began to pelt them. The wind quickened, whipping at the leaves of new cotton in the field next to the cellar. Glancing in the direction of a lightning flash, she saw the weathervane now spinning like an airplane propeller She grabbed the cellar-door handle and pulled it as a powerful gust caught it like a sail, slammed it open, and scraped painfully at the skin on her fingers. Charlie eyes were wide with fright.

Keeping him close, she hurried down the cellar steps, below the reach of the wind, and put a match to the newspaper she had rolled into a torch as she ran. Thrusting the blaze into each corner of the entrance, she cremated any black widow spiders that might lurk there, and then pulled Charlie past her and into the darkness below. A few large raindrops spattered against her face. The rope strained taut as she used it to haul the door closed. Then she descended into the damp cellar, the smell of mildew and mold thick about her. The dying light of the burning newspaper on the floor helped her locate the coal-oil lamp always kept in the cellar for moments like this. Ruth struck a match that flickered in the dark, causing shadows to dance on the walls. Rain splashed heavily against the door as she lifted the lamp's globe and put a match to the wick, filling the cellar with the heavy smell of sulfur and burning coal oil.

Straight-backed oak chairs, too rickety for everyday use in the kitchen, sat next to a homemade bench built along the back end of the narrow concrete room. Shelves that lined two walls were filled with rows of empty jars and some of last year's uneaten canned fruit and vegetables. She stood, trembling, catching her breath, calming the rush of her heart. With the palm of her hand, she wiped away the raindrops that had pelted her face. She shivered and wondered why she hadn't had the presence of mind to pull on one of Papa's or Mother's old sweaters before charging out the door. Charlie pulled two chairs into the middle of the cellar floor, and she collapsed into one of them. Charlie sat down beside her in the other one, and she put an arm around his shoulder. "Come here, close to me," she said, pulling at him.

"Mama, you're shuddering." Charlie stared at her, wide-eyed, his breathing heavy and fast.

"I'm just a little winded. And cold," she said. The everyday, blue, polka-dot housedress she had on was thin and destined soon for the rag bin, and the old, sensible, down at the heels work shoes she'd borrowed from her mother.

A gust of wind rattled the door, and Charlie pressed closer.

"We're all right now. Don't worry," she said, but she could feel her pulse beating in her throat. She swiped at some of the rain's wetness on her arms and then hugged Charlie even closer.

She was startled when Charlie half-whispered, "I wish Dad were here."

Ruth did not want to talk about Chester right now, afraid she might cry. "I do, too. But since he's not, how about I tell you a story? Goldilocks and the Three Bears? Or the Three Little Pigs, maybe?"

"Naw. Will Jr. and Carl told me those a dozen times. Tell me something about Dad. You don't say much about him anymore."

"I know one about Beauty and the Beast. Or Cinderella." Ruth's voice broke as she felt the choking sadness and fear that Charlie's reminder of Chester had stirred.

A loud crash of thunder sounded outside, and Charlie peered nervously at the cellar door. His lip trembled. "Please tell me a story about Dad."

Ruth stiffened. "I don't want to do that right now, Charlie. Maybe another time."

"Aw, please, Mama? You never want to talk about Dad. Nobody wants to talk about him."

Ruth felt hot even as she shivered at the prospect of talking about Chester. She brushed at her forehead, where drops of sweat had gathered, and shook her head, swatting her hair against Charlie's mouth. He brushed it away, pulling out one hair that had caught in his teeth, causing a pinprick of pain. She yelped, and he pulled away. Tears finally started to run down her face, not so much at the pain but for thoughts of Chester.

"MaMaaa! You scared me." Then, tilting his head and looking more curious than guilty, he said, "You're crying."

"It just startled me when you pulled my hair," she said. Lately she had been pulling out the hateful gray strands that were beginning to show up in her shoulder-length, coal-black hair, and it didn't hurt enough to yelp about.

CHAPTER I ✦ RUTH

"I'm sorry." Charlie repeated, his own eyes threatening to fill with tears.

"No, Charlie. I'm the one who's sorry. I didn't mean to scare you."

"That's okay. But I still want you to tell me a story about Dad."

A wave of sadness broke over her. Although Chester wasn't anything she wanted to talk about right now, she had to put her fear and sadness away to talk to Charlie. And he wouldn't stop pestering her until she did. "Okay. I don't want to talk about him being overseas fighting in the war. How about if I tell you about the first time I went out with your dad? That OK?"

He nodded and settled in close to her again.

At least that was a long time ago and was more funny than sad. She'd have to leave out parts of the story and tell Charlie only things he would find amusing. "Well. Your grandpa Scarsdale had taken a load of cotton into town and left Chester to do some chores. He finished the work and then hitched up a young gelding that really hadn't been well-broken to the buggy yet and came tearing over to our place. He drove buggies too fast back then. Like he drives his cars too fast now."

She paused, staring into the cone of light burning at the center of the lantern globe, and breathed in the raw smell of burning coal oil. Remembering back, she said, "He insisted I go on a buggy ride with him. Mother and Papa were both busy doing something in Hobart—I don't rightly recall what—and I was there watching out for my sisters—your Aunt Pearl and Aunt Joan—and my brother, your Uncle Winston, who was just a few years younger than you are now. I figured that Pearl, who was twelve, could manage till I got back. Joan and Winston, thank goodness, were down in the hayloft or they'd have put up a fuss to go with us. Pearl tried to tell me I'd be in big trouble if I went with your daddy, but I didn't pay her any mind. You get to be fourteen, and it's hard to tell you anything."

Chester and his two brothers had a reputation with the girls that Ruth knew about; every girl from twelve to sixteen who lived within five miles of the Scarsdale farm had some story to tell about them. And some of those tales didn't include the word "no" in them. Her papa had told his girls he'd strap them within an inch of their lives if he ever caught them with one of the Scarsdale boys.

Charlie pulled at her sleeve, dragging her back into the story. "What'd he look like back then, Mama?"

"Why, he was six feet tall, but he always slouched a little, so he didn't look it. Still does, as you know. He was a year older than me, fifteen, and he had this nice head of black hair. You've seen your daddy only after he was bald. Back then, he had lots of hair. And those big blue eyes. Just like yours. They could almost look right through you and know what you were thinking about him." She laughed and shook her head, and Charlie put up a hand protectively, warding off another mouthful of hair.

"You've got brown eyes, Mama. So, I'm just like my dad, then. Not you."

I sure hope you're not just like your dad, she thought. *There're things about him—I never want you to grow up just like him.* "There is a way you're like him. "He always had dirt in that little notch under his neck." She outlined with her finger the depression under Charlie's chin where his neck met his chest. "Just like you would if I didn't keep after you. I don't think he knew any better. Your Granny Scarsdale wasn't exactly the kind to care about such things." She reached down and stuck her finger inside the rip in the left knee of his overalls. "And he always had one or both the knees out of his overalls. Just like you."

Charlie laughed and swatted her hand away. "That tickled," he squealed as he jumped to his feet and backed away.

"Okay. Okay. I won't do it again." She reached out to him. "Come sit down, and I'll finish the story." Looking past him in the dim light of the lantern, she saw movement in the corner of the cellar. "Oh, God, Charlie—there's a mouse."

Index finger pointed like a gun, Charlie walked to the corner of the cellar and yelled, "Bang!" as he stepped on an insect scampering

CHAPTER I ♦ RUTH

on many legs toward the safety of a crack. "Isn't nothing but one of them thousand-leggers," he bragged, "and I got him with the first shot." The chair groaned as he flopped down and looked up at her. "It's okay now, Mama."

Relieved, the stricture in Ruth's throat relaxed. That had been one of the things back then that drew her so to Chester, his ability to do things like Charlie had just done. Keep her safe from mice, thousand-leggers, and rattlesnakes. But that had changed over time. With Chester prone to take off sometimes and not be seen for days, she'd not felt so safe being married to him. Still, she couldn't stop loving him, no matter what. Even last year, when he'd gone missing for a week without any word, she couldn't get mad enough to stop loving him.

"Thank you, Charlie. I really appreciate you killing that old thousand-legger."

"You're welcome. But did you get into trouble, going on a buggy ride with Dad?"

Clearing her throat, she swallowed hard and went on. Now that she'd started, it didn't seem as hard talking about Chester as she'd imagined. "Get in trouble? Well, yes, I did. But be patient. I'll tell about that later." She smoothed out her apron and picked at a thread that lay across one pocket. "I swore Pearl to secrecy on penalty of severe torture and violent death." Ruth made her voice deep and threatening, crooked her fingers into talons, and pinched at Charlie's arm.

He flinched away in mock terror but grinned from ear to ear. "You aren't all that scary," he taunted. "What about Uncle Winston and Aunt Joan?"

"I said that, when they came to the house, Pearl should tell them I'd run over to the neighbors to borrow something. And then I climbed in that buggy with your dad. He drove us over to Tallchief Mountain, the same as you can see from the front porch." Remembering back to that ride, she felt a shiver run down her spine. He had that horse running most of the way. Chester was hard on his pa's horses, one of the reasons her own papa never liked him all that much. Chester was a wild one and a Scarsdale, his pa coming from Kentucky people who had a mean streak in them. There'd even been some feuding amongst his and another Kentucky family that made Pa Scarsdale light out for the territories. But that wasn't anything for a boy Charlie's age to know.

"We climbed around in the rocks. Lucky one of us didn't get bit by a diamondback rattler. They were thicker'n fleas back then. We saw nary a one, thank the Lord."

"Did he hold your hand?" Charlie giggled and grabbed her hand. "I'll bet he held your hand, didn't he?"

"Why, Charlie Scarsdale. I wouldn't've let him do that. It was a first date. You wouldn't get so forward on a first date, now, would you?" She slapped playfully at his hand.

The truth about things that went on between her and Chester that day was not something you told a boy Charlie's age. Or anyone else for that matter. Chester's hands had been all over her up there among the rocks, slyly seeking out those private places he had no business finding. She had fended him off, scolding him about his busy hands and wondering if she had been wise to drive off with him. But then, before anything really bad happened, a fast-moving thunderstorm blew in. Much faster than today. She was so busy warding Chester off that she hadn't realized it was threatening until there was a forked flash of lightning and a crack of thunder. It had been all the warning she got before a torrent of water poured over them. It scared her to death, but with nowhere to run, she'd just stood with Chester, their faces upturned, the water soaking them. The thin dress she'd worn let her skin show through and, as if hypnotized by the steady fall of rain and too scared to move, she'd stayed still, her eyes closed, as Chester's hands undid the top buttons of her dress, letting her breasts fall free. He had sucked rainwater from her nipples, and it felt so good, it was if her fears were melting and flowing away with the mountain

CHAPTER I ✦ RUTH

runoff that ran in rivulets at their feet. Then he'd begun to rub her thighs, slick with water, yet burning with his touch as he moved even higher.

A slash of lightning, so bright she had seen it through closed lids, stabbed into a gnarled oak a hundred yards upslope from where they stood, and it was as if an ax had split it from crown to base. Then a crack of thunder jarred her. Ruth screamed. She jerked away from Chester and ran to the rig where the young horse was standing with his head bowed to the wind and rain. Chester stood there on the mountain slope, laughing at her like a madman, slapping his thigh. As she fumbled with the buttons on her blouse, she cried, guilty that she had let him go so far but hating that she had run away. Her head felt light, and, when she looked up at Chester, after-images of the lightning flashes spotted the mountainside with small green polka dots.

Chester ran down the mountain then, jumping from one slippery rock to the other, splashing through puddles until he reached her, and then, swooping her up in his arms, set her down in the buggy seat. He grabbed the reins and sent the horse slogging through the muck toward the road. Neither spoke, though she stole enough glances in his direction to see that he was barely looking where he was driving but instead keeping her in his eyes that were bright and full of mischief.

"Come on, Mama. What are you thinking about? Is that all that happened?"

"No. We got caught in a thunderstorm, and, on the way back home, the buggy got stuck in the mud. Your daddy and I had to get out to push. By the time we got the buggy moving again, we were muddy as your grandpa's two fat pigs."

Charlie jumped up and squealed with delight, turning in a circle, and then settling in beside her again. "Two fat pigs. Two muddy fat pigs," he chanted.

"Oh, you like that idea, do you? Well, that wasn't the worst of it. After we climbed back in the buggy, it got stuck again, and we climbed back out into the mud. Your daddy and I were behind that old buggy pushing as hard as we could when, all of a sudden, it came unstuck, and that crazy young gelding ran off with the buggy, and there was your daddy and me running down the road after him. Just before I caught up with your daddy and that horse he'd finally caught, down I went, flat on my face in the mud. I just lay there, not knowing what else to do. Your daddy tied the horse to a bush and came around to help me up, but he started laughing again so hard he couldn't see, and I was so mad I grabbed him by the legs and set him down beside me. Then we just wallowed around together in the mud."

Her face grew warm with the memory. With the rain swatting at them, they'd rolled to the side of the road, and Chester had ended on top, her with legs spread and him fumbling at his overall straps with one hand, trying to pull them off his shoulders, while he pulled at her panties with the other. When he got his britches down to his knees, there was only one white spot left on him, and it looked big and dangerous as papa's shotgun. It was aimed right at her. A spasm of guilt and shame at what she was allowing made her push away from him. She grabbed a fistful of mud and let fly with it. Then there was not one spot of him that wasn't muddy, and his shotgun went limp as an old rope. He looked as surprised as a hound caught sucking eggs.

"I want you to know we was really such a mess that your daddy wouldn't let us get back in the buggy. Made us both walk back to the house."

Charlie was lying across her lap now, tears rolling down his face and laughter shaking his young body. He slapped his thighs, too, just like she remembered Chester doing. Gasping for breath, he sat up and shook his head at her. "I bet Grandmother and Grandpa sure gave you what-for."

"They wanted to be mad. They really did. But when we walked into the yard, leading that wore-out horse pulling the mud-spattered buggy, we looked like a couple of drowned rats. Winston jumped from one leg to the other and laughed his fool head off while he pointed a finger at us. The rest of the family just stood there and laughed. I think that was the worst thing they could have done to hurt me, anyway." She paused, remembering. "I think Pa gave me a couple of swats with his razor strap—you've seen it hanging out there in the washhouse—just to let me know he was good for his word. But he was always a pushover for us girls. It was Mother who harped at me for the next month. Funny, though, after we got married, she got to liking your daddy. Your grandpa just could never abide him. Said I couldn't see him again."

"I don't think Grandpa likes me all that much, either, Mama. He don't ever say much but to tell me not to do something or another—not gather the eggs because I might break one, not milk Isabelle 'cause I might make her milk dry up, or not ride one of his horses 'cause it might throw me off and break my neck."

"Now, Charlie. Your grandpa has got a lot of worry on his mind, having the two of us here living with him and your grandmother. And he never was too good with boys, particularly after your Uncle Brian passed away." Charlie was partly right, of course. Papa and Mother mostly living hand to mouth, Papa didn't really want her and Charlie living there with them. She wasn't so sure about Mother; she held in her feelings better than Papa did. Papa took his dislike of Chester out on Charlie.

"Grandmother Ida doesn't seem to like me all that much, either," Charlie mumbled. "She hardly ever says anything to me."

"Nonsense, Charlie. That's just the way she is to everybody."

"But what about you and Daddy? Did you go out with him again?"

"Well, not exactly right away. But your grandpa couldn't do anything about it when your daddy outbid everybody else at the box supper to win my box. Papa even entered the bidding himself at the end, when he saw your daddy was going to get it. I never did know where the money come from, but your daddy had enough to keep raising the bid on Papa.

"At two dollars and a dime, when Papa didn't bid right away, that old auctioneer called out, 'Going once.' He waited a second, givin' Papa a chance to bid higher. I was so excited and breathless that I dug my fingernails into my palms so hard that they left marks.

"At 'going twice,' the room was so quiet you could have heard a pin drop, and it seemed to me that not a person in the schoolhouse breathed while they waited. I'd never been happier in my whole life when I finally heard, 'Going three times, and sold! To that handsome young man with the bluest eyes I ever saw.'"

Your Grandpa looked like he'd swallowed a green persimmon, and he was so upset he up and walked outside, slamming the door. The crowd clapped for your Daddy, and all his friends jumped up and down and cheered. My Uncle John bid on, and won, Sister Pearl's box, and Papa was supposed to bid on sister Joan's. But he was so put out he didn't come back in to bid on it. Bless her heart, she started to cry so hard that Mother had to go outside and shame your grandpa into coming back in. Joan would have been heartbroken if he hadn't bid on her box. He glared at your daddy all through the supper, saying hardly a word to your Aunt Joan—she had tears in her eyes the whole time she and your Grandpa nibbled at the sandwiches she'd helped Mother make."

"He sure did show Grandpa, didn't he?" Charlie eyes glittered just like his daddy's. Ruth grabbed and hugged him.

"Now don't you go saying anything to your grandpa about what I told you. He's still smarting from that, even after all these years. He wouldn't take kindly to being reminded."

Tears again came to her eyes, almost spilling over. She too, was smarting from losing Chester to the war and having to come live with her folks. The late afternoon she arrived at the farm, she had gone out into the thicket and lay under the new spring leaves for most of two hours, the canopy covering her loneliness and sadness. As darkness crept over her hiding place, she crawled over to the edge of the thicket, the darkness still hiding her, but then the three-quarter moon had come up and cast away her protection. Stars had winked on, more stars than anyone could count, adding their light to the moon's glow. She wanted at that moment for all the lights in the sky, and even all those in the world, to blink out, leaving her in total darkness. Of course, it didn't happen. So finally, picking herself up off the ground, she trudged back to the house to face Charlie and her parents. Charlie had been frantic, not knowing where she was, feeling that something was terribly wrong—that she had abandoned him, too. Like his daddy had.

"I won't say anything to him. I promise," Charlie said, his mouth twisting into a one-sided grimace as he stood up. "How much longer we going to have to sit down here?"

Realizing that she no longer heard the wind or the spatter of rain on the cellar door, Ruth walked up the stairs and pushed the door up six inches to peer out. A rooster crowed, as if the restored light that crept in behind the dark clouds was really the dawn of a new day. Throwing the door all the way back, she climbed out, Charlie dogging at her heels. The sun, now low in the west, set the wet mulberry tree's leaves to sparkling.

Charlie ran through the mud, kicking at puddles with his bare feet, and sending up great geysers of water. Barking his fool head off, Spot, the old hound, came tearing up from the wash house and ran circles around Charlie.

The world smelled clean and well-washed, and something inside Ruth felt cleansed a bit as well. Before today, she'd not talked of Chester since they had arrived on the farm, and what she had just told Charlie of a distant and happier time, had released some of the pressure on her sore heart.

Ruth took a deep breath and started walking toward the kitchen. It was time to set the table. Time to mix the cornbread and get it in the oven. Time to peel potatoes. Time to get the pork chops ready to fry. Time to set the water bucket under the cistern pump and begin turning the handle. Time to end another day living on the place she grew up calling home.

It no longer felt like home.

CHAPTER 2

Ida

Ruth nearly had dinner on the table when Ida came back from visiting Pearl; the smell of pork chops sizzling in the iron skillet greeted her at the door. "My, that does smell good," she said and sat down at the table with Bob and Charlie. Ruth forked the meat onto the everyday platter that Ida had been using for thirty years, at least. She liked it, though; the faded roses on the old thing reminded her of her grandmother, who'd given it to her all those years ago.

Ruth set the platter on the table, interrupting Ida's thoughts. After first serving herself the meat, potatoes, and green beans, Ida passed each dish on to Bob, who piled his plate high. When it came Charlie's turn to help himself to the potatoes, he would have followed Bob's example if Ruth hadn't reached out and taken the serving spoon from him.

CHAPTER 2 ♦ IDA

Bob glanced from Ruth to Charlie, pursed his lips, and shook his head. Ida scowled at him, and he turned his sour attention back to his food.

"That's enough, young man," Ruth said. "Just take one spoonful. You can always have seconds if you're still hungry when you finish what's on your plate."

Wasn't that just like men and boys, Ida thought. Her daughter Joan's two little girls, even though they were only two and four years old, had better table manners than Bob or Charlie.

Charlie shrugged his shoulders in resignation and turned to her. "Did you have to go to the cellar, too, Grandmother? Mama and I had to."

"Your Grandpa, me, Pearl, Bill, and the boys were in their cellar for as much as an hour. That was quite a storm."

"It sure was. Mama and I were down there a long time, too. She told me all about her first date with my daddy."

The sour look on Bob's face deepened, and his face flushed. He did not like Chester Scarsdale, and Ida wished Charlie hadn't brought him up, knowing it would drag out hateful words from Bob. "Why don't you tell us about being down in the cellar, Charlie," Ida said before Bob opened his mouth. "Did you see any black widows?"

Charlie looked from her to his grandpa and then at his mother. He stuffed a bite of pork chop in his mouth before beginning his description of what went on during the storm. She didn't like him talking with his mouth full but said nothing. She didn't listen, either, but kept her eyes on him so he'd think she was. She could tell that Bob was about to bust a gut because he was aggravated at having to listen to Charlie. Thank goodness he kept his mouth shut.

She was relieved when they all finished and, since Ruth had cooked, Ida started doing the dishes while Ruth wiped down the stove and table, and pumped the water bucket full. Finished with the kitchen, Ida went to her chair and began sewing a quilt piece. Ruth joined her and began to patch one of Charlie's overall knees. The boy went through more knee patches than anyone else she had ever known. Bob sat near the radio, turned down low, listening to news of a Nazi bombing attack on England. She tried not to listen to all that horror; reminded her too much of her son, Winston, being in Burma. Charlie sat quietly on the floor beside Ruth, rereading the Sunday funnies he'd keep until the next Sunday paper came.

When dark fell, Ida lit two coal-oil lamps and sewed by their weak light. *None of us really have that much to say to one another,* she thought. And if they did, it would be unpleasant. As nine o'clock neared, she stood and said, "Good night," once, before disappearing into her bedroom, a chorus of "Good nights" following her.

Peering at her face, reflected in the mirror and covered in cold cream, Ida was reminded of the photograph of a white-faced female that her soldier son had sent home from that far-off, Japanese-infested Asian country. Burma, she recalled. Using slow, deliberate strokes with a freshly laundered but tattered cloth that once served as a dishtowel, she smoothed the cleansing oil into her skin and then, carefully, wiped it away. Face powder and rouge left a pink smear on the remnant. The uncovered image in the mirror, pressed with worry lines and too much sun, barely resembled the last studio picture taken of her that, for sixteen years, lay abandoned in the bottom of her vanity. She was Ruth's age back then, her skin without the wrinkles that now furrowed it worse than a newly prepared cotton field, her hair black as coal, her brown eyes fixed on something off behind the camera. She had another picture taken with their old box camera a few years later, and she was smiling, shading her eyes with one hand and waving with the other; it was an unhappy wave to Bob as he rode away on one of their horses, she recalled, and then pushed the memory away. She'd not been much happier then than now. Bob was running around on her, and she'd found out. She wanted to brush that memory out of her head. Couldn't be done. From among a collection of brushes and combs, she selected a pink brush with a medley of carved flowers on its back, and, pulling her hair forward over her left shoulder, she brushed through its waist-length fullness, sweeping carefully down through each gray-streaked lock. A tangle, like her bad memory of Bob, pulled at her scalp. She frowned but brushed on.

Finished with her hair, Ida laid her glasses on the bedside table, turned back the covers, and sat on the bed for a moment, looking around her room. Every wall was covered with shelves that held her figurines. Those glass and porcelain figures spoke of her life, held many of her memories. Her eyes fell on the small ceramic boy holding a kite, and pain stabbed her heart, making it hammer with grieving nostalgia.

When he was eight years old, her son, Brian, had bought this kite-flyer for her birthday. Saved the pennies he'd earned from picking cheat-grass heads out of the oats. Tightwad Bob paid him a penny for every hundred head. Little Brian earned himself a dime and used it to buy the present.

Brian was her first thought when she realized Charlie and Ruth were coming to live here with them. It was like a knife in her heart, knowing she would have to see Charlie every day and, seeing him, be reminded of Brian. Sweet boy that Charlie was, she'd still hardened her heart to him, kept him at a distance with her stern looks and criticisms that sprang too quickly from her lips.

Tears threatened Ida's eyes, and, impatient with herself, she wiped roughly at them. Looking at her bare feet, lined with blue veins that wandered up her legs like the ugly meandering of a swollen creek, she slipped into a pair of worn house shoes and stole noiselessly through the darkened house, pausing at the front door. Beside her on the wall, where it had hung for eighteen years, was a picture of her Brian. She'd had an old photo enlarged and tinted so that there was a sense of life to the fourteen-inch figure standing so straight and proud. To be sober was like him; he never smiled for a camera. Those darling knee-length britches and the laced cuffed shirt had been borrowed from her sister, Clara, the only one in the family that could afford those kinds of clothes for her children. There were rosy cheeks on her Brian in the picture, and she looked at him every day to dispel that last picture of him she carried in her nightmares, the pale, drawn face she saw when he was dying.

That boy would be alive today if Bob Choat hadn't been more interested in his money than his own flesh and blood. The day after Brian died, she moved out of their bedroom. She'd never been back.

She reached out in the darkness and caressed the oval frame before moving on to the front porch to sit in the swing suspended from the rafters. The stars were out, and there was a quarter moon. During the storm that day, the rain had washed away all the dust and barnyard odors, and the earth smelled new. Her swing creaked rhythmically as she pushed gently back and forth against the concrete slab with her foot. The throb of uncountable cicadas' nighttime calls quickened and then subsided but never stopped. It was as if something in nature were repeatedly pressing against an accelerator and then slacking off. She thought of it as the motor of the night, pulsing. If it stopped, someone might die. She'd carried that silly thought with her ever since her little brother, Claude, had died. She had to have been fourteen or fifteen at the time.

Her little brother was deathly ill, and her mother asked if she would take her other brothers and sisters outside to sit under the mulberry trees so the night air would help cool their fears. Sitting together on the blanket, talking in quiet and hushed tones, she'd tried to comfort them.

They'd sat there for only a few minutes when they heard Mother scream. Then, for a moment, the thrum of those night creatures ceased. They all sat frozen on the spread blanket. She felt for the hands of two of her sisters and gripped them hard. Her two baby brothers began to cry. Another of her sisters buried her head in Ida's lap to muffle the choking sobs that shook her small body.

Then their papa came out and told them what they already knew. "Your poor little brother has passed on."

The next day, she gathered her brothers and sisters around her and told them that the insects stopped thrumming the moment Claude

CHAPTER 2 • IDA

died. "Time stopped for a moment," she'd said. "And Claude's life stopped, too." She believed it then. They'd believed it, too. To this day, when the cicadas' night sounds stilled, she felt her throat tighten and her pulse quicken.

From up the road, headlights bumped and flickered as a car approached. The road was deep in mud from the downpour this afternoon, and, as the car came near, Ida heard its wheels sucking at the mud. After it passed, she could see one taillight, like a large firefly, blink off and on. She wondered if anyone in the car had seen her there on the porch, dressed in white, like some ghost gliding over the surface of the porch as she gently moved back and forth in the swing. There'd be rumors in town tomorrow if they had. "Saw something on Bob Choat's porch last night. Looked pale as a ghost," they'd say. Then the gossip would start, and, before long, somebody'd be saying, "There's ghosts on the Choat farm. So and So saw one sitting on their front porch."

She heard the rasp of hinges left too long without oil and turned to see her grandson standing there with the screen door held open. He was almost invisible in the dark, owlishly staring at her as she brought the swing to a stop. He was certainly Chester's son and looked like Chester had the first time she saw him. Almost the same age, too, her being twenty-six and Chester ten. That walloping of his little behind she'd given Chester for pushing her youngest girl in the dirt almost caused a fight with his mother. Elly Scarsdale's boys could do no wrong in her eyes.

"What're you doing up, Charlie Scarsdale. It's way past your bedtime." Her lips tightened.

"Can't sleep. Thought I heard someone out here."

"Well, bless you child, you did. It was me. Now get on back in there and go to bed before your mama wonders where you got off to." Ida shooed him with her hands like she would a pesky fly, but the boy remained there, stepping from one bare foot to the other, as if he were standing on hot cement.

"Can't I sit a spell there with you?" He took a half step in her direction and then stopped. "I dreamed about my daddy and woke up. I miss my daddy a lot."

She wavered for a moment. She must do her best to keep at arm's length from this child. It was bad enough that he stirred so many memories of Brian. And of Chester. If she let him get close, it might let all that bottled-up hurt, grief, and hot anger about Brian and her slow-burning guilt over Chester consume her, and then it might never stop burning, destroy what little life she had left. God help her if that happened. Life with Bob was bad enough, and having Ruth and Charlie living here made things worse.

"We're going into town tomorrow. You'll be as cross as a bear if you don't go on back to bed. Now go along." She heard the meanness in her own voice, and it made her want to cry.

"Please."

She took a deep breath and let it out slowly, hoping he would leave, but he remained stock still, waiting, like some small animal caught in the headlights of a car. And she could understand his missing Chester. It had to be hard for him. "Oh, all right, come on. But for just a moment." Her muscles tight, she scooted herself over as far as she could, and Charlie pushed himself up beside her, sending the swing rocking into motion again. The softness of his body against hers burned her. The wild hammering of her heart made her think it might break away from its mooring.

Before either of them spoke again, flickering lights appeared on the southeastern horizon over Tallchief Mountain, where the big guns from Fort Sill's artillery range began their night-time practice. Seconds later, the hollow boom from their firing, sounding like distant thunder, reached them.

The cicadas muted their night song.

She felt faint.

CHAPTER 2 ✦ IDA

They sat quietly as they glided slowly back and forth, watching the flashes of light and listening to the boom of the cannons every minute or two.

Charlie pointed at the mountain that separated them from the cannon's boom. "You think there might be ghosts over there on Tallchief Mountain?"

Recovering some, she said, "Absolutely not." She gathered her nightgown tightly around her. "Those flashes and booms over there are from cannons."

"I know that, Grandmother. Mama told me that. But I was thinking about something Mr. Buchanan told me—that there were ghosts over there on the mountain. Grandpa got real mad about that when I told him. Called Mr. Buchanan a liar and a horse thief. But Mr. Buchanan buys savings stamps from me."

"Well, Charlie. I think there might be ghosts over there for Mr. Buchanan. And your grandpa. But there aren't any over there for you."

Charlie scratched at his head as if puzzling over what she said. "You believe in ghosts, Grandmother?"

Charlie moved closer to her, trembling. Ida wanted to put her arm around him but let it go limp in her lap, like a useless piece of frayed rope. She stiffened. "I don't know, Charlie. There's things go on in this world that can't be explained any other way. But me? I never saw one. Never heard one. If you really want my honest opinion, anyone with a good conscience don't have to worry about such things."

The cannons ceased fire, and all was eerily quiet. A winged night creature, a bat or a loon, darted overhead. A moment later, its muted call sounded, and, as if on its signal, all the cicadas took up their cadence again. Ida shuddered.

The night that Brian's force in this world ended, there had been a moment of eerie calm just before he went into convulsions. The wind that had buffeted the house all evening quieted, and all she could hear was the muted sobbing of Brian's sisters and little brother huddled in the next room. It was Christmas Eve night, and she yelled at Pearl because she couldn't quiet her sister and get to sleep. Then, going to the door, she called in an apology before sitting down at Brian's side. His labored breathing calmed, and he opened his eyes. To Ida, cooling his brow with a damp cloth, it seemed he had a faraway look in his eyes, like someone not long for this world. She was stunned, death having slipped into the room and stood before her with so little forewarning.

She knew her boy was sick, knew he needed to be in town seeing a doctor. She'd begged Bob for hours to take Brian—she would have gotten down on her knees and pleaded if it would have done any good. It wouldn't have. He kept harping on how near broke he was.

"Ida, we just don't have the money for a doctor. I've got fifty dollars to my name, and most of that goes for seed. We don't plant a crop, we don't eat next year. We don't eat for the next week if I take that boy in." Bob stood there in the doorway, not coming in, afraid that if he got too close, he might see for himself how sick his son was. "And for a bellyache. He's had half a dozen bellyaches in his short life, and you never wanted me to drive him to town."

"Bob, he's never been this sick before, for God's sake. Can't I get that through that thick head of yours?" She turned then and saw that look of surprise on her boy's face, his eyes widening and his mouth falling open. Then he began to jerk with a fierceness that shook the whole bed.

When Brian took that last look at her and convulsed, terrifying her, surprising Bob, maybe even surprising the good Lord that made him, she screamed. Stood up and yelled, "For the love of sweet Jesus, Bob, get the horses, or I swear I'll walk to town carrying him."

Bob rushed to the boy's side, disbelief written in the slackness of his face. And he didn't say another word as they rushed outside into the stinging December snowstorm, or while Ida sat in the buggy as he hitched his best horse to it; didn't speak even as their boy grew slack and lifeless in her arms.

CHAPTER 2 ✦ IDA

With stinging words, she forced Bob to lay his buggy whip to the horse in a way he had never done before or since, flogging it almost to death as they plowed through the deepening drifts. At the doctor's house, Bob tried to take the boy in his arms. She wouldn't let go. Through knee-deep drifts, she staggered to the door and screamed for the doctor to open up. When he didn't come right away, she screamed, "Pound on the door, Bob, or he'll never hear us out here." Bob began to pound with his fists for what seemed to her forever.

Blurry-eyed and frowning, Dr. Bailey finally appeared at the door in his nightshirt, carrying a coal-oil lamp. "For heaven's sake. What is it?"

She burst into tears then, as Dr. Bailey took one look at Brian and then led them to his office, where he listened to her tell of what had been going on. The ragged breathing of her boy filled the small space in the examining room, crowding out the air. Her head began to spin, and she couldn't get deep-enough breaths as she lay Brian on the table and cradled his head in her arms.

The doctor gently pulled her away, lifted Brian's eyelid and peered closely, as if to find some hope within the feverish depths of that eye. He felt the boy's poker-hot forehead and pressed on his belly. Brian's face hardened in anguish. Dr. Bailey then shook his head just once, but it was as if that small movement shifted a fragile balance. Brian took his last precious breath and settled into eternity. The doctor closed Brian's eyes and pulled the sheet up over his angelic face. Ida almost fainted away, and, had Bob and the doctor not helped her into a chair, she would have ended up on the floor. She sat there as hot tears scalded her face.

Bob then stepped over and looked down at Brian, shaking his head in disbelief. "He just can't be dead," Bob murmured, still not wanting to believe, still holding on to his thick-skulled hope.

"You killed him, Bob Choat," she yelled, the bitterness in her heart choking her as she spit out the words. "You killed him, and you won't even accept he's dead."

"God help me, I didn't mean to," was all he'd answered, before he turned and walked out of the doctor's examining room. From the living room came four throbbing notes of a grandfather clock, and, as Ida sat looking at her sweet boy, she fainted dead away.

"Grandmother?" Charlie was tugging on her nightgown sleeve and moving restlessly in the swing.

"I'm sorry. I got lost in a memory just now and plumb forgot I was sitting here with you." She wanted to lift him into her lap and for him to mold into her, like Brian had done when he was a little boy, brush her lips across the top of his head, and let her own tears fall among his curls. She took hold of the swing's chains with both hands and held on.

"Are you OK?" He laid his hand on her arm.

His touch was like a hot knife, sharp and piercing. She wanted to move away, flee into the bedroom and surround herself with all her china figurines. "Yes, I am." Trembling, Ida stood. "But we have to go inside now, Charlie."

The boy slid down from the swing onto the concrete porch and quietly followed her inside and stepped around her when she paused just inside the door. "Good night, Grandmother. See you in the morning."

"Good night, Charlie." Hot tears rolled down Ida's cheeks as she leaned against the doorjamb, her hand on the smooth glass of Brian's picture frame. When they laid Brian in his grave, she swore never to hold a little boy so close to her heart ever again. And now, as she stood there, unable in the darkness to see that precious image on her wall, her chest began to lose its fullness, as if her very heart was shrinking, growing smaller until it squeezed out all that which Charlie threatened to stir to life there. She groaned.

"Grandmother?" Charlie turned back and tugged at her sleeve. "What's the matter?"

Startled, she pulled away. "I thought you'd gone on to bed, Charlie. There's nothing the matter. I'm just a little sad thinking about my boy Brian, who passed away a long time ago." She took hold of the doorjamb with both hands and held on.

CHAPTER 2 • IDA

"You sure you're OK?"

"Yes, I am." Trembling, Ida took a step away from the door. "But you have to go to bed now, Charlie. It's time you got to sleep."

"I'm sorry he died, Grandmother." Charlie moved up close and patted her arm.

"You are really a good boy, Charlie. Thank you." More tears sprang to her eyes, though she tried to hold them back. "Now you go on to bed."

When the boy left the room, she couldn't hold back the tears. She walked back outside and rocked in the swing until she had let loose every last one. Then, peering into the night sky, where a million stars drifted, sharing their brightness with a quarter moon, she wondered if her Brian was up there somewhere beyond the stars in heaven, waiting for her to join him. Another lone car crept toward them, bathing the porch in light, and then passed by, its taillights unblinking as it slowly disappeared into the distance.

CHAPTER 3

Bob

↣ ✤ ↢

Bob Choat came awake slowly. He sat up in the dark, swung his legs off the bed and stared blurry-eyed at the floor. It was five o'clock, give or take five minutes, and he was awake and ready to face the day. As long as he could remember, he had awakened on his own. There was no need of an alarm clock. He stood, slipped on a shirt and overalls, and then stepped barefoot into his brogans. Feeling his way in the dark to his coal-oil lamp, he struck a match, lifted the mantle, and set the blackened wick burning. The heavy odor of coal oil and sulfur trailed behind him as he carried the light into the kitchen and set it down on the counter. He washed his face in cool water dipped from the water bucket, dipped again, took a mouthful and spat in the sink, then drank deeply. Thin, predawn light began to filter in from the curtained windows. A rooster crowed insistently, challenging the day. Bob reached for the slop bucket Ida kept under the sink, pushed open the screen door and stepped outside.

On the porch, he gazed east, past the mulberry trees standing sentinel along the road. Shards of crimson backlit the purple clouds lying close to the horizon. He turned to look west, beyond the barn, and saw straight rows of young cotton that stretched to the end of his land a half mile away. He had a good stand of cotton this year, for which he was grateful. Yesterday's storm had done little or no damage. Now if they didn't get any hard rains to drown it out and the boll-weevil pests were light this year, he could make a half-bale of cotton to the acre. That, the two hogs he'd butcher, and the money he'd win at dominoes would get him through a winter of feeding all four mouths now sitting around his table. A week after Charlie and Ruth drove in and she'd announced they were there for the duration of the war, he'd purchased those two hogs to fatten and butcher. Cotton, hogs, and dominoes. That and the milk from Isabelle should keep them from going hungry. Maybe leave him with a little to put back for a rainy day. Or a drought-plagued day. He'd had some money saved back when the crash of '29 happened—and thank God it wasn't in a bank. Hid under the floorboards in his tack room, no snooping kid like Charlie around to find it. With what was squirreled away, he'd managed to keep body and soul together during the dust-bowl days that followed. Thank God, too, that those days had ended.

He picked up the garbage pail sitting just outside the door, stepped from the porch, and trudged up the muddy clay path that led to the washhouse and then on up to the barn. The left shoulder strap of his overalls, which he had left unfastened, bounced against his back at each step. He reached for the strap, sliding it through his palm to the brass buckle and anchored it in place with a jerk, not spilling a drop of the hog swill he was carrying in the slop bucket.

He stepped inside the small, one-room washhouse, took down from the wall a milk bucket with his free hand, and walked on down to the barn. The front door creaked as he opened it, and a rush of warm air—pungent with the acrid stench of hog and horse manure, hay dust, and oiled leather from the harness he used with his horses—wrapped around and embraced him. He hung the milk bucket on a ten-penny nail he'd driven into the wall near the cow's stanchion.

From inside a small pen nestled in one corner of the barn, the two hogs he was fattening set up a racket, squealing and snuffling their demands that he feed them. As he emptied the swill into their low wooden trough, the larger of the two animals stood with its front feet and one back foot bathed in swill as the other squealed and shoved at him.

Bob slapped the greedy porker on the hams, knocking him off his stingy perch. "Suuee. Get over there. Stop hogging it all for yourself, Roosevelt." Roosevelt squealed indignantly but moved away as the smaller animal plunged its snout into the trough and began to eat, his angry protest drowned in the gruel. "You don't start eating more, Churchill, I'm not gonna get enough bacon off you to fill a frying pan." Bob poured a measure of hard kernel corn into each end of the trough. Roosevelt tried to eat at both ends, but Churchill gained a purchase, braced his forefeet, and stood his ground.

Old Tony nickered, and his other horse, Big Jewel, thrust her head over the stall, watching Bob out of her one good eye.

"Morning, Old Tony. Big Jewel." Bob patted each of the two work horses on the shoulder and rubbed their noses before he led them out of their stalls and to the water tank. Old Tony blew out his breath, fluttered his lips, and shook his head as if trying to dislodge an imagined harness before plunging his nose into the water. Bob unloosed the brake that held the windmill's fan-blades in check; they caught the morning breeze and then began to turn. The screech of metal on metal as the pump shaft turned scared up a brace of quail that flew into a clump of milkweed and hovered quietly, not moving.

As the horses drank, Bob stared at the far-off hump of Tallchief Mountain, sitting on the horizon as a reminder of past years—years when, as a small boy and all this land still belonged to the Kiowa Indians, he'd spent time riding through it with his brothers and Pa on the way to Mangum, Texas, to visit a married sister. Couldn't have known back then that one day he'd be livin' on some of that land. Or that the government would take Mangum and a whole other big parcel of land away from Texas and give it to Oklahoma.

When he started walking the horses back to the barn, one-eyed Big Jewel walked sedately along behind, like the well-mannered and aging old lady she was. Tony tossed his head and danced away, pulling on the halter. Bob yelled, "Gol-dang you, Old Tony, quit acting like a colt." As if he understood Bob, the horse fell in with Big Jewel's sedate plodding walk. Putting the horses back in the barn, Bob grabbed a pitchfork and tossed sweet-smelling alfalfa into their stalls. He reached over and gave Old Tony a slapping pat and then rubbed Big Jewel's ears. The horses tossed their heads, sending a shower of the loose hay fluttering to the ground. In a long sliver of light stealing through a crack in the barn wall behind them, hay dust danced and swirled.

Bob opened the barn door again and hollered, "Sue, boss. Sue. Sue, there, Isabelle." His jersey cow raised her head from the grass and began an awkward trot to the barn, her milk-distended udder bouncing against the insides of her back legs. Isabelle would need breeding again soon, he mused, which would get her milk production up. And he'd have a new calf to raise and sell off. When the cotton was all harvested, he'd do just that. With Charlie drinking nearly a quart of milk a day, there was barely enough left for Ruth, him and Ida. Bob made a face at the thought of the boy. A Scarsdale through and through. And Bob couldn't stomach the Scarsdales. Chester in particular.

He'd raised his own family of five, and that was enough. Pearl and Joan had the good sense to marry decent men, and they never asked for anything from him. Neither had ever borrowed money after they walked down the aisle. But now, he had to help bring up his oldest daughter's kid.

Having them cost him and Ida, and money was scarce. And there were his domino winnings he'd hidden away for his own use that the little snoop had stumbled on to. When Ida found out about it, she threw a fit. Like with everything else she held against him, she would never let him forget hiding that money from her. That was just one more nail in the coffin of their marriage. And all because of a Scarsdale.

Mooing softly, Isabelle shoved past him and stuck her head into the manger; then she turned and eyed him as if to show disappointment that he had not yet poured her grain.

"Doggone it, Isabelle, I'm coming. Stop giving me that cockeyed stare." He spilled a full measure of oats into the trough, and, when Isabelle dipped her head into the feed, he pulled a wooden bar over against her neck, fastening it into place, making sure she couldn't decide to walk away and leave him "holding the bucket." Taking up the milk bucket, he grabbed his one-legged stool, walked to the cow's right flank, sat down, and pushed at her thigh to make her step back and expose her distended teats to him. Resting his forehead on her flank, he took each teat in his right hand and rubbed it free of dirt and filth. *Probably should wash them off,* he thought, but this wasn't the first time he'd forgotten to bring a wet rag with him. Ida and Ruth wouldn't have to know, and, by the time he strained the milk before bringing it to the house, they couldn't tell whether it came from a clean or unwashed teat. And it didn't much matter to him.

With the bucket gripped firmly between his knees, he began a rhythmic stroking, trapping the milk by squeezing the top of the teat with his thumb and forefinger and then, pressing one finger at a time, coaxing out a steady stream of cream-rich milk. At first it pinged hard against the bottom of the bucket in a whiny, drawn-out sound like nothing he had ever heard anyplace else. As the bucket began to fill, the long ribbons of milk streaming into a fast-deepening, frothy puddle at the bottom, the raw, heavy smell of it wafted up. He relaxed into the pleasure of it.

CHAPTER 3 • BOB

A mother cat crept out from under the floor of the granary and sat waiting. Her brood, two tiny yellow toms and three spotted females, peeked from the edge of the shadows. Bob aimed a stream of milk at the mother cat, and she opened her mouth as if it, too, were a bucket that needed filling. She hardly missed a drop. Finished squeezing out that full teat of milk, Bob turned the flow back into his bucket. The cat backed under the floorboards where her young would root and suck.

He'd been squirting milk at an old yellow tomcat back in 1904 when his pa had called for him to saddle up two horses when he was done milking. "Somebody took off with Blackie last night," his pa told him. "Took my mare right out of the pasture, and that worthless hound of yours didn't say boo." Bob had felt a passing twinge of shame for his dog's laziness. But it wasn't shame that mounted the horse along with him to keep company as he rode after his pa. It was anger. His pa wasn't being fair. That dog belonged to the rest of his brothers and sisters as much as it did him.

All that morning and into the afternoon they had followed Blackie, going into the Wichita Mountains and then out the other side before the trail was lost. "We could be following those tracks on into Texas for a week, even if we picked up the trail again. Can't do that," his pa had said and turned his horse back toward home. A long-horned cow and her calf browsed through a meadow of tall prairie grass he and his pa crossed, and a small herd of deer sprang up and lost themselves in the scrub oak. Bob sat his on horse a moment, watching their bobbing white tails disappearing. That's when they saw those two no-account boys, Nash and Buchanan, with a rope around Blackie and leading her in the direction of Cooperton, where they likely planned to sell him.

When he'd heard Charlie was talking to Buchanan, trying to sell him a saving stamp, telling him tall tales, hinting at knowing something about his grandpa, Bob almost screamed at the boy. Told him he better not be going around that old horse thief, or he'd have to answer for it. Maybe even get a lickin' for it.

Lost in memory, he pulled too hard on Isabelle's teat, and she stomped one back leg and mooed in protest. He jerked the bucket from under her, sloshing milk onto the barn floor. "Dag-nabbit, Isabelle, I gotta quit remembering so hard when I milk you."

Placing the near-full bucket back under her again, he stripped the last of the milk from the displeased cow, loosed her from the manger, and let her and the horses out into the pasture.

Going to the tack room, Bob moved aside two hundred-pound feed sacks full of chicken feed and pried up a loose floorboard, revealing a small hiding place. This had been where he'd kept his money for years. Neither him nor his pa believed in banks and never used them. Good thing, too. When all those banks failed back in 1929, all his and Ida's money was in two safe hiding places, part of it under the floorboards of the barn and known only to him and part in the false bottom of Ida's trunk. He'd been in a hurry two weeks ago when he stuck that fruit jar of money behind a bale of hay. Then that fool kid found it. Now instead of a Mason quart jar near full of money, there was one with a few nickels, dimes, and quarters rattling around in the bottom. He poured out a few coins, counted out a dollar and a quarter, and slipped it into his pocket. He dropped eighty-five cents back into the jar, placed it under the floorboard, and, with a grunt, set the feed sacks back on top of his bank. Luck and well-played domino hands today in town would win him enough to put back more than he'd taken out. He'd give Ida half of it and tell her that was all he'd won.

He heard Ruth calling, her voice still drugged with sleep and sounding like she had a summer cold. Exiting the barn, he could see her standing on the porch waiting to see if he'd heard her call. Since arriving here she'd looked more and more unhappy. She'd begun to put on weight since that no-account son-in-law had run off and joined the Sea Bees. Maybe getting shot at by the Japs would help make a man of him, get him back home with some sense of responsibility. He could sure use that. Or, even

CHAPTER 3 • BOB

better, one of those bullets just might . . . He didn't finish the thought. Shamed him too much.

With the full milk-bucket pulling at his arm and shoulder, he walked to the wash house, where he kept his cream separator. Leaving the milk to be strained and separated after breakfast, he turned to leave and glanced up at his pa's double-barreled shotgun hanging above the door. His pa had traded a lame mule for the gun in 1863, a year after he'd deserted from the Confederate Army. Carried it with him into the Cherokee Indian Territory when he moved there with six of Bob's older brothers and sisters. Had it when Bob was born down in the Choctaw Nation and when they moved on to the Chickasaw and then the Kiowa Nations. Bob's Pa and the old gun had traveled through a lot of Indian land.

Pushing out the wash-house door, he walked toward the house, and, as he passed the coal-oil barrel that sat beside the coal bin, he gave it a gentle pat. He'd watched his own kids, and now Charlie, straddle and ride the barrel, beating on the metal sides with a stick. When near empty, the blows made a hollow boom, like the far-off sound of cannon fire you could sometimes hear coming from the big guns over in Fort Sill. He'd told all of them that was no way to treat a horse. They'd just looked at him and nodded, but the next time they took a notion to ride, there was that stick in their hands again and they were banging away. Kids did love the racket booming out from beneath them.

He scraped mud from his shoes on the mud scraper by the porch before he entered the kitchen; the scent of bacon, mingled with that of baking-powder biscuits, made his mouth water. Folgers coffee, shooting up like a small geyser, sprayed the glass lid of the percolator. Ida had poured sweet milk, cooled in the icebox, into Quaker Oats glasses that sat stoutly on the table, gleaming white as new crystal. With a satisfied sigh, he lowered into a chair opposite Ruth and Charlie.

"Bob Choat. Did you scrape any of that mud off those shoes before you came in this house?" Not waiting for an answer, Ida set a plate of fried eggs and bacon on the table and went back to the stove, muttering.

Bob looked around at the doorway to the kitchen and saw that he had, indeed, left some mud from his shoes on the linoleum. Not enough to bellyache about, though. "Guess I didn't scrape them enough," he admitted.

Ruth looked up from stirring her coffee, and Bob wished that she would take his side, sass her mother. She ducked her head instead and said nothing.

"That man goes down to the barn and then walks right back in here without wiping his shoes good enough." Ida took steaming hot biscuits out of the oven and carried them to the table. "Thirty-four years he's been walking into my kitchen without cleaning the mud or the barnyard dirt off his shoes."

Not responding to her criticism, Bob chewed a bite of well-buttered biscuit and watched Ida stir flour into hot bacon grease and then add milk while she stirred. They had been married for all those years, and it had never seriously crossed his mind to leave her. When it had crossed his mind to walk away, it seemed as if his stomach turned to water. There was too much fear of what would happen to him if he were alone. He'd never been on his own. Had lived with his folks till he married Ida. Could count on less than ten fingers the number of days they hadn't been sleeping under the same roof. He'd felt really lost when she'd gone into town to stay for a week when Joan had her second girl.

Charlie, his egg and bacon vanished from his plate, reached and took another biscuit. "These are really good, Grandmother."

Ruth set the biscuits out of the boy's reach. "I swear, Charlie, you can put away as much food as a grown man."

"But when it comes to helping out around the place here, I don't see him doin' much," Bob said as he forked two pieces of bacon and an egg onto his plate.

CHAPTER 3 • BOB

Charlie scowled at him and said, "You won't let me do anything."

That dirty look reminded Bob so much of Chester Scarsdale that he wanted to reach out and slap the boy's face. Instead, he picked up another hot biscuit, broke it open and dropped it into his plate. Steam rose from the biscuit's center. "Biscuits are good and hot this morning," he said, reaching for the gravy bowl Ida had set on the table.

"Would be every morning, if you would get here on time and sit down with the rest of us," Ida carped.

Bob felt an ache beginning to grow under his breastbone, an ache that often started when Ida, her words sharp as a newly filed hoe, scolded him. She'd been doing that more often since Ruth and Charlie showed up. He figured that she was takin' her aggravation out on him instead of them. Believing that didn't make it any less hurtful.

Ruth set down her fork and said, "Papa, Joe Williams told me he needs cotton choppers. I'm going over to his place next week unless you have something here for me to do." She took the bowl of gravy and ladled some on Charlie's and her biscuits.

"I have nothin' needs doing around here for a while. Cotton's pretty clean this year." He wiped his plate, sopping up gravy with the last piece of his biscuit. "With that new tractor of his, Joe Williams can't plow deep enough to kill most of the weeds. Takes a good team of horses to raise cotton right." There was silence in the room as he downed a swallow of sweet milk. Not even Ida could criticize the way he farmed his land. Since the rains came back after the dust-bowl drought, he'd done well.

Ruth coughed, and he saw a nervous twitch of her mouth before she said, "But what I wanted to ask is, until I can earn some from chopping, would you loan me a dollar or two so I can get some things I need?"

He sat quietly, not wanting to answer, not wanting to come up with a dollar of the change he'd put in his pocket, needing every bit of it for his gambling at dominoes today. Sometimes he would be down a dollar before he had figured everything out about the other men's tells or repeated mistakes, and could then take back what he'd lost and then some. Teetering back on the rear legs of his chair, he stuck both hands inside his overall bib and slowly rocked himself. "I can only let you have a half-dollar, and you can pay me back when Joe Williams pays you."

"I'll loan some to you," Charlie said, driving a wedge into the silence that followed, and Ruth, her dark eyes softening, turned to Charlie, who dug in his pocket and held out a dime toward her. He pushed his jaw defiantly forward. "And you can borrow what I earn chopping cotton."

Ruth's eyes softened, and she patted the boy's arm. "You're sweet to offer, Charlie. But you need those for your savings stamps."

Bob hated that he was made to feel cheap by the boy's offer. Feeling spiteful, he asked, "You think Joe Williams is going let a half-grown city boy in his cotton field?"

Charlie looked back and forth from him to his mother and then, his eyes screwed up into a hateful stare, came to rest on Bob. "I'll bet he'll let me chop cotton."

"I'll ask him and see," Ruth said.

Bob pushed away from the table, reached in his pocket and pulled out two quarters. "This is all I can let you have. You'll just have to get by on that. Or ask your mama for some of that money Charlie found in the barn."

Ruth grew red in the face and looked at her mother, who, not meeting her eyes, began gathering the dirty breakfast dishes. Ruth stood and carried her and Charlie's dishes to the sink and began washing them. Bob knew he and Ida had shamed her. But he wasn't about to apologize.

"I didn't know that money was yours. You should've hid it better if you didn't want me to find it," Charlie blurted.

"Don't sass your grandpa, Charlie." Ruth spoke with angry bitterness in her voice. "He's the one's feeding us both now."

Darned if she isn't right about that, Bob thought.

CHAPTER 4

Ruth

⇥ ✤ ⇤

Standing beside her papa's thirty-six Ford squatting in the side yard like a shiny black beetle, Ruth watched her nine-year-old son charge out of the one-story, frame farmhouse, his overalls riding an inch above his brogan shoes and stretched tight across his stomach. An untucked shirttail bloused out from one side of his overalls, which he left unbuttoned to give him room to breathe. She'd sewn his shirt from muslin flour sacks, a dark green paisley on a lighter green background. His sandy-colored hair, which Ruth had combed so neatly ten minutes ago, looked like a haystack after the cattle got at it. He bounced into the back seat, and then bounced some more, sending a fine spray of red dust billowing up, thick as smoke.

"Charlie Leon Scarsdale." She leaned into the window and lifted her hand to swat him, but he scooted to the other side of the car, out of her reach. In her irritation, she was careless and rubbed her new flowered print dress against the dirty car door. She wanted to cry. Mother had found a pattern and made the dress from bags that had held a month's supply of chicken feed before coming under her sewing-machine needle. She wiped at the smudge but was unable to brush all the dirt away. Her eyes squinched to keep the tears back. She ducked, scooted in beside her son, and frowned at him but let it go at that.

Charlie ducked under his upraised arm to avoid the worst of any halfhearted slap she still might aim at him. Paying no further attention to him, she settled herself back, her soft bulk sinking so far into the seat that it pulled Charlie toward her. He quickly grabbed the back post of his open window, hung one arm down outside the car, and pulled away. He rested his chin on the windowsill, keeping as far from her as he could manage. He needn't have worried; she was over her aggravation with him.

Mother, her back stiff as a hoe handle, lowered herself into the front and turned in her seat, frowning. "I swear, if the heat isn't the death of me today, that dust Charlie stirred up will be." She then turned and looked straight ahead, holding herself erect. "And it isn't even summer yet." A thin seam of sweat began to form on the back of her flowery summer dress. With a white handkerchief she dabbed at her neck. "Living through the dust bowl, I shouldn't complain, I guess."

Ruth's papa opened the driver's door and slid his six-foot-three frame under the wheel, his nose erupting in a small explosive sneeze before he started the car rolling slowly toward the road. Even on hot afternoons in town, he wore his denim shirt and overalls and sported a short-brimmed fedora pulled down firmly over his thick, graying hair. In the rearview mirror, Ruth saw his eyes, deep brown and disapproving, staring back at her and Charlie.

A familiar ache in her stomach began to nag at her. It had twisted there often since arriving at the farm and had become even worse after Charlie discovered that fruit jar half-full of nickels, dimes and quarters

CHAPTER 4 ✦ RUTH

and brought it to the house, excited that he had found it. "Look what I found in the hayloft. A real treasure," he'd said proudly. But Mother had snatched the jar from him, angry spite furrowing her brow, and she had hardly spoken a kind word to papa since. Nothing much was said to Charlie, but he'd been battered by his grandpa's hard-thrown looks. She knew that her papa was taking the loss of his money out on Charlie, being harsher and more critical of him than usual.

Charlie held onto the window post as the car lurched and swayed over the deep ruts left by other cars since the heavy shower the day before. Ruth's mother, as if hinged at the middle of her ample waist, swayed with each lurch of the car. Ruth closed her eyes and thought of Chester, pulled a picture of him out of that special place in her mind where she stowed away the pleasant memories of him. She couldn't wait till the day when a boat would bring him back from the South Pacific. When that happened, she wouldn't be living with her mother and papa. She wiped at a tear but could not rub away the ache throbbing behind her breastbone.

Approaching the only other house on that mile stretch of road, she saw nine-year-old Sarah Williams come bursting through the screen door, her long blond hair billowing out behind her as she ran helter-skelter into the cotton patch bordering the road.

On seeing Sarah, Charlie waved both hands at her. Sarah jumped high and threw a kiss at them. Ruth smiled then. She was glad that Joe Williams' daughter and Charlie had taken a shine to each other; Sarah had no mama, and, right now, Charlie had no daddy. Sarah tried to keep pace with the car for a few yards, her feet flying over the wet plowed earth. Coming to a stop, bathed in the light of a midday sun, she waved them to the corner where they slowed to turn.

Mountain Valley School, where Charlie would soon be poring over this winter's lessons, stood empty on one corner. Its white clapboard siding was peeling paint in places but really hadn't changed that much since she and Chester had gone to school there. She had loved being in class from the first day of grade one on through the end of grade eight, which she'd taken a second time because there'd been no way for her to travel the ten miles into town for high school. She'd loved learning. And she adored the teacher, Miss Jones, who had been there all nine years she attended. She hoped Charlie would have as good a time there as she had. Papa's irritated voice interrupted her thoughts as he turned north toward Babbs School.

"I swear, that Joe Williams couldn't plant a straight row if his life depended on it." Papa shook his head in disgust. "Farming for over ten years, the man ought to know how to plant cotton."

Both she and Charlie knew only too well the words that would follow. She watched Charlie as his mouth moved wordlessly along with his grandfather's: "Can't play dominoes worth a pig's tail, either." She suspected Papa thought *a pig's ass*, even said it around other men at the domino parlor, but he didn't curse in front of Mother, her, or Charlie.

Ruth wanted to smile but was afraid her papa would glance back and see her. Want to know she thought was funny.

Papa slowly sped up to the patriotic speed limit of thirty miles an hour.

"This seems so slow," Mother complained.

"It saves on gas," Papa said.

"And you're the tightest man with a dollar this side of the Mississippi," Mother said. But Papa still just creeped on, so she added, "Even before the war, you was slow as the seven-year itch."

Charlie turned on his knees and, braced against the car's door, stared out the open side window, and gave an order, "Forward. MARCH," to the long rows of new cotton plants they were driving by.

Ruth thought the fields of new cotton could, to a boy with an imagination, look like small green-clad soldiers standing at attention. As the car crept forward, laying down new ruts for anyone following them this day, the green brigades double-timed alongside them, never breaking their perfect ranks.

CHAPTER 4 ✦ RUTH

"I swear, Ruth, that boy does nothing but talk to hisself lately." Her papa shook his head and then reached to scratch the side of his thick nose.

"The boy's just playing, Papa. He's been doing that ever since his daddy joined up."

From the rearview mirror, her papa fixed an eye on her before quickly looking ahead once more. "Chester Scarsdale had no business volunteering to go off and fight in this war, Ruth. A man his age should've stayed back here in a safe civilian job taking care of you and Charlie."

Hanging close by her mother's ear, a strand of long hair, now loose from the twisted knot behind her head, swept back and forth across her neck. She reached back for it, shoved it into place, and said, "He's off helping us fight this war, Bob. Just like our Winston."

Ruth would never tell her parents the real reason Chester joined the Sea Bees. She tried to beat back that memory every time it forced its way into her mind. Thankfully, Charlie spoke up and interrupted the memory before it took hold.

"Yeah, my daddy's gone off to build bridges for the jeeps, trucks, and tanks to use. He told us in his last letter he was working twelve to fourteen hours a day."

Her papa just shook his head. Ruth retreated into silence.

Looking out her side of the car, Ruth watched telephone poles move past at a turtle's speed. She thought of the headlines in last week's Hobart paper: FIERCE AIR AND SEA BATTLE RAGES in the Pacific. On first seeing that, a sick dread had made her lay it aside. She couldn't bring herself to read it. Chester might be somewhere in the middle of that fighting. At this very moment, enemy planes could be dive bombing the bridges Chester helped build. She tried not to think of those explosions, bridge parts hurled out into space, the whole span collapsing, men, jeeps, and tanks sliding into the river and going under. Then she thought of her brother, Winston, somewhere overseas as well, trying to keep rowdy soldiers on leave from starting little wars among themselves or with some of their allies' soldiers. That's what MPs do," he'd told her when he was home on leave just before shipping out to Lord knows where. Burma Mother had told her when she got his first letter.

Two birds launched themselves from the sagging electric line that connected miles of wooden poles along the roadway. Charlie, reaching across her and pointing his index finger, shot at each one. "I never miss," he crowed. Another bird took off from the pencil-thin runway and came under his deadly fire. "Bogies at two o'clock. Ka-pow."

Ruth reached quickly before he could dodge away and grabbed Charlie's hand. "Would you stop that nonsense, now? It's giving all of us a headache, and it's making me worry about your uncle and dad."

Charlie turned and squeezed into the corner, wiping his nose with the back of his hand. Silently, he turned away from her and, with his other hand, shot from the hip, his aim trained on a small brown thrush sailing in for a landing on a lone tree by the roadway. "Got him," he whispered, glancing sideways at her.

Not having the energy to correct him again, she sat looking straight ahead, her head cocked to one side, her mind on those awful days before Chester had shipped out, how painful they had been for her.

"Everybody's got to help with the war effort, don't they Mama? Just like daddy."

She looked at him and raised an eyebrow. "How does it help to pretend shooting down airplanes?" She reached over and brushed a strand of hair drooped across his eyes.

Pulling his head back, he faced her. "It won't, but I'm talking about reselling those two savings stamps I bought. Then buying two more. I just hope I make enough chopping cotton that I can buy even more to resell."

"Chopping cotton'll teach you that money don't grow on trees," Papa growled, stabbing a look at Charlie from the rearview mirror.

"Well, Bob, the boy thought money grows in quart jars. That's the kind of lesson he got from you," Ida said.

CHAPTER 4 ✦ RUTH

Ruth, turning her head to look out the window, fanned herself with the cardboard church fan she kept up behind the back seat. But she laid a protective arm across Charlie's shoulder. "And he's wanting to help out with the war effort. Help his dad. And his Uncle Winston. You ought to be proud of him for that, Papa."

The storm had missed pouring rain down on the road as it neared Babbs School, and Papa "harrumpfed" as he jerked the car further on to his side of the road as the mud gave way to dry, rutted clay and gravel.

Ruth's mother scowled at him and said, "I wish you'd pay more attention to driving than criticizing Chester."

"Any man who'd go off and leave. . . ."

"Papa." Ruth growled as she sat forward in her seat, her eyes narrowed and her mouth tight. Charlie had never heard her use that tone with her papa, and it must have frightened him, because his eyes grew round, and he moved closer to her. Papa hunched his shoulders and said nothing. She sat back and patted Charlie on the leg; he relaxed and stared out the window without speaking or fighting the war.

In the silence, Ruth breathed in red dust kicked up by the tires. It filtered through the windows, danced in the air around her, and like fine paint-spray covered the seats, her clothes, and her hair. She'd be spitting red phlegm by the time they got to the blacktop. The sun beat down, heating the car roof to a temperature she knew would fry an egg. Mixed with the dust and heat and sweat, the scent of her mother's toilet water also floated in the heavy air. The hum of the motor vibrated through the floorboards, and loose gravel, kicked up by the back wheels, hit like birdshot on the undercarriage.

Three miles west of Mountain Valley School, they turned north onto the blacktop at the Babbs Switch School, and, from the smooth surface, Ruth could hear the muted hum of Papa's worn tires. Soon Hobart's water tower and grain elevators came into view and grew larger and larger, ever so slowly, as they drew near.

Ruth remembered rides she'd taken with Chester before the war. He never paid attention to speed limits, rocketing along at sixty miles an hour. Scared her to death. After the first time or two riding with him, Mother never got in a car with Chester at the wheel.

They approached Dixon Heights, which was the only small hill in the otherwise flat eighty square miles of farmland surrounding Hobart. Ruth gazed at the house sitting on top of the gentle rise. It gleamed white in the morning sun. Ever since she was a child, she'd had the fantasy that it was something like a fairy house and the people who lived there were happy and carefree.

On reaching the corner of First and Main, the heat had made itself fully known to Ruth, and she felt sweat running down the small of her back as she sat forward in her seat. Her papa nosed the Ford into the curb, slipping it in between two dusty white lines painted there weeks earlier by the city maintenance department. "We should leave around six o'clock," he said. Without another word, he heaved himself out of the car and walked across the street to the domino parlor.

Ruth let herself out of the car into the heat of the sun beating on the concrete sidewalk and, with Charlie and her mother, walked to the courthouse square. There were tall, native elm trees that had been planted years ago to shade wooden benches scattered about beneath them. They were grown tall, and their shade held some blessed relief from the heat. "Let's sit here in the shade for a bit, Mother. It's as comfortable as sitting close to Joan's water cooler. And she's not expecting us yet for another thirty minutes or so."

"Just for a few minutes. Joan might need help with the girls while she's fixing lunch for us," her mother said as she sat down. She took a cardboard fan from her large purse, and began to fan herself. "Your papa and I sat under these trees two or three years after they were planted back in 1903. Didn't give much shade, though. My own pa had just won 160 acres of land in the 1901 lottery. Your papa wasn't that lucky, so he had to sharecrop for a few years after we married."

CHAPTER 4 • RUTH

Ruth had heard this story Lord knows how many times before, but she did not interrupt her mother. She anticipated now hearing about Oklahoma becoming a state in 1907, but Mother only sat fanning herself and looking off into space. Ruth thought, *I guess she has memories of the past same as me.*

She watched Charlie wander off to examine the Women's Christian Temperance Union fountain and then walk toward the business district, where he hoped to sell his savings stamps to some passersby. She yelled out to him, "Now don't you go off wandering from out of downtown. And be at your Aunt Joan's in forty-five minutes for lunch."

The shade cooled the harsh air to a bearable degree, and she and her mother sat quietly together, each with their own thoughts, until her mother said, "Whatever possessed Chester that he up and volunteered for the Sea Bees? Knowing him, that was the last thing I'd think he'd do."

Her mother must have seen the furrows Ruth felt lining her brow because she reached across, patted Ruth's knee, and said, "You don't have to talk about Chester if you don't want to."

That kindness of her mother melted Ruth's resolve not to remember what led up to Chester's volunteering for the service, and the memories rushed in of those awful months before she was forced back to her parents home in Oklahoma.

CHAPTER 5

Chester

↣ ✺ ↢

In the bleak darkness of early morning, a blaring PA system awakened Chester from a fitful sleep. The dull thudding in his temples and sour taste in his mouth were a glum reminder of last night's alcohol-enhanced carousing. As the unwelcome glare of bare overhead bulbs showered the barracks, disgusted groans and shouted curses beat harshly against Chester's aching head. His feet flat on the cool concrete floor, he sat forward, both hands covering his eyes, blocking out the stabbing light. His body was covered with sweat. He wiped one hand across his bald head, and his palm came away slick. With his thumbs, he tried to massage away the pain in his temples. *Scotch whisky headaches are the worst*, he thought. And the goddamn Aussies? They alone would give you a headache.

CHAPTER 5 ♦ CHESTER

"Come on, you sleeping beauties, we've got work to do," yelled Richard Bell, the platoon leader, who was standing at the light switch. "Chow's on in fifteen minutes. And you better eat hearty. We've a busy day ahead."

"Why don't you shut the hell up?" Chester groaned.

"Can't do that, Chester. Got to make sure you're up-and-at-'em."

"What? Are the Japs attacking?" Chester bitched, not lifting his hands from his face, hating Bell's nasal whine. Goddamn, he shouldn't have listened to that lawyer and enlisted in the Sea Bees. He was working his ass off. Better to have joined a tank crew and have it shot off. It would be a quicker death. On second thought, he should have listened to Ruth and spent two years locked up. He couldn't hate the jailers any more than he hated Bell.

"No," Bell shouted, "The Japs will never get this far south. They're getting their asses kicked. The Marines stopped them before they got here to Brisbane."

"But if they did get here, we'd give them one hell of a fight," growled Johnny Polk, a large, brooding man who slept two bunks away. "That is, if we're all awake and ready."

"Shut up, Polk. My head hurts enough already without my having to hear you mouth off," Chester said, looking up and staring at Polk, who was already dressed and prepared for the day. A former railroad worker out of New York City, Polk was more muscled than one of Chester's pa's work horses. But meaner than a Jersey bull. Chester thought of how he'd had to put up with Polk on the ship all the way from Port Hueneme to Brisbane. They'd picked at each other from the first day, and he'd grown to hate the bastard.

Thinking of the day he'd left the States, watching the open water widening between their ship, the *Monroe*, and the shore, he'd felt depressed as hell. Crowded for days that turned into weeks aboard that floating target for Jap subs with 2,500 other men all jammed into space intended for a thousand, he thought at times he might go crazy if he didn't punch somebody. And a couple of times he did. Not Polk, though—the man wouldn't even feel it if Chester hit him. That damn trip—with or without Bell and Polk—was sure as hell not a pleasure cruise. On the trip, a sister ship had been blown up by a Jap sub, and he'd helped bring survivors on board the *Monroe* while mine sweepers chased down the sub and blew it to kingdom come. But seeing that ship sinking while men were drowning all around it had left him even more fearful the *Monroe* would be next.

He wished, not for the first time, that he'd walked away from that fight in Tulsa. When that bozo started hitting on his girlfriend, Alice Jenson, he'd just lost his temper and cursed him out. Then the son-of-a-bitch broke a beer bottle and came after him, so he had to defend himself. Well, that should have been all—just self-defense—but he'd lost his head and put the man in a hospital. And much to his regret, that had led him to becoming a sitting duck for Jap subs.

To make things worse, after traveling 6,000 miles and reaching Vanuatu Island, for eleven days they'd had to wait on board the *Monroe* as it sat in the waters of the Espiritu Santo harbor. Some had suffered heat stroke in the sweltering confines of the ship. He'd never sweated so much in his life, and he'd sweated *a lot* back in Oklahoma while wrestling hay bales, hoeing cotton and pulling bolls, or following his papa's mules all day in the heat as they pulled a two-bottom plough through acres and acres of a dusty field.

Then that last 1,150 miles to Brisbane had been brutal, and everyone had been ready to kill each other—if not some Japs—by the time they tied up at New Farm Wharf, Brisbane. He and Polk had once almost come to blows, but thank God his friend, Hough, an oil-driller from Ponca City, Oklahoma, and the only other Okie in the platoon, had stepped between them. If he hadn't done that, Polk would have wiped the floor with Chester.

Hough had buddied up with Chester when they first landed in Port Hueneme, California. He wasn't sure he'd have made it through those

CHAPTER 5 ♦ CHESTER

weeks on the boat without that friend. Thinking of Hough, he raised his aching head and peered at the bunk next to his.

Hough was still lying there on his bunk, glaring at him like a newly awakened barn owl. "You bitchin' already, Scarsdale? You're not even out of bed yet."

"Go to hell, Hough."

"I will. The devil would be better company than you are. You bitch more'n my wife, and I can't get away from you like I did from her." Hough, down on his luck and broke, claimed he had joined up just to get away from a nagging wife, three kids, and a shitload of debt. He liked having three meals a day and a roof over his head most of the time. His wife's allotment took most of Hough's pay, but that was okay with him; he just needed a few dollars in his pocket to get shit-faced when off the base and could find an Aussie girl to sit on his lap. Or do more.

Bell started down the narrow path between the bunks, swatting the iron frames with a baton. "Get your butt moving, Scarsdale, so's you won't miss breakfast." He gave an extra hard whack to Chester's bunk and, as he continued on, catcalls and whistles following him. Anger bloomed in Chester's face, and he had to restrain himself from grabbing the baton from the man's hand and flattening his skull. If he ever caught Bell on the street after the war, Chester vowed he'd break both the man's legs. Well, maybe not; last time he beat the hell out of somebody, it had landed him in the bitchin' service. Big mistake. He wished he had stayed in bed with that woman he'd been lying with last night. With no one to interrupt him. Not even Hough, who had rousted him out of her bed so they could get back to the base on time. The thought was interrupted by Bell, who wasn't through yet.

"Okay, girls—listen up. We have to offload equipment from the ship so the boys from C Company can haul ass getting that roadway we've been working on finished."

Chester had a fleeting thought of going AWOL, hitting the local bars, hooking up with that woman he'd met last night. Another sharp pain rocketed through his temple, forcing that thought out of his mind. Moving slowly so as not to disturb his brain, he dressed in his green fatigues and work boots, then shambled along behind the others to the mess hall. His plate filled, he sat down at a table by himself and devoured the syrup-drenched pancakes and greasy sausages on his plate. Sitting over the empty dish with his lower lip pooched out, he stared at a spot somewhere in front of him, his mind blank to everything going on around him. Holding a smoldering cigarette between two fingers of his right hand, he placed the same two fingers of his left hand against his temple and, supporting his jaw by the ball of his thumb, let smoke curl about his face. He'd been in this God-awful backwater less than two weeks. It felt like it had been forever.

And it wasn't just the hangover that made him feel so bad. He'd had two letters from Alice, the woman he was running around with before shipping out. In the first one, she'd written about missing a couple of periods. When the second one came, he'd read the few short lines over and over again, hoping he'd see something different each time. The words remained the same.

> *My Dearest Chester,*
> *I hope this is as wonderful news for you as it is for me. We're going to have a baby, Chester. And when this war is over, the three of us will be together. You be sure to take care of yourself. I want you to come home safe and sound. So will our baby.*
> *Love you.*
> *Alice*

He'd downed a half dozen beers that night and wasn't sure he'd been fully sober since. Thinking now of those words and wondering for the thousandth time what he was going to do about them, tightened a knot in his belly that pained him more than his headache.

CHAPTER 5 ✦ CHESTER

"You got that faraway look on your puss, Scarsdale. You done deserted our little work party before we even walk over there?" Hough slid in beside Chester and slapped him on the back.

"God damn, Hough. Don't do that. My head is killing me."

"Sorry. I thought you were thinking about last night. About Ivy."

"Ivy? Was that her name?"

"Yeah, Ivy. And Layla. You thinking about them?"

"No. My head hurts too much to think about last night. I'm thinking I hate this whole damn mess I've got myself in."

Hough wolfed down his plate of food without another word and then said, "Come on. Get your lousy butt off that bench, and let's go."

The last of the breakfast crowd was heading out the door to the loading docks. From two tables away, Johnny Polk stood to go. His impassive eyes landed on Chester and lingered there for more than a heartbeat.

"What're you staring at, Polk?"

Polk shrugged and walked away without comment.

"You better leave that one alone," Hough cautioned.

Chester smashed out his cigarette in the dregs of maple syrup left in his empty plate. "Yeah. Forget Polk. Let's go get this damn day over with."

"Yeah, Scarsdale. And hopefully get this damn war over."

Shoving back the bench, Chester joined Hough and the others. None of them looked any happier than he felt.

CHAPTER 6

Ruth

Her mother reaching out to physically comfort her was a rare thing. Her pat on the knee loosened Ruth's thoughts and feelings, much like Charlie's insistence on hearing about Chester had when they were in the cellar. She spoke haltingly as she said, "I know I don't have to talk about him. But mostly it's him that I've thought about since that son of mine encouraged me to tell a story about his dad." She reached out and broke off a leaf from the bush next to her, brought the bitter green smell of it close, wrinkled her nose, and said, "When they bloom, this bush's flowers will smell so much better than its leaves."

"Now what does that have to do with anything, Ruth?"

Ruth grunted and threw the leaf down. "Nothing, I guess. I have no idea why I smelled it. Maybe my feelings are as bitter as that leaf smelled."

CHAPTER 6 • RUTH

"Well, I suspect you feel like you're not exactly living in a bed of roses these days. Life for you seemed so much better when your sister Joan and I visited you up in Tulsa last year."

"It was, mostly," she said, but her memory went straight back to her last ten days there before they moved to Oklahoma City. It was almost a year ago today. They'd been living in Tulsa for a little over six months, and Charlie had finished third grade there. Chester had kept his job for that whole time without once getting in trouble with his boss and getting fired. But then he told her one morning that the construction company he worked for had a job that would take him away overnight. When he didn't show up that second night, or the third, or the fourth without any word from him, she had begun to feel the heavy weight of fear growing like a hateful tumor, filling her chest. She knew Chester had a wandering eye and sometimes absented himself. But never for that many days.

"Chester was making pretty good money there, Mother, and I liked the duplex we were living in. There was a good school for Charlie. You and Joan had a good time those two days in July you visited. The weather was really nice. August wasn't a hot month last year in Tulsa, either."

She wasn't thinking about the nice weather when Chester went missing. On the third morning after he was gone, she awakened with a start and reached for the other side of the bed, feeling for the warmth of Chester's long frame. Her palms only glided over the smooth sheet on that side, still fresh and unused. She took hold of his pillow, pulled it in close to her and imagined she smelled the faint odor of Old Spice shaving cream lingering on the pillowcase.

After that, she began lying awake until the wee hours of the morning, while passing cars danced their headlight across the ceiling. In that shadowy flicker, the flowers in the wallpaper seemed to dip and sway, disturbed by the deep breaths of anxiety she exhaled into the room. One night a car had turned into the drive, and she threw off the covers to rush outside, only to hear the car backing out and driving away. She and Charlie were all alone, with no money, the only food in the house some sugar and a box of oatmeal, with only two servings between them and starvation. The past two days she'd gone without eating anything but one serving of oatmeal, so there would be more for Charlie. That morning, there was only enough for his breakfast and for lunch. If she'd heard nothing by then, she'd determined to swallow her pride, call home, and ask Papa for help. For his grudging help. She sat on the edge of the bed, squeezing the mattress with both hands as worried tears forced their way out of her eyes. She pulled up the top bedsheet and wiped the tears away.

Charlie called impatiently from the kitchen, "Mama, I'm hungry."

"I'm coming, honey. Be a good boy and put on some water to boil." A loud groan came from the kitchen, followed by banging of pots and the scritch of a match on the side of the matchbox. "Don't you burn yourself, now." Ruth pulled on her robe and smoothed at the tear in it that she'd made the night before when it caught on a loosened nail in the screen-door. She'd gone out to the front porch hoping Chester would drive up, holes now in both her robe and her heart.

She pulled at the tangles in her hair, making faces at herself in the mirror and wishing her eyes weren't so red and swollen from tears. Wishing even more that she was a beautiful woman. A younger woman. A woman that could keep Chester more interested in staying home. Not absenting himself for days at a time. In her girlhood diary, she had written, "I was a pretty baby, but I grew up to be plain." Men had denied that when she was younger, saying she was beautiful, but men were apt to say that for their own reasons, and those were not always good ones. It was likely she had lost five pounds over the past week. That and another ten pounds would get her back to a weight that was more pleasing. But starving to death was no way to lose weight.

"Mama, the water's boiling. Hurry up."

Walking into the kitchen, she found Charlie drooped forward in his chair, his chin resting sullenly on the kitchen table as he stared at the box of

CHAPTER 6 • RUTH

oatmeal. From its side panel a long-haired man wearing a funny hat smiled at him. He did not smile back.

"I wish my dad were here so we could have something else to eat."

"I do, too."

"Where is he anyway?"

"He's out on a job. Took longer than he thought." Sometimes she wondered if she should tell Charlie the truth but always decided to keep it to herself. No sense burdening the child with that kind of truth.

"I hate oatmeal."

"So do I but it's oatmeal or nothing."

With his two ring fingers, Charlie pulled at the corners of his mouth, while pushing up the corners of his eyes with his two forefingers, then completing the ugly face by sticking his tongue out at the man on the box.

Ruth startled when her mother broke into her reveries and asked, "What are you scowling about Ruth? You look positively put out about something."

Ruth relaxed her face and tried to smile. "I was just remembering something about Charlie. Do you recollect that awful face Winston used to make, pulling at his eyes and mouth? The one he taught Charlie when he was five?"

"Lord, yes. I came near slapping Winston every time he made it."

"Well, your grandson took to doing it. I tell him, 'Your face is going to freeze like that someday, and then how are you going to feel?'"

Back there in Tulsa she recalled Charlie leaning forward onto the table, laying his head on his arm, and letting out a big sigh. "You always tell me that, and it ain't ever happened."

She'd likely told him, "Don't say 'ain't.' And just because it hasn't happened yet don't mean it won't." Lot of good it did. She couldn't remember. But she couldn't forget Charlie complaining again that he was hungry. She'd poured herself a cup of hot water and then spooned in half of what was left of the oatmeal. Short of starving again, she'd vowed never to allow that smiling Quaker face in her house again if she lived to be a hundred.

A small breeze drifted through the courthouse grounds, rustling the leaves overhead. Ruth shifted her weight on the hard wooden bench and lost herself once more in the memory of that morning and how, gripping the cup of hot water in both hands, she'd sipped slowly, trying to pretend it was coffee, hoping some warmth would seep in and dispel the ugly coldness that had spread out from somewhere deep inside her. But the cold came from fear. Fear that Chester had gone for good, and there was no way to warm up if that were true. Fear that, if he did not return, for the rest of her life, she would feel a chilling loneliness.

Her mother interrupted her thoughts again, saying, "I don't think you ever did write and tell us why Chester up and moved you and Charlie to Oklahoma City. I realize he's not one to put down roots. You all have certainly moved around a lot over these past few years. You did say things were going good there in Tulsa. Why did you move?"

"It was something of a surprise to me, Mother. That's for sure. Though to tell you the truth, I gave up a long time ago expecting he'd stay put in one place for very long. As I recall it, I learned one morning while Charlie and I were just getting ready to sit down and have breakfast. Charlie's least favorite. Oatmeal."

"I remember that boy of yours always did like his bacon and eggs. And biscuits and gravy, too. He once told Pearl that her sausage gravy was his favorite."

"I had just spooned some oatmeal into a bowl and added half of the sugar that was left. Charlie sat looking at it with disgust written all over his face, but he was so hungry he picked up his spoon—and then I heard the front door open. Chester had been away overnight for a few days, working in Broken Bow, but that morning he walked in looking sassy as a bantam rooster, his hat cocked at an angle and pushed back onto his forehead. You probably remember how he liked to wear his hat that way."

CHAPTER 6 • RUTH

"I do." Her mother stood up and smoothed down the back of her dress. "I think Joan's water cooler may be a little cooler now than sitting under these trees. Let's go on over to her place."

"You go on. I want to sit awhile. Keep an eye out for Charlie and make sure he gets over to the house in time for lunch."

"Suit yourself." Her mother put the fan into her purse, pulled out a white handkerchief, and rubbed it across the back of her neck. "You won't like sittin' out here much longer, though. Another little while and the sun will be baking you to a crisp—shade or no shade."

As her mother walked away, Ruth was almost breathless at the memories of Chester's return after his weeklong absence. The minute she saw him, relief had swept away the hurt feelings that had built over the week, and she'd run to him. He pulled her into a bearhug and whirled her around, then planted a kiss full on her mouth. She kept back the tears that threatened to fall, held the kiss, and would have stayed in his arms no telling how long if he had not set her down and turned his attention to Charlie, who was clinging to Chester's waist.

He ruffled Charlie's hair and put an arm around his shoulders. "Hi there, little man. Glad to see your old daddy?"

Ruth didn't know whether to scold, laugh, or cry.

"Breakfast ready?" Chester asked; he took one look at the oatmeal and turned up his nose. "Not oatmeal."

Charlie stood back, scowling, and said, "I hate oatmeal."

"Fry us up some bacon and eggs, Ruth."

Ruth swallowed her gorge and kept back from expressing most of the week's fear, anger, and concern, not wanting it to spill out and drown his good humor. She couldn't help saying, "Chester, this child and I have had nothing to eat but oatmeal for most of this whole past week. And not enough of that. He's hungry. I'm starving."

Chester's large blue eyes, snapping with unsuppressed excitement when he'd come in, widened in surprise. That was followed by a storm cloud of aggravation, and, for a moment Ruth feared he would turn around and leave them to the last of the hateful, hot cereal.

Charlie moved up close to Chester, and then, with his legs apart and his hands doubled into fists said, "Daddy, I want some bacon and eggs. I don't want to eat oatmeal ever again as long as I live."

"Boy, that stomach of yours is all you ever think of." But Chester grabbed him, gave him a hug, looked at Ruth, and said, "Hell, what happened to that money I gave you last week?"

The bubble of pride at Charlie's demand of his dad brought more iron into Ruth's voice and she said, "You borrowed most of it back before you left. That's what. And the two dollars I had left in my purse couldn't feed us for a week. You just can't do that to us."

"God-damn if I didn't go and forget that I borrowed it. And I didn't plan on being away for so long. It just happened."

"Well, we've gone without for a week while you were forgetting. "We've been worried to death. . . . "

A spark of guilt flickered in Chester's eyes but quickly disappeared. "Well, hell, then. You two get dressed and take those hangdog looks off your faces, and we'll go get something. How about we go to Shirley's and order up some bacon and eggs."

"Biscuits and gravy, too," Charlie yelled.

"Hell, yes. All you can eat."

Ruth didn't have to tell Charlie to go get dressed but once. He flew to his bedroom. Going to hers and Chester's bedroom, she quickly pulled on a flowered print dress. Her stomach was knotted, and she had begun to sweat even though the summer's heat was just now making itself felt inside the house. She fumbled with her belt and then threw it aside in disgust when her hands, shaking and unsure, could not fasten it. Chester, impatient in the other room, yelled for them to hurry. His cigarette smoke, like a noxious fog, seeped under the bedroom door, making her sneeze. The front door slammed, and she hurriedly slipped her feet into a pair

CHAPTER 6 • RUTH

of down-at-the-heels shoes and ran to the porch, the fear that Chester might disappear dogging her footsteps.

He and Charlie were waiting for her in the car, and, when she crawled into the front seat, her heart was beating so fast, she had to take several deep breaths to slow it. Her mind was in a whirl, relief and anger mixed in equal proportion. She wanted to yell at him for being so selfish. But she wanted him to know how happy she was that he'd returned. "Can you tell me where you've been for the past week?"

He let out a sharp irritated breath, sending the last drag on his cigarette swirling out his mouth and through the open window. The cigarette butt followed. "I was hired on by a construction company in Broken Bow to drive one of their crawler-tractors with a bulldozer on its front end. Head foreman took twenty minutes to show what they wanted me to use the damn thing for, and then kept me busy all week. They had a rush job at this big construction site. I've just been eating, sleeping, and working. Nothing else."

The anger welled up again, and though she knew he would only get more aggravated, she said, "Why couldn't you drop us a card? Call?" And though she did not want to ask and hear an answer, she wondered how he could have kept his clothes so clean and pressed if, indeed, he'd been working so hard and long.

"Now that's enough, Ruth. It cost money to make a long-distance call. With this God-damn rationing, I didn't have enough gas to drive back and forth. And I was too tired at the end of a shift to think of going to the post office to mail a card."

Ruth, her belly hollow as an empty milk can, looked straight ahead, wondering if there was some answer to how a man could be so contrary and selfish. All she could see was the image of trees sliding past on the slick paint of the hood. He'd certainly found time to take care of his car. It was not the first time she'd let herself fully admit that Chester Scarsdale was looking out for himself first, and her and Charlie a distant second.

Or was it third, fourth, or fifth? But what was she to do? He was her husband, and she couldn't make it without him. And God help her, she loved the man.

They trooped into the restaurant, Charlie in his excitement pushing hard against the door and almost hitting a man standing at the cash register. On entering, Ruth thought she would faint from the good smells coming from the kitchen. Chester smiled at the pretty waitress who showed them to their booth and took their orders for breakfast. Charlie bounced up and down in his cushioned seat as he waited for the waitress to take their order. *If my bacon and eggs don't come soon,* Ruth thought, *I may be bouncing up and down as well.* The waitress appeared with two cups of coffee, and Ruth, her hands encircling the heated cup, drew coffee-laced steam deep into her lungs. It had been three days since the last of the coffee ran out. Taking a sip, she sighed and set back.

Chester lit up a cigarette took a deep drag and let it flow slowly out his nose before he began telling them about the work in Broken Bow. To Ruth, it was all she could do to concentrate as she watched the waitress carrying orders of bacon and eggs to other tables. When Charlie had ordered the same, plus biscuits and gravy on the side, she and Chester echoed him. Now, each time the waitress appeared from out of the kitchen with her tray loaded with plates of food, Ruth prayed it was for them.

Charlie broke out in a big smile, repeating, "Boy, oh boy, oh boy. Here it is."

Ruth thought the words to herself but did not want Chester to think she was acting like a starving child. Though she was famished, she took the time for one more sip of coffee. The first bite of eggs tasted better than anything else she had ever eaten.

His mouth full of biscuits and gravy, Chester said, "I've been bustin' to tell you something, Ruth, but figured I couldn't get your full attention till you started filling your stomach." He sat forward in his chair, his eyes widening in excitement. "With all the younger men off fighting this war,

CHAPTER 6 ✦ RUTH

it's easier for me to find a good-paying job now. It's men my age doing all the specialty work with dozers, and there's not enough of us out there to meet the demand." He took a huge bite of biscuits and gravy, and then waved his fork in a circle, as if he were conducting an orchestra. "This company I've been working for don't seem to get that yet. I'd asked for a raise two months ago, and all I got from them was, 'When you've worked for us six months, we'll talk raise.'"

Ruth's fork paused halfway to her mouth, but she lowered it then, and asked, "You're surely not thinking of quitting, are you?"

He dismissed her question with a wave of his hand. "Remember us giving Jerry Jenson and his niece a lift back to Tulsa last time we visited Hobart?"

She nodded, remembering very well, Jerry's niece, Alice, who had been hanging on to Chester's every word when they'd driven the pair to Jenson's house. He'd liked it, too, having a twenty-four-year-old moon-struck over him.

"Well, a couple of days ago, Jerry was working at the same site as me. We got to talkin' and he told me he'd hired on with this fellow he knows down in Oklahoma City who'll pay fifty cents to a dollar more an hour than I'm getting now." Chester pointed his fork at her and shook it, sending biscuit crumbs sprinkling onto the table. "Now that ain't all."

Charlie giggled and wetting his finger, picked up the breadcrumbs one by one and licked them off.

"Don't do that Charlie," Ruth scolded. "You've still got biscuits and gravy on your plate." Interrupting Chester gave her a second to take in the idea they'd likely be moving again.

"It sounded to me like a God-damn good job, let me tell you."

"That's wonderful, Chester," Ruth said, not really feeling it, the sick bubble in her chest ballooning at the thought of another move.

"You betcha. And the good news is that Jerry called and told him about me. The man hired me sight unseen. You won't have to worry about paying the bills or having enough to eat anymore. And, Charlie, I can get you those clamp-on roller-skates you've been wanting."

"So, it's decided, Chester? We're moving to Oklahoma City?"

"I have to be there to start work the day after tomorrow. So, let me get you back to the house, and you can start packing up while I'm at work today. We leave tomorrow after I finish working and get my paycheck."

Ruth was so surprised and worried she didn't know what to say to Chester as he hustled them up and out the door before she finished her second cup of coffee. Somewhat dazed by the news and the feeling of satiation from the food, she could think of nothing to say except, "We have to stop and get something to eat for today and tomorrow before we leave."

"I don't get paid till tomorrow, and all I've got is four dollars. I need enough to buy eight gallons of gas with my rationing card. That's enough to get us to Oklahoma City. So, here's two dollars. Don't get anything that'll spoil before we get there."

He didn't need to state the obvious, she thought. But that wasn't something you said to Chester when he was in this giddy mood if you didn't want him to get huffy.

Chester drove them to the grocery store and then took Charlie to scrounge cardboard boxes while she spent almost every last cent of the two dollars on bread, a jar of peanut butter and one of strawberry jam, a box of Kellogg's Corn Flakes, bologna lunchmeat, potato chips, cookies, and milk. She scrunched her nose up as she passed the Quakers lined up close by the corn flakes and thought, *Charlie would stick his tongue out at them.* They were waiting for her in the shade of the store awning when she came out into the heat of the morning. The trunk and back seat of the car were piled with cardboard boxes, and Charlie, excited by having filled his stomach with something more than oatmeal and the expectation of taking off on the adventure of moving, squirmed like a two-year-old.

When Chester pulled into the driveway of their rented, furnished duplex, Ruth sighed. She'd thought of this as home, had hoped it was

CHAPTER 6 ✦ RUTH

permanent, but couldn't think of it as a home, now, knowing she was leaving tomorrow.

"You-all get everything packed, and I'll load it when I get back from work," Chester said as he pulled boxes from the trunk and handed them to Charlie to carry into the duplex. "We want to get an early start." He waved as he backed out of the drive, leaving her and Charlie to fill the empty boxes. Ruth was afraid the empty space his week's absence had created could not be filled before he hurt her again. But if she couldn't fill her emptiness, she could fill the boxes, so handing one to Charlie, she said, "You put your toys and clothes in this while I get the rest of the things packed."

She started by folding the extra sheets and pillowcases they had for their beds. The pretty daisies she'd embroidered on the pillowcases were still bright with color even after months of washing them. By the end of the day, she had packed their clothes, extra bedding, toiletries, and cookware into cardboard boxes, a couple of suitcases, and the large trunk that held keepsakes and anything else of value.

Chester's shift was over and he hadn't showed up so she and Charlie set down to sweet milk, bologna sandwiches, and cookies. Ruth's feelings of emptiness began to deepen.

Charlie began to fidget and asked, "Where's dad? He said we were leaving tomorrow."

"He's just busy, Charlie. He'll be home directly." But she was frightened that they were going to be left alone again with what she'd bought today. She hated the thought that they would end up being alone till she and Charlie finished emptying the jars of peanut butter and jam. Then she'd learn to hate them like she had the oatmeal. Charlie, too.

She drew a deep breath and let it out slowly when Chester dragged in two hours late, smelling of alcohol and cigarettes. The fear and hurt feelings she let disappear into the emptiness inside her as she listened to him make excuses.

"Some of the boys decided that since I was only going to be back one more day, and this was my last night before we left, that we should go out for a couple of beers," he explained. I had a hamburger. Don't need any supper."

Ruth turned in early, leaving Chester and Charlie listening to *The Great Gildersleeve*. Her night was filled with restless dreams, even after Chester finally came in and filled the empty space on his side of the bed. She dreamed of feeling starved and awakened so hungry that she fixed and ate a peanut butter and jelly sandwich. Then, feeling spiteful, she stuffed the smiling Quaker into her trash bag even though he had one more serving of oatmeal to give them. Through much of the remaining night, she lay half awake, dreading the thought of getting into the loaded car and driving somewhere new. She was not sure why the dread. Moving somewhere else was something she'd done throughout their marriage. She always made do.

Chester was up at daybreak, wolfed down the milk toast Ruth made him, and was out the door, promising first that he'd be back right after work, and then adding, "Make sure you're ready for us to pack the car the minute I get back."

Ruth didn't hold her breath waiting for him to return on time and wasn't surprised she still hadn't seen him when two hours had passed. By then, she and Charlie had everything they'd need for the day packed, and she had cleaned the four-room duplex from floor to ceiling, leaving it spotless.

"Why did we have to clean house, Mama? We're leaving here."

"Nobody is going to move into a house I've lived in and say, 'That woman who lived here last was a horrible housecleaner.'"

Chester pulled up five minutes after she'd said this to Charlie, opened the luggage compartment, and yelled, "Come on—come on. Time's a-wasting."

And who wasted two hours, she thought but kept that to herself as she helped load her large trunk and two suitcases. Those heavy items took

CHAPTER 6 ♦ RUTH

up most of the car's boot, but in the nooks and crannies around this luggage Ruth stuffed winter coats, their good shoes, a small radio, and their soiled bedding. They filled the back seat with cardboard boxes, leaving only room for Charlie between them and the door.

Complaining, "There ain't enough room for me back here," as he opened the back seat door, Charlie squeezed in beside three cardboard boxes stacked next to him. Ruth had to shut the door for him.

As they pulled away from their home of more than six months, a few tears rolled down Ruth's cheeks, but she hid them from Chester and Charlie. She reached down into one of two large purses, one filled with what she called, "my feminine needs," and the other with handkerchiefs, her makeup, rationing stamps, part of a loaf of bread, a jar of peanut butter, and one of jelly. With the handkerchief she'd retrieved, she dabbed at her cheeks and, peering out over the loaf of bread she'd laid on the dashboard, watched the city of Tulsa fade away. The cramped interior of the car soon began to smell of their day-old sweat and the fine dust Chester's earth moving machine had kicked up. Things didn't get any better when he lit up his first cigarette, and, though he directed the smoke out his open window, it blew back in, claiming its place and making Ruth's eyes begin to burn.

Ruth was cramped and irritable, Charlie whiny and complaining, and Chester in one of his blue funks at the end of the three hours it took to drive the 90 miles to Oklahoma City. They spent an hour looking for a place to rent, but by the time it was fully dark, they'd found nowhere they could afford to stay. Ruth lay awake in the front seat of the car much of the night and listened to the soft breathing of her son and the heavier one of Chester. When morning came, they ate peanut butter-and-jam sandwiches she made in the front seat and passed to Chester and to the back seat for Charlie.

"This tastes better than oatmeal," Charlie said as he bit into his second sandwich.

"I have to admit you're right, Charlie—it sure does taste better than oatmeal."

"You two going to keep harping on that?" Chester asked. "Won't ever happen again. So just drop it."

Please God, let that be true, Ruth thought.

Driving through a part of the city near his job, looking for something to rent, she was worrying they would be spending another night in the car, but, by dark, they'd found an affordable, furnished duplex. Chester was morose and quiet as they moved into what she hoped would be their new home, not just a rented space.

*

"Mama, I'm hungry."

Ruth started at the sound of her son's complaint. She'd been so absorbed in her memories she'd not realized how much time had passed. "Well, let's get on over to Joan's, and if your grandmother and those two cousins of yours haven't already eaten everything, you can get something to eat."

"They're just little girls. They don't eat that much."

Which was true. Still, they were already five minutes late to lunch, and Joan and Mother would be fussing at her for sure.

CHAPTER 7

Ruth

➤➤ ✾ ⬅⬅

That evening, after all the chores were done, supper over, dishes washed, Mother at her sewing, Papa listening to the new, and Charlie in the midst of reading a Hardy Boys book, Ruth sat in the porch swing and gently rocked as she let the cooling night breeze waft over her. She had resisted letting all those upsetting stored memories of last year rise to the surface, but they had a force of their own that she couldn't control. Now she stopped fighting to keep them pushed down and let them fill her mind, hoping they would exhaust her, and she could finally get some sleep. She recalled settling into the new duplex they'd rented in Oklahoma City with some ease because the family next door had a girl Charlie's age, and the two of them hit it off right away. The girl's mother quickly became Ruth's friend, and she didn't feel so lonely during the day. Charlie adjusted to his new school, which, God bless him, was the sixth one he'd attended since first grade.

Chester did well in his new job and didn't get in a fight with his boss or any of his coworkers. Ruth didn't like it that he worked long hours and often spent nights away when the company sent him out of town on a construction job. She had known, not long after marrying Chester, that he was a restless soul. And one too easily led to testing limits; he was unable to cope with anyone telling him what to do. Still, Ruth hoped the Oklahoma City duplex was a more permanent home for them than the last few had been. She felt settled and looked forward to the Christmas holidays. They were going to spend Christmas Eve and Christmas Morning in Oklahoma City, and then hoped to visit Chester's folks, who lived on the family farm near Hydro, Oklahoma.

The Christmas season started out with Chester not raising a fuss when she sent her sister Pearl's two boys each two dollars and Joan's two- and four-year-old girls a dollar each. He seemed happy, too, when she brought home presents for Charlie—more than any past Christmas. Most of them were practical gifts, things Charlie needed, but not all of them. Chester was making good money, and they had some to spare. He smiled a lot and didn't scold Charlie as much. Gave her a hug and kiss more often. She latched on to the hope that this Christmas and the coming New Year heralded the beginning of a new and better chapter in their lives.

On Christmas morning, she was awakened by Charlie yelling, "Get up, Mama. Hurry! Daddy and I want to open presents." Throwing on a robe and going into the front room, she found them both sitting in front of the Christmas tree, Chester leaning back on the couch, smoking one of his Lucky Strikes and Charlie bouncing up and down on a chair he'd pulled close to the small Christmas tree that Chester had brought home. That was a first. He'd always left that to her. Two days earlier, after unpacking the ornaments and a string of colored lights from her trunk of valuables, Chester, Charlie, and she had removed the dead bulbs from

CHAPTER 7 ✦ RUTH

the string and screwed in new ones. They'd laughed a lot while draping the lights over the tree. Chester even gave them a hand putting on the ornaments. Now it all looked so festive, she had to smile.

"We let you, Ruth, you'd stay in bed all morning," Chester teased.

She didn't say but thought to herself, *as if I weren't the one who set up late wrapping presents after you and Charlie went off to bed. Otherwise, there would be fewer presents under the tree.* "Those presents aren't going anywhere, so you two just hold your horses until I make myself a cup of coffee."

"I already perked some coffee, Ruth. Get me one, too," Chester called after her as she pushed through the kitchen door.

"And bring me a glass of milk," Charlie yelled. "Santa didn't eat all his cookies."

Well, she thought. *This* Santa ate three of them while she was putting presents around the tree. She was so pleased to see the two of them excited and Chester sounding like he was in a good mood. She hoped he liked what she was giving him and was excited by the three presents with her name on them.

Two minutes later, with coffee and milk in hand, she said, "Okay, Charlie. You get to hand out the gifts."

His eyes shining with excitement, he handed them each a gift. Chester praised him for the pair of gloves Ruth had helped Charlie pick out. She gave Charlie a big hug and a kiss when he gave her a picture of the three of them he'd drawn and colored in class. The three stick figures were holding hands, and all three had enormous heads with wide smiles plastered on their faces. A bright sun poured rays of sunshine down around them, and a dog stood near, a large bubble above its head with the words, "arf, arf, arf Merry Christmas," scribbled in Charlie's childish hand.

"I'll get this hung first thing after we finish opening gifts," she promised.

She was amazed that Chester had splurged on presents for her. She was thrilled to death when she opened her two gifts from him. He had given her a warm chocolate-colored shawl and a silver heart-shaped locket she'd admired in a local jewelry store they'd walked by one evening not long before Christmas. The touch of his hands against her neck as he fastened it around her neck made her shiver with pleasure. He then received the same treatment as Charlie, though the kiss lasted longer.

After Chester unwrapped the new leather wallet she'd saved for out of her grocery money, his blue eyes sparkled and crinkled with good will. He said, "What a pretty picture of yourself you put in here," and then pulled her close and kissed her.

He kissed her again when he tore the red-reindeer-and-Santa-sprinkled paper off his next gift and saw the new belt. Her whole body warmed with his kisses.

With growing disappointment, Charlie unwrapped and laid aside a new shirt, socks, and underwear. He brightened a little when he tore open a tube of Pick-up Sticks. His eyes lit up when he tore open a small package with a red and yellow wooden spinning top that changed to orange when spun. But he whooped with joy when he opened a package with the clamp-on skates he'd been wanting for months. It would have been a good Christmas for him with just what he'd already received, but then Chester handed him a package that had been out of sight behind the couch till then. Charlie was speechless, then his face lit up like a Christmas tree when he tore into this last, special gift from his daddy.

He squealed so loud that Ruth was afraid it would disturb the neighbors as a bright-red metal box came into view. He pointed to the letters printed on the lid and read aloud, "The New Erector, The World's Greatest Toy." He opened the lid and peered inside with a more reverent look than any person Ruth had ever seen during church services. "And it's got seventy-two-pieces!" He clapped his hands. "Plus a motor!"

"You really fooled Santa somehow," Chester said. "The way you've acted lately, I was sure all he would bring you was some coal and a few switches." Charlie paid him no mind and began unpacking the box. Ruth smiled as Chester plopped down on the living room floor and reached for some erector pieces. "Old Santa must have known your daddy's a construction worker. Wanted you to be one, too." Charlie's smile was plastered all over his face during the whole half an hour Chester helped him put together one of the structures suggested in the directions, a simple four-legged tower with a lift at the top. His excited face added to the warm glow emitted by the string of lights she'd woven through the branches of the Frasier Fir that Chester had installed in the corner of the living room.

She loved even more that, after breakfast, wearing his new belt and with all his money and driver's license changed over into his new wallet, Chester agreed to playing a quick game of pick-up sticks. Charlie beamed even when Chester took the highest scoring stick, won the game, and proudly declared, "I'm the pick-up stick champion."

Charlie then pleaded, "Let's play again, dad. Please."

"We'll play again, I promise. But it will have to be some other time." He ruffed Charlie's hair, then took coffee, cigarettes, and the newspaper over to his favorite chair. Leaving Charlie to his erector set, Ruth sat across from Chester feeling happiness well up and overflow along with her tears of gratitude.

She was sure life could get no better than this.

*

It was getting on toward nine here on the farm, and the cicadas were singing their night's song as the air cooled. Old Spot the hound started barking, and she wondered if he were down by the chicken house chasing off some unwanted critter like a coyote or possum. But these sounds were not enough to distract her mind from wandering on beyond that perfect Christmas as she continued to swing slowly back and forth.

*

Things had felt freer and easier between the two of them during the days between Christmas and New Year's Eve. Several times a day, Ruth touched the locket she'd been wearing since Chester fastened it around her neck on Christmas morning. With the start of a new year, Chester began coming home late some evenings. On a brutally cold, late winter evening, after Charlie had fallen asleep, Ruth stood ironing Chester's shirts and waiting for him to come home. The slow-ticking clock on the kitchen counter moved its large hand monotonously around and around its face, marking the minutes passing that Chester did not come home or call.

It was after nine o'clock, and she had just picked up another shirt to iron when the shrill ring of the phone startled her. She grabbed for it. Thank God. Chester. Hopefully letting her know he'd soon be on his way home. A wave of relief broke over her as she first heard Chester's voice.

"Ruth, I got in a fight with this bastard in a bar who was mouthing off to me, and the cops arrested me. I'm in jail. They tell me you'll have to come up with five hundred dollars for a bail bondsman to get me out."

Ruth's right hand tightened around the receiver pressed hard against her ear, while with the left, she reached for the edge of the kitchen counter to steady herself. Leaning over the sink, she choked out, "Where am I going to get that kind of money?

"Goddamn it, Ruth, you think I don't know that?" he spit out at her. "I'm just telling you so you can bring me some things down here tomorrow morning. Looks like I'm in here till I go before the judge."

"I'll get there in the morning as soon as I get Charlie off to school," she said, and the phone clicked off without Chester saying goodbye. She sat staring at the floor and not wanting to believe what she'd just heard. Why couldn't he control his temper? Grow up? And where on Earth could

CHAPTER 7 • RUTH

she find that kind of money? A wave of dizziness overtook her. What would she tell Charlie if Chester had to spend time in jail?

As if he'd heard her thoughts, Charlie appeared in the doorway to his room. "Was that daddy? Will he be home later?" With the heel of his hand, he rubbed at the sleep in his eyes, waiting for her answer.

"I'm afraid your daddy had a little accident at work today, honey. He won't be able to get out of the hospital for a few days. I don't know how many."

Charlie's eyes grew large, and his mouth dropped open. "Is he hurt bad? Will he be all right?" He hurried over to her, and she put her arms around him and drew him close. "He's not hurt bad, but he'll still have to be away for a while. Now let's both go to bed, and we'll talk to daddy tomorrow on the phone."

Charlie was back asleep almost at once, but Ruth, unable to keep her mind quiet, lay in their bed staring at the ceiling and worrying. Chester going before a judge? She just couldn't believe it.

Arriving at the jail next morning, she almost cried when she saw two long scratches on his left cheek, a bruised jaw, and a purple blotch the size of a silver dollar under his left eye, which was swollen shut. His right arm was in a sling, and he couldn't move without grimacing in pain. "Oh, sweetheart," she said. "I'm so sorry."

Being Chester, he laughed and said, "That bastard I got in a fight with is a hell of a lot worse off than me."

He wasn't smiling, much less laughing, three days later, when he went up before the judge on charges of a Class B Misdemeanor. His court-appointed lawyer argued that the other man was a local troublemaker, known to the police, and that Chester had no prior arrests. Despite his bad temper and not-infrequent fights, Chester had never been arrested before. Sitting in the courtroom, she was stunned when he was found guilty of aggravated assault. She almost fainted when the judge said, "I'm giving you a choice, Mr. Scarsdale, of spending two years in jail and paying a $500 fine, or," he paused, as if for effect, and then continued, "or enlisting in the one of the armed services. You and your lawyer go talk this over, and get back to me directly."

Immediately after the verdict and the judge's offer, they were escorted by the court-appointed lawyer to a small room, which Ruth was sure had once been a storage closet for housecleaning supplies. She was not surprised that when the door closed, Chester erupted.

"Goddamn that son-of-a-bitch. It was all I could do to keep from telling him what an asshole he is."

The lawyer pursed his lips and shook his head. "Good thing you didn't. The judge was a bit more lenient on you than he usually is. Must have been he took pity on this pretty wife of yours sitting there in the courtroom with tears in her eyes. And he gave you a choice of enlisting or going to jail. He could have just sentenced you to a lot longer jail term and given you a much larger fine. You have to remember that the judge had a good look at those photographs of the man you were fighting with. You sent him to the hospital bruised all over and with a serious concussion, a broken arm, and internal injuries from the stomping you gave him. And the testimony from the man's friends about how you acted wasn't so flattering, either."

Chester seemed to wilt. "God Almighty, Ruth. These past three days in jail have been a bitch. There's no way I could take two years of it."

"There's no way you can go overseas and get shot at, either," Ruth said, her voice rising to a shout. "Going to jail would be better than putting yourself in harm's way. You just can't think of joining up. What would become of Charlie and me for the rest of our lives if something happened to you? At least, if you went to prison for two years, you'd come out whole."

Chester bowed his head and shook it back and forth. "I'd come out a jailbird is what would happen. Be so stir-crazy I'd be talking to myself. You want a husband like that? Prison's just out of the question."

CHAPTER 7 ✦ RUTH

"Mr. Scarsdale, Mrs. Scarsdale, I have a suggestion. I have an uncle who at age forty joined a navy battalion called the Sea Bees. He told me they only do construction work. Build airfields, make roads and bridges, and anything else that needs construction. It's not that they are completely out of harm's way, he tells me, and they do carry guns. But unlike a marine or grunt soldier, they're seldom if ever on the front lines. The Sea Bees might be a safer service to consider, folks. And, Chester, you can arrange for Mrs. Scarsdale to receive a small allotment each month out of your pay."

"Hell," Chester said, "I'd much rather work my butt off than rot in prison."

"Please don't do it, Chester," Ruth pleaded.

Ruth wasn't sure whether to be relieved or hysterical when he was released from jail and three days later enlisted in the Sea Bees. She had to keep herself together for Charlie's sake. Her son had been concerned when he saw the bruises and scratches on Chester's face but only looked puzzled when Chester said, "I'm enlisting in the Sea Bees, Charlie." Thank the good Lord Chester lied to their son as easily as she had earlier, telling him, "Listen, boy, I'm joining up because I gotta help whip those Krauts' and Japs' asses and make sure you and your mama are going to stay safe back here at home."

*

Chester was ordered to report to Fort Peary, Virginia, on January 20 for his initial three weeks' training. Sitting at the kitchen table together after Charlie was asleep when he told her, Ruth let the tears roll down her cheeks. "I have to go with you, Chester," she said.

"We just don't have the money for that, Ruth. On what they'll be paying me, we can't afford to pay rent and have anything left over for you and Charlie to buy food. Makes more sense for me to just live on base and send money back to you here."

The headache came on then, splitting her brow in two as if a wedge had been driven between her eyes. "What are we going to do? Charlie and I can't stay in Oklahoma City for the same reasons. We just can't afford living here." She remembered Mr. Quaker all too keenly and wished never again to invite him or one of his ilk like Cream of Wheat or Grits to be the sole tenant in her pantry.

"You'll have to go live with your folks," Chester said.

"I can't do that, Chester. I think Charlie would be miserable. My folks can hardly bear to be around him, given the way they feel about you. They think he's a chip off the old block. His Pa and Granny Scarsdale love him do death."

"My folks have got a houseful right now. They've got Jerry and Dianna's five-year-old, Pierce, and Dolly and her three kids crammed in that shanty of theirs. You and Charlie would have to sleep in the barn with Pa's old cat, Duncan, and all the rats and mice he's too old to catch any more."

She had shivered at the thought. "What about your uncle Pete down there in Weatherford? He's been nice to Charlie and me. Out behind his filling station he's got those six one-room cabins he rents out. I'll bet you could talk him into letting us stay in one of those for next to nothing. I really don't want to go home to Mother and Papa."

"I'll give him a call, Ruth. See what he says. I really don't want Charlie having to put up with Bob Choat, either. Or your mother." He put his arm around her shoulders and pulled her close. "My folks over in Hydro can look in on you—bring vegetables, milk, and eggs from the farm when they can spare any. Pa will bring you some meat from the smoke house when he butchers this fall. And Ma will bring you some of the fruit and vegetables she cans this summer and fall. You and Charlie should do just fine."

Ruth didn't see much of Chester for the next two weeks as he worked fourteen-hour days. "I'm trying to earn enough to tide you and Charlie over until you start getting those checks from the government," he assured her. "Uncle Pete says you can stay, rent free, in one of his tourist-court cabins

CHAPTER 7 ♦ RUTH

if you help out around the gas station and with his other five rentals." Still, her fear and concern knew no bounds as she packed their things.

The day Chester drove them to Weatherford, Ruth felt the tears behind her eyes would break any minute and she wouldn't be able to stop them. As they left Oklahoma City, Charlie began asking questions he'd kept bottled up till then. "How long you going to be gone, Daddy. Can we come visit you? Will you write me a letter? Will they let you come home sometime soon? Will you ride all the way across the ocean on a big boat?" It was as if a damn had broken as he asked his questions in quick, jerky sentences, the sheer volume of words drowning out his fear of losing his daddy.

When they reached Weatherford and parked in front of Uncle Pete's service station, he came out to greet them. Ruth had always thought he looked a little like a picture of Will Rogers she'd once seen. Uncle Pete had the same homey smile, and a worn fedora. A lock of hair escaping from underneath the crown almost reached his eyes. Giving her and Charlie a hug and Chester a handshake, he led them to the one-room cabin that would be her and Charlie's new home. After helping unload their things, Uncle Pete left them to say goodbye to each other. Chester was in a hurry to get back to Oklahoma City before dark. Ruth wanted him to stay with them and cried as they stood at the front door, Charlie on one side of his daddy and holding on while she clung to Chester with both arms around his neck. Chester stooped down and hugged Charlie even though Ruth did not let go. "You take care of your mama now, Charlie. And be a good boy."

Through his tears, Charlie said, "I will."

"Now stay in here while your mama walks me to the car." His arm around her, he guided her outside into the cold and walked to the car with his arm around her shoulders.

Though in her winter coat and melded into Chester's warm arm and body as she clung to him, a coldness pierced her, chilling her to the bone.

"I don't know what to say, Chester. I've never been so scared and unhappy in my life," she whispered.

"Hell, Ruth. I'm scared out of my britches. I keep wondering if you were right and I should have just gone on to jail for a couple of years." He pulled her arms from around his waist and held her away from him for a minute. "You take care of yourself, Ruth. And take care of our boy. I love you both." He reached down and gave her a lingering kiss as they both clung to each one last time.

Ruth broke into tears and gripped him in her aching arms as if she would never let go. He reached up and slowly pried her arms away, opened the car door, and sank into the seat as she pushed the door closed, the snap of its catch sounding so final she broke into tears. The first angry growls of the starter did not promise that the motor would catch, and she hoped it failed to start. But the engine did catch, the gears turned, and the car slowly pulled away. As Chester turned onto the highway, Charlie ran out of the house into the cold without a coat and flailed both arms wildly, as if to coax one last goodbye wave from his daddy. But Chester disappeared and never looked back. Ruth ran to Charlie and, holding him close, shepherded him inside. Neither of them slept well that night. Ruth for many nights thereafter.

As she settled into the one-room cabin, found a country school nearby for Charlie, and hoped for letters from Chester, she couldn't get over being frightened at thoughts of what was to become of her. What if he were killed? Even if he wasn't, this war could last for years. How could she survive on her own?

In the first letter she received from him after he drove away, he wrote:

"I'm being sent from Fort Perry to Port Hueneme Naval Base in California, where I'll train seven or eight weeks and then ship out to God knows where. I know you would like to join me here, but we both know that living on the money I get paid isn't enough for us to

CHAPTER 7 ✦ RUTH

live on. I hope things are working out with Uncle Pete and the folks. Give Charlie a big hug for me. I hope he's learning to build some damn fancy things with that erector set. I love you both."

At first, Chester's parents came into town every week or two and brought food from the farm—she and Charlie would have starved on what Chester had left with them when he drove away. She didn't get any money from the government for several weeks after they arrived. As spring approached, Pa and Granny brought less and less. "We're havin' an awful time tryin' to feed all of us out there on the farm," Pa told her. What little he'd been able to leave for them had to be stretched as far as she could manage, but the reality was becoming more and more evident every day that Mr. Quaker was thinking of coming to visit them again. Thank goodness Charlie never tired of biscuits and gravy, which was what she sometimes served them twice a day.

One bright spot for Charlie was that his teacher made all the kids warm chocolate pudding every day at lunch time. Paid for it out of her own pocket. Another was that the school, unlike others Charlie had gone to, didn't have a resident bully. Probably helped that most of the students happened to be girls.

In the second letter Chester wrote, he told her he was shipping out overseas on March 23. She cried when she read it and was awake all night worrying about his safety. The news of the fighting on both the western and the eastern fronts was filled with reports of fierce battles.

Two days later she answered a knock on her door and found Uncle Pete, standing on the step, holding his fedora, and sporting a hangdog expression on his face.

"Howdy, Ruth," Uncle Pete began. "I've something I need to tell you."

"Come on in, and have a cup of coffee, Uncle Pete. I just made a pot."

He sat at her small table and waited quietly while she poured two cups and tried to steady her breathing as she set them on the table and placed her sugar bowl and creamer closer to him. She waited to say anything until he had taken a sip of the coffee. "Everything all right, Uncle Pete?"

Uncle Pete cleared his throat and said, "I hate to tell you, Ruth, but I sold this place, and, come first week of May, I'll be moving down to Altus, where my daughter Elizabeth lives. I'm gettin' on toward sixty-five and just can't keep doin' this work."

"I certainly can understand you needing to do that," Ruth said, though a part of her wanted to say different. She had to hold back her tears as she asked, "When do we have to move out?"

If Uncle Pete's face hadn't been burned dark by the sun, Ruth figured it would have turned bright red; as it was, it turned two shades darker brown. "Fellow bought it. Paid cash on the barrelhead. Said he wanted to take ownership first of May." He finished his coffee in one swallow and stood up. "I'm real sorry, Ruth. I hope Chester's folks can take you in." He walked to the door but turned and said, "Thank you kindly for the coffee," before escaping out the door.

What am I to do, she thought but could come up with no good answer. She wrote to Chester and asked that question, hoping he'd have an answer but deep down knew he did not have a good one. When she got his next letter, her fears were realized. He wrote:

> *I know you don't like the idea, but I think you'd have to go stay with your parents till the war is over. Ma wrote and said they're having a pretty rough time of it trying to take care of Jerry's boy and Dolly and her three. She wrote that she was feeling really bad about not helping you more. Last summer's vegetables from the garden Ma canned are gone and until she can depend on this year's produce, there'll have to be some tightening of their belts. Bob and Ida are in a much better position to keep you and Charlie.*

CHAPTER 7 • RUTH

Ruth sat down at the tiny kitchen table and cried when she finished reading his letter. She still sat there an hour later, the half cup of coffee grown cold, and her mind numbed by what she knew must happen. Her only skill lay in being a mother and wife. She had no other skills to speak of other than those she'd used helping out Uncle Pete and the seasonal farm work she'd done when she was young. The prospect of finding some other kind of work scared her too much. She was a housewife. Had always been a housewife. Never wanted to do more than be a housewife. Taking a deep breath, she looked at the feedstore calendar hanging on a nail next to the table. It told her it was April 10, 1943. Above it was a picture of a farmer standing in a field of cotton that had just peeked through the red soil of an Oklahoma farm. The picture could have been taken looking out on her papa's field. Looking away and shaking her head in denial of what the reality was, she began making plans to pull up stakes and find a way to get to Papa's and Mother's farm, a place she dreaded having to live. She'd married at fifteen partly to get away from home, and now she was forced to return.

Uncle Pete agreed to drive her part way and let her use his phone in the service station to arrange for her Uncle John to also get her part way to Hobart. When she placed the calls to her two sisters, each agreed to drive them a few miles distance and eventually on to the farm.

Until the first week in June, Ruth pinched pennies and lived off the goodwill of Uncle Pete and the Scarsdale's eggs, an occasional jar of last summer's canned vegetables and fruit, and the last of Pa's and Granny's salt-cured ham and bacon. She took Charlie out of school a few days before the end of the term, packed up their meager belongings, and, early on a rainy Sunday morning, loaded them into Uncle Pete's car.

Out of the goodness of his heart, he'd agreed to drive her and Charlie to Clinton, where she would meet up with Uncle John, who, when she called him, had been surprised to hear from her, but on learning of her situation, had said, "I can spare enough gas to get you from Clinton to Cordell." She was thankful for his sacrifice; it was a thirty-two-mile round-trip drive for him and would take a third of one week's worth of gas stamps. Her sister Joan had agreed to pick them up in Cordell and bring them to Hobart. Sister Pearl would see to it they got to the farm. And here they were.

CHAPTER 8

Ruth

⇉ ❊ ⇇

"Guess what, Mama," Charlie said.

Ruth startled and put her hand to her heart. "I wish you wouldn't sneak up on me," she said. "You liked to have scared me to death."

"I didn't mean to scare you. But I just finished reading The Disappearing Door. My cousin Carl said he would lone me The Mystery of the Flying Express when I finished with this one."

Ruth took a deep breath and let her ruffled feathers settle down before she said, "That's nice, Charlie. I'm glad. But please don't come up on me like that. Please?" He closed his hand around the book, and she took his wrist and pulled him down onto the bench. "When I get my wits about me again, we have to think about getting to bed. You'll be cross as a bear tomorrow if I let you stay up any longer."

"Why are you still sittin' here? What are you doin'?" He began pushing the floor with his feet making the swing move.

"Just calm down, Charlie. I know you're excited, but calm down." She reached out and smoothed a lock of hair that had fallen down over Charlie's forehead. "I was just now thinking about our trip from Weatherford to the farm."

Charlie's eyes lit up. "Yeah. I remember seeing all those army trucks. And remember we saw antiaircraft guns and cannons. And trucks with huge bombs on them. Or maybe they were torpedoes."

Ruth nodded. She remembered the military convoys all right, but her eyes did not light up at the memory. They had been pinned between trucks headed west on 66, those behind hugging their bumper until they saw enough empty highway ahead to give them room to pass. Other convoys came at them from the east, heading west, lumbering by with their loads of huge shells, guns, tanks, and whatever else was in those with a covered top. Thinking about them now, like then, brought up visions of war more nakedly vivid than the pictures she saw in the paper or on the movie screens at the Kiowa theater. And, of course, amidst all these memories and thoughts, Chester's danger at the hands of their enemies who launched missiles at him just as these weapons on the trucks would hurl death back at them.

"I remember getting sick, too," he said. "And Uncle Pete having to stop. I really hated standing there with all those truck drivers seeing me upchucking." Charlie made a sour face at the memory. "And the car smelled like puke all the way to Clinton."

"Just be glad I caught most of it in a paper bag before we stopped," Ruth said. Even though the car had smelled of Pete's chewing tobacco and his motor-oil-stained pants when they'd started out, inside the car, it became almost unbearable. The raw stain of what had escaped the bag sat moldering on the back-seat floorboards. She wouldn't have been able to sit in the car if the smell of Uncle Pete's tobacco hadn't cut the stink.

"And you were lucky that Uncle Pete didn't have a fit about it and leave us beside the road."

"He wouldn't have done that," Charlie challenged.

He was right. But when the weather changed for the worse, she wished he'd stopped and let them run to the nearest storm shelter. The approaching front had appeared on the horizon not more than five minutes after they drove on. Ruth remembered that when she saw they were heading toward a bank of roiling black clouds, the bottom dropped out of her stomach. She'd pleaded, "Can we pull off and try to find a storm cellar?"

Uncle Pete only looked at her with a puzzled frown. "It's just a rainstorm. I heard nothing on the radio about any tornados coming this way. I need to get back to the station as soon as I can. Sam Willard is going to be in to get that flat tire, and I won't have it ready. We have to drive on." She swallowed her panic, sat back in her seat, and wished she had another paper bag handy for herself.

A long line of army trucks roared past them, spewing water onto the windshield, turning it white, momentarily blinding them until the speeded-up back-and-forth of the windshield wipers flushed it away. Uncle Pete had to reach up every minute or two and wipe away the film of moisture that formed on the inside of the windshield. She felt the terrified beating of her heart against her chest all the way to Clinton.

Forty minutes after they left Weatherford, Uncle Pete turned off the highway, pulled under a service-station canopy, and helped her unload her suitcases and trunk next to a soda pop cooler. "You say your Uncle John's supposed to pick you up here shortly? Should I wait?"

She shook her head. "You've been real good to Charlie and me, and that's enough. I know you've got things to do back at the station. We'll be all right till he gets here." Ruth's voice caught in her throat as she made this statement. Nothing would be all right until this storm had passed.

"It was good having you around these past few weeks, Ruth. Sorry it couldn't be longer." He gave her a quick hug and a gruff, "Goodbye," crawled into his car, and turned back onto 66, where he disappeared into the rain-misted flow of military convoys.

The storm had quieted for a while with only an occasional flicker of light, so when a bolt of lightning flared nearby and a peal of thunder shook the air, it sent a shiver of terror through her, the shock turning her hands and body to stone. She couldn't move for a few seconds. In the glare of the lightning, she stared at the raw outline of a native elm growing next to the station, its leaves heavy with moisture, its limbs dancing wildly in the murky wind. Her nerves were so frazzled she wanted nothing more, right then, but to sit down on her trunk, drop her face onto her hands, and weep. Or better still, find a storm cellar. No hope for that, so, instead, she took hold of Charlie's hand and led him inside the station to a window looking out into the sheeting rain. "Heaven help me," she whispered low enough that Charlie wouldn't hear. "I wish Uncle John would get here."

"I'm hungry, Mama," Charlie whined, pulling at her arm.

"How can you be hungry?" She said, speaking sharply. "You ate two biscuits you'd drowned in gravy not more'n two hours ago." When her son teared up, she relented and gave in to the pouty silence that followed her question. "Here's a nickel. Buy yourself a Hershey's bar."

Moments later, as Charlie stood biting into a bittersweet Hershey's chocolate bar, Uncle John pulled in under the station canopy driving an ancient Ford sedan.

*

The Fort Sill cannons on the other side of Tallchief Mountain began to boom and flashes of light split the darkness, interrupting her thoughts. "Goodness, Charlie, we have to get to bed right now. Not another peep

CHAPTER 8 ✦ RUTH

out of you. You hear?" She tucked her son in for the night and then lay down in her own bed. Staring at the ceiling, she could not sleep but thought about the rest of that unhappy trip home.

After tucking her son in and crawling into her own bed, she lay still thinking about the end of that trip. After Uncle John drove her to Rocky, her sister Joan was there to drive them from Rocky to Hobart, and then her sister Pearl drove them on to the farm. By the time they reached Babbs Corner, the clouds had all blown on past, and Ruth's anxiety had followed them. Then the miles fell behind her like loose cotton blowing off a loaded cotton wagon. It had not rained much at the Babbs Switch School juncture, so, when Pearl turned off on to the hard-clay road, it was not as muddy as she'd expected it to be. Shady Creek was swollen, but the ditches were empty of water. Pearl made good time, and, all too soon for Ruth, they made it to her parents' driveway.

That May morning, as the car came to a stop in the farmyard drive, she thanked her sister for helping her and then unwound from the seat, stood in the drive, and turned a slow circle. With mixed feelings of love and hate, she took in the sight of the house and barn, the chicken house, the wash house, outhouse, and the fondly remembered the metal coal-oil barrel. Ever since Papa first set it up out by the coal bin, it was every one of his children's and grandchildren's pretend horse. As a child she'd straddled, pounded with a stick, and directed that old horse to faraway places, almost allowing herself to believe it was a real pony she was riding.

Beyond the farmyard lay fields of young cotton washed clean by the rain this morning. It lay in long, straight ribbons of leaves, which just at that moment, blessed by sunlight piercing the retreating clouds, glistened like green satin. Rubbing sleep from his eyes, Charlie joined her and stood silently.

She remembered all those years as a girl watching the same cycle of rain and sunshine. The same cycle of cotton growth and harvest, the young plants pushing up from the soil, the weeds being chopped to give the cotton room to grow, to flower, to develop bolls that took on the color of a purple plum and which, in the late fall, burst into white balls of cotton. As a child and young woman, she'd spent many hours in backbreaking work in these fields. She had left that life, hoping never to return to it, but she'd been forced to come back to a welcome she knew was thin as the wispy clouds she often saw drifting lazily over the pasture, the house and barn, and the rows of ripening cotton. As other memories drifted through her mind they became as wispy as summer clouds and then disappeared as she floated into sleep.

CHAPTER 9

Ida

Another week gone by, thought Ida, as she glanced out the car's passenger-side window at their neighbors' young cotton that was a few inches taller than last week and now covered the bare earth, decorating the red fields of clay with ribbons of green. Bob's eyes were on those acres of cotton, too, and she wasn't surprised when he spoke up.

"I think I got a better stand of cotton than Joe Williams and Burt Johnson. Don't seem the plants are as high. I suspect they didn't get as much of that rain during that last storm as I did. Brought moisture to some and passed the unlucky ones by."

He didn't say, but she knew he was also comparing how the rows of cotton were lined up less straight. At some point he would be calculating how much money he'd make if his cotton came in at a half bale an acre.

That was all he ever thought about this time of year. Or talked about. Blessedly, he stopped talking after delivering the broadcast about cotton conditions on his and the neighbors' crops.

Her thoughts wandered to Ruth, who, complaining of a headache, begged off leaving the house, and Ida knew it was just an excuse to be alone with her misery. That last trip into town had put her in a mood. Said she couldn't get her mind off Chester out there in the South Pacific. Charlie was curled up in the back seat, preoccupied, she was sure, with daydreams about war but, thank the Lord, he was not making any of those irritating battle noises. Inevitably, when the idea of war entered her head, Ida wondered how her boy was doing over there in Burma. Winston was a sensitive young man, and she was sure he was suffering from being in the army. Bob's mother certainly suffered when her son John fought in the First World War. And came home wounded. None of Ida's brothers had gone overseas even though they'd been in the service.

Ida's musings drifted to the visit she'd have with her mother when she got to town. She hoped to find her in a good mood and not aggravated by that drunk she'd married after Pa died.

Over the past twenty-two years Ida had made this trip into town every Saturday except when the road was axle deep in mud or snow, or she was sick in bed. Her eyes drifted away from the cotton and focused on the weed- and grass-choked ditches that were also decorated with Indian paintbrush, bright-yellow flowers with purple centers, an occasional bluebonnet, and other spring wildflowers she couldn't name, all basking in the early summer sun. The hard-clay road they were driving on was a long, reddish-brown partition that, along with barbed-wire fences, separated the fields of growing cotton one from another. Ida believed she had thoughts like this, that not many others seemed to have. At least no one spoke to her about them.

She supposed that, had she not been born to a dirt-poor farmer with umpteen kids to feed, she would have grown up a sensitive poet or artist.

CHAPTER 9 ♦ IDA

Or a musician. Like her son, Winston. She had some talent. Back in fourth grade, she'd earned an award for a picture she'd drawn. She often wondered what would have become of her if she hadn't dropped out of school when she was twelve. Her papa had won 160 acres in the land lottery of 1901, and they'd moved from a small town in Kentucky to Rocky, Oklahoma, in a covered wagon. Being the oldest, she'd been needed at home to help with all the young ones who came along almost every year till there were fourteen of them. No time for her to be in school, even had there been one close she could have attended. Then she married Bob and moved to his tenant farm when she was sixteen and had Ruth when she was seventeen. She'd spent her whole life in the heat and dust of farm life. Living out her days with a man who would end his in a cotton patch or a barn. Except for the children, her life had been a waste.

But thank the good Lord she had passed her talents on to Winston. That boy could draw the likeness of just about anybody. In high school, he'd caricatured quite a few teachers, something she could never fully praise him for; too many times he got into a peck of trouble when the images weren't too flattering. But she'd admired him for that talent, secretly enjoying the thought of his teachers' discomfort. And could he sing! Like a nightingale. He could span two whole octaves with that voice of his. Ever since a sprinkling of wispy fuzz began appearing on his cheeks at adolescence, he could pick up a musical instrument and play it well enough within a month to entertain at box suppers. And all that had come from her side of the family. Her grandfather had been a fiddle player of note in their part of Kentucky. Bob Choat's people couldn't carry a tune in a bucket or draw a full bucket of water out of a cistern, much less draw a picture.

A scissor-tailed swallow raced alongside the car, and enjoying its antics, Ida said to Bob, "Slow down. I want to watch." She loved the way those pretty birds split their tails when they dipped and sailed. No other bird she'd ever seen or heard tell of could do that. Special is what they were, and she needed something special in her life every once in a while to keep her going.

"I think that bird is flying to town with us," Charlie said. He banged on the window and waved as the bird flitted across in front of the car and disappeared somewhere behind them.

She wished she'd not disturbed the boy with her comment and, aggravated with him, spoke sharply, "I swear, I think you scared that bird off, Charlie. And I so enjoyed seeing him fly along with us." Ida stared ahead, feeling pouty and like a little girl who had lost her pretty balloon. In this mood, her mind went to last week when she and Joan were talking before Ruth and Charlie showed up to lunch. Joan had leaned across the table and lowered her voice to say, "I heard a rumor yesterday that Chester was running around with Alice Jenson while him, Ruth, and Charlie were living in Tulsa and after they moved to Oklahoma City."

"Good Lord—I hope it's just rumor."

"I also heard she may have been in California with him the two months he was at that Port Hueneme Naval Base. "Now she's back in Roosevelt living with her sister—and is pregnant."

"I just hope to goodness it isn't Chester's baby," Ida muttered.

"But if I know Chester, it won't surprise me if it is," Joan said.

Speaking with Joan about Chester and Alice had forced an unwanted memory to come crushing down on her. Years ago, there was a time when she was so angry at finding out Bob had been running around with that Edens woman that she hadn't slept with him for months. One day when Bob took Ruth to the doctor to see how her pregnancy with Charlie was coming along, they'd left her and Chester alone together. She was only thirty-three years old at the time, and hard work on the farm and the unforgiving sun had not yet taken their toll. She had a pretty face and a slim body back then, and she had sensed from the time Chester first started looking at girls and women, he'd looked at her. At eighteen, he was young and charming, and, partly out of spite and partly out of

CHAPTER 9 • IDA

need, she'd given in to those charms. She'd sweated bullets for a month afterward. That was the biggest and scariest mistake of her life, chancing a pregnancy with Chester. Thank God she'd skipped only one period before starting again. There was no way she would have had his child. Before that happened, she would have taken a trip to that filthy little cabin she'd heard of down by Lone Wolf and lay on that abortionist's kitchen table. Before she had that period and knew she wasn't pregnant, there had been dreams—no nightmares—of the heavy smell of her own blood and body fluid as that old Indian woman pushed a mesquite switch deep into her womb and twisted like she was turning a critter out of its den with a length of barbed wire. She would awaken terrified and sweating, curse Chester and herself for their stupidity, and then lie awake for hours wallowing in guilt over betraying her own daughter. How could she ever explain what she'd done to the good Lord come judgment day?

In times past, when Ida would see Alice Jenson in town, the pretty young thing was awfully flirty with men, married or not. So yes, if Chester had been around Alice, it was not a far reach to think she was pregnant with his baby. A leopard doesn't change its spots, and a man like Chester never changed his reckless behavior, either. If Alice was carrying Chester's baby, it was going to be a hard thing for Ruth to accept. And how could they let Charlie know he had a half-brother or -sister? She shuddered at the thought and shuddered again when she asked herself how many other half-brothers and -sisters Charlie might have out there. Knowing Chester, there could be a lot more than one. She startled when a lament from the back seat jarred her out of her reveries.

"I wish Mama'd come into town with us today."

"She didn't feel like making the trip, what with her laid up with a headache." *Or, more likely, she was laid up with a bad case of heartsickness,* Ida thought, wondering if Ruth had heard the rumor. And if that wasn't enough, now Ruth might have to contend with saying things to Charlie he oughtn't have to hear.

With Ruth staying at the farm, it falls on me to look after Charlie, she then thought. *I hope he spends all day trying to sell those infernal savings stamps.*

She glanced back and caught sight of Charlie throwing something from the back window. "Charlie, what did you just do back there?"

"Nothing, Grandmother."

"Don't you *nothing* me, young man. I saw you pitch something out the window."

Bob began to brake the car to a stop. "Answer your grandmother, Charlie."

"It wasn't anything important."

"You let us be the judge of that."

"My rabbit's foot."

"Your rabbit's foot? Did I hear you right?" Bob turned in the seat and threw a quick frown at the boy, sending Charlie's mouth into a quirky pout. The car swerved into the other lane, and Bob's eyes snapped back to the road. "I declare, didn't those cousins of yours ever tell you to give a rabbit's foot away? Or bury it? It's bad luck to just throw it away. We got enough bad luck around the place as it is without you adding to it."

Ida glared at Bob and opened her mouth to scold but clamped her jaws shut. She gave no mind to foolish ideas about a rabbit's foot. What was happening to Ruth and Charlie wasn't about bad luck. It was about Chester's bad behavior. Charlie, his voice filled with the disgust and disappointment, said, "I ain't had nothing but bad luck since I got that rabbit's foot from Carl. Since then, I lost the pocket-knife my daddy gave me, my daddy went away to the Navy, and I'm not having a lot of luck selling savings stamps. Carl must have used up all the luck in that rabbit's foot before he gave it to me."

"Well, you could have passed it on to me. God knows I might have squeezed a little luck out of it at the domino parlor today." Bob pulled his fedora tighter to his head and stared straight ahead.

Bob's attempt at humor gave Ida a twinge of irritation. "I hear tell you don't need much luck at dominoes, Bob." She felt a fluttering in her chest

CHAPTER 9 ♦ IDA

and an ache between her shoulder blades. The deep breaths she took would not fill her lungs. The road ahead wavered as Bob slowed to a stop at the blacktop. These spells came with some regularity now. They took the sap out of her, making her feel as dried up and deadened as a gnarled old mesquite bush. She barely listened as Bob turned onto the blacktop, sped up, and then answered her.

"Mostly that's true. But the luck of the draw counts for something." Bob wasn't driving over the speed limit, but he slowed as they approached a black-and-white police car, its red light flashing, parked behind a red pickup.

"Look," said Charlie, "Bet they were driving too fast."

Charlie's words came to her from somewhere else, like birdsong from the leaf-heavy limbs of native elms guarding the courthouse, or from inside a shut-off room in her house. They were muffled and indistinct. She would have to tell him to speak up. But she was too tired right now to do more than lean her head on the dashboard. Her pulse beat out a fast rhythm in her temple, and that rhythm was off. There were extra beats. Then it seemed her heart would stop a beat or two and then speed up, as if it were making up for the skipped beats.

"Ida? Are you OK?" Bob slowed the car even more and cast a quick glance at her.

She raised her head and passed the back of a hand across her eyes, hoping to wipe away the blackness that seemed to hover there. "I'm fine, Bob. Just fine. I had a spell of tiredness there for a minute." Her heartbeat became familiar again, steady as the old mantle clock sitting on top of the radio. She was going to see Doctor Hollister one of these days soon and tell him about these spells she was having, get him to prescribe a little something for her nerves. The good Lord only knew she had enough going on right now to put her nerves in a state.

"You don't look so good, Grandmother."

When she turned in her seat and looked at him, Charlie's eyes appeared to have grown to large, sky-blue saucers that mirrored concern and not a little fear. It caused a flicker of nervousness in the pit of her stomach, and she twisted back around, letting her eyes fix on the water tower that in the distance loomed above Hobart like a fatheaded giant. Its shadow would be falling across the front of her mother's house right now, depriving the front porch of direct sunlight. She'd go there and sit a spell, let the weakness pass.

Bob glanced at her again, worry lines creasing his forehead. "The boy's right. You don't look so good, Ida."

"Don't you worry yourself about it. And don't you dare say anything to Ruth. She's got enough on her mind right now. That goes for you, too, Charlie." She was sure, though, that Charlie's troubled eyes denied his quick nod and whispered, "OK." Bob's tight-lipped silence did not reassure her that he'd keep his mouth shut, either. "Now let me off at my mama's. I promised I'd visit her awhile today and in case she needed anything from the grocery store, I'd get it for her."

When Bob pulled to the curb and stopped the car, she gathered herself together, climbed out of the front seat and, straightening her shoulders, took a deep breath, hoping she could make it to the front porch. Her mother stood there, watching. Ida didn't want her to see that anything was amiss. Before Bob pulled away, she called out, "You come on back here, Charlie, soon as you're done peddling those stamps. You hear?"

CHAPTER 10

Ruth

⇢ ✾ ⇠

Charlie had sworn her to secrecy and then told Ruth about his grandmother's spell in the car. Ruth wasn't sure what to say to her mother. Worried as she was, she couldn't just pretend to not know. But she'd been saved from going back on her word with Charlie when Papa told her, "You need to keep an eye on your mother; help out more if she'll let you. Instead of hoeing cotton for Joe Williams, stay home with Ida."

But her mother, who was no fool, threw a fit when she quickly figured out what was going on and demanded that Ruth go on to the field. "I won't have you sitting around here watching me like a hawk when you need to be earning some money. And Joe can't let Charlie into the field without you there to watch him. And see to it he knows what to do—and behaves."

Ruth had caved to her mother's wishes. It was harder to say no to her mother than it was Papa.

The sun was barely up over the horizon on Monday as she watched Charlie pace from one end of the front porch to the other, waiting for the plume of dust that Joe Williams' battered Ford would pound out of the red clay road. It had been a month and a half since Pearl had driven her and Charlie into the yard, and, since then, the young cotton plants in the fields around the country had grown knee high. Ruth was secretly glad that Mother had insisted she go to the field. Now she could make some much-needed money to keep her and Charlie in clothes and necessities. No money had yet come from Chester since she'd left Weatherford, and she wondered if he'd forgotten to change her address so the allotment would come to her. No letter had come from Chester for over a week, making her almost frantic with worry.

She'd learned in a letter from Chester's mother that her youngest boy, Jerry, had turned eighteen, been drafted into the Navy, and was at end of his training. Would likely be sent to the Pacific Theater. Now Ruth included him in her worries along with Winston and Chester. She heard every day on the radio about attacks on American ships by Japanese subs or air force, and if Chester and Jerry survived, it would be a miracle. Though Winston was a military policeman, he was still in dangerous parts of the world. And no telling where he was. All that and now worries over Mother's health. A short few months ago, she'd been so thankful that Chester, at thirty-five, was too old to serve. And God knows where in the South Pacific he now was.

Thank God Charlie was too young to serve. He couldn't even imagine the horrors of a war. She called to him, "Why don't you sit down by me, Charlie? You're going to be too tired to work before we even get to the field. Or wear out those shoes you're wearing."

"Will not."

"Okay, but don't say I didn't warn you." Charlie sat down by her for a moment and then, his face screwed up into a knot, stood, took the hoe his

CHAPTER 10 ✦ RUTH

grandfather had grudgingly loaned him for the day, and dragged it though the dusty yard, gouging crisscrossing six-inch wide pathways. It was the same thing she and her sisters had done as girls, imagining the narrow paths as roads to walk along, one foot placed carefully in front of the other, as they pretend-rode a buggy or Model T to Hobart. Or Altus. Or even as far as Oklahoma City. Their limited imagination did not take them out of Oklahoma. They'd played tag, too, chasing each other endlessly while trying to keep their balance on the tight paths. Step outside the path or get slapped on the back, you were it, and the pursuit would reverse.

Coming close to a sticker-patch, Charlie began a vicious chopping onslaught on the spidery tough plants.

"Charlie, you're going to be too tired to chop any of Joe Williams' cotton, you keep messing around in the yard like that."

He stopped his vicious attack and stood leaning on the hoe, staring off down the road once more. "I wish Joe would hurry up and come," he said.

Thinking of Joe took her back to when she was only thirteen or fourteen, and just before she became sweet on Chester. She and Joe had made calf eyes at each other for most of one semester of school. He'd kissed her out behind the building where the boys kept the horses while they were in school. Her first kiss. Her feet hadn't touched the ground for the rest of the day. To tell the truth, it had occurred to her once or twice since then that she'd been a fool not to stay with Joe. He'd have given her a much different life than Chester. A more settled one, anyway. But Chester had been more exciting and aggressive with her, and she'd become a Scarsdale instead of a Williams. Now Joe was a widower living half a mile away with a young daughter, Sarah, who became friends with Charlie not long after they'd arrived. Living only a half mile away, they played together often. Sarah seemed to enjoy helping build with Charlie's erector set as much as he did.

Ruth stood up and caught sight of her shadowy reflection in the windowpane and was not pleased with the look of her mother's worn, old long-sleeved work-dress that came to her ankles. She peeked out from under one of her mother's equally old and worn settler's bonnets. She liked that it hovered about her face, hiding her eyes from the sun—and her sad, worried expression—in its shadow. A pair of her brother's scuffed, unpolished brogans protected her feet. She had put on two pair of his heavy socks, frayed and mismatched, to fill out the oversized things. She was a sight. She wondered what Joe would think when he saw her. Silently scolding herself, she thought, *I'm hoeing cotton for Joe, not doing a fashion show.* She turned away from her grim reflection in the glass, laid her gloves on the swing, leaned her chin on the top of a hoe standing by the door, and gazed off toward Joe's farm, wondering why he hadn't yet appeared. With a deep sigh, she sat back down in the swing.

From the side of the porch where he was standing, Charlie yelled at her, "Mama, you look like the old lady in the shoe." She rose from the swing so quickly she left it swinging as she stepped down off the porch and raised the hoe as if to chop him down. He turned and ran down his newly plowed road, his hoe held in front of his body like a high-wire pole, balancing him.

"You don't talk about your mother that way, young man, or else I'll part your hair with this hoe." But she laid the hoe aside and prepared to sit down to wait for Joe.

"Yhaan yhnn. Can't catch me," he yelled.

"Oh, I can't, can I," Ruth yelled back and then charged at him.

Holding on to his old straw hat, he threw his hoe aside and darted around the house, with Ruth right on his heels. They rounded the last corner of the house, and Charlie started for the mulberry trees at the road but skidded to a stop and yelled, "There they come."

Ruth stopped, too, and peered out from under her bonnet. A red dust cloud spilled down the road behind Joe's green Ford truck with its black front fenders and wheels. Sarah had told her it was almost brand new and said, "My daddy really likes driving it." As it neared,

CHAPTER 10 ♦ RUTH

Charlie waved his hoe back and forth over his head, and Sarah waved back from the cab where she sat with Joe at the wheel. Two adolescent boys standing at the front of the truck bed leaned over the cab letting the breeze curl and snap their hair into dark tendrils that whipped at their faces. Most of the Roosevelt townspeople, hired by the day, sat in the truck bed. As the truck slowed and stopped at the turn-in to Papa's farm, Charlie grabbed his head in two hands as if a stab of pain had hit him between the eyes.

"What's the matter, Charlie?"

"I just got a little headache is all."

Ruth felt his forehead to see if there was any fever and though his face was flushed, there was no real heat. Still, she was troubled by his sad expression. "What's wrong, Charlie?"

"I bet everybody here has a daddy with them. Except me."

Ruth felt tears come to her eyes, and she patted Charlie on the shoulder. "You've got a daddy, too. And I know he loves you." *Chester ought to be here, though*, she thought, with her and Charlie, and not thousands of miles away. They could still be living in Oklahoma City and not getting ready to do the back-breaking work of chopping cotton. The men in the truck were no older than Chester, but they weren't overseas getting shot at. If Chester had been smart enough not to get into a bar fight, he wouldn't be, either.

Joe Williams slid out of the driver's seat and, standing on the running board, leaned over the top of the cab and waved for her and Charlie to join them.

As she approached, Ruth nodded to the people standing in the truck's bed. With their sun-darkened skin, they could be Indians from off the reservation over by Cache. Two of the men with lit cigarettes sent smoke dancing into the clear morning air. One of the men nodded back, some of the children waved, and a women called out, "Hello." Joe helped them into the back and then stuck an unlit pipe into his mouth, sucked hard, as if to bring back to life what dead coals still lingered in the bowl. He then called out in his deep voice, "Everybody hang on now," and climbed into the cab.

As the truck rolled into motion, Ruth's mother come out on the porch and flapped her apron, spilling dry breadcrumbs into the yard. A scattering of chickens raced toward the house, surrounding Mother as she stood with one hand to her eyes, shading them as she watched the truck drive away. Ruth had killed a couple of the young roosters and dressed them earlier that morning. She knew her mother would do it otherwise, and doing things like that seemed to take the wind out of her. But Mother passed the breathlessness off as nothing; wouldn't go see a doctor because, "they'd just find something wrong with me." As if it were their fault then, that she'd have something wrong with her.

Charlie yelped and cried out, "A grasshopper hit my ear." He ducked down in front of Ruth, who was standing with her back to the cab.

Ruth sat down beside him, braced her back against the sideboards and tried to rub the hurt away with one of her cotton gloves.

The two town boys laughed at Charlie, and one yelled out to him, "Stand up, and take it like a man."

"You behave yourself, and stop tormenting that little boy," one of the men called.

The boys laughed. They held their forearms in front of their eyes, facing into the breeze, unconcerned about the butterflies, grasshoppers, midges, and dragonflies whipping by them, sometimes delivering sharp smacks to their arms and face.

On reaching the field, Ruth jumped down from the truck bed. With the hoe in her hand, she stood near the cotton. The small buds that had begun forming on the new branches that were fanning out from the main cotton stalk would in a short time burst into flower. She'd always enjoyed waking up one morning and seeing white and yellow cotton blossoms decorating the fields. The morning after that she'd awaken to see that, overnight, the flowers had all turned from white to pink. And ten days later, see that had they turned dark red for a day. Then, dropping to the ground, they left behind tiny cotton bolls.

Joe Williams sauntered over to Charlie and said, "Your mama told me this is the first time you've chopped cotton. You know what to do?"

"Yeah, I think so," he answered, looking out over the field.

"Just make sure you don't chop to close to the plant, or you'll disturb the roots. You can reach down and pull up by hand any weeds growing too close to the plant."

Ruth smiled at Joe's helpfulness. He was so much better with Charlie than Chester could ever be.

Sarah said, "He's going to do just fine, Daddy." She was smiling, but, to Ruth, it seemed more a grimace than a friendly smile. She likely had not yet completely forgiven Charlie.

Sarah had been mad at Charlie since the day before. They'd left their shoes off while they played in the barn loft. When called to the house, Sarah thrust her feet into the shoes without putting on her socks or shaking her shoes out. She ought to have known better. She'd screamed and danced about while kicking her shoes off and letting them fly in two different directions, one landing in the loft and the other over the edge of the loft into a horse stall below. With Charlie right on her heels, she went running barefoot to the house, crying and screaming, "Something' bit me on the toe, Mrs. Scarsdale."

When Ruth looked at the toe, she saw that the big toe was red and swelling. "You sit right here, Sarah, and I'll go get something that will help it stop hurting." She went out to the ditch that ran along the road in front of the yard, picked some wild growing mullein leaves, and, while Sarah looked on, made a poultice and spread it on the toe.

She sent Charlie to find Sarah's shoes, and, when he returned with them and a dead scorpion on the end of a stick, he said, "When I found Sarah's shoe, there was this dead scorpion lying beside it." He laughed and pointed a finger at her, "You should have seen Sarah when that old thing bit her. She did a new dance. I'm going to call it the *scorpion stomp*."

Sarah made a face at him, wrinkling her nose and twisting her mouth into a pinched circle before she flounced out the door, limping on her sore toe and refusing to forgive Charlie even after he followed her to the road, apologizing and begging her to stay. Ruth hoped she was over it now.

"I know you'll make a good worker, Charlie," Ruth said and patted him on the shoulder.

"I'm a good worker. I'll really chop a lot of cotton today." Charlie squared his shoulders and pursed his lips like Chester always did.

"OK, then, folks, let's get those hoes a-choppin'." Joe walked back to the truck and set a ten-gallon milk can of water and a dipper in the shade beside the truck.

Before he followed Joe's direction, one of the men lowered a dipper into the can and drew it out full, took a mouthful of water, swished it around in his mouth and then spat a stream of tobacco-stained saliva out through a gap in his two front teeth. Taking another dipperful, he downed it. Ruth was used to sharing a water bucket with the family, but she was not so sure she wanted to with a tobacco-chewing stranger. She'd have no choice but to do it, she knew. That or near die of thirst.

As she, Charlie, and Sarah walked over to their rows and began chopping, Ruth heard a car door slam, and, looking over her shoulder, saw Mildred Alred, Alice Jenson's older sister, and her son, Corky, walking toward them. Corky had an unpleasant sneer on his face. Mildred's full gaze fell on Ruth; the woman's eyes hardened, and her mouth turned down. Surprised and confused, Ruth looked away, not wanting to hold the woman's disapproving gaze. She had absolutely no idea why the woman looked so cross; she'd never had anything to do with the woman and hadn't spoken to her in years. Her brow creased with aggravation when she heard Corky laugh and yell, "Did you ever see the likes of the straw hat that boy's wearing?"

CHAPTER 10 ♦ RUTH

Ruth was reminded of the braying young jackass Papa had once owned.

Sarah went striding over to Corky, her pretty face puckered in a frown. Both hands on her hips, she yelled, "You better not start anything, Corky Alred."

Ruth was relieved to hear Joe Williams, who was standing by his truck, call to his daughter, "Sarah. You get to work."

Sarah scampered back to her cotton row but threw angry looks back at Corky.

"All right, Corky," Joe said as he walked up to the boy. There was a frown on Joe's face, and he had his pipe clamped hard between his teeth. "What's going on here, now?"

"Nothin'," growled Corky. "I just think that boy has on a funny-looking hat."

Charlie sputtered, "Nothin's wrong with this hat."

Mildred Alred snorted and said, "Corky's right. That hat's too big for the boy. It'll keep falling down over his eyes."

"Now, that'll do, Corky. Mildred. Why don't you all get to work, and I'll help Charlie here fix his hat," Joe said.

Without another word, the two Alreds walked away, and each started off down a cotton row, their hoes swinging. Charlie's eyes widened, and his face turned a bright red as he looked at Ruth, who had come over when the Alreds walked away. He demanded, "Why didn't you find me a hat that fit?"

"I'm sorry, son. It was the only one I could find."

"Don't' fret, Charlie. I'll make it fit," said Joe. "Come on over here with me." He walked to his truck, took out a piece of stout cord, asked Charlie to hold his hat where he wanted it to sit on his head, wrapped the cord around the hat's crown, and pulled it tight. "There you go, Charlie. That'll keep it out of your eyes."

"Thanks," mumbled Charlie as he turned and stormed off down a cotton row, swinging his hoe at every weed. Ruth suspected he was pretending they were Axis enemies he was mowing down. Or Corky Alred.

She stood there, embarrassed, a deep frown pulling her mouth down as Joe turned to her, smiling.

"Can't blame the boy for being angry," Joe said. "But I think it's more at Corky than at you."

Ruth's tension melted in the goodness of his words and the warmth of his smile.

CHAPTER 11

Chester

Pausing only for short rests, water, and a bite of food, Chester worked nonstop for twelve hours. Building this new runway—the one he was sweating over now—was behind schedule, and they had put him, and every other Sea Bee who could stand up and walk, to work finishing it. He cursed under his breath at gung-ho Richard Bell, who pushed everyone to their limit. He wanted more than ever to catch him out behind a tent somewhere and knock the shit out of him. But he wasn't going to press his luck. At moments in the late afternoon, though, if he hadn't been so bone-tired, he thought he just might cold-cock the little bastard.

Stumbling back toward camp in the early evening, Chester saw one of the men jerk off his clothes, jump into the ocean's waves, and begin splashing water at the others on shore. Hough and others, their exhaustion forgotten, began diving in, yelling, and splashing. Chester peeled off his sweat-stained cap, threw it high in the air and then, with a yell, ran to the ocean's edge and dove into the water, clothes and all. Coming up behind Hough, he grabbed him and pushed him under.

Hough came up gasping and sputtering. "You crazy son of a bitch. You trying to drown me?"

"If you drowned, I wouldn't have to hear you snore all night, now would I?" Chester grabbed for Hough again but missed, and with a push from Hough, he stumbled face first into the water.

Hough gripped Chester by the scruff of the neck and shouted, "You're the one that snores," and then forced Chester's head under and held it till he was sure he was drowning.

When Hough let go, Chester came up coughing and spitting. Catching his breath, he swung at Hough, catching him on the shoulder and sending him staggering back. "You bastard. You damn near drowned me."

Hough drew back to throw a punch of his own but pulled up short when he heard Bell shout, "Hough. Scarsdale. You two, cut it out. And the rest of you. Out of there, now, and get your butts to the chow hall. We got a hell of a lot more work to do in the morning," Bell paused and then said, "And everybody needs their beauty sleep. Especially you, Scarsdale."

Chester splashed toward shore, kicking water as he went, sending a geyser spraying over Bell and Johnny Polk, who was standing nearby. "Whoops. Sorry." He stood grinning, daring Bell or Polk to react.

Instead, Polk turned and walked away, leaving Bell staring at Chester, his eyes mean. "You're pressing your luck with me, mister," Bell said.

Chester took a step closer to Bell and stood nose to nose. "I think maybe you're coming close to running out of luck yourself."

Hough grabbed Chester from behind and carried him in a bear hug back to where his own clothes lay in the sand. "I don't want you to spend the rest of this bloody war in the brig while I have to do your work and mine."

CHAPTER II ✦ CHESTER

"Put me down, you son-of-a-bitch. Or I swear I'll kill you."

And who'd you go whoring and drinking with?" He spilled Chester onto the sand. "You punch me again, though, Scarsdale, by God, and I'll bury your sorry ass six feet in the sand and go whoring on my own anyway."

"Yeah? And how are you going to find a woman without me helping?"

"What's the matter with you anyway, Scarsdale? You're spoiling for a fight."

Chester took a deep breath, lifted himself off the sand, and shrugged. "I'm just all-around pissed off, I guess. Got a girlfriend back home that's pregnant and a wife and boy waiting for me to come home to them. Worrying over what to do keeps me awake at night. It makes me so goddamn mad every time I think about what I've done to myself. And when one of those assholes Bell or Polk is around, all I can think of to do is kick the shit out of them." Chester took three deep breaths, stood, brushed at the sand covering his work blues, and then fell in behind the last of the men. Trudging alongside Hough to the mess hall for supper, he spat on the sand and swore, "So help me God, I hate this whole goddamn Navy—and particularly Polk and Bell."

"Yeah," said Hough, "but you can bet they hate you, too. Like I said before, you've been pushing your luck with them, buddy."

*

In the total darkness, as Chester lay in his bunk, trying to fall asleep under mosquito netting that seemed to hold in the heat of the night, his mind roiled with thoughts of Alice, Ruth, and Charlie. And of that baby Alice was carrying, whatever its name would be. He didn't want to think about what Ruth and Charlie were going to feel if they found out about Alice. And God knows that, with Alice back with her sister, they'd find out sooner or later. Partly to spin his mind away, he let thoughts of

Bell fill his mind. If this wasn't the goddamn service and Bell wasn't his superior in rank, he'd beat the crap out of him and take his chances with that overgrown redneck, Johnny Polk. "God damn it," he said aloud.

"Why the hell are you talking to yourself, Scarsdale? How do you expect me to sleep?"

"Well, piss on you, Hough. If I could go to sleep like you and snore as loud, I wouldn't be talking to myself." Chester let out a sigh of frustration. "I was thinking about the shit I'm in back home."

Hough sat up and lit a cigarette. "That woman Alice you shacked up with before we shipped out?"

"Yeah. That one." He'd been a fool to agree to let Alice join him for his last few weeks in the States instead of Ruth and Charlie, but Alice'd thrown such a fit to come be with him, he'd agreed. He knew he'd have a great time with her. Better than he would with Ruth and Charlie. And he was soon heading off somewhere and might never come back. Better to lie around in bed with a good-time woman like Alice than with Ruth. He didn't know how to think about Ruth. Those weeks with Alice had made him think of how little fun he had with Ruth. Since Charlie was born, she'd given up on going dancing and drinking with him as much. She'd always hated him smoking. And sex was just something she put up with. Alice loved to smoke, go dancing with him, and could drink him under the table. She was a goddamn live wire in bed. Loved every minute of it. "I had a lot of fun with her. Not much with my wife and kid."

Hough said, "Hell, I know what you're up against. I had to join this man's Navy to find any peace from that nagging wife of mine. Whoring around with you has been the most fun I've had since I was a kid."

"Pipe down, you two. You're keeping me awake," someone called.

"Why don't you-all go to hell," Chester shouted.

A rustling in the dark around them started then, and then some whispered voices. "Hough? What the hell's going on?" Before Hough could answer, Bell's voice came from of the darkness nearby.

CHAPTER 11 ✦ CHESTER

"Scarsdale. Get your ass up and come with us. Me and some of the men want to talk to you."

The barracks door opened and from the moonlight outside the door, Chester saw several men pass through.

Chester took a deep breath and said, "I don't like the sound of this, Hough."

"I don't, either. Sounds like there's a mob forming out there in the dark. You better make a run for it or go see what they want."

"You coming with me?"

"Sure. Wouldn't want to miss a hanging if that's what they're here for."

Chester, his heart racing, his bare back and shoulders shining with sweat, pulled on his pants and walked out into the pale light of stars and a half-moon. He saw Bell and all the other men in their barracks standing around in their skivvies, all looking at him. "What the hell's up?" he snarled. "We havin' a party?"

Bell stepped from out of the crowd of men and said, "You've been aching for a fight ever since we got here, Scarsdale. I figure you're not going to be happy till you get one. So, I'm going to see you get one."

Chester felt a quiver of anxiety clutch his stomach and his heart began beating even faster as he looked at the others milling around. He wondered if he had a friend among them other than Hough. Certainly not among Polk's friends, who made up most of the men present. They'd not hidden their dislike of him. But then, he had not hidden his dislike from them, either. "Am I going to have to whip the whole bunch of you?" he challenged.

Bell gave a short laugh. "No. But I suspect you could have your pick of any one of them you take a notion to. They're all sick of you. And I'm sick of you. So, come on, and let's get this over so I can get some sleep." Bell turned and led the way through the darkness to an open space between the dozens of barracks that lined the camp and handed Chester a pair of boxing gloves—and then a second pair to Polk. "Polk here has graciously volunteered to do the honors."

For a second, Chester wasn't sure what Bell meant, but when it hit him, he felt his rage growing. "You don't fight your own fights, Bell?"

"I don't fight the men under me. Polk here volunteered to be my stand-in."

Polk, his muscled bare chest gleaming from sweat in the moonlight, stepped closer. "I guess I made this my fight, too. I don't like you very much, Scarsdale."

Chester took the gloves and, never taking his eyes off the big man, backed several steps away from him. He held his gloved hands out to Hough to tie and whispered, "This SOB is going to make mincemeat out of me, Hough. And it's Bell's ass I want to kick."

Hough shook his head. "You haven't exactly hid your feelings about Polk."

"Bell's a sissy, you ask me."

"Just go on over there and take it like a man. Fight won't last long, so you ain't going to suffer too much."

"That all the encouragement I'm going to get?" Bouncing his gloves together, Chester walked over to where Bell and Johnny Polk stood backed by the hostile faces of a dozen other men. The excited quiver in his stomach turned into a clenching knot, and the feeling brought back a memory of the time he and his brother Joe had been waylaid by the three Horton brothers, big farm boys with eyes meaner than Johnny Polk's or Bell's. He'd been scared to death, but he and his brother had won that fight, though Joe had had to use a scoop shovel to brain one of them first to make it a fair fight. He couldn't think of anything at the moment to make this a fair fight.

Bell, his mouth twisted into a sour grin, his white teeth glowing in the moonlight, stepped between Johnny Polk and Chester.

"There ain't going to be any kicking or biting. First man down can end the fight by not getting up. Or not being able to get up. Any questions?"

Chester spat close to Bell's shoe. "I got one. I still want to know why you aren't fighting your own fight. I don't buy that shit that you don't fight the men under you."

"I figured Polk'd give you a better fight than I could."

"But this is your fight. Not Polk's."

"It's both ours," said Polk "You ready?"

"I think so. Yeah." Chester brought his fist up from the waist and caught Bell square on the chin, then followed with a left jab to the eye. The man dropped like a shot hog and lay still. Johnny Polk stood, his gloved hands poised to fight, still as a board.

But Hough gave a loud guffaw and stepped between Chester and Johnny Polk. "You boys heard the rules. First man down and don't get up, loses. I declare Chester Scarsdale the winner here. And Bell the loser. Now, let's all get some sleep."

Johnny Polk grinned and shook his head. "I don't much like Bell, either," he said, and slid the gloves off. He pointed down at Bell. "What're we gonna do with this one? Can't leave him out here all night."

Chester poked Bell's leg with his shoe but got no response. "You want to grab his legs while I get his arms? We'll carry him to his bunk. If I'm lucky, he'll sleep all night before he sends the MPs after my sorry ass."

Johnny Polk reached down and hefted Bell across his broad shoulders. "Don't need no help from you, Scarsdale."

Stung, Chester balled his fist but thought better of pushing his luck, so he followed Hough and the others back into the barracks. It took what seemed hours for his stomach to unclench and the tension in his muscles to relax. Then he slept uneasily through the rest of the night.

*

Next morning, Chester stood with his platoon, every one of the men wearing a knowing grin. He darted glances out of the corner of his eyes at Bell, who sported a black eye and bruised jaw. Half expecting the MPs to come calling that morning, he'd crawled from his bunk, bleary-eyed, from a night of poor sleep. No MPs showed up. But it still wasn't too late.

Bell stepped to the front of the men and cleared his throat. "OK. Most of us are unloading those barges that came in last night. Scarsdale, you report to the detail working on mucking out the cesspools." A chorus of guffaws followed as he paused to stare right at Chester. "Any questions?" When there were none, he dismissed them. Bell and the other men moved off, leaving Chester still rooted to the spot.

Before he moved on with them, Hough said, "I guess he plans to just keep you in deep shit instead of throwing you to the Military Police," Hough said.

"Probably didn't want the brass to know he put Polk up to beating my brains out."

"And he sure doesn't want it to be known any more'n it already is that you made a jackass out of him in front of the men."

"Get on out of here before Bell wonders where you are. Comes back to find you. Sees me again and changes his mind."

*

That following weekend, as darkness fell, the barracks were empty except for Chester, who stood guard duty, and Hough, who was the last to leave. *That's all I need, to be on guard duty with this load of shit on me,* he thought. *Probably better off since I can't seem to wash off the smell of all the shit and piss that's spattered over me the past three days.* If he hadn't let that bastard Bell provoke him. If he'd just gone ahead and taken a beating from Polk. If. If. If. So damned many *ifs* that left him here instead of in a pub with that Aussie woman swilling a few rum drinks. Could forget about home and the way he smelled—for a while, anyway. Hell, if he'd

CHAPTER II • CHESTER

not beaten the shit out of that man back in Oklahoma City, he could go to a bar with Alice and drink himself shitfaced.

He was pulled out of his thoughts by Hough. With his Dixie Cup sailor hat cocked rakishly to the side of his head and a shit-eating grin on his face, Hough walked up to him and said, "Sorry, pal, but I guess shoveling shit and losing liberty is better than sitting in the stockade for God knows how long."

"Tell Ivy why I won't be showing up. Tell her I would like to bury all my worry in those sweet arms and lay my head on those big titties of hers."

"Hell, no. I'm going to tell her you said I should look out for her because you'll be doing guard duty for the duration of your service."

"You do that, and I'll break this rifle over your head."

Hough laughed. "See you, buddy."

Left alone at his post, his legs beginning to ache, he tried to hold on to images of Ivy's big tits, but instead, his mind wandered to what was going on at home. He'd sat on his bed many a night asking himself, "What the hell am I going to do?" over and over again. Should I stay with Ruth and Charlie? He did love that boy. He wasn't so sure about Ruth. She'd stood by him for eighteen years through thick and thin. But he wondered if, down deep, she thought the Choats were a cut above the Scarsdales. At least Ida and Bob did. But to go with Alice and the baby? He wasn't so sure Alice would be as forgiving of him as Ruth. Shit fire, he didn't want to live around another baby mewling and puking night and day. But come to think of it, that wouldn't necessarily be the case if this war dragged on. The kid could be in school by the time he got home. If he got home.

It did not cheer him to then think that it might be years before the war was over and he saw Alice or Ruth again. Hopefully by then, one of the two might have forgotten him and gone off with somebody else. Fat chance. They both were the type who stuck with a man no matter what.

Hell, he thought, *before the war was over, the Japs, Johnny Polk, or one of Polk's friends—or Richard Bell—would see to it he never made it back.* That thought depressed him even more.

CHAPTER 12

Bob

⇢ ✤ ⇠

Bob swirled the dominoes about, setting them whacking against one another in rhythmic bursts. The shuffle, the draw, then the play, dominoes took him out of the ordinary, allowed him to be somebody. DOMINO CHAMPION OF OKLAHOMA read the certificate on his bedroom wall. He rode the train all the way to Oklahoma City and back to play that tournament. First and last time he was ever on a train. When he got back, he spent one whole sawbuck to have the certificate framed. He was the man to beat, and everyone in this smoky domino parlor knew that. His family, friends, and acquaintances played knowing what the odds were, that they'd go away from the table poorer. Otherwise, they played somebody else. Few did. They liked to take him on, brag a little when they did win—with lucky draws.

"Bob, you're going to wear a hole in the table before George gets here to play, you keep stirring those rocks." Sitting across from Bob, Bill Dennison, his son-in-law, lit a cigarette and blew out a lungful of smoke. Bill was dressed like the farmer he was—overalls, work shirt, and brogans—could be a younger version of me, Bob thought, if he'd just grown another five inches. And had a full head of black hair like me instead of that whispery-thin, brown mess that always looked like he never combed it. He liked Bill, who was, and always had been, even as a boy when Bob first knew him, a hell of a lot more steady than Chester or Joe Williams.

A thin-as-a-rail, bald-headed man dressed in jeans and a western-style work shirt sauntered over from a nearby table where he'd been sipping coffee from a white mug. "Name's Potter," he said, "I'm from over by the Rainy Mountain Indian Reservation. You boys need another hand?"

Bob didn't like playing with strangers; sometimes they were such amateurs that they were no challenge. Still, they had good money, and, since there were two empty chairs, he nodded and said, "George Peterson is coming in any minute. We'll play soon's he gets here."

More men drifted in to play dominoes at one of the other five tables or to play snooker. Bob had never seen a woman in here. Only men. On Saturdays, they came to gamble away the long morning and afternoon, or just to chew the fat or kid around while they watched the play and the money change hands. He gazed around the large, smoked-filled room at the domino players and then let his eyes come to rest on the snooker players standing around two large tables covered with green felt. Bob didn't cotton to snooker; it was too much about a steady eye and not enough about brains. Dominoes exercised the mind, but snooker only exercised the elbows.

"George don't show up soon, we ought to ask someone else to join us," Bill said. "We're wasting good time here."

As if hearing his name called, the door to the parlor opened, and in walked George. He was a bear of a man, bigger than the other two but

CHAPTER 12 ✦ BOB

shorter than Bob. He lumbered over, sat down in the fourth chair, and quipped, "Mind if I sit in as fourth?"

"Don't see why not," Bob said. "I'd just as soon take your money as I would anybody else's. I've shuffled them, so now you got here, we can draw to see who goes down first." Bob swirled the dominoes once more, the clicking and clacking of the black tiles music to his ears.

Watching the other three men's movements and expressions, he waited his turn as they drew their dominoes. He studied the newcomer's face as he picked up. Bob had learned a long time ago that winning demanded knowing things about the men he played with. He'd also learned to remember who had played what and who had passed up putting down a winner because they didn't have in hand the right domino. During countless hours of playing the game through the years, he'd also come to know that there were things he could learn from the others' behavior that could help him win. Nowadays, after play had gone around a time or two, he could be pretty sure to know something about what the others still held in their hand. He'd learned that Bill's wide smile when he first picked up his dominoes was a dead giveaway; he'd drawn four or five of the same numbers, one of them most likely a double he hoped to make the spinner. When George drew a hand, he'd move his dominoes around in front of him, putting them together in groups of two, three, four, or more. Later, when he played one of those from a grouping, Bob would have a better idea what his other dominoes were. Potter had a twitch in his left eye that Bob would learn to read after they'd played a hand or two.

They each drew a domino to see who made the first down, and Bob turned over the five-six, the highest number drawn by the four men. He turned his domino and scooted it into the pile, and, when the others did likewise, Bob shuffled the pile once more. Each then drew seven dominoes, and Bob, who'd done the shuffle, waited for the others to draw first. He pulled the last of the dominoes, stood two facing him on the table, and carefully placed the other five in his wide hand, one stacked on the top edge of the other, the raised dragons on their backs rough against his palm.

"Give me a nickel," Bill said as he slapped down the two-three and scooted it to the middle of the table.

George played the three-six from his cluster of dominoes, and Bob knew he likely held two more sixes.

"I'll give us a spinner and take a dime." Potter, the twitch in his eye now gone, played the double-two. He sucked on a corncob pipe he lit after he sat down, drawing smoke through the stem and letting it out in dribbling clouds.

Smoking? Disgusting habit, Bob believed. Almost worse than chewing tobacco and spitting in a coffee can. But truth to tell, the place wouldn't have seemed like a domino parlor without a haze of smoke dancing around the bare bulbs dangling above the tables, and stinking spittoons squatting down beside the old boys with dips or chaws in their mouths.

Bill played the two-four. "Guess we'll just have to take that dime, too."

Bob laid down his domino as if it were delicate enough to break. "I'll just have to kill that old double six of yours, George," he said, cutting off the three-six with his five-six.

"You been lookin' at my hand again, Bob?" George's frown deepened as he played the blank-four.

The first hand ended with Bob thirty points behind Potter, but, by the end of the game, he had won by twenty. Bob went on to win the next two games as well.

As he played the first domino of the fourth game, Potter nodded at the front window and said, "That boy standin' like a wooden Indian outside there has got more gumption than I do. He ain't coming in here and playing dominoes with you."

"Potter, that boy is Bob's grandson Charlie." Bill laughed and followed Potter's play with his own. "And my nephew."

"Fool kid's trying to sell savings stamps," Bob said.

CHAPTER 12 ♦ BOB

"That's not all he's doing," Bill said. "He's been out making a few dollars chopping cotton for Joe Williams. He's put a couple of dollars of his own money into stamps. You gotta give him credit for that." Bill waved at Charlie, who had turned to peer through the window. He waved back.

Bob grunted a half laugh. "He ought to stick with chopping cotton. He's not doing so well at sellin' stamps. And quit waving at him. He's liable to come in here and pester you to buy one." He slapped down his domino, and then realized he'd missed a better play. And all because of that kid out there on the street breaking his concentration.

"Hell, I'd at least have something to take home with me if I bought one," George said.

The play went on around the table, but Bob had lost his concentration. For a while he'd put out of his mind the two extra mouths he had to feed. Now he couldn't stop his gorge from rising, couldn't push the thoughts of that fool grandson of his trying to hawk those damn savings stamps. With too much anger showing for his own comfort, he slapped down his last rock. "Domino."

"Damn, boys, we better watch out today, Bob here's in a huff." George began stacking the dominoes and turning them face down.

As the morning wore on, hand after hand was shuffled, drawn, and played. "I'm going to give us that double five and make twenty," one or another would say, or "I like that double six for a spinner; give me fifteen." By the third hand of the third game they played, Bob had learned to read Potter's eye twitch that appeared when he tried to misdirect with a false comment about the play. It was a liar's twitch. As the day wore on, Bob called "domino" more often than the others, leaving George and Potter still holding dominos in their hands. It took him by surprise to hear the noon whistle go off, signaling that it was time to take a break for something to eat. By then, most of the winnings belonged to him and George.

After a short noon meal at Leona's restaurant, where he'd had to spend a whole fifteen cents for a hamburger and a nickel for a cup of coffee,

Bob returned to the domino parlor and settled into a chair, impatient for the afternoon crowd to filter in. From the back, he could hear the proprietor hammering on something, cursing with each blow. The water cooler whined as it forced a steady flow of moist air over him. Through the front window, Bob spotted Charlie on the sidewalk again, still pestering people to buy a stamp. The boy's curly hair, windblown, stood out in all directions like a scarecrow's straw hair in a bean patch. His nose would grow even more freckles the longer he stayed out there in the sun. Charlie selling savings stamps was silly; you could just walk into the post office and buy a stamp if you took a notion. It was an idea put in his head by his other two grandsons, Pearl's two boys. Where they got the idea, he hadn't any notion, nor did he know why they weren't doing the same thing if they thought it was such a good idea. It was on the same level as snipe hunting. They'd taken Charlie on that wild goose chase once when he was too young to know any better than to sit out in the dark with an open tow sack thinking he'd catch the snipes his cousins were scaring up. Now he didn't know any better than to stand around on street corners hawking those stamps.

The vein in his neck began to pulse and his brow tightened. Ruth and Charlie's coming had stirred up Ida, made her restless and harder to get along with. And those spells she was having worried him. Chester was at the center of all this. When Ruth was a girl, Bob had warned her about taking up with the Scarsdale riffraff, and she'd paid about as much attention as a skittish mare. Now she and her half-brained kid had been put out to pasture on his land. And Chester Scarsdale wasn't paying any rent.

The door opened, letting in a blast of hot afternoon heat along with the tall frame of Joe Williams. He was wearing jeans and a denim shirt that stuck to him in places where he had sweated through. He had known Joe Williams since he was a no-account kid running around with Chester Scarsdale, looking for trouble. Ruth'd been sweet on Joe till Chester took her on a buggy ride. On the rebound from Ruth, the son-of-a-gun had

CHAPTER 12 ✦ BOB

taken up with Bob's daughter, Pearl, and then dropped her six months later, breaking her heart. Later, Joe cleaned up his act, settled down with a good woman, and did pretty good for himself until his wife, Theresa, died a year or so ago. Since then, he'd lived alone with his daughter on the Williams' place a half mile from Bob.

As Joe Williams came by the table he stopped, nodded, then said, "Having any luck today, Bob?"

Bob picked up the double-blank domino and began to tap it on the table-top. "Playing dominoes doesn't have all that much to do with luck. Luck is catching a good rain when you need one, Joe."

Joe Williams grunted a laugh, sauntered over to a rack of pool cues, and took one down. He sighted down its length before he said, "These sticks are getting so warped I'd do better using a table leg to shoot with." He racked the balls and centered them, then took the stick and slammed it against the cue-ball, plowing it into the packed nest, sending all fifteen balls flying in every direction. He pocketed three balls in a row without missing. "Your cotton looks like you're going to do well this fall, Bob?"

"Doing all right."

"You look for the war to be over soon? Get your boy, Winston, back home."

Bob tossed a domino into the air, caught it, then twiddled it between his fingers. "I suppose it depends on how long it takes us to whip the Krauts and Japs."

Joe stopped shooting to chalk his cue. "Charlie's been playing with Sarah a lot lately. Tells me he worries about his dad a lot. Ruth's pretty worried about Chester, too."

Bob stared, his face wrinkling so hard he could feel the skin folding in on itself like new furrowed soil. A small ache began in the deepest furrow, the one in the center of his forehead. "I heard from Ida that since they finished chopping for you, Charlie and Ruth've been visiting you all some. You a widower, and her with a husband overseas, it don't look right to some. You know how this town is. People talk."

"I don't mean to cause any trouble for her, Bob." Joe Williams stabbed at the cue ball, sending it rocketing toward one of the last three balls left on the table. "But the kids do like each other, and both are minus a parent. I think they're a comfort to each other."

The loud thwack of the balls as Joe Williams rammed them into the pockets unsteadied Bob, made him want to pick up a pool cue and whack Joe Williams up beside the head. "I can see that. But I don't want you getting any ideas about Ruth. You and Chester had quite a reputation back when you were younger."

Joe Williams sauntered back over to the domino table, hooked a chair with his foot, pulled it close to Bob, and sat down. "There's some things you got to let go of, Bob. I'm not the hell-raising kid you knew fifteen to twenty years ago."

"I'm not forgetting what you did to Pearl, either, Joe. Poor thing suffered when you stopped seeing her." Bob dropped the domino he was holding, and it skittered under Joe Williams' chair.

Joe Williams scooted his chair back, picked up the domino and said, "Pearl forgave me a long time ago. She feels she got a better deal marrying Bill. Probably did." He laid the domino down and flicked it with his finger, sending it shooting across the table like a cue ball, scattering the other dominoes like frightened sheep.

"That girl always did have a short memory," Bob said and then herded the scattered dominoes into the center of the table. "But I don't."

Bill and Potter came in from off the sidewalk, greeted him and Joe Williams as they started for the table, but stopped short. They looked at each other, and Bill shook his head. Then they turned to the window and peered out, not speaking. Bob figured they saw the slow burn between him and Joe. He stroked his cheek, wondering if his face was as red as Joe's. If those two were fool enough to come on over, they'd ignite themselves from the heat. "This ain't the time or place for any more of this conversation, Joe," Bob said.

"Begging your pardon, but I don't know when the goddamn right time'll come, or where that place'd be," Joe snapped. His eyes narrowed, and a dark frown creased his brow as he stood, turned, and walked out, slamming the door behind him.

Good riddance, thought Bob.

Bill and Potter sidled over then, walking slowly, as if not sure they were welcome.

He snapped at them, angry that they'd seen what had just happened. God knows what they'd make of it. "Go on. Sit down. We've got some dominoes to play."

CHAPTER 13

Ruth

→→ ✾ ←←

Summer had slipped away, creeping along like one of those box turtles she'd seen on the road or in the field. Time had slowed when she was pulling bolls, and one day was so like the next it all seemed to have been like one long, tiresome, never-ending day. Then one morning she woke to the crowing of that old rooster of Papa's, and it was almost September. August 30 and Charlie's first day of school. It had surprised her, though it shouldn't have. There was a note on Mother's feed-store calendar hanging on the wall right beside her place at the kitchen table. She came to her senses three days ago when Pearl asked her if Charlie was ready for school. He wasn't. She wasn't. And now as they walked the three-quarters of a mile to Mountain Valley School, neither of them were yet ready.

CHAPTER 13 • RUTH

They were still two or three hundred feet from the schoolhouse when the morning sun came from behind a cloud and, reflecting off the tall, schoolhouse windows, stabbed at her eyes, leaving after-images playing across her eyelids and adding to the ache in her temple. *Headaches are what a mother gets when their son acts like Charlie has all the way here,* she thought.

"I don't want to go to this stupid school," Charlie mumbled.

Ruth reached out to take his hand, but he pulled it away, and his mouth turned down into a pout. "I'm too big for that," he mumbled, putting his hands behind his back. The hand-me-down, newly washed overalls his aunt Pearl had given him were already dusty and his hair, sticking out in three different directions, looked as if he hadn't put a comb through it. His nose, wind-burned and freckled, was scrunched up as if he were passing a dead animal on the road.

A sudden burst of loud voices and high-pitched laughter of children washed over them. Ruth saw flashes of color as children in bright new patterned dresses or rolled-sleeve shirts, darted across the schoolyard to the merry-go-round. Charlie stopped, sullen and mulish, and shook his head.

"Behave. I don't have any patience with you left."

"I don't want you to take me. I'll go by myself." Planted in the middle of the road with his forehead wrinkled and his lips tight, he glared at her.

"I have to talk to the teacher sometime. Might as well be today." A step toward him was all it took to get him moving again, walking stiff-legged, like a calf being pulled by a rope, slower and slower as he approached the Williams' driveway.

"They're all going to think something's wrong with you, you go walking into the schoolyard looking like your overalls have too much starch in them."

"I want to wait here. You can go on and see the teacher, and I'll come along later." He walked over to a grove of mulberry trees in front of Joe Williams' house, squatted down, and picked up a dirt clod.

"Now quit pestering me. Act nine instead of like you're six."

"I'm acting nine." A hateful look disfigured his face, and Ruth wanted to slap it off.

"You stop that now, Charlie Scarsdale. And if I have to, I'll hold your hand all the way there." Ruth started walking across the ditch to the mulberry trees and hissed at him, "If you don't stand up this minute and come with me, I'm getting a mulberry switch and using it on you all the way to the schoolyard."

Charlie stood, crossed the ditch, and began walking down the road still carrying the dirt clod. "I don't know hardly anybody here, and I'll bet there's a bunch of bullies just waiting to devil me," he said between clenched teeth as he scuffed his shoes against the dirt. He threw the dirt clod at a fence post, sending up a spray of dust, then, his shoulders squared as if he were being led to slaughter, walked on.

"Pearl's boys are there. Sarah Williams is going to be there, too, and you know her. You've been playing with her all this last spring and summer."

"Every time I go to a new school, there's someone who wants to start trouble. Sarah told me Corky Alred goes here. He's sure going to pester me to fight."

"You get into any fights; I swear I'll skin you alive. I won't have you turning into a hoodlum."

"I don't start fights."

"I don't want to hear any more about that. Just stay away from trouble, you hear?"

The schoolyard was filled with children, and the closer he came to the gate, the redder Charlie's face became. Ruth saw eight children, spaced around an iron merry-go-round and holding on to the wooden handrail. All together, they pushed hard and made it go around faster and faster until someone shouted, "Now!" and they all jumped on, some landing on their knees, and others on their stomachs, their feet kicking out behind them.

CHAPTER 13 • RUTH

Corky Alred lost his grip and spiraled off, landed hard, rolled on his side, and lay with his elbow cocked and his palm supporting his head. He looked straight at the two of them and yelled, "Looky who's a comin'." The twirling children dragged their feet until the merry-go-round slowed. A shrimp of a girl, too small to run with the others, jumped on as it made a last turn. Then they all sat, staring as she opened the gate and stepped through.

Charlie dragged himself in close behind her and then inched away. The hand-me-downs Pearl had given him were a size too large, and Ruth knew he wanted to sink into them and escape.

Corky Alred dusted off his patched-at-the-knees overalls, squinted, and knitted his brow. His long-sleeved shirt was worn through at one elbow. There was a smear of dirt on his left temple from where he'd landed in the dirt. He flicked a twig that had stuck to his sleeve, and it landed close to Charlie's foot.

When Charlie scuffed the twig into the dirt, Corky gave him a mean-eyed stare. Ruth knew for sure there would be trouble between Corky and Charlie before the day was out. She'd have to let the teacher know. Nodding to the children she said, "Hello, everybody. I'm Mrs. Scarsdale, and this is Charlie."

A tall girl with uneven pigtails, the oldest looking of the group, said, "Pleased to meet you," and most of the others said hello. The shrimpy girl, now sitting on the merry-go-round, called out a singsong, "How-dy."

Corky spat into the dirt and ground his heel into it.

Ruth quirked her mouth and frowned at him but said nothing. What she wanted to do was tell him to wipe that smirk off his face and behave. Instead, she smiled at all the children and said, "You all can go back to playing. Charlie and I are goin' to meet Miss Zickenfoose."

With Charlie dogging her heels, she hurried to the schoolhouse, climbed up three steps, slap-dusted with eraser chalk, and entered a small room that held a standing water pump. Coat hooks were attached above hard wooden benches lining one wall. "Put your lunch in one of those cubbyholes over there, and go on out in the yard while I see if Miss Zickenfoose can speak to me."

"That's a stupid name." He took the sack lunch she handed him and stuffed it into an empty space.

Ruth had made a lunch of cold fried chicken, an apple and three saltine cracker cookies. Between two saltines she'd spread chocolate frosting she cooked up using sugar and powdered Hershey's chocolate. That was something she knew he'd look forward to. That and making it home without a run-in with Corky or one of the other boys. She turned to enter the classroom and was startled when Charlie slammed the door on his way out. Her heart began to race. She took a moment to calm herself and then opened the inner door.

The schoolroom smelled of chalk dust, old books and coal fumes. The air seemed to pulse with dust-motes dancing heavily in the harsh sunlight that pushed through the tall windows. Hardwood flooring was slick from the red clay young feet had tracked across it through the last fifty years. When she first started school here twenty-eight years ago, her teacher, Miss Oliver, would ring a cowbell, and all the children would line up and march down the aisles as music played on a wind-up Victrola. They would recite a morning prayer and, then, their hands held firmly over their hearts, stand tall as they pledged their allegiance to the Flag of the United States of America. In a salute to the flag, they would throw their hands out toward the flag, but they didn't do that anymore. The gesture was so like the salute to Hitler that that had stopped. Back then, Ruth would pretend to sing, mouthing the words as the other children half-shouted "God Bless America." She would do math problems, read or recite through the long morning until noon recess, when most of the others would troop out the door for an hour. She and her two girlfriends sat at their desks whispering secrets, reading, or doing homework.

CHAPTER 13 • RUTH

As Ruth now approached her desk, the teacher rose, came around, and extended her hand. She was a short, slender woman who looked to Ruth like a younger version of Miss Oliver.

"I'm Miss Zickenfoose. And you are?"

"Ruth Scarsdale. I'm Pearl Dennison's sister. Will's and Carl's aunt." Ruth liked the looks of Miss Zickenfoose even though she agreed with Charlie that her name sounded awfully strange. The teacher was dressed in what looked like a loose, comfortable wool skirt and had a small watch pinned to the gray sweater that matched her skirt. Sensible shoes rested on the floor. Having to be on your feet a lot of the day corralling a classroom full of active children would probably make your feet sore if you didn't have comfortable shoes. Like Miss Oliver, she smelled of chalk dust and lavender perfume.

"You must be Charlie's mother."

"You know Charlie?"

"My guess is that at least half the county knows him by now. He's out on the streets of Hobart every weekend with his savings stamps and going up to people to introduce himself. I've heard a lot of good things about him."

"He's got a good heart, but he gets a little stubborn at times. I hope he doesn't give you too much trouble."

Miss Zickenfoose laughed. "Charlie will do just fine. Is there anything I might need to know about him from you?"

"I suppose all the kids here have their dads at home, them being farmers. Charlie's dad is overseas. Charlie worries a lot about him."

"Everybody here has an uncle, brother, or cousin in the service, so there's a lot of worry to go around."

"You need to know that he got off to a bad start with Corky Alred."

"I'll take a strap to that boy the first time he acts up with Charlie. Or else send for his daddy and let him do it for me." Miss Zickenfoose extended her hand. "I'm sure everything will work out."

*

Forty-five minutes before Charlie would be dismissed from school, Ruth walked the half mile from her parents' farm to Joe Williams' place, and when he didn't open the door to her knock, she walked down to the barn, where his truck was parked. She found him with a scoop shovel in hand mucking out the stalls for his milk cows. Dressed in work jeans and a plaid shirt, he was sweating as he pitched shovelfuls of manure out the window onto the manure pile. She admired the strength in his arms and back as he bent to his task. It troubled her that she paid attention.

"Hello, Joe."

He was startled, and his last scoop almost missed the window as the shovel's blade struck the window sash. "Goodness, Ruth, you gave me a start." He took a red bandana from his back pocket and wiped sweat from his forehead. "You come to collect Charlie?"

"Sorry, Joe. I didn't mean to scare you, but I got here a little early and thought we could visit a while." Ruth had visited with Joe on occasion since arriving at her papa's farm. But now she felt awkward, shy that she was here in the barn alone with him. At a loss for anything more to say as she remembered back to the time Joe had kissed her out behind the horse shed, the smell of horses then not much different than his barn smelled now. Her face grew warm with the memory, and she prayed Joe would not notice.

"I'm glad you did, Ruth. I like your company." He smiled and nodded to some hay bales. "Why don't we sit a spell till I cool off, and then we'll go to the house. I'll make us a glass of iced tea. Sarah and Charlie will be along soon, and I'll give them a snack before you head back to your papa's place."

Ruth lowered herself onto a haybale and sat facing Joe. "On the way here, I saw your cotton was coming along. Looks like you and Papa will have a good crop this year." Even as she said it, she knew this was the kind of small talk that the men engaged in when they met in the field or on the downtown streets. She didn't know what else to say.

Joe stuffed the bandana back in his pocket and sat facing her on one of the hay bales. "That's true. I'm hoping you and Charlie can help pull bolls in three or four weeks. I think my crop will come in before Bob's. Was Charlie excited to start school?"

"I don't think so. He's started so many new schools. Chester never seemed able to stay in one place long enough for him to have a full year. And Charlie always has to contend with the school bully those first few days. That Corky Alred has already started giving him dirty looks."

"Yeah, Sarah and I know all about Corky. Believe me, Charlie'll have to whup Corky's little behind before that stops."

"But I won't have him fighting. That's what got Chester in the mess he's in now." She wished that hadn't slipped out and hoped he would let it pass unnoticed.

Joe did not respond but, stuffing his bandana into his back pocket, said, "I probably ought to tell you something Ruth, if Bob hasn't already said something to you about it. I ran into him at the domino parlor on Saturday, and he wasn't all that chummy with me. Brought up you and me spending time together now and then. Said we'd be starting rumors if we weren't careful."

Ruth closed her eyes, knotted her brow, and shook her head. "Papa's been awful mean headed since Charlie and I arrived. I'll have to have a talk with him about this nonsense."

"With Bob, I'm not sure how much good that'll do. He hasn't particularly liked me for a long time. But I want you to know, I'm comfortable with our short visits. Busybodies be damned." He stood and reached out a hand to her. "Come on, now. Let's get up to the house. It probably smells better up there though I won't promise it."

"That, and if anybody sees us hanging out in the barn together, think what they'll say then."

As they walked out into the barnyard, dust swirled up in a gust of wind that caught a tumbleweed and sent it rolling past the house and down the driveway, where it caught up against a corner fence post. Once at the door to the house, Joe Williams stopped, looked at her hard, and said, "I'm not forgetting about what you said about Charlie and Corky. It's just that I don't think you'll like what I'm going to say. You're just trying to put off the inevitable, Ruth. Corky's going to bully Charlie till he does something about it."

At that moment, she heard a collective yell from beyond the trees hugging Joe's frontage to the road. She heard Charlie shout, "You're full of beans, Corky." And that was followed by Sarah's high-pitched scream of, "Why don't you just get lost, Corky."

"Sounds like you're a little late with that thought," Joe said. "Let's go see what all the ruckus is about." He quickly outdistanced Ruth, reaching the road while she was only halfway there.

Through the branches of the mulberry trees, she could see a pack of children milling about on the road and heard Corky yell, "Your daddy knocked up my aunt Alice."

Charlie, anger and disbelief sounding in his reply, yelled back, "My daddy would never hit a woman no matter what. He ain't no coward."

Corky laughed and then taunted, "You are one dumb cow turd, sissy-boy. What I was saying is that your daddy put a biscuit in my aunt's oven."

Sarah yelled, "You hush up, Corky Alred. That's a nasty thing to say."

Ruth's heart was beating so hard she thought she would faint. As she reached the road, she saw Corky draw back his fist and step in close to Sarah, but Joe yelled at Corky. "You better not lay a hand on Sarah, Corky, or I'll tan your butt right now." Reaching Sarah, he put his arm about her and said to Corky, "I'm going to see to it your daddy and mother knows about this. You hear?"

His lip curled, Corky spat on the ground and danced back a few steps. "I hear. But my folks won't care."

CHAPTER 13 ✦ RUTH

The wind picked up, and everyone's hands went to their eyes, protecting against the blowing road dust as Ruth shouted, "Charlie, get yourself up to the house. Corky Alred, you get on home before I tan your hide myself."

Corky sneered and pointed at Charlie. "Saved by your mama." He took off, running backward, chanting, "Mama's Boy. Mama's Boy."

But Ruth wasn't thinking about the fight anymore. She was enraged by what Corky had said about his aunt. She hoped to God it wasn't true. What would she and Charlie do if it was? She just couldn't face the idea. Or even look at Joe. She was too embarrassed. Calling to Charlie, she started off down the road, throwing a quick goodbye over her shoulder to Joe.

As they approached Papa's and Mother's place, the wind picked up even more and sent her and Charlie's hair swirling about their faces. Papa's white hound-dog came trotting down the road to greet Charlie, wriggling its back end as if trying to wag more than its tail. Charlie fell to his knees and put his arms around the dog and buried his face in its soft neck.

The wind blew harder and colder.

Fall was upon them. Winter was just around the corner. *The Farmers' Almanac* had promised a hard winter.

CHAPTER 14

Ida

*E*ntering the outskirts of Hobart, Bob said, "First time we've had some peace and quiet on the way into town in a while."

Ida shrugged. "Charlie was happy enough to ride into town early with his uncle Bill and the boys. Thought he might have more time to sell those savings stamps now he earned enough chopping cotton to buy two dollars' worth. Ruth and Pearl decided to make apple jelly out of the last of those apples Pearl bought over west of Roosevelt."

"Charlie ridin' back with us?"

"No. Ruth told me he's meetin' up with Joe and Sarah Williams. Joe's folks invited him to stay for supper. Joe will drive Charlie home before bedtime."

"I like Joe's folks, but I don't cotton to him. And I think Ruth is spending too much time at Joe's place. Been using the excuse it's to keep

CHAPTER 14 • IDA

Corky Alred away from Charlie after school. Let him have time to play with Sarah."

"Can't argue with that," Ida said.

Driving up past the city's junkyard, Bob pulled over in front of a house badly in need of paint. "Your mother don't get somebody to patch that roof and fix the gutters, that place is going to fall down around their ears."

"Can't argue that, either," Ida said as she spied her mother's second husband, Walter—someone she couldn't stomach being around—sitting on the front porch reading a newspaper. "Come pick me up at Joan's when you're ready to drive home." She climbed out of the car and reluctantly walked to the house. The moment she stepped onto the porch, Walter started exercising his gums with all the self-righteousness of the ignorant.

"Howdy, Ida. I missed seeing you last time you were here." He picked up a Folger's Coffee can and spit a glob of snuff-laced phlegm into the mess in the bottom.

If she were asked by someone if there was one thing about Bob she appreciated, she'd tell them it was that he didn't sit around smoking, chewing tobacco, or dipping snuff. To Walter she said, "You were off to the grocery store, and I didn't stay too long last time, Walter." *And I wish you had gone again today*, she thought. It was too bad her mother ended up with this mean-spirited old reprobate after losing Papa. But when you get older, you don't have much choice in a man if you wanted to keep food in the pantry and a roof over your head. If ever something happened to Bob and she had a chance to remarry, God grant she did better for herself than her mother had.

"D'ja read yet about how they're letting them niggers carry guns now?" Without waiting for an answer, he said, "I sure as hell wouldn't want a nigger with a gun behind me on the lines. Might just shoot me in the back."

And it would be good riddance, Ida thought, but said, "Well, now—isn't that something?"

"Yes, it is. Back in the World War One, when I was in the trenches, weren't no niggers carrying guns. I did have to put up with some damn worthless French fighting alongside me, though. It's a damn wonder we won the war with allies like them." He spit once more into his can and set it down by his chair, where it was welcomed by a couple of houseflies. "Them French seem pretty worthless in this war, too, letting the Krauts run all over them like they did."

Ida could not particularly abide coloreds any more than the next person here in Hobart, but she didn't air those feelings every time she had someone's attention. She wrinkled her nose in disgust and tried to think of something sensible to say back that wouldn't get him all riled up. Only hateful thoughts came to her. Thankfully, her mother opened the door and invited her in, so she didn't have to respond. They left Walter to the company of his snuff, spit can, the two flies, and hateful thoughts. Exchanging knowing glances, they passed from view of his rheumy eyes. Ida knew her mother could hardly abide Walter any more than she could. As they settled back into soft cushioned chairs in the parlor—which smelled of tobacco, dust, and her mother's talcum powder—she let out a relieved sigh at being off her feet. Even that short walk from the car had winded her. Or maybe it was the aggravation with Walter.

As her mother had grown older, the order of things in this little house had changed; disarray was everywhere, and dust covered surfaces her mother'd once kept clean and shiny with furniture polish, feather dusters, and hard work. "There isn't enough time now to get to everything," her mother would claim. But with age had come long catnaps, and sometimes she fell asleep while Ida was in the middle of a sentence. Just not much energy left in her these days.

The house was filled with the belongings of the past, whatnots, outdated papers, family pictures, and doilies. Bottles of perfume Ida had given her years ago cluttered the bathroom shelves. Old stains remained embedded in the furniture and rugs like hard-to-forget memories. A

CHAPTER 14 ♦ IDA

crumpled newspaper and a wadded-up 3Musketeers candy wrapper lay side by side on the end table. On the coffee table, there was a silver-plated spoon and an inexpensive China tea set, valuables her mother held too precious to give away, but not valuable enough to sell, or the old man would have already had them in the pawn shop. Social Security and the few dollars the children sometimes sent didn't go far enough. Didn't keep Walter in snuff.

Her mother spoke up as soon as they were settled. "I'm going to be 80 next year, and I suspect I'll go soon." She said that every time Ida visited. "I want you to look around and put your name on anything you take a fancy to that isn't already spoke for."

"Thank you, Mother—I'll do that." Ida always thanked her mother and then meandered about without finding anything her sixteen brothers and sisters had left unmarked. Did she really want anything from this house? Probably not. Her mother's mementos of the past were old and dusty, some worn smooth by years of her mother's handling them. And besides, Ida had her own treasures. They were encased in a halo of her own memories that made them precious.

"You look a little peaked today, Ida. You OK?"

"I been getting these dizzy spells lately, Mother. Feels like I'm going to faint."

"I been having those for years. Doctor told me I needed more iron. I told him I lived next door to a junk yard, and did he think I ought to chew on a rusted fender." Her mother laughed, almost losing the uppers of her false teeth before reaching up and pushing them back in place. "He said I might, but seeing as how I didn't have no teeth to speak of, it would be better to take me an iron pill every day. Get my blood to thicken a little."

"I think these spells of mine are nerves, myself," Ida said. "Too much aggravation with Bob. Having Ruth and Charlie to look after. My boy over there in Burma maybe getting shot at. Don't leave me much peace." She didn't mention the worry she had that Alice's baby might be Chester's.

Ruth had confided in her what Corky Alred said. No telling how long Ruth and Charlie would have to live with her and Bob if that were the case. But she didn't let her mother know about that worry and would be thankful if the rumor didn't reach those old ears.

Her mother looked at her out of eyes dimmed to a faded, watery blue and then shook her head. "When I was your age, I still had six young'uns living with me. And two with a husband and baby of their own. Thanks goodness, though, for those two son-in-laws livin' with us and doing the farm work, or we wouldn't have made it. Still, it was like a three-ring circus around there, one baby or the other squalling its head off, and those kids of mine bickering like they was five-year-olds instead of being practically growed."

"I figured that having raised and married off nine of us by then you'd had lots of practice." That came out with a bitter edge that brought another wrinkle to her mother's eyes.

"Don't you go sassing me, Ida. You're still my child, you know." Then her mother's voice softened. "I know you have yourself a burden right now with Charlie and Ruth livin' with you. But you only got four to worry about now. There cain't be no room for self-pity."

"I just wish I'd have married some other man than Bob. He was so grown-up looking when I married him. Responsible, I thought, if I thought at all. He was nineteen, three years older than me. And was handsome. But nineteen-year-olds don't have much sense, either. Bob had less than the ordinary, even after growing up in that family of his. Though none of them went beyond a third-grade education, most of them turned out okay."

"People grow up in good homes and still end up doin' wrong, Ida. Look at your brother Stanley. And your sister Maggie. Who'd ever think they'd go bad? Maggie, I can understand a little better; she married into that riffraff from Willow Springs. But Stanley? He was such a good boy growing up."

"Leastwise when your back wasn't turned," Ida said, feeling anger well up in her, the bile she'd collected all those years ago when her younger

CHAPTER 14 ♦ IDA

brother had made a mess of his life while pretending to be the obedient son. Going to church on Sundays and stealing horses during the week. Graduating to cars and getting sent away for ten years for armed robbery. A deep ache began in her chest and ran to her left arm, making it throb. She spilled a drop of tea on her dress, her hand trembled so.

"What's the matter, Ida? You look like you just saw a ghost." Her mother's face blurred, the creases that defined it melting together into bland smoothness.

Ida's mouth turned dry, and her pulse hammered in her ears. Short, labored breaths seemed blocked behind her breastbone, so that she couldn't pull enough air into her lungs. "I'm having one of those spells again, Mother." Pinpricks of light flitted across her vision, and the room grew darker, as if the sun were setting before its time. A hollow roar began, and it was as if a black tornado cloud were approaching, much like the one that years ago had almost sucked Ruth right off the ground. Now it was lifting her up and bearing her away, whirling her about and tossing her like Bob would a bag of chicken feed. Her mother fluttered there below, calling, trying to reach out and snatch her back. But she was hurled further away, caught up by the force of the storm that beat against her chest.

The last thing she remembered before passing out was her mother yelling, "Walter! Git yourself over to that domino parlor and fetch Bob. Right now."

When she came to an hour later, her mother and Bob urged Ida to go to the doctor. "I might ought to, but I'm pretty sure these spells are just nerves. I'm not about to go see a doctor for something he can't help anyway."

CHAPTER 15

Chester

⇥ ✽ ⇤

Before the sun came up on the first warm spring morning in Brisbane, Australia, Chester helped load a ship that would carry him and the other Sea Bees in his unit to an island somewhere north of where they had been. Once the ship was loaded, he stepped on-board with all the other men and as they steamed out to sea, stood looking wistfully at the shore. Though he'd worked his ass off for months on that shore, he had been safe from the Japs. Now they were sailing right to the edge of the shitstorm.

The water was calm, a sea of glass that his ship skimmed over like a wild duck on his pa's farm. Trucks, bulldozers, jeeps, field ranges and refrigerators, building materials, and men were crowded in the convoy's ships. The men of his company were perched on the equipment or crowded

CHAPTER 15 ✦ CHESTER

together on the deck near him, all of them smoking and shooting the breeze. Chester sat near the rail with a lit cigarette in his hand and blew a lungful of smoke into the air as his eyes scanned the waves. "I've got this itch I just can't scratch, Hough. I'm sittin' here smokin' this cigarette, and it could be my last one. Damn Jap submarines wandering through these waters could blow my ass to kingdom come."

"Didn't you hear that most have been sunk or chased out?" Hough said and then spit over the side of the ship.

"Yeah, I heard. Loud and clear. They said 'Most.' If just one Jap sub's still around, it might find us."

Five hours later, relieved that no Jap sub had found them, he sat in the lee of a tractor he would drive ashore when they reached Kiriwina Island. This was a training exercise, but he still had an army of butterflies invading his stomach. Smoke from his last Camel cigarette drifted up and, caught by the wind, swirled crazily and disappeared.

As Chester saw the dim form of the island come closer, Richard Bell stepped onto a tractor-crawler and yelled over the roar of the landing ship's motor, "Attention. Break out the K-rations."

Chester snuffed out his half-smoked cigarette and flipped it over the side. "Damn, but I'm going to be sick of Spam before this miserable war is over." But he took out his rations, tore the lid from the dull army-green can, began scooping the contents out with his fingers and sucking them into his mouth.

Hough snorted. "You better enjoy that while you can. Won't be nothing else till we get all this crap on shore and set up for tomorrow."

An hour later, through scorching sunshine, his flat-bellied tank lighter approached the island's sandy beach as waves battered the bow, rocking and rolling the craft. Three men took death grips on the boat's side and lost their K-rations into the water. Tight-lipped, Chester braced himself against the side of the lighter and watched the palm-fringed island edge nearer. Over the bow, he could see small puffs of smoke blossom as

Aussie snipers in the palms began shooting blanks at the coxswains in the approaching craft. The pop of 25 caliber rifles cut through the hum of the lighter's motor as it was driven closer to the beach. Even knowing those weren't real bullets aimed at him, Chester said, "Damnation, Hough. They're scaring the shit out of me." He crouched down and clenched his fists till his fingers cramped. In his shirt pocket he carried a letter he'd received from the States, one from Charlie writing about his worry over Chester's safety. Charlie sure as hell was more concerned about his daddy right now than the Navy brass sending him out here to help build a runway in this godforsaken part of the world.

As the boat churned through the heavy surf, gallons of salt water poured in from the sides and splashed over Chester. "God damn it. I'm going to drown before anybody ever has a chance to shoot me."

Johnny Polk, standing on the deck a few feet from him, spit into the water sloshing at their feet and said to no one in particular, "This is a piece of cake. If them planes I hear comin' in was Japs, we'd have something to gripe about."

"And you're talking from experience, now, aren't you?" Chester challenged.

"You got a mouth on you, Chester, you know that?" said Polk.

Chester's released his grip on the side of the boat with one hand and, as the airplanes' raced closer, he touched his shirt pocket, felt Charlie's letter resting there, likely wet as a dishrag. At least the letter from Charlie in his pocket might bring him the luck he needed to help him get through the next few days. Next time he wrote, he'd tell Charlie just that.

Bell stood and yelled at the top of his lungs, "OK. Let's go."

Chester's numbed legs would hardly let him move. He felt a knot form in his stomach and his pulse quicken. He took a deep breath and held it, feeling his heart bucking inside his chest like a skittish stallion. *This is just an exercise*, he told himself, aggravated that he was reacting as if he were going into a real battle.

CHAPTER 15 ◆ CHESTER

"Come on, you wet bastards, let's move." Bell shook his fist at them. "We gotta get these damn supplies ashore." Chester wondered if Bell thought him deaf, dumb, and blind when he yelled, "You heard me, Scarsdale—get ready."

Muttering "Christ Almighty," Chester watched the first ones on shore jumping down into the water, each hoisting a load of materials, then disappearing into the maze of palms. Other ships disgorged bulldozers and tractors that began flattening the underbrush. Some bogged down in the muddy sand at once.

His lighters slid to a halt in soft sand, and the ramp dropped. As Chester splashed ashore, he heard Bell yell, "Scarsdale, Hough, Polk, help get some of that mesh unloaded and in place. We don't get that down, none of those machines will get far."

Chester and the others, all sweating like mules in the ninety-degree heat, began unloading mesh, laying it down on the sand and then on into the jungle where a roadway was being cleared by hand. A man Chester recognized as Commander White, USNR Civil Engineer from Tulsa, a pint-sized son-of-a-bitch with the energy of a jackhammer, moved up and down the beach, prodding the men on like a slave master. Chester was glad he was at the jungle's edge and moving away from the man. Under his breath, Chester muttered, "Damn the Nazis, the dagos, the Japs, the sun, and all those other boats bringing in supplies. And damn White." He glanced once more at the beach and saw dozens on dozens of lighters delivering mesh to the beach for his tired and aching back to carry into the tropical hell he found himself in. *At least it's hot as hell*, he thought and walked on with his load. Chester and the others laid yards and yards of mesh into place on the mud of the jungle floor and then returned to the beach, where the ships continued to disgorge machinery, building materials, and more mesh on to the sand. On one of the trips into the jungle, he watched as a section of mesh he'd helped lay, designed to "snowshoe" vehicles over soft sand or mud, failed to hold, and two of the cats and a truck carrying supplies bogged down.

"You men go help carry those supplies inland," Bell ordered. "That's the only way they're going to get delivered."

"Son of a bitch," Chester said, then kicked off his shoes, shouldered a box thrown to the ground by a truck driver who had climbed in the bed of his truck that was up to its axle in mud. Time after time, Chester plowed barefoot through the sand to the depots and back. Soaked to the skin with his own sweat, he shucked his pants and shirt. Soon, every man around him had thrown off theirs, and now all were working in their skivvies. The other men, slick with sweat and struggling through the mushy sand, reminded Chester of the slimy bullfrogs living back home in his pa's rocky draw. As the sun burned his skin darker, Chester wiped sweat from his eyes, cursed his slick hands and tired body, *and somehow kept on.*

When enough sturdier mesh was finally laid down by midafternoon, he returned to his tractor and started the motor, hooked up to a trailer loaded with more mesh and then weaved his way through the men and supplies and on into the jungle. The mud and muck on either side of him brought a memory to him of Ruth and the first time he'd taken her on a buggy ride. Thinking of Ruth pained him. He'd felt angry and guilty ever since her letter had come, telling him what Corky had said to Charlie. She wanted to know if it could possibly be true. He wondered, too, about Charlie. He'd had to chuckle when he read that Charlie said, "My daddy would never hit a woman no matter what." He was sure that Pearl's two boys would take him aside and educate him. Ruth would be too embarrassed. But what could Charlie be thinking once he knew? He'd like to throttle that nephew of Alice's. He should write Ruth and tell her . . . What? That he was leaving her for Alice? Staying with her and Charlie? God help him—he couldn't decide.

Finally parked a half mile from shore, he helped unload and when finished, climbed back on the tractor, sat on the hard metal seat, and let his thoughts continue to wander back to Oklahoma.

CHAPTER 15 • CHESTER

"Quit your wool-gathering, Scarsdale," Bell yelled. "We got too damn much work to do for you to slack off."

Chester jumped, startled to be caught doing nothing but let his mind wander. Gunning the motor of his tractor, he drove back to the water's edge.

*

Before sundown Chester helped unload ten landing crafts' cargo onto the trailer hooked to the back of his tractor or hauled supplies and equipment inland on his back. Countless more Sea Bees waded onto the island, and, when night wrapped the shore in darkness so black, he couldn't see his hand in front of his face, Chester, Hough, and the others finally stopped. Exhausted and grit-covered, he looked for but couldn't find a place in the dark to set up shelter, so he rolled up in his tent on the sand next to Hough and tried to sleep. Night birds called out, and insects set up a hum, a racket that reminded him of summer nights in Oklahoma when the cicadas sang. His ma had once told him she'd thought the sound of cicadas was a soothing sound, but somewhere out in the dark of this world were men who would like nothing better than to kill him. He could not be soothed by the cicadas' song.

"Hough?"

"Yeah?"

"You think we'll survive this war if we keep getting closer to those damn Jap soldiers?"

"Damned if I know."

"Son of a bitch, I hope we do."

CHAPTER 16

Bob

→→ ✾ ←←

Bob had worried about Ida ever since that spell at her mother's but was grateful she'd hadn't had another for two weeks. As the evening six o'clock whistle sounded, he pulled up in front of his daughter Joan's place and waited for Ida. Together they drove downtown and parked in front of the hardware store to wait for Charlie and Ruth. In the chilly, late September afternoon, a few people still sat in their cars or lounged against their fenders, getting in some last-minute gossip, a final few pulls on a cigarette, or a moment of people-watching before going back to chores or preparations for supper. Out his open window, he nodded to acquaintances and spoke a greeting to neighbors but didn't want to draw anyone into a conversation. He was ready to go home. He and a frowning Ida waited longer than he wanted for Ruth and that confounded boy to show up.

CHAPTER 16 • BOB

"You manage to make enough to start another fruit-jar savings bank?" Ida began to fan herself with her open hand as if, Bob thought, the anger that always lived inside her could be fanned away into the air.

Bob grunted and pulled seventy-five cents out of his pocket. "I had a little luck today."

"I don't want your winnings. I just detest the thought that I was having to skimp when you had that much saved up just moldering out in the barn." Ida's face could curdle milk; it looked that sour to Bob.

"Go on and take it." He dropped the change into Ida's lap. "You'll be hollering before the evening is over that I didn't let you have it. Anyway, I kept half; it's enough for next week." He looked at Ida carefully, tried to tell if she were really all that upset. Last week, Ruth got her two sisters to back her up and argued their mother into going to see the doctor. Would have drug her there if she'd absolutely refused. News wasn't good. Bad heart. Told Ruth and the girls they'd need to lighten their mother's load. No more heavy lifting. Turned out that having Ruth home might be a godsend after all.

Ida gathered the change from her lap and dropped it into her bag. "You seen Charlie today?"

"He might'n-near wore a hole in the concrete walking up and down the street. And it'll be up to me to have to pay the city for the damage."

"I swear, I never saw you so downright mean-spirited as you are about Charlie. Except with your own sons. I never seen anybody as mean to their boy as you were to Winston. And you don't say anything much about him being in the war."

Bob wanted to say that they were talking about Chester Scarsdale's son, not theirs. Next thing he knew, she would be carping at him again about Brian. Trying to change the conversation back to his grandson, he said, "I just think Charlie's a chip off the old block, always leaping before he looks, and not giving a damn about the cow manure he might land in."

"I don't think you're right about that, Bob. That boy is good-hearted. And Ruth has tried to raise him right."

"What about last week, when Charlie and Sarah found that billfold, and he decided to keep the money that was in it? Convinced Sarah to go along with him. Got into trouble with the sheriff because of it and worried Ruth to death. We'll have more trouble with that one. I'd darn near bet the farm on it. And speaking of the devil."

Charlie came moping along the street without a glance in their direction. He was bent as a broken fencepost, dragging himself along like an old man with the miseries. From the corner of one eye to his ear, a shallow, dried gully made by tears cut through the street dust that had lightened his freckles. He remembered that Chester had the same kind of freckles as Charlie's.

The boy flung himself into the back seat and slumped there with a look so sullen that Bob was sure no good had come from the day.

"Didn't go so well, huh, Charlie?" Ida reached back and laid a hand on Charlie's knee.

"I only sold three stamps today," Charlie grunted and raised his chin, looking defiant, as if daring them to comment. "And I'm not going to get paid for one until next week."

Bob wanted to say what a damn fool Charlie'd been to still think it possible to sell all that many savings stamps. Damn foolish notion. "Well, I don't know what . . . ?"

Ida caught Bob's eye with a look that said, "You say one more word, you'll have the dickens to pay."

Charlie eyes widened, and he looked at Ida and then at Bob before he said, "I did get this, though." He held up a bomb-shaped penny bank. "The man at the bank said it was worth fifteen cents, but he gave it to me 'cause it advertised the bank, and I was selling savings stamps."

Hobart First National Bank was printed on one side and on the other were instructions that Bob read as the boy held it out for them to see.

Bomb bank. Fill this bank with your spare change. When full, break it open and purchase a WAR BOND at your nearest post office. This bank

CHAPTER 16 • BOB

will hold $18.75 in pennies, nickels, dimes, quarters and half-dollars which is the price of a $25.00 WAR BOND. Bomb the Japs from your own home.

Ida patted Charlie on the arm. "That's real nice, Charlie."

"You work your tail off all day long and all's to show for it is that?" Bob felt his aggravation slop out, like spilled hog swill. Charlie sat back as if he'd been hit in the face.

"I'm going to use it to save enough to buy a whole war bond." Charlie reddened beneath the powdering of dirt, making his freckles stand out like flyspecks on an unwashed window. "I found a penny on the street and put it in with another one I had in my pants pocket." He held up the bank and gave it a shake, making the two pennies rattle around like seed in a dry gourd. "Mama said when we pull bolls later this month, I can put some of what I earn into stamps. But I'll just put it in my bank."

"Good thing you have to break it open to get the money out. Won't be tempted to spend it," Bob said.

"Shame on you, Bob." Ida reared back against her seat and screwed her face into a scowl. "At least the boy won't be squirreling his money away in a fruit jar for gambling and the good Lord only knows what else."

Bob was relieved to spy Ruth walking down the street toward the car so that now they could head home. Glancing in the rearview mirror, he saw Charlie slink as far into the corner as the door would allow, his face screwed up in pinched defiance.

Ruth entered the car just as Ash McGregor came out of the hardware store, waved to them, and walked over to the car. He placed a hand on the windowsill and leaned over to peer inside. The grime from the hardware store's tools and supplies rimmed his fingernails, and Bob admired that. Meant the man worked for a living. "Evening, Ruth. How are you, Mrs. Choat? Bob? You've got quite an enterprising boy there, Ruth. He's going to help us win this war and bring his daddy home." He reached in the back window and ruffled Charlie's hair. "How'd you do today?"

Charlie sat up straighter. "Not so good. I only sold three today. Mr. Buchanan's going to pay me for his stamp next week."

Bob almost pissed his pants when he heard that. George Buchanan was one man he disliked more than Chester Scarsdale. And he'd told the boy not to go around his place again.

McGregor shook his head. "You talking about George Buchanan, Charlie? Old man who lives over there in the Nash Hotel?"

Charlie ducked his head when he saw the look Bob gave him, but he answered McGregor. "Yes, sir. Last week Mr. Buchanan wanted to buy a stamp from me, but I didn't have change for a dollar, so he said he'd have it for me today. And today he was visiting with Mr. Horner and didn't have any money on him, but said he'd give me the twenty cents next week. Trouble is, I won't have the money to buy more stamps for next week."

"You might as well kiss that twenty cents good-bye," Bob said.

"This has happened before, and he always paid me a week or two later."

"Still, that old man would steal the nickels off a dead man's eyes. And almost never pays his debts, does he, Ash?"

"I've heard tell."

"And he probably fills Charlie's head full of tall yarns about when he was friends with Jelly Nash."

Charlie said, "Today he told me all about how him and Frank Jelly Nash were friends before somebody put out Nash's lights. Said you knew him, too, Grandpa. And there was something about you and Shady Creek, but I didn't know what he was talking about."

Bob felt the blood rush to his face. "You can't listen to anything that old jackass brays about, Charlie. And I better not hear of you going to his place again."

"I told you not to go out of downtown, Charlie Scarsdale," Ruth added. "There you go not minding me again."

"Now, Ruth, I know it's none of my business, but there's no harm will come to a boy around here," McGregor said. "Even from the likes of Buchanan. That old man's no good, but he wouldn't hurt a child. He might sell more stamps if he went out into the neighborhood if he isn't having any luck downtown. And I hate to see a kid with his kind of backbone get discouraged."

"He won't ever sell enough of those stamps to amount to a hill of beans no matter where he tries," Bob said. But what his blood was boiling about was that Buchanan had mentioned Shady Creek. He could wring that old devil's neck for that.

"If he goes out into the neighborhoods, he'll get better known," McGregor said. "Then, I bet, he'll find more people willing to buy. And in the meantime, Charlie, let me have one of those stamps. That's what I came out to the car for."

Charlie's eyes widened as large as saucers and he looked so charged with false hope, he fairly bounced on the seat like a rubber ball as he pulled out a stamp and handed it over to McGregor. "That's great."

Bob held up his hand. "Now, just a minute. You shouldn't have to do that, Ash."

Ida said, "You'll not interfere with this boy's chance to sell one of these stamps, Bob Choat."

"I didn't mean to get in the middle of a family disagreement." McGregor stepped back from the car and stood looking back and forth between Ida and Charlie and then back to Bob, like he didn't know which way to look.

"My apologies, Ash. Go on and buy it. But I won't have him bothering you every time he comes to town," Bob said.

"No bother what-some-ever," McGregor said as he handed Charlie a dime , took a stamp and then backed up on to the curb and waved. "I'll see you all next weekend. Don't be discouraged, now, Charlie, you hear?"

"No sir, I won't be. And I'll do a better job sellin' next week." He leaned out the window and waved to McGregor when the man paused at his door and looked back.

Ruth pulled him back inside. "I'm glad you can bank on selling to Mr. McGregor every week, son. And speaking of banks, where did you get this one?" She picked the bank bomb from out of Charlie's hands.

"Man at the bank give it to me." Charlie then rattled on faster than a road-show hawker. "And I met a lot of people today. There was a lady, Mrs. Braun, said she knew you, Mama, and that I should say hello for her. I saw Joe Williams. He said to say hello to you, too. But I didn't like it much 'cause he said he and my daddy had been a couple of scoundrels."

"That's true enough," Bob said. "Joe's cut from the same cloth as Chester. And Buchanan's a thief and a liar, so, Charlie, you stay away from him." He gripped the steering wheel, his knuckles white. He wished to God that son-of-a-female-dog hadn't mentioned Shady Creek. He did not want Ida to ever know about Sally Tate. Her husband, Richard, had won a piece of land in the 1901 lottery. The man thought he was the luckiest man in the world that day. It wasn't many years after that when Bob thought he was the lucky one, lying on the bank of Shady Creek with Sally a few times while Richard sweated behind a mule and a one-bottom plow.

Bob remembered being a good-looking man back when he was in his thirties, six-three with a shock of hair as black as Old Tony's mane and a smile so winsome that he turned many a pretty girl's head. He would leave Ida and their two kids at home and square dance all Saturday night, get up and go to church the next morning, then sweat all the next week behind a plow and be ready for another go-round come the weekend. He'd danced with Sally only twice before she invited him out to pick pecans along Shady Creek. Wasn't pecan picking that either of them had in mind. He tied a saddle blanket on behind his piebald mare's saddle; told Ida and the kids he was going into Hobart to get a wheel bearing for his cotton wagon. He and Sally sat for a few minutes on the blanket cracking pecans, and then he reached over and kissed her. She stood up and let her dress fall around her ankles. He had never seen skin so

CHAPTER 16 ♦ BOB

mouthwateringly creamy as hers. When he reached out and touched it, he thought he'd died and gone to heaven.

Buchanan had come upon him and Sally once but beat a hasty retreat when Bob yelled, "I'll kill you if you ever say a word about what you just seen." Still, he'd been uneasy ever since, his secret known only to Sally and that old crook. Now the jackass had started spilling his guts to Charlie. *Well, I'll see to that*, he told himself.

"What's the matter with you, Bob? You look ready to pop a blood vessel." Ida stared at him, her eyes screwed up with curiosity and her mouth a crooked line of concern.

"Are you sure you're all right, Papa?" Ruth asked. Like Ida, there was concern in her voice.

"Never mind." He gunned the motor, grinding the gear as he jerked the car forward and sped up past the twenty-mile-an-hour town limit.

"You're going to strip those gears right out of this car, Bob Choat. What in the world's gotten into you?" Ida turned toward him and spoke as if he had lost his hearing, if not his senses.

"I'm not going to let that old skinflint Buchanan rooky-doo Charlie out of twenty cents what's rightly his."

"Highway patrol or a sheriff's deputy sees you, you'll pay more'n twenty cents," Ida said.

"I'll be the one paying the fine, won't I?" He turned a tight corner and slammed to a stop at the front entrance of the Nash Hotel.

"Papa, I don't think you ought to go up there."

He looked at his daughter and scowled. "You stay out of this."

"But Grandpa, he'll pay me next week," Charlie said. "I'm sure of it."

"You stay out of it too, Charlie."

Bob slammed the car door, stormed into the lobby, and demanded Buchanan's room number from the balding young man behind the counter.

"I can't give that to you, sir. Not unless Mr. Buchanan's expecting you." The man's lip trembled, and he stepped back from the counter.

"Then I'll have to bang on every door in this place till I find him," Bob said.

"Room 307, Sir."

Ignoring the stares of two old men sitting in the lobby's oak rocking chairs, he stomped up the two flights of stairs and down the hall, beat on the door panel until his hand stung and, hearing nothing from inside, wanted to kick the blamed thing off its hinges. Buchanan had been released from prison years ago after serving ten years for cattle rustling. When he'd come back to Hobart, he was pretty shiftless but hadn't again run afoul of the law. Bob had been uneasy every time he saw the man on the street, wondering if the day would come that Buchanan would run off the mouth about Shady Creek. Now it had.

The doorway across the hall opened, and, when he turned to look, an elderly woman peered at him, her faded blue eyes sparking annoyance and caution. The gaudy, flowered wallpaper with its large leaves that swept around her door made it appear as if she were standing in an arbor. His glare sent her ducking back inside and closing the door.

From the other side of Buchanan's door came a slapping and thumping that stopped with the click of a lock. "What in thunderation's going on out there?"

"It's Bob Choat. I want to talk to you."

Buchanan opened up, his rheumy old eyes big as quarters, and his lips screwed up in a pout. "You're makin' enough noise to wake the dead, Bob."

Bob almost stepped back from the musty odor of chewing tobacco, cheap alcohol, and unwashed humanity that assailed him. Instead, he stepped forward and, towering over Buchanan, squeezed out between clinched teeth, "You old reprobate. You've been running off at the mouth to my grandson. Cheated him out of twenty cents. Didn't you figure that'd get back to me?"

Buchanan stared at the floor. "Why, I wouldn't do that. I like the boy too much. And I told him I'd pay him next week, didn't I?"

"Yeah, I know. He said as much. But if you act true to form, you won't."

CHAPTER 16 ✦ BOB

"You don't go spreading ideas like that around, Bob. There's some just have it in for old George Buchanan, and you're one of them. But Charlie ain't. That's why I like him and would never cheat him out of even a plugged nickel."

"You damn fool, you're just as crooked as you ever was."

Buchanan winced. "Well now, Bob, I've always knowed you was no gilded lily yourself."

Bob thrust his face close to Buchanan's and the smell of old tobacco and rotted teeth almost made him gag. "You go mouthing off about Shady Creek to Charlie, or anyone else, so help me I'll cripple that other leg of yours."

Buchanan's face turned deep red, and he backed up a step. "You just get out of here now, or I'll get the law on you."

Bob advanced on Buchanan and said, "You think I'd give a damn? I'll come back and nail your mangy hide to that wall yonder if I hear of you telling tales out of school again. I told you once you ever mention me and Sally, I'd kill you. I've a mind to do it, too."

The old man stumbled back, and Bob followed.

"I really didn't tell Charlie anything, Bob." Fear now clouded Buchanan's eyes. "Hell, I realize I'd be in a jam with you iff'n I really was to tell all I knew about you and Sally to that boy. And I wouldn't steal from him." Buchanan took a deep breath and seemed to swell up like a horny toad.

Bob wanted to hit him in the belly, force out all that hot air that was holding him up. If he did that, there wouldn't be anything left of the man but skin and bones and he'd collapse right on the floor, never to get up again. "And as if going on about me, and cheating the kid, wasn't bad enough, you had to fill his head full of stories about you being Frank Nash's buddy. I ain't forgot how you two stole my daddy's horse that time."

"Now looky here, Bob, you oughtn't to go talking about me that way." Buchanan turned away, shuffled off to his rocker, and sat staring out the window. "Me and Frank found that horse grazing out there, and it was so gentle, it didn't run when we rode up. We figured it couldn't be that tame and not belong to somebody. We was going to take it in to town and leave it."

Bob followed Buchanan to his chair. It was the only time he had been inside the old goat's place. The odor coming from the open bathroom door stunk worse than a pigsty. "Well, you were right about that. It belonged to my pa. If he hadn't trained his shotgun on you two, I'm not sure you'd have given her up so easy."

Buchanan stared up at him, not agreeing or denying, his sickly pallor reminding Bob of soured milk.

"Give me the money you owe Charlie right now, and put a damn zipper on that mouth of yours."

Buchanan hastily opened his purse, poured out a handful of coins, picked out two dimes and handed them to Bob.

"You stay away from Charlie, you understand?" He waited till Buchanan nodded, turned, and stalked out of the room, slammed the door, and stomped back down the stairs to the lobby. Behind the counter, the night clerk cowered with a phone in his hand.

"No need to call the law," Bob said. "I didn't hurt the old man, just put the fear of God in him." Walking to the waiting car, he climbed into the driver's seat and handed Charlie the twenty cents.

Charlie stared, open-mouthed.

"Now listen to me. You stay away from that old buzzard. He's no good. People like him'll cut your heart out for a thin dime. I've had truck with him before, so I know what I'm talking about."

Charlie, his eyes shining, kept nodding as if dumbstruck. Ida sat with her mouth all drawn up in a disapproving line. Ruth just stared at him.

CHAPTER 17

Ruth

⇥ ✿ ⇤

Ruth and Charlie rocked gently back and forth in the front-porch swing, watching for the mailman's car to stop at the rural mailbox a quarter of a mile away. She sat close to Charlie for warmth and hoped against hope that this would be the day another letter from Chester would arrive. Since writing Chester, she had waited, fear and anticipation growing as she grew more depressed and unhappy. When Corky's words about his aunt Alice came to mind, she would ask herself the question, "If what Corky said was true, how could that husband of mine wait for me to hear about him and another woman from out of the mouth of a child?" And on a dusty road, yelled out by Corky for everybody to hear? Say nothing when he must have known about Alice being pregnant for Lord only knows how long. Ever since she stood out front of Joe's house and heard Corky shout it, she'd not known what to think. What to do. What to feel.

"You think we'll get a letter from Daddy today?" Charlie asked, his tone one Ruth knew he used when there was not much hope of getting what he wanted.

"All we can do is hope, son. Leastwise that's what I'm doing." She reached over to Charlie and swept the hair out of his eyes. It was an unusually warm September late afternoon, and she'd finished all her chores for the day; getting Charlie off to school, separating the cream from Isabelle's ample milk; churning the cream for its butter; giving the front room a good cleaning; cooking and doing the dishes. Sitting here wishing for a letter was a few minutes of rest till she started supper. And Lord help us, Charlie was eating like a horse since he started school. A far as she knew, nothing more than trading insults had happened between him and Corky. She'd heard those kinds of things from Chester and the other boys when she was a girl. The thought of Chester back when they were young and innocent—or at least she was—got her to thinking of her present troubles with him.

Despite all his wild behavior and infidelity, Chester and she had had eighteen years of sitting down most days to three meals, listening to George and Gracie Allen on the radio, lying together most nights wrapped in the other's arms. Now he was overseas, maybe being shot at and might even be killed before this was all over. And if he wasn't? Would he still be with her? She couldn't bear the thought of never being in his arms again. She so wanted a letter from him saying that what Corky said wasn't true. She shuddered as a slight breeze picked up and cooled the air.

"Mama! Mr. Buchanan was sitting in the courthouse square on Saturday, and he bought a stamp from me. Said he was sorry I had such a mean-headed grandpa!"

"I thought we made it clear you weren't supposed to have anything to do with that man."

CHAPTER 17 • RUTH

"You all just said I couldn't go out of downtown to visit him. I didn't. I just talked to him downtown," Charlie said, looking up at her with soulful blue eyes.

Those eyes, so much like Chester's, made her want to cry. "You're just splitting hairs, young man."

"It's Grandpa who really cares about me seeing Mr. Buchanan, isn't it?"

For an answer, she tickled him under the arms, and he squirmed away, giggling. She wasn't sure that had been a good thing to do. Likely just encourage him to go on seeing that old man any chance he got. Looking up, she saw the mailman pull to a stop, and she pushed Charlie away. "Get on with you. Go get the mail. There might be a letter for us from your dad."

Charlie's face brightened but then clouded over. "You say that every time," he said, jumped off the porch, and ran full tilt toward the mailbox a quarter of a mile away. Charlie's dearest hope, Ruth knew, was that they would get a letter from Chester today. And it was her dearest hope, too. He'd failed to snap one of his overall straps, and it flopped against his back as he ran. It reminded her of Papa, who half the time went around with one of his shoulder straps undone.

She watched him run most of the way, not pausing for breath till he was even with the thicket that protected that end of the farm from dust storms. Then he reached the mailbox, waved a letter over his head, started running full tilt back toward the house, and yelling over and over again, "There's a letter from Daddy. There's a letter from Daddy."

She jumped off the porch and rushed out of the drive and down the road to meet him and take the letter from his hand. Tearing it open, she stood in the middle of the road and scanned the short page covered in Chester's scrawled handwriting. Then, not wanting to believe what she'd read, tried to read it again through her tears.

Dear Ruth,

I am doing OK right now. Haven't seen any real action yet which is OK by me. People are getting their butts shot off right and left out there somewhere though and I probably will be joining them some time in the near future. I can't tell you where I am; the censors would just cut it out anyway. Listen, I've been awful busy without any time to just sit around and think. But I want you to know I've cried over this thing I'm about to write you. As you have already found out from Corky and probably some of the gossips there in Hobart, Alice Jenson's pregnant. More than likely it's with my baby. Now what I need to decide isn't coming easy. The damn hardest thing is that I love you and Charlie. But then how am I going to leave Alice's baby a bastard without a last name. That isn't right, either. I'm sorry, I wish I hadn't put us all in such a pickle. I'll just have to decide what to do as soon as this damn war is over.

I know I'm leaving you the job of helping Charlie understand about having a half-brother or sister the best way you can. If he doesn't hear it from you, it will be from somebody else. You tell him I love him.
Chester

Ruth's eyes filled with more tears, and her forehead began to throb. Charlie dance around her asking over and over again, "Mama, what's the matter? What did Daddy say?" Charlie grabbed for the letter, but she snatched it out of his reach.

"Just a minute, Charlie. I've got to let my head clear."

"Is my daddy all right? Did he get shot or something?"

"Your daddy is all right. I'm just a little overcome is all."

"Can't I just read what he said?"

"No, it's too personal. Here, I'll read the part about you." She rubbed her eyes and, her voice unsteady, read some and made up the rest.

CHAPTER 17 • RUTH

Dear Ruth and Charlie,

I am doing OK right now. Haven't seen any real action yet which is OK by me. I can't tell you where I am; the censors would just cut it out anyway. Listen, I don't have a lot of time on my hands, time to just sit around and think. But I want you to know I think of you two a lot. Charlie, I love you and miss you.

The crunch of car tires on dry clay alerted Ruth that someone was approaching. It was her parents. She wiped at her eyes, wishing they could not see how upset she was. But when they stopped and she walked up to the car, frown lines of worry scored deep furrows in her brow.

"What's the matter, Ruth? You look like you've seen a ghost," her mother said.

Charlie spoke up, "We got a letter from my daddy. He says he's OK."

"Well, that's wonderful, Charlie," Mother said, looking at Ruth expectantly.

"I'll tell you all about it later, Mother, but right now I want to be alone for a bit. Charlie, you go on up to the house, I'll be up directly." Ruth walked down the road a way, stepped over the barbed wire fence and cut across the pasture toward the thicket at the far end of her papa's farm. The bitter smell of the crushed weeds were no worse than the bitterness crushing down on her. She pushed her way into the thicket's center and lay down under the prickly branches of the thorn trees that grew there. It was the same spot she'd retreated to when she first arrived at the farm. Shadows of the late afternoon advanced, giving way to dark as night slowly descended, covering her grief with its concealing touch. Her parents had lived together for thirty-one years, through all kinds of tragedy, and they'd stuck it out together. Even with all her papa's running around on her mother. Even now, with Ida never uttering a single kind word around him, and not always for good reason, Ruth believed, her papa was not about to up and leave. *Maybe Chester won't, either,* she thought. There was no conviction in that thought, and then she let the tears flow.

A three-quarter moon came up, and stars winked on, adding their light to that of the moon's. She wished, like she had before, when she'd first arrived and walked down here, that all the lights in the sky, and even all those in the world, would blink out, leaving her in total darkness. It hadn't happened then. It didn't happen this time, either.

She had no idea how long she lay there, but as the air cooled and with the ground beneath her hard as rock, she began to shiver. *The longer I stay here,* she thought, *the harder it will be for me to face my parents—and Charlie.* She just couldn't face telling her parents, or Charlie, about the letter, about the fact Chester had doubts about coming back to her and Charlie. She was afraid to face Charlie with that awful possibility.

Exhausted and stiff, Ruth made her way out of the thicket and began walking down a cow path toward the barn. Nearing the barnyard, she saw a light flare from somewhere near the barn door and its light began to swing gently back and forth as someone carried it into the pasture and down the cow path toward her.

She trudged toward the light and, drawing near, saw it was her papa. "You didn't have to trouble yourself to come down here, Papa."

"Not knowing where you was, Charlie's been frantic, believing that something was terribly wrong. Wouldn't settle down till I promised to come to see about you."

"I'm sorry. I just had to be alone for a while. Papa, Chester wrote he wasn't sure what to do about Alice Jenson. It's his baby she's carrying." Ruth could not keep back the tears as she leaned into her papa.

He patted her on the shoulder with his free hand. "I figured it must be something like that. Otherwise, you wouldn't go running off down into the thicket, and stay out here alone after dark." Papa sniffed and took his hand away from her shoulder to wipe across his eyes. "I feel real bad for you, Ruth. You don't deserve this. Neither does Charlie, for that matter."

CHAPTER 17 ♦ RUTH

"Thank you, Papa." Ruth was surprised that he was crying over her misfortune. It wasn't like him. His saying that about Charlie wasn't like him, either. Her heart went out to him, and his tears and concern made her feel stronger, ready to go face her son with the lie she had to tell him. He'd understand better when he was a little older, or when Chester returned. That could be his job, explaining his actions to his son. "Don't tell Charlie just yet. I'm not ready for him to know."

"You may be making a mistake there, Ruth. Ain't good to keep that from him. He'll learn it from Corky Alred or someone else for sure. Pearl's boys more'n likely."

*

Days crawled by as she stayed locked in her black mood. It was hard to pull herself out of bed in the morning, and she hated crawling into bed at night, unable to do more than stare at the dark ceiling once she was there. Two weeks passed, yet there was never a time she could bring herself to tell Charlie about the baby; she'd tried several times, sat him down with all good intentions to let him know, but the words wouldn't come.

Near the middle of October, Ruth wrapped a blanket around her shoulders, sat in the front porch swing, and slowly glided back and forth, the chains anchored to the rafters groaning softly as if in pain. She stared out over her papa's cotton field and tried to get the picture of Chester and Alice out of her mind. But then, other troubled thoughts and feelings crowded in. Tensions with Mother and Papa. Mother's heart trouble. Guilty feelings of the warmth she felt for Joe Williams.

Gravel popping on the road brought Ruth out of her reveries, and, looking up, she saw Sheriff Cashe drive into the yard. He waved to her, rolled down his window, and called out. "Your Papa here, Ruth?"

"He's down at the barn," she called back. *Speak of trouble, she thought. The Good Lord help me. Has Charlie gone and done something else?*

CHAPTER 18

Bob

⇥ ✽ ⇤

Hearing the squeal of brakes in need of new brake pads, Bob came out of the barn to see the Sheriff's car sitting outside. He walked toward the car as Dutch Cashe pulled his long legs out the door and stepped onto the ground in his cowboy boots. "What brings you back out here, Dutch? More trouble with Charlie?"

"No. No trouble. I just need a couple minutes of your time. You got somewhere we could get out of the wind?"

"There's my tack room," Bob said and then led Cashe into the barn.

As the two of them entered, Cashe wrinkled his nose and said, "I'm not sure I can stay in here. How do you stand to be in here with them two hogs all the time?"

CHAPTER 18 ♦ BOB

Bob became aware of the rancid smell of the pigpen. He'd grown so used to spending time in the barn, he seldom noticed. The two shoats began to snuffle and grunt as Bob led Cashe into the tack room and closed the door on the stench and the noise from the pigs. He pushed the only chair in the room toward the sheriff, saying, "Take a load off, Dutch." They'd been acquainted for thirty years, but he suspected this wasn't a social call. "Why the visit?"

The lawman squatted down on one leg, cowhand style. "You take the chair, Bob. I ain't going to take the only one you got in here." He reached into his shirt pocket, pulled out a pack of Camels, and pulled a cigarette out with his lips. "Mind if I smoke? It'll help kill the smell of those porkers."

"Go ahead, Dutch."

Cashe took a small box of matches from his pocket and, removing one, scratched the head across the seat of his pants, bringing alive a flame.

When the match flared, Bob thought of the first time he'd seen Cashe, sometime back in 1913. The man almost got burned to death helping put out a fire in Hobart when the town was barely six years old. His flesh had crawled when he saw Cashe fall through the roof of a burning building and he had been sure the man was burning to death. So'd everybody else, and they started screaming and crying. But then, coughing and spitting and still holding on to the hose, Cashe was dragged free by two other men on the roof.

Cashe reached down and picked up a few loose grains of seed wheat that lay spilled on the floor. One by one, he began tossing them toward a knothole in the floorboards. "Cotton looks good, Bob. About time to get field hands in there."

"I figure about another week if it stays dry. A little longer it comes a hard rain."

"You goin' to have that grandson of yours in the field?'

"He's chompin' at the bit. But he'll be pulling bolls for Joe Williams first. Joe's crop's comin' in earlier than mine. Charlie says he's goin' to make enough to finally buy hisself a war bond. Maybe two." Bob chuckled at the thought. "He's still a little light in the britches to bring that about."

"I don't know about that, Bob. He's been awful serious about selling those stamps. And something else's come up, too."

Roosevelt gave a high-pitched squeal that was followed by grunts of protest from Churchill. Bob went to the door. "Sueeee there, Roosevelt. Sueee, Churchill." At the sound of Bob's raised voice, the hogs' angry squeals turned to loud snorting grunts.

Cashe laughed and squatted once more. "Whose side are you on, anyway, Bob? It was me, I'd be calling those two Hitler and Mussolini."

"I like them pigs. Wouldn't insult them like that." He picked up the hame and started smoothing it with an oiled rag.

"So why do you call that old hound Hitler? You don't like him?"

"Nah. I guess when I named him that I was thinkin' what a low-down dog Hitler was. There was something you wanted to talk to me about, Dutch?"

"George Buchanan and Charlie," Dutch said.

Bob sighed deeply. "That old fool'd say or do anything right now. He ain't been the same since that mule kicked him in the leg and crippled him up. Must've caught a piece of his skull, too."

"Well, that's the God's truth. But that's not what I came out here for, either."

"What is it then?" Bob asked, wondering why the old sheriff was taking so long to state his business.

"Well, the old rascal had a heart attack, and it took him."

Bob's mouth fell open. "Well, I'll be," he said. "That's sure a surprise. But I don't suspect you'd be coming out here just to tell me that."

"That's right. It seems that grandson of yours had been going by Buchanan's for some time and selling him savings stamps. Would spend time with the old man. When they called me, and I found him dying in

CHAPTER 18 ♦ BOB

his apartment, one of the last things he said was that Charlie was the best friend he had."

"I told Charlie he shouldn't go around that old horse thief."

"Now don't speak ill of the dead, Bob." Cashe reached in his pocket and pulled out some bills, a coin purse, and a wristwatch. "Before they trucked him away on the gurney, George handed me his watch and all the money he had to his name. Came to almost forty dollars. Said he knew he was dying and that he had a little burial policy that'd take care of putting him in the ground. He wanted Charlie to have the money and this here watch. Said he might as well have it as anybody else." Cashe chuckled. "Buchanan said that if he pulled through, I should tell Charlie to bring him a couple of savings bonds. Said the little fart had damned well better keep coming by, too. The old cuss really got to caring about Charlie. I'd have asked you to let Charlie visit him one last time, but he didn't last more'n a couple of hours after I spoke to him."

George dying felt strange to Bob. The old thief had been around so long that it was hard to believe he was gone. "Must have been a smidgen of good in that old carcass after all," Bob said.

"I think that grandson of yours is what brought it out, though." Cashe handed over the crumpled bills and the change purse Bob had seen when he went to the apartment for the twenty cents he owed Charlie. Dutch pulled Buchanan's watch off his wrist and handed it to Bob.

Bob put the change purse and watch into his overalls' pants pocket. He leafed through the bills and then stuck them in the bib pocket of his overalls. "Up till now the boy's been nothing but a nuisance about those war bonds. There's enough for two bonds. He's got a bomb bank that First Federal gave him. He's been putting loose change in it, hoping to save enough for his own bond. I just hope this helps him settle down. Maybe stop him from making a pest of himself in town."

"I wonder if you've missed seeing the good in the boy, Bob." Cashe threw the remainder of the wheat grains onto the floor, like he was hand

173

sowing a field. The cigarette at the corner of his mouth, bobbing with each word, dislodged ashes that drifted to the tack room floor. When I came out here about that wallet, I gave the boy a talking-to that put the fear of God in him. Something his grandpa and grandma Scarsdale never did with his daddy. I don't think Charlie'll want another conversation with me."

"Hope you're right about that, Dutch."

Cashe chuckled. "Charlie told me he planned to use Billy's ten bucks to buy stamps for his war bond. Sort of a wartime Robin Hood. Rob the poor and give to the war. Not like Chester. He'd have spent it carousing if I remember him rightly. I believe it was probably Chester told Charlie, 'Finders keepers, losers weepers.'"

"Even thousands of miles away, Chester's aggravating me. Leaving his wife and kid to fend for themselves or to live off someone else's charity is damn pitiful," Bob said.

"That may be so, but you're keeping an eye on Charlie while he's under your roof. And I'm obliged to think you're making sure he's not growing up just like his dad." Cashe stood up, picked up a well-oiled hame, and examined it, rubbing his hand along the smooth wood. "You taking care of that grandson and that daughter of yours for long?" Cashe shifted his weight to his other leg and scratched at his crotch.

"I'm not sure. But I'm trying real hard to take good care of them while they're here. It ain't easy. There was that trouble with the wallet, him and Corky Alred are givin' the teacher a hard time, he was hanging around with that old bandit, Buchanan, without letting me or his mama know, and he's been trying to peddle those savings stamps in town almost ever since he got here. Talking the leg off people and telling them he's trying to sell enough to equal a war bond.

"But selling those stamps is a sensible thing for the boy to do. Better than keeping wallets that don't belong to him," Cashe said and hung the hame back on the wall.

"But I sure don't cotton to his being a pest," Bob said.

CHAPTER 18 ✦ BOB

Cashe shrugged. "Oh. And one more thing. During that last rainstorm when you and the family were in town, I got a call from a neighbor of Doris Walden. She said she saw Charlie go into Doris's and wondered if I better check on him. Wanted to know what a nice little boy like Charlie was doing visiting the town prostitute."

"Lord God."

"Don't get all excited now, Bob. She's been buying stamps from the boy. He'd been out in the rain and got all wet. She just had him in to dry his clothes. Nothing bad went on."

"Can you trust the word of that woman?"

"About most things, not. But she's been a customer of Charlie just like Buchanan. Not the best company to keep, but for some reason Charlie brings out the best in people. When he's not tempted to keep wallets that don't belong to him, anyway."

"I'm going to have his mother give him a talking to again. She's told him not to go all over town knocking on doors. He don't listen. It's little wonder he fell in with those two—and God knows who else."

"Have it your way, Bob. By the way, you get a hard-on for anybody else in Hobart, I can't have you coming into town and acting a vigilante. It ain't no more right than that boy keeping Billy Longbow's money."

Bob grunted. "Buchanan brought up with the boy some old business concerning me he had no call to gossip about. And I thought he had gypped Charlie out of the price of two savings stamps. I guess I lost my head there for a minute."

Cashe nodded. "Well, now, I've got to be getting along. You and Charlie both stay out of trouble, you hear?" He chuckled as he turned to go.

Bob ambled back with Cashe to his car with old Hitler sniffing at their heels the whole way. Cashe reached down and ruffled the dog's ears before crawling into his car and driving away.

Going back inside the tack room, Bob sat polishing and re-polishing his hame. A mouse scurried out of a hole at one corner of the room, sniffed its way along the wall, and then darted back to the hole. He rubbed Buchanan's watch and looked at the time. *Gettin' near suppertime,* he thought. *Charlie won't be able to sleep tonight he'll be so excited. Maybe Cashe is right, and I've been too hard on him. Fact is, Charlie's not like Chester in a lot of ways. All I've seen, wanted to see, were how he was.*

Bob stood and stretched, something he had to do these days when he sat too long. His hand drifted to his bib pocket where he'd put Charlie's folding money and then he patted the change purse stashed in his other pocket. He thought about finding a fruit jar in the wash house to put the money in and taking it up to the house. Tell everybody he found it in the hayloft. The thought tickled him, but he'd never do such a thing.

Bob did wish he hadn't made himself look bad in the sheriff's eyes. But despite what Cashe said, if Buchanan was still alive and he had to do it all over again, he'd damn well do it.

CHAPTER 19

Ruth

→→ ❀ ←←

Ruth awakened to the crowing of a rooster and reached for the other side of the bed, trying to imagine she was lying next to Chester. But the spot next to her, as it had been since the day he left her in Weatherford, was empty. On these cold mornings, his chilled spot in the bed was a reminder of the cold reality of him and Alice. And of what to do about telling Charlie of Alice's baby. The way he might react to that news, frightened her. Charlie gave her a lot to worry about these days as it was.

She'd almost had a heart attack when Cashe showed up a second time—she was sure Charlie had gotten into trouble again. And when Papa came to the house and told Mother and her what Buchanan had left Charlie, they had been flabbergasted. Charlie had broken down and cried when he came home from school that day and Papa told him Buchanan was gone. Papa had been more shocked than she and Mother were to hear that Buchanan had given Charlie all that money—and a watch.

None of them had been surprised when, the next time Papa took them all to town, Charlie headed to the bank and bought two war bonds. He put most of what was left in his bomb bank. Ruth was surprised that Papa didn't find something hurtful to say about all this. He'd even suggested that Charlie hold back two dollars to buy more stamps to peddle on the street. Told Charlie that he wanted him to pull bolls for him when his cotton was ready.

Ruth knew she'd have to fight with Charlie to get him to spend some of what he earned pulling bolls on a new pair of shoes. He was dead set now on buying a third bond. She wondered if he would still want to buy and sell savings stamps once she told him about Chester and Alice; that Chester might not be coming home to her—and to him.

Thinking of Chester, her mind turned to the letter she'd received from him the day before. She could remember it almost word for word and thinking about it now brought back some of the tension. He'd written:

October 23, 1942
Dear Ruth and Charlie,
 Yesterday we got our first mail in a while, and I was glad to hear all is well with Charlie. After mail call everybody just sat around all nice and quiet till someone would jump up and shout something like, "My grandson, Billy, just made straight A's on his report card." Or "Edna sent me a box of cookies." I yelled out about Charlie using that money he got from old man Buchanan for war bonds and that he was going to be pulling bolls to buy even more. They all laughed when I told them about finders keepers losers weepers. Hell, I'd done the same as Charlie. After all, it was just an old Indian's dole from the government.

CHAPTER 19 ♦ RUTH

Then we all gathered around the guy who was opening a box of cookies his folks sent him, hoping he would share one. Ha! But we all laughed when he opened the box and all those cookies had been shaken so much in transport they wasn't anything but cookie dust. But he let all of us take a spoonful. Best dust I ever ate—and I ate a lot of it during the dust bowl. Tell Charlie I love him and everybody else that I said hello.
Chester

p.s. I'm sorry, Ruth, but I'm still struggling with this thing about what I'm going to do when I get back.
Chester

Not even "Love, Chester." At this point she, too wasn't sure what she was going to do when he came home. Her hurt and depression had turned more and more into anger.

Rousing herself from sleep torpor and the thoughts roiling around in her head, she forced herself to get out of bed and then dressed in old work clothes before leaving for the kitchen. She found her mother at the stove, putting bacon on to fry.

"Sit down, Mother, and let me do that."

"I know everybody around here thinks I'm an invalid, but I'm well enough I can fix you breakfast when you're gettin' ready to head out to the field."

Ruth sat down at the table and watched as her mother turned the bacon, and when she judged it nice and crisp, fork it onto a platter and began breaking eggs into the hot bacon grease. The smell of fried eggs and bacon brought Charlie into the kitchen. Half asleep and with a frown on his face, he sat down across from her and began buttering a piece of toast. Taking a bite, he mumbled, "Corky's probably going to be at Joe's place today."

"Oh. Well, I'll give him his comeuppance if he bothers you." Wondering if Corky was still talking to Charlie about his Aunt Alice and Chester, she felt heat rising in her neck and face. She had to tell him what he heard was the truth, but so far hadn't had the courage to break his heart.

An hour later, Joe Williams drove up in his truck. He had fastened tall, latticed rails all way round the bed to hold in the cotton. Laborers he'd picked up in Roosevelt hung on as he bumped over the ruts left after the last hard rain. He came to a halt at the road and motioned Ruth and Charlie to ride in front with him. As she climbed in the cab after Charlie, Ruth felt self-conscious getting this special treatment and wondered what those folks in back made of it. Or what her Papa, who stood at the door, watching, would say to her come evening.

"Sarah's already in the field, Charlie," Joe said and reached up to tousle her son's hair. "She's got a head start on you, so you'll have to work hard to catch up."

Charlie only nodded and Ruth suspected he was feeling mad about something Sarah had said to him the day before. But she said nothing. There was little talk on the half-mile drive, Joe only talking to Charlie about pulling bolls for the first time. Ruth was glad. She didn't know what to say to Joe. There were other field hands already in the cotton when they arrived, and she saw Mildred Alred's old, battered car parked next to a worn-out-looking pickup. She was happy to see Mildred and Corky already bending to their work halfway up the cotton row.

Joe pulled to a stop, and the ones in back climbed down, snapped their cotton sacks out to their full length, fitted the shoulder strap in place, and bent to their work. Strong, gloved hands flew as they tore the cotton bolls from the stalks and shoved them backwards into the mouths of their sacks. Ruth could see they were old hands at this task. There was no way she could keep up. It had been too many years since she'd been in a cotton field at harvest time. She dreaded what her hands would look like at the day's end and how sore they would be despite the gloves she was wearing. *I just hope there's no blisters*, she thought as she pulled the strap of the cotton sack over her shoulder. "Come on, Charlie. We got to get you to work. Where's your cotton sack?"

"Grandpa said Joe had one."

"Well, sure," Joe said, "I have one you can use."

The sack Joe handed Charlie was no larger around than a five-gallon milk can and only twice as long. It had been made for Sarah to use. Ruth was not surprised when Charlie objected.

"This sack's awful dinky."

"All the other cotton sacks are eight to ten feet long. Made for adults. Not a ten-year-old. You fill one, and it could weigh seventy-five to a hundred pounds. That's more'n you can pull," said Joe. "This one was just made for you."

"Corky and all the other kids have big sacks, and they'll all tease me."

Joe Williams grinned and shook his head. "You just come tell me, and I'll set 'em straight. But there's no way you're going to pull a big sack around. You try and they really will tease you."

"I wouldn't have to fill it," Charlie said.

Joe Williams nodded at a pile of sacks in the back of the trailer. "Okay. Go on and take one, then."

Ruth opened her mouth to object, but Joe touched her arm and shook his head.

"Let him learn for himself," he said.

Dragging the long sack behind him, Charlie returned, stopped, and pointed at the pickers far down the field who had been there before they arrived, "Corky'll find something to make fun of me."

"Corky Alred is nothing but a bully. Don't pay any mind to his teasing." Thinking about what else Corky might say, Ruth added, "Or anything else coming out of his mouth."

"He says anything, you come to me," added Joe.

"Everybody'll say I'm a tattletale."

"Then stay with me. I'm going to be in the field with you all day."

"Corky already says I'm a mamma's boy. If I hang around you all day, he's sure to believe he's right."

Exasperated, Ruth said, "Do what you want, but get to pulling bolls."

"My daddy'd let me to wipe up the ground with Corky if he was here."

That coming from Charlie made her want to slap him. She took a deep breath to calm herself and said, "I don't care what your daddy might do. I didn't raise you to be a roughneck."

"That's true of Chester, all right. He'd have done that," Joe said, taking off his hat and running a callused hand through his thick hair. "Even if his mama told him not to."

Ruth's face hardened, but she turned away so Joe couldn't see her scowl. He shouldn't go butting into this. She appreciated Joe's help and kindness to her and Charlie but didn't want him encouraging bad behavior.

"See, Mama? Joe and Daddy was friends. I'll bet Joe would let me fight just like Daddy would."

Joe's brow furrowed, "I'm sorry, Ruth. Charlie. I shouldn't have got in between you two. You ought to do what your mamma says."

Charlie glowered back and forth at her and Joe and then stomped off to a cotton row and began pulling bolls and thrusting them into his long sack.

On hearing Joe take her side and correct Charlie, Ruth felt her irritation with him give way to a warmth spreading from her chest into her face. Chester would never have done that, only egg Charlie on to defy her. Catching her eye and holding it, he said, "Charlie's a lot like Chester, Ruth, but he's got a lot of good in him that I never saw in his daddy. I really don't think if he takes up for himself that he'll grow up to be as much like Chester as you worry about."

Ruth nodded, hoping Joe was right, and said, "I'd better get to work, or Charlie will pull more bolls than I will."

Joe smiled. "Can't let that happen now, can you?" His gaze had held hers longer than she was comfortable with, and she felt color rising to her cheeks.

CHAPTER 19 • RUTH

"You look pretty when you blush," he said.

Shaking her head, she looked down at the ground, turned away, and walked to the row next to Charlie's. With the first frost, the cotton leaves had withered, loosened, and drifted to the ground, leaving a heavy blanket of cotton exposed. At that moment she felt as exposed. There was no mistaking that Joe was flirting with her. And she'd liked it. Been mortified by it. But liked it. Sighing, she bent to her work, bending side to side and stripping cotton of the rows on either side of her. Catching up with Charlie, who had paused and was staring at the other cotton pickers who had reached the end of their rows and started back, she said, "You going to stand there and gather wool all day, Charlie?"

"No," he growled and began pulling handfuls of the brittle bolls filled with white puffs of cotton, and stuffing wads of them into his sack. Though not fast, he was determined. As Ruth stripped cotton from two rows, Charlie did so from his one. He almost kept pace with her, and, when they met the others who had started back, he didn't look up, only waved a hand at Sarah, and his cousins, who shouted hello to him. Pulling ahead of Charlie, Ruth came to the end of her row and started back with her half-filled sack. When she reached him, his sack was almost too heavy for him to pull, but he insisted that he could go on. She insisted that he go on to the wagon to weigh in. Sullen, he trudged back down the row, dragging the heavy sack a few feet with both hands, and then resting before he doggedly kept going.

She began working faster, hoping to weigh in when he did. She was sure that if she left him on his own, when he passed Corky again, there could be trouble. Her sack was crammed full when she reached the end of the row where Charlie sat waiting in the cotton trailer's shade for other field hands to weigh in. Two little girls were playing in the shade next to him, but he was paying them no heed. Taking hold of his sack's shoulder strap, she helped him drag it to the cotton scale, where Joe stood waiting. She kept her eyes from catching Joe's, afraid she would blush again.

"Charlie, you've got a good start there," Joe said.

Charlie sunk to the ground and sat cross-legged, watching Joe lift the sack onto the balance scale, weigh it, and write the weight down in a bound ledger.

Joe nodded to Charlie and said, "You brought in a good-sized load, Charlie. You'll make you some real money before this crop's in. Now, crawl up in the back of the trailer, and I'll hand your sack up so you can empty it."

Ruth's face grew warm, and the tightness she had been feeling since Joe had gazed at her melted some. It pleased her so much that Joe was giving Charlie some attention and that Charlie was responding without an argument. Even her resentment of Joe's encouraging Charlie to fight lessened. She wanted to tell Joe how much she was pleased, but she couldn't allow herself to say anything lest she betray what she was feeling. Charlie climbed into the truck bed and sunk up to his knees in the cotton bolls, and Joe threw the sack up to him. Charlie grabbed hold of its middle and shook, disgorging wads of bolls that separated as they spilled out. Grabbing the closed end, he whipped the sack up and down as if he was popping a dishtowel and spilled out the rest, leaving the sack limp as an old rag. Dust trickled down into Ruth's nose. She sneezed as Charlie flung his sack on the ground and bounced to the front of the wagon on the spongy cotton bolls. As he started to crawl out of the wagon bed, Joe Williams called out.

"Might ought to stay up there and empty your mama's sack while you're at it."

"Whyn't she do it herself?" Charlie asked.

Joe Williams' face clouded over as he heaved her sack up onto the trailer.

"Don't sass like that, Charlie." Ruth glared at her son, a scowl that usually made him sit up and take notice. "You heard what Joe said. Now get busy and empty that sack, or I'll tan your hide for you." *Why was it he could be so nice one minute and sassy the next?* she wondered.

CHAPTER 19 • RUTH

"It'd be nice of you to do that for your mamma, Charlie," Joe said.

Bo, the hired man who had his cotton weighed, now climbed onto the wagon and hauled his sack up beside Charlie. "Looks like they got you outnumbered, boy. I reckon you best jist get on with it." He spat out a smelly cud of tobacco, sending it over the side of the wagon in a high arc. He then shaved another piece from off a twist of Old Missouri and stuck it inside his cheek. Charlie grabbed Ruth's sack and held it a moment. His baleful gaze turned to Joe Williams' dog that had come up from the house and lay in the shade of the trailer near the little girls.

Ruth's eyes were drawn to the old dog, too, as it heaved up from the shade, ambled to the wad of tobacco, sniffed once, and then turned back to its resting place. In a way, Ruth envied that old hound—it didn't have to worry about a rude son, a husband fighting in some far-off jungle, another woman pregnant with her husband's baby, or what he would choose to do if he lived to return.

As if reading her mind, Charlie said, "That old dog can do anything he wants to."

"That old dog's got fleas and lives outdoors all winter. Best you remember that, boy, and why don't you get busy with emptying that sack," Bo said and flipped his sack up and down, spilling the loose bolls around Charlie's legs, burying him to the knees.

Starting at the open end of his mother's sack, Charlie shook out all the matted clumps of cotton into the wagon, then flung it over the side, and climbed down. Taking his sack, he trudged back to a row of cotton.

Ruth called after him, "Go on down to the end of the row and pick back this way. You won't have to drag your sack so far." Charlie started pulling bolls and stuffing them inside. "You all just watch. I'll make it back."

"See how he takes advice." Ruth walked over and stepped on the sack. "You mind what I say, now. Go on to the end." She then turned to Joe and said, "I'll do two rows up and only one back. I can keep an eye on Charlie that way."

Charlie jerked the sack forward and started trudging toward the far end of the field, rubbing at the spot where the strap had cut into his collarbone. Ruth watched as halfway down the field, he passed some of the younger oncoming boll pullers, their heads bobbing as they bent and straightened to the work. Charlie put his head down. The other hands kept on pulling, but the boys all stood and stared, wide grins on their faces. Will Junior and Carl both called out "Hi" to him, but, in return, he only raised a limp arm in a half-hearted wave. Corky Alred, his sack fuller than Charlie's had been, waved to him from fifteen rows away and yelled, "How're you doin', Charlie?"

To Ruth's relief, Charlie didn't answer, and Corky let it go.

At the end of the field, Ruth started back, turning from one row to the other as she pulled fistfuls of bolls laden with cotton and stuffed them in her sack. As she approached a group of women, they stopped for a few minutes to rest their backs and wipe their faces with handkerchiefs. They glanced her way and stopped talking. Ruth saw Alice's sister shake her head and lean in close to speak to the women but in a low voice that Ruth couldn't hear. Believing now that everyone there in the field knew about Alice and Chester, Ruth gritted her teeth. She could only wonder what the women must think of her. Several rows over, Sarah, her hair tied up in a knot under a settler's bonnet made from a daisy-flowered feed sack, stooped awkwardly to her work. She stopped to peer out at Ruth as if from a cave, the front edge of the bonnet half a foot from her face. Her eyes were indistinct, hooded in daisies growing on a blue field of cotton cloth. She had on one of her daddy's old shirts, the sleeve rolled and then buttoned, the shirttail hanging loose, the collar fastened under her chin with a safety pin. She'd donned long stockings of white cotton. The dress's hem was unraveled on one side, making it seem that Sarah listed to one side like a small bent tree. Were it not boll-pulling time, Joe would have discarded it. Sarah, holding her elbow to her side as if hiding her hand from the

CHAPTER 19 • RUTH

eyes of the women, waved once at Charlie and returned to her work. Ruth hoped Sarah wasn't overhearing the gossip about Chester and Alice Jenson.

Farther down the row, the stares of the women likely still following her, Ruth stopped and breathed in a lungful of the crisp, late-autumn air, and let her breath out in a small cloud of vapor that was whisked away to disappear into the cold, dry air. She bent to snap more cotton from the stalks, stuffing the cotton into her sack and then hitching it forward. Her face warmed as she labored, and its warmth was like that she felt on a cold morning when she sat next to her papa's potbelly coal stove. She stopped once more, straightened, and stretched her back.

A lone hawk circling the cotton field caught her attention. A bobwhite darted away from the cotton and landed in the adjoining pasture, where it gave a cautious cry. A cottontail rabbit froze in a fence row, hoping, Ruth suspected, that the hawk would not spot him. All the migrating birds had already flown south, and the opossums, rattlesnakes, skunks, and prairie dogs had burrowed deep. And here she was, wishing she could climb out of the hole she was in and find a little sunshine in her life.

Her burdened sack grew heavier and, feeling like one of papa's draft animals with too large a load, she had to haul it forward in short jerks. The strap began to cut into her shoulder. Fattened by all the double handfuls of cotton she shoved into its open end, the sack looked like a giant canvas snake, stalking her. If Chester did come home to her, she swore she'd never find herself picking cotton again.

Ruth worked closer to the end of the row and, looking up, saw Joe Williams finish weighing Charlie's sack of cotton; then he handed the counterweight to one of the little girls who was sitting with the others, playing house under the wagon. She saw her take the heavy piece of metal in both hands and tip it forward, looking as if she were pretending it was a coffeepot and she was pouring coffee into imaginary cups. Joe stood waiting, slouched against the wagon, a cigarette dangling in his lips, his eyes on her. He waved. She waved back, then quickly tucked a stray fall of hair behind her ear and bent to her work.

"You like Joe, don't you?" Charlie said as he came to meet her.

"Can you keep your voice down?" she said just as a burr from a cotton boll jabbed through her gloves, pricking her finger. She took off the glove and sucked at the hurt. The raw taste of blood made her feel sick to her stomach. "I do like him, Charlie. He's nice to you and me." She lowered her voice, hoping Joe couldn't hear this conversation.

"I heard Grandpa say you was spending too much time sittin' on Joe's front porch waiting for me to get out of school." Charlie spoke in a whisper now, but every word he muttered sounded to Ruth like a shout.

She put a hand in the small of her back and stretched. "Joe's just a friend, Charlie. He was good friends with your daddy when they were growing up. I like him." *Not too much, I hope,* she thought to herself. But when he'd looked at her, called her pretty, she had felt much too pleased. *I'm a married woman,* she thought. *But will I be when Chester comes home?* She stared at the trailer where Joe was leaning against the eight-foot, slatted sideboards of the truck, top-heavy now with cotton. It looked as if one good shove by Joe would send it over onto its side. Charlie broke into the silence. "I miss my dad. I'll be glad when he comes home."

If he's coming home to us, she thought and then blurted out what she'd held in for too long. "He may not be coming back to us, Charlie." It seemed to her that she said it so loud everyone in the cotton patch had heard.

"Why?" The look of utter fright and hurt on Charlie's face made her want to cry. *Should I stop? Let it go?* she thought. The answer to her question was the flood of words that came pouring out. "You've probably heard that Corky's Aunt Alice is going to have a baby. Well, that baby may belong to your daddy, and he might have to go live with her and the baby when he gets back."

"I don't want him to do that." The hurt in Charlie's eyes changed, his face hardened, and he looked ready to scream. Or cry.

"I don't, either. And he may not. But it's something we have to start thinking about." But even as she said this, she wished the genie weren't out of the bottle, that she'd kept her mouth shut till she knew for sure what was going to happen.

"Now, come on—we can't just stand here all day. Walk on up to the other end of this row and start back pulling bolls."

Breathing hard, Charlie whirled around and marched up the cotton row, only stopping when he reached Sarah, who was seated on the ground, the top of her head barely showing above the cotton stalks.

Ruth began pulling again, faster than before, shoving cotton into her sack as if it were something hateful she had to thrust away from her. There was little warmth from the sun, which now sat lower in the southeastern sky, but sweat trickled down her back and off her face, and in the cool, dry air, it evaporated quickly, chilling her.

CHAPTER 20

Charlie

→→ ✲ ←←

Sarah peered up at Charlie from out of her settler's bonnet and smiled, "I was a-waitin' for you." Charlie flopped down across his empty sack, rubbed at his eyes so Sarah wouldn't notice he had shed tears from them, and peered at her from between two stalks of cotton. Their breaths fogged out into the chill, late-October air, rose and mingled, then disappeared into the sky above them. His stomach had begun to ache, and he wanted to scream out that it wasn't true what his mother had just told him, but Sarah wouldn't know what he was talking about. And though she was his best friend, he didn't want to tell her. He reached out, and picked up a sluggish grasshopper that was nibbling at a dead leaf, and sailed it as far as he had strength to send it.

CHAPTER 20 ✦ CHARLIE

"What'd you do that for, Charlie?" Sarah asked and took off her bonnet. Charlie pulled his mouth tight, gritting his teeth, and said nothing as Sarah wiped away a rivulet of sweat that ran down one side of her face. Her hair, damp with sweat, tumbled out, hiding her face. She shoved it back and twisted it on the back of her head.

"Are you mad at me?" Sarah's brown eyes grew large and teary.

"No. But I thought maybe you might still be mad at me," he said. "Didn't like me anymore."

"Why'd you think that?"

"'Cause of what Corky's been sayin' about my dad and you said my dad was awful. I got mad at you and you got mad back."

"I was just mad for a little while." She put her palms behind her in the dirt, leaned back on them, and tilted her head to the side as if to encourage him to say something more.

She was the best friend he'd ever had. But how could he tell her about what his mamma had just said. He couldn't possibly do that. He wanted to cry but he couldn't do that either. Not out here where people might see him.

Sarah sat up and then her eyes widened. She pointed her finger over the tops of the cotton plants behind him and said, "Uh, oh. Here comes trouble." She stood up and put her settler's bonnet back on, shadowing her face once more.

Charlie turned to look and then screwed his face into a frown. Corky Alred was advancing on them from across the field. Charlie started breathing hard, and it felt as though the anger and hurt swelled his chest to bursting.

"What you all doing lying around in the cotton like that?" Corky yelled. "Won't get no work done thataway." The ever-present, sneering smile he usually glued onto his face when making trouble, was more crooked than usual.

Sarah stood up, planted both feet in the soft ground, and balled her fist. Charlie was sure there were sparks coming out of her ice-blue eyes. "We was just talking. Saying what a trouble-maker Corky Alred is."

"Aw. You ought'n't talk about me that way." Corky reached down, and from off a cotton stalk, jerked a boll that hadn't opened because a boll-weevil had drilled into and killed it. "My aunt heard what you did in town, Charlie. Couldn't believe my ears when I heard it. Didn't know you had that kind of guts it took to visit Doris Walden."

Charlie didn't know what to say to that. He gripped the edges of his cotton sack, afraid that if he let go, he'd start punching Corky. "Whyn't you go suck an egg, Corky."

"And I bet you gave something more'n stamps to Doris Walden." Corky cupped his balls and thrust his hips back and forth.

"You shut up," Charlie yelled. "And get away from here."

"Or what?" Corky asked.

Sarah cocked a hand on her hip and her face pinched up in disgust. "Corky, you-all are about as nasty as your old flop-eared hound. And a lot meaner. I'm gonna tell my daddy on you."

Corky side-armed the cotton boll at Sarah, hitting her on the arm.

"Ow. Stop that right now, or I'll tell your mama on you."

"Go ahead. I don't care." He picked off another stunted, unopened boll and drew back his arm.

She stepped back and put her fingers across her eyes, fear replacing the rage.

"We didn't invite any split-tail girls to butt in here." Corky drew back and threw the second cotton boll. Sarah ducked to one side, and the dried, hard boll caromed off her elbow. Her fists clenched, she ran at Corky, but he dodged aside, stuck out his leg, and sent her stumbling face first into the dirt.

Tears came to Sarah's eyes as she pulled herself up and began dusting her skirt. "You big old cow pile," she yelled. "I hate you."

CHAPTER 20 ✦ CHARLIE

"You ain't nothing but dog puke, yourself," Corky crowed like a cock-eyed rooster.

Charlie, his face burning hot was still trapped in place by the old fear of his mother's punishment if he got into a fight. It made him dizzy.

"And you was sure lying in the cotton with Charlie a long time, Sarah. You two playin' like you're Doris Walden?" taunted Corky.

All the hatred Charlie had been swallowing and storing away for weeks flooded him as he jumped to his feet. Thoughts of his mother's threat of punishment for fighting made his gore rise, but he swallowed it down like a dose of castor oil. Shaking his head to clear it, he bent, scooped up a dirt clod, and let it fly. It exploded in a shower of dust on Corky's chest.

Wide eyed with surprise, Corky stood like a storefront dummy as Charlie charged and slammed into his tormentor, sending him flying onto his back. Charlie dived on top screaming like a wild animal, "You shut your filthy mouth!"

Sarah yelled, "Give him what for, Charlie!"

Charlie straddled Corky and began pounding his mouth, nose, and cheeks. Rage made Charlie feel so hateful and vicious, he no longer cared if his mother made good on her threat to beat him black and blue if he ever lifted a fist to anyone.

Blood spattered from Corky's split lip as he yelled, "Get off me. Get off me," spraying drops of bloody spit over the front of Charlie's coat.

"Charlie. Here comes Daddy and Ruth!" Sarah screamed.

From across the field, Charlie heard his name called, but he didn't stop pounding the arms that Corky had thrown across his face. Then he was swinging at empty air as he felt grabbed from behind by the back of his coat and lifted off Corky. His ears rang from a flat-handed slap delivered by Corky as they were pulled apart. He tried to jerk free and dive back at Corky but was held back.

"You stop that this minute, Charlie," Joe commanded. Corky, sniveling, with tears running down his cheeks, and blood pouring from his nose, scooted back using his elbows and feet like pistons to scramble away as Charlie continued to try to pull away from Joe.

"Now I said stop it. You listen to me now." Joe Williams turned Charlie to face him.

Charlie took a deep breath, and, seeing Joe's tobacco pouch that had jiggled out of his pocket and fell to the ground, kicked it and then stopped trying to pull away. Scowling, he said "You ain't my daddy. You got no right to tell me what to do."

"That's right, Charlie, but I don't want you out here fighting in my cotton field when there's work to be done."

Before Charlie could say more, Sarah yelled, "Corky started it, Daddy." She stomped over to Joe leaving little puffs of dust behind her and stood in front of him, her hands on her hips and her mouth puckered up in an angry pout. "Corky was throwing cotton bolls at me and deviling Charlie and me about Doris Walden. He was saying nasty things about me and Charlie. Charlie was just takin' up for me."

A small crowd gathered, curious looks passing from one person to another, sniggering erupting from the children and older boys.

Anger sparking in her eyes, Charlie's mother arrived out of breath and puffed out a sharp rebuke, "Charlie Scarsdale. You've been fighting—after all I've said to you?"

"Calm down, Ruth. Sarah says that Corky was throwing bolls at her and deviling Charlie and her about Doris Walden. He was just taking up for the two of them."

"What's this about Doris Walden?" Her heated eyes seemed to turn from brown to coal black as she spat the words at Corky.

"Aunt Alice told me that Charlie was carrying on with Doris Walden in town last Saturday." Corky pointed a finger at Charlie. "And when I asked about it, he threw a dirt clod at me and then jumped all over me."

Breathing hard, his mother said, "Did you do something you haven't told me about?" Her bonnet had slipped off her head and hung by its tie

CHAPTER 20 • CHARLIE

around her and a black tangle of hair, sweaty and matted, was plastered across her brow, making her look even angrier. Charlie's heart began to pound faster and it was a fight to hold back his tears.

"Whatever it was, I don't suspect this is a place to talk about it," Joe said.

Mildred Alred, who had been at the other end of the cotton field, came striding up, jerking her half-filled sack behind her. She moistened a handkerchief with her spit and began dabbing at Corky's bloody nose and mouth. "What happened here, Corky?"

"Charlie jumped me for no reason."

"What are you going to do about that boy, Ruth?"

His mother, her eyes now screwed up in anger, said, "He was tormenting Sarah and Charlie."

Joe spoke up, "Threw cotton bolls at Sarah and pushed her in the dirt. And what he was saying about Doris Walden wasn't very nice, Mildred."

Charlie felt a wave of relief to see Joe's and his mother's angry eyes turned on Mildred. He hoped they'd now forget how angry they were at him.

Mildred hissed. "Sounds like it's become the whole county's business now." She nodded at the crowd, which had grown larger. "And that boy, like his daddy, is up to no good most of the time, Ruth."

Charlie's mother's face hardened to granite, and she spit out her words like he'd never heard before. "It's no business of yours, that bully of a son, nor anyone else around here. Someone in your family's got more to answer to than my boy."

"Far as I see, it's that boy's daddy who has something to answer to. And Chester's boy here is wild as his daddy. He's been bothering Corky in school ever since it started, and now he's beating up on my Corky."

"Corky here's the one with a reputation for causing trouble," Ruth said.

Joe took a deep breath, and, to Charlie, it was as if he swelled up and grew taller, like some comic-book character with special powers. His face grew dark and the end of his nose red. "I don't like saying this, but Corky here seems to be the one causes the most trouble. With my girl as well as

Charlie." Joe looked down at Corky. "Get your butt to work right now, or I'll send you and your mother home and hope she lays a stick to your backside. And I hear you bother Sarah or Charlie again, I'll use a stick myself."

Corky's mother glared at Joe and said, "Sorry you feel that way, but it don't change nothin'. And hearing how you see it, I don't want to pull bolls for you. There's plenty others need me." She took Corky's hand and started pulling him toward her car.

Corky yelled back over his shoulder, "You're still a yellow-belly who won't fight fair." He threw angry glances back as he was driven away.

If they had been knives, they would have killed me, Charlie thought. But now, as his anger cooled, his stomach began to clench and his chest to feel like someone was sitting on it. A wave of guilt over what he'd done to Corky washed over him. He felt sorry for Corky, and it surprised him.

Joe looked at the crowd of people gathered about. "Ain't no bolls gettin' pulled long as we're standing around."

The workers turned back to the cotton rows, their hands flying as they pulled the cotton from loaded stalks and stuffed it in their sacks. Two of the men dragged their full sacks to the scales and stood waiting for Joe to come weigh them in. One field hand glanced out the corner of his eye, his mouth turning down in disapproval. Of what, Charlie didn't know, but he guessed it was directed at him. His mother glanced from him to Joe, shaking her head. A tear trickled down her cheek.

"We're causing you a lot of trouble here, Joe."

Joe took out his pipe and drew air through it once and let out a puff of air that, in the cooling air, drifted out like a cloud of smoke that danced and then disappeared. He said, "Not so, Ruth. It was Corky caused me trouble." He turned to Charlie, "And I suspect, Charlie, that you and Sarah won't have too much trouble from Corky from now on."

His mother, her shoulders sagging, looked at him. "I want you to go to the car now, Charlie. I think we're done here for today."

CHAPTER 20 ♦ CHARLIE

"I don't want him getting in no trouble. Corky started it," Sarah said.

Whatever happens to me now don't matter. Sarah's on my side, Charlie thought. "I want to stay in the field," he said, setting his mouth in a determined line.

His mother opened her mouth to say something, but Joe interrupted. "With Corky gone, there won't be any more trouble. Let him stay, Ruth."

Without waiting for his mother to say anything more, Charlie picked up his cotton sack.

Before he could walk away, he felt Joe Williams' hand on his shoulder. "This September we got some rain, and it was a lot warmer'n usual. Not all that good for my crop. But we couldn't have had a better October. Mild and dry. Gave the cotton time to mature. I knew then it would make a good crop if an early freeze didn't take it. I got lucky. It's going to make at least a half a bale an acre this year." He patted Charlie on the shoulder. "What's happened to you this past few weeks is a little like my cotton crop. You had a poor planting and growing seasons, but I suspect things'll work out for you just fine. And don't worry your head about that fight with Corky."

His mother's face clouded over even more, and she said, "I don't like you encouraging the boy to fight, Joe."

"I'm not encouraging him to fight. Only to take up for himself. Or my Sarah. That's different." Charlie felt drawn to Joe now. Joe wasn't his daddy, but he was treating him like he'd have wanted his daddy to if he wasn't off fighting the Japs. He was relieved that his mother only shook her head and said nothing more about fighting.

"But what's this thing about Doris Walden that Mildred was talkin' about?"

Charlie took a deep breath and let it out slowly. "I got all wet and she had me go into another room and take off my clothes while she rummaged up an old blanket to wrap around myself. While my wet clothes dried in her clothes dryer, she brought me a cup of hot cocoa and we talked and waited for my clothes to dry. Grandpa said it was not a big deal."

"Papa knew about this? He didn't say anything to me about it."

Charlie shrugged. "He said it was none of his business and that I should tell you."

"And why didn't you?"

Charlie began to feel the angry heat rising into his face as he'd felt minutes ago with Corky. "Why didn't you tell me about daddy?"

His mother frowned, started to say something, and then just shook her head.

Joe spoke then. "That thing with Doris Walden. I heard about it at the domino parlor. I didn't want to say anything to you about it, Ruth, till we had a chance to talk private. But now that it's out, I'll tell you what happened. Sheriff Cashe told Bill that a nosy neighbor of Doris's had called and told him she'd seen Charlie go inside with her. Cashe went by and talked to Doris, who said Charlie was wet as a used washrag and she dried his clothes for him. And Cashe believed her. Said she wasn't really such a bad sort, just a little loose with her virtue."

Hearing Joe say that caused a stirring in Charlie's stomach, like a flight of butterflies were loose in there. It wasn't like when he was scared, and they fluttered about; it was as if they tickled him and made his insides relax. "She always treats me nice and buys a savings stamp from me." Charlie looked up at his mother. "She ironed my stamps dry that got wet. Wrapped them in wax paper so they wouldn't get wet again."

Joe took a large white handkerchief from his pocket and blew his nose. "Ruth, people say a lot of nice things about Charlie. Seems he's made a lot of friends in town selling those stamps."

His mother's face was lined with doubt and confusion as she stared at Charlie. "That doesn't excuse him going all over town and going into people's houses. Particularly Doris's."

CHAPTER 20 ♦ CHARLIE

Joe Williams laughed. "Can we talk about this later, Ruth? Right now there's a cotton crop I've got to get in. And I've lost two pickers on account of you, Charlie, so you'll have to work twice as hard."

Charlie heard the lightness in Joe's voice, not aggravation, and he vowed to work as hard as he could to help bring in Joe's cotton crop. And maybe if he worked hard, he wouldn't think about what his mamma had told him about Daddy and Alice Jenson.

CHAPTER 21

Ruth

⇢ ✸ ⇠

The morning dishes done, the beds made, and the floor swept, Ruth sighed and lowered herself onto a chair sitting next to her mother. She thought of what had gone on between her and Charlie when they were in Joe's field. He hadn't brought up what she had told him about his daddy since then, and she was glad for that. Still, he looked sad at times, and she was sure he must be thinking about it. She couldn't bring herself to ask. He still tried to sell savings stamps in town and had bought some stamps with the money he'd made pulling bolls, though most of it she had insisted he save for later or use to buy some shoes and long underwear. She'd said nothing more to him about Alice and Chester. Or about Doris. She had been angry when asking Papa why he hadn't told her about Charlie going into the town prostitute's house. He'd just shrugged and repeated what he'd said to Charlie—in a way that was a welcome change. Not too long before, he would have used Charlie's lack of good sense to devil the boy with.

Taking up needle and thread, she began to hand-sew quilt pieces, a pastime she was not particularly happy doing. Her arms, back, and legs were still sore from all the bending she'd done pulling bolls for Joe and Papa and from dragging cotton sacks that often grew to weigh as much as sixty pounds. Come to think of it, she mused, sewing helped pass the time and was easier on her body than field work. "I'm glad all the crops are in," she said to her mother. "I'd almost forgotten how hard it was to be in the field all day, day after day for two or three weeks."

Her mother looked up from her embroidering and said, "I'm sorry, Ruth, that you had to go back into the field. But I guess a lot of women are going to work these days. There aren't enough men around with so many of them off to the war." She took another stitch in the rose pattern on the pillowcase.

"I'm thankful that Charlie and I have enough money in our pockets now to buy essentials for the coming few months." *And*, Ruth thought, *I'm thankful I won't have to ask Papa for money anymore.*

Papa spoke up, surprising her by saying, "Charlie did better than I expected. Made himself some money. I have to give him credit for that."

Thank goodness you can finally come away from all that criticism of Charlie we've heard since we got here, Ruth thought but said, "He made enough to get some clothes he needed, buy a few victory stamps, and to have some left over to save."

"Keeps that up, he'll have quite a nest egg when those bonds mature," her mother said. Looking up from her work, she paused as if thinking whether she should ask about something on her mind. "Bob finally heard and told me about that ruckus in Joe's cotton field. How do you think Charlie's handling all that?"

Ruth knew her mother was fishing for information about how Charlie was taking the news of Alice and Chester, but she wasn't ready, if she ever would be, to speak of it to her parents. "He's been back in school for a week, and Sarah told me there's been no trouble with Corky. Thank goodness." She had gone down to meet Charlie and walk him home the first three days of that week to make sure there was no trouble. There had been none, but she kept going so she could talk to Joe. They'd spent a little time on Joe's chilly front porch, drinking coffee and visiting, while she waited for her son to get out of school or while Sarah and Charlie played. She'd confessed to Joe about Chester's letters to her and about what she'd told Charlie about his daddy. Joe'd reached over and patted her hand. That was the kindest thing that had happened to her in a long time. She'd cried. He'd blushed to the roots of his hair and apologized. None was needed, she told him.

Interrupting her thoughts, Papa said, "That dusting Charlie gave Corky his first day in Joe's field gave the boy a taste of what Charlie's capable of."

"Now, Papa, don't you go encouraging him to that behavior. Joe doing it is enough."

Her papa harrumphed, reached for, and turned off the radio. "On the news they said a cold front's moving in first of next week. I'm going to butcher them hogs. Ruth, I'll need your help. Your mother shouldn't do any of the hard work."

Ruth made a face. She hated seeing those hogs butchered. Always hated helping with it when she was younger and living at home. Charlie would be crushed when he found out the pigs had been killed. And her papa would be so unhappy having to kill them, he'd likely cry. As a girl, she'd always hated to see him cry; it made her cry all the more. It would make her cry even now. Not only for the hogs but for the reminder of all the killing going on overseas. "Of course, I'll help, Papa."

"I'll do what I can, Bob," her mother snapped. "Just stop treating me like an invalid."

Ignoring Mother, he said, "I'm driving into Hobart today to pick up some feed for the horses. While I'm there, I thought I'd play a few hands of dominoes. Either of you want to go?"

CHAPTER 21 ✦ RUTH

"You might have mentioned it a little earlier, Bob. We'd have had some time to get ready."

Ruth's papa shrugged. "I don't want to sit around here too long before I leave, but go on and get ready. I'll wait."

"Tell you the truth, I really don't want to ride into town. You go on, Bob. You, too, Ruth if you want."

"I'd like to visit Joan for a while, but I don't want to leave you alone, Mother."

"Nonsense. You go on."

"You're sure you won't need me here?"

"No. You go on. This may be the last day it's warm enough for me to sit out on the swing to do some sewing and not be all cooped up inside. And don't you worry about me being here alone. Pearl lives five minutes away, and I can call her to come over if I get to feeling poorly."

"So, you coming, Ruth?" Her papa asked as he started for the door.

"Just one minute." She didn't want to make him wait, and, even though she hated going into town wearing her everyday clothes, she laid her sewing aside and, pulling her coat on, followed him. Stopping at the car, she looked out over the bare fields. The stark, dead cotton stalks made her feel sad. They held no promise now other than being plowed under to make way for the spring planting. Lately she was feeling a lot like that herself, worried that she, too, held no promise now.

"You going to get in, Ruth, or just stand there staring off into space?"

Ruth slid into the front passenger seat, and, as her papa drove out of the yard, she saw her mother sitting on the side porch basking in the unusually warm, late-November morning sun. "I'm worried about Mother," she said after riding in silence for half a mile.

"I am, too."

Ruth was surprised that her papa admitted his concern. It wasn't like him, and it frightened her to see it. "Do you know something I don't, Papa?"

Her papa's brow wrinkled as he said, "No. Nothing more than you do. But Ida just isn't the same. She's aged overnight. Doesn't have energy for much. You be sure not to let her do any heavy lifting when we butcher those hogs."

Ruth sighed and looked at Joe's dreary cotton field as they drove past, his brown stalks depressing her more. If anything happened to Mother, she wasn't sure what that would do to Papa. "I'll see to it she doesn't," she promised. Little more was said as they drove the last nine miles to Hobart. There was little to talk about with Papa. The war, his animals, weather, dominoes, and cotton were the only subjects he was really interested in, so she was happy to sit mostly in silence. Neither of them, she knew, wanted to discuss butchering Churchill and Roosevelt. When he finally nosed the car into a spot at the south corner of the courthouse and killed the engine, she stepped from the car and looked out over the courthouse grounds. The benches were no longer shaded by the native elms, which had lost their leaves. The Bermuda grass was a dusty green and would remain so till the spring rains washed the dust away, and new shoots of grass would appear.

"I'll be heading to the farm around two," Papa said. "I'll meet you back here by then." He ambled across the street and never looked back.

In no hurry to get to Joan's house, Ruth sat down on one of the benches and gazed at the buildings across the street, Bill Webster's barbershop, Ellie's Café, Johnson Drugstore, and The Five and Dime. Unlike on Saturdays, they were drawing few customers. Few country-folk came into town except on a Saturday. Her thoughts turned to Chester as they always seemed to do when she was alone with nothing particular to occupy her. It had been difficult being in the cotton field with Alice's sister, feeling the eyes of the other women on her, some spiteful and some pitying. It was worse with what happened with Charlie and her. Even after talking it over with Joe, her spirits felt lower now than they had ever before. She couldn't seem to wrap her head around the reality of Alice and Chester.

CHAPTER 21 ✦ RUTH

Tired of sitting with her morbid thoughts, she stood to leave and, taking one more sweeping look across the street, saw Joe Williams emerge from the barbershop. He held his hand up, waved once, and then started crossing the street, his eyes more on her than the traffic. No matter, there wasn't a single car driving down the street at the moment. Her first thought was the wish that she'd changed into something nicer than her work-a-day house dress. Had bothered to put on makeup. She was not surprised that her heart began to beat faster, and her face to feel hot. She'd grown more and more comfortable talking to him on his porch or at his kitchen table, but, here, on the courthouse grounds, they were in plain sight of anyone who happened to look this way.

He sauntered up to her a warm smile lighting his face. "I saw you over here, Ruth, and thought I'd come over say hello." He sat down on the bench, removed his hat, and ran his strong fingers through newly cut hair. "Can you sit a while with me?"

Ruth sat back down on the edge of the bench, thinking she'd best say just a word or two and leave. "Just a few minutes, Joe. Then I have to get to Joan's."

"What are you doing in town when it's not a Saturday?"

"Nothing in particular. I just get bored sitting out at the farm. When Papa decided to drive to town and play some dominoes, I came along to visit Joan." She felt shy and unable to meet his gaze, so focused on the hand that held his cigarette. "I was on my way over to Joan's, but it seemed so pleasant out here that I decided to sit a spell." The cigarette in Joe's fingers was burning close to his knuckles and she wondered if she should say something. Keep him from burning himself.

"How about having lunch with me, instead?"

Startled, Ruth stood, wanted away from temptation. "Oh, Joe. You know I can't do that. There'd be talk. There's enough of that already. Besides, every busybody in town would know by nightfall and make up all kinds of stories. And with all the gossip about Chester and Alice, I don't want to guess what they'd be saying about us."

"We can drive over to Rocky, where nobody knows us."

She looked into his brown eyes and hated having to say, "I'd like to, but I don't want to give a bunch of busybodies something more to talk about, Joe. What would our kids or parents think if they found out? And I'd be surprised if Chester didn't know about it the first time he gets mail from around here. You know it'll get back to everybody." She didn't add that she'd have a lot of anxiety and guilt to handle even if no one saw them together. Much as she had grown to like Joe, she wasn't ready to face dealing with that.

"The town's busybodies be damned. As for our folks?" He shrugged his shoulders. "As for Sarah? She told me the other day that she really likes you." He grinned, and Ruth thought for a moment that he looked like a mischievous boy. "And she said she wouldn't mind having you for a mother."

"I declare. No telling what a child is likely to say," Ruth said as her face flushed warmer, and she wondered if it would burn her like Joe's cigarette was going to burn him any second now. She needn't have worried because he ground the glowing end of the lit cigarette into shreds of tobacco and ash against the rough sole of his shoe and dropped what was left to the ground. "After what I told Charlie in the cotton patch, I don't know how he'd deal with coming to think we were up to something."

Joe gave her a crooked, one-sided grin. "That's true. But we could talk further about that over lunch."

She felt her heart beating too fast for comfort. His words tugged at her, pulling her toward something she wanted to do, but was frightened of doing. She looked around the park, felt her stomach knotting, hoping no one they knew was gawking. She saw only three people on the sidewalks, and they all looked preoccupied with something more than her and Joe. Not paying any mind to them. Not wondering what a married woman was doing talking to a widower.

She pushed closer to the edge of the bench, ready to stand up. "No, we can't do it," she said. "I need to get on to Joan's house."

CHAPTER 21 ✦ RUTH

"I can get my truck and meet you on the street behind the courthouse. Let you off there when we get back. Hardly anybody's ever walking that street except on a Saturday."

Why does he have to be so persistent? she wondered as she scooted back, leaned against the backrest, and took a deep breath. Her heart in her throat, she took another deep breath. *I'm going to say yes if I don't get up and leave this minute*, she thought. But she felt glued to her seat. Seconds passed as she thought of Chester. A picture of that Jenson woman came into her mind. She began to shake her head as if to deny the truth in those thoughts.

"It's nice being with you, Ruth. And we've never shared a meal."

"It would be nice," Ruth said. It didn't sound at all like her to say that. Or to follow with, "I can't get home if I miss my ride with Papa. He said he would be leaving by two o'clock."

"I'll have you back by 1:30. I promise. And remember, if Bob leaves without you, I live only a half mile from his place. You can wait with me for school to get out and walk Charlie home."

"Papa will wait. Be madder'n a hornet. But he'll wait."

Joe laughed aloud. "Come on, now. Say yes. I'll see to it you're not late."

She felt light-headed and scared, but said, "I'll go see Joan for a few minutes and explain where I am and tell her to keep it to herself. She'll do that for me." She swallowed hard, trying to choke down the dry taste of sawdust that was gathering in the back of her throat.

Joe stood. "I'll meet you in half an hour. I have to run by the feed store and pick up a sack of chicken feed and get a few groceries while you see Joan. I'll be ready to go in fifteen or twenty minutes."

Flustered, she sat and watched Joe walk away, desire and guilty fear roiling beneath her breastbone. She pictured Chester overseas, working hard, being shot at and bombed by the Japs, while she, safe and sound, went to lunch with an old friend of his. But then she pictured him and Alice together, and a spark of anger propelled her to her feet. She walked with determined steps to Joan's door and knocked so hard her knuckles hurt.

When the door opened and Joan greeted her with a hug, Ruth felt the resolve to go to lunch with Joe begin to evaporate. Her stomach tightened when her sister held her by the shoulders and stepped back.

"What's the matter, Ruth? You look like you've seen a ghost."

Wordless, Ruth pulled away from her sister's grasp and walked over to a soft chair sitting at the window looking out over the courthouse and its grounds. Taking in a deep breath and slowly letting it out, she said, "I think I may be getting ready to do something that I really shouldn't."

"Oh, for heaven's sake. I've not known you to be in the habit of doing that."

A rush of heat burned her cheeks as she said, "I've been visiting with Joe at his house a lot lately. Letting the kids have some time to play together after school."

"Yes, Papa mentioned that to me recently. Wasn't too happy about it."

Well, Joe saw me in the courthouse grounds a few minutes ago. Told me he enjoys us being together and asked me to go to lunch with him over in Rocky. If I do it, I suspect by tomorrow, everyone in this county will know about it."

Joan's eyebrows rose, and a faint smile broadened her lips. "Maybe not. No one would know you two over in that town."

Ruth studied her sister's face to see if there was any hint of displeasure, but Joan kept smiling. "It's okay with you?"

"Of course, it's okay with me. After the way Chester has acted, I like the idea of you spending some time with a decent man. See how it feels. You might find the strength to leave Chester then. It's about time."

"He's over there fighting the Japs. I don't think I should be faithless to him."

"If I know Chester, he's probably over there shacked up with some twenty-something, cute island woman."

Tears sprang to Ruth's eyes, and she felt a stab of hurt and anger. Joan's words were too near the truth. It hurt. "You don't know that, Joan.

Don't you think with the mess he's got over here, he'd have more sense over there?"

Joan's laugh had no humor in it. "Enough about Chester. You going to go to lunch with Joe?"

Ruth buried her face in her hands, and her voice came out hoarse. "I told him I would. But I can't go through with it."

"Of course, you can. And should."

"I should? You mean it?"

"I mean it. Now, go!"

"You won't think I'm a terrible person?"

"Well, I've thought that ever since you gave me a spanking when I was four years old. But that's beside the point. Just go. We can talk about it later."

*

On the way out of town, Ruth forced down her rising gorge and brought up only safe topics. She did not want to talk about what they were doing. Speak to the consequences they both might face. She caught herself breathing too fast and becoming a little dizzy, so she took one last deep breath, held it for a few heartbeats, and slowly let it out. A strained silence filled the cab, and seeing Joe's death grip on the steering wheel and his tense shoulders, she figured that he must be as tense as she. Ruth felt her stomach tightening even more; she had to force herself to take measured breaths. If her sister had shown the least bit of disapproval, Ruth would not be sitting here with Joe, terrified and speechless. She startled when Joe broke the silence.

"I remember the first time I saw you, Ruth. You were a new first-grader, and I was a second grader. You wore those long, black braids that came down to the middle of your back, and your skin was burnt brown, I expect from being outdoors most of the summer. You could have been an Indian from off the reservation."

Ruth laughed at the forced memory, but it was a nervous laugh. "Well, I remember sometime in first grade you and Chester pulling those pigtails and making me cry."

"That was only because we wanted you to know we liked you."

"Funny way to do that."

"You know how boys act around girls when they're that age. Sarah had the same thing happen to her. Actually, something worse; last year, Bobby Goforth dipped her pigtails in an inkwell."

"I remember the two of you deviling me in one way or another all the way through to my seventh-grade year."

"Yes, but we stopped then, didn't we?"

"No. You just changed tactics and started teasing me, and then, after a while, pestering me to let you walk me home—or go for buggy rides."

"I thought I'd won out on that score for a while," Joe said, and Ruth caught a wistful sound to his admission. "But then Chester won your heart. I was mad at both of you for a long time. I guess till I met and married Theresa. I stopped hanging out with Chester much after that."

The outskirts of Rocky came into view, and, in seconds, they were parking outside the Hometown restaurant. There were even fewer people on the street here than in Hobart, which made her feel a little less conspicuous. The rich smell of frying hamburgers enveloped them as they entered the restaurant, and Ruth drew in its comforting aroma, hoping to calm herself. As she looked around the room, Ruth swore the eyes of the few people sitting at the tables shifted to her and Joe as they were being seated. *God,* she thought, *let it be only idle curiosity.*

The waitress walked over with a coffee pot and asked, "What can I get you folks today?" She smiled at them the whole time she was taking their orders of coffee and hamburgers with fries. Ruth thought, *Thank God it isn't a knowing smile.* As they then sipped coffee. Joe's eyes caught and held hers, and then his quiet smile warmed her heart. A delicious mixture of exhilaration, fear, and longing made her feel more alive than she had been in months.

CHAPTER 21 ♦ RUTH

"You're looking real pretty today, Ruth. I swear your face doesn't look drawn and tired like it did when I came up to you sittin' on that bench at the courthouse."

Her tense muscles and clenched stomach began to relaxed as she continued to look into Joe's warm eyes. Before she'd climbed into Papa's car that morning, she'd stared out over the field of cotton and thought that life held no promise for her. Things felt so different at this moment. *I love being here with Joe*, she thought. She didn't want to respond to his compliment but only to prolong this moment without interruption. She lowered her eyes, unable to keep looking at Joe; afraid that she could not restrain the impulse to reach across and caress his hand.

Joe set his cup down and said, "This is really nice, Ruth."

She nodded and then sat back as the waitress placed the hot fries and steaming hamburgers down in front of them. Still smiling, Joe picked picked up his burger, took a bite, motioned to her plate, and said, "Better dig in before it gets cold."

They ate in silence at first. The raw onions, dill pickles, and thick patty of meat filled her mouth and her senses, making words unnecessary. This was so different, sitting down to a meal with Joe rather than on his front porch with just a cup of coffee. Finished with all but her fries, she met Joe's eyes again and opened her mouth to say something, but words wouldn't come. She wished now he would say something.

As if reading her mind, he said, "I like sitting on my porch or in the kitchen talking to you, but it's hard to talk seriously with those two kids of ours chaperoning us most of the time. And there's something different about being here eating lunch with you. I like it."

Heat rose to Ruth's cheeks. She was not sure she liked her thoughts being so transparent to Joe. In an effort to calm herself, she said, "I was thinking of those two. I'll bet they both would love these hamburgers if they were here." If she could have kicked herself, she would have. He had asked for something in that comment, and she hadn't given it. With effort, she lifted her eyes to his and said, "But you're right. It really is nice being here with just you." Her blush deepened, and she looked down at her coffee.

"Since when you told Charlie about Alice and his daddy and then all that nonsense with Corky and Mildred happened, things have changed between us. You've opened up to me about how hard it's been living with all that. Living with your parents. Not being able to really talk to Charlie about what the future holds for the two of you."

Ruth nodded. "I don't know why, but much as I love my sisters, I couldn't bring myself to share all that with them. I've appreciated it so much that I could talk to you." She drained her cup, took a deep breath, and said, "But I'm not sure if I'm doing the right thing being here with you. Still, I've not been so relaxed and happy in months." She ducked her head and choked up at the words. Joe sat quietly while she recovered. "I think we best be going, Joe." She stood up. "But first I have to go to the ladies' room." She hurried into the bathroom, peered into the wall mirror and saw that her face had a glow she hadn't seen in months. Even without makeup, she looked less like a haggard farmhand than when she last checked a mirror.

When she returned to the table, Joe stood, and, as they walked to the car, his hand rested on her back, leaving chills and goosebumps crowding her arms. Both were quiet as they drove the first mile. Then Joe turned the conversation to the war in Germany, a long way from where Chester was stationed. Still, the mention of war brought back thoughts of him. As they entered Hobart, pangs of guilt warred with gusts of excited fear that filled her throat with dry heat, choking her. It sent her into a coughing spell just as he pulled onto the street behind the courthouse to let her out.

"I think we got away with it," Joe said, grinning.

Ruth only shook her head and gave him a wan smile, too afraid of what she might say to discourage—or encourage—his obvious pleasure.

Dropping the smile, he said, "We just had lunch, and that's no crime."

CHAPTER 21 ✦ RUTH

"I just wish the rest of the world believed that," Ruth said as she slid out of the front seat and walked away, turning only once to see him watching her. She waved and then hurried on to Joan's apartment, wondering if anything like this lunch with Joe could ever be repeated. The unsettling image of her parents', Charlie's, or Chester's reaction, were they to know, nagged at the back of her mind, making it hard to hold on to the pleasure of having been with Joe. She knew that if she was found out, Charlie would be more confused than ever. Papa would throw a wall-eyed fit, and Mother would give her a cold shoulder. Then she remembered that papa had said they would butcher soon. That sorry job, she hoped, would take her mind off everything else.

CHAPTER 22

Ruth

⇥ ❋ ⇤

Ruth finished taking her last bite of cold cornbread and washed it down with fresh milk from Papa's generous jersey cow. Then, picking up her cup, she sipped at the dregs of morning coffee and watched Charlie crumble one last piece of cornbread into his bowl. He poured milk over it and stared at the sugar bowl before he started lifting a spoonful of cornbread and milk to his mouth. He'd heard that not sugaring his cornbread or iced tea was another way to help with the war effort; sugar was being rationed so it could be made into alcohol that was used to make explosives for the military. He'd sworn off using it. Bless his heart, if he stopped to think of how much sugar was used in his grandmother's cakes, he might just stop eating that, too. *Maybe not*, she thought.

CHAPTER 22 ✦ RUTH

Thinking about Charlie's sacrifices for the war effort made the heat of guilt rise to her face. She had been so happy driving to Rocky with Joe for lunch, something so pleasant she'd been unable to put it out of her mind. She felt a mixture of pleasure at the thought, but then Chester immediately came to mind, and deep guilt burned her face and clenched her stomach. Thank goodness her sister wasn't as stuck in the mud as her papa and mother. Or the gossips. Joan even encouraged Ruth to go on visiting with Joe when she picked up Charlie at school. But then, Joan hated Chester. Would be happy if Ruth dumped him for Joe.

Ruth was startled from her thoughts by the rattle of her papa's coffee cup in his saucer and his strained voice, "I hate to do it, but it's got to be done. We got to get busy this morning butchering those hogs." He rose from the chair and disappeared into his bedroom.

Charlie bolted out of his chair, grabbed his coat, and ran out of the house to get away to school. She didn't blame him. He'd cried when his grandpa first said he was going to butcher the hogs sometime soon. She'd like to run away, too. But it was necessary to help Papa or her mother would be right in the middle of the hard work.

She watched Papa come out of his room, his eyes bright with unshed tears. She had seen him cry in years past when he had to slaughter an animal. He was hard on his family but soft on his animals and was saddened when he had to kill them. But Ruth, like her papa, knew they had to do this, or they'd go without grease to fry things in and have no pork chops, bacon, or ham to eat this winter. Everything was scarce and getting scarcer. Not enough shortening for baking because it went for making explosives, nor enough gasoline because it was needed to power the tanks, guns, ships, and planes. Not enough sugar. Rationing stamps for what little of these things you could get. And red meat? Butchering his own animals was the only way Papa could afford to get meat on the table. This year, because of her and Charlie, he'd decided to fatten and butcher not just one, but two hogs.

"I'm going on down and help Papa," Ruth said.

Her voice bitter as alum, Ruth's mother said, "It's me should be down there stoking the fire under the scalding pot and carrying the meat to the wash house to salt down and the fat up here to the house to render, not leaving most of that to you."

"You got no business doing heavy work with that heart of yours."

"Ruth, you're already doing more than your share of the work around here."

"No, I'm just doing my share." Ruth wasn't sure of that sometimes, but helping Papa might even the score some.

She walked out of the kitchen and onto the porch; then she stared out over the field of bare, dead cotton stalks that stretched out in front of the house. The first year Papa had sharecropped this piece of land, she'd been six years old. They'd moved up here from Sugar Creek down by Velma, Oklahoma, all their belongings piled high on the bed of a wagon, leading an old Jersey cow her great uncle had given them. A calf had run alongside, bawling its fool head off for the first five miles of the trip. That calf was the great-grandmother of Isabelle, who had provided the milk they'd drunk at breakfast. They all slept on the ground every night of that trip. Mornings she'd bustled around the campfire, helping to make coffee for her papa in an old iron coffeepot her grandmother had given her parents for a wedding present. Mother had thrown a handful of coffee grounds into the pot of boiling water, then let Ruth drop in a couple of eggshells to settle the grounds. Back then Mother told Ruth she was a pretty little girl. With her long black curls down to the middle of her back, cotton socks that came high on her legs, and a dress her grandmother had made out of store-bought muslin, she'd gone around happy and smiling, bright as a new penny.

She remembered sleeping out under the stars and the excitement of knowing that, the next day, the family would have a new place to live. One with three bedrooms. She'd been happy that night, curled up with

CHAPTER 22 ✦ RUTH

her mother and sister Pearl while her papa threw more wood on the fire and made the rounds of the animals, making sure they were well hobbled so they couldn't wander off. They'd had a sow and a shoat, that followed the wagon like a pair of dogs and bedded down so near, she'd had trouble going to sleep because of their snoring. Papa had liked to brag that the sow had thrown four fine litters for him. Four months later when he'd butchered that shoat, she'd cried. So had he.

She flinched when she heard the crack of Papa's rifle and the high-pitched death squeal of one of the hogs. For a few minutes, she couldn't bring herself to go look but, when she did, saw Papa hoisting one of the hogs—she wasn't sure which one—by its hind legs hooked to her papa's version of a block and tackle—a fence stretcher attached to a tripod contraption he'd constructed out of four-by-four lumber. Ruth stepped down off the porch and, dragging her steps, started for the outdoor slaughter. Her breath steamed out, and the vapors rose into the cold morning air.

She saw her papa slit the hog's throat, sending blood gushing like a faucet into a washtub. Some of it sloshed onto the ground and on Papa's shoes. Turning from the animal, he walked over to the scalding vat, added more coal to the firepit, squatted, and held his hands out to the fire. He stood and walked back over to the animal and slashed open its belly from one end to the other, letting its entrails spill into a wheelbarrow as he cut them away. Heavy steam rose from the vat of boiling water. Tendrils of vapor drifted up like a fine mist from the warm bucket of blood. A White Leghorn hen, bolder than the rest, pecked at the spilled gore. Ruth wanted to be sick.

Her papa wiped his hands on a bloodied rag. "I thought I was going to have to do this all on my own, Ruth." He hung the bloodstained rag on the point of one leg of the tripod and then grasped it and another. "Take hold of that other leg of the hoist and help me walk it over to the vat."

The stench of blood and pig shit wrinkled Ruth's nose in disgust. In a nearby pen, the other hog paced and squealed, as if knowing its turn was coming. "Papa, I hate to have to help you with this, but I know it's necessary," Ruth grunted as she helped him walk the hoist over to the boiling water. Hot vapor swirled up and blew off toward the barn as they lowered the carcass into the scalding vat.

"This ain't the first time you've had to do this work, Ruth. You was raised on a farm, after all," her papa said, aggravation hardening his words.

"You're awfully snippy with me, Papa."

"I don't like killing these hogs is all. But I was also thinking about that no-account husband of yours not being here and you having to do all this work. And I get mad every time I do," he said adding more coals to the fire.

Ruth wondered why Papa would bring up Chester at a time like this; she stood silent for what seemed to her a long time before asking, "How long do you plan to leave that animal in there, Papa? The hairs are going to set up, and we'll have to shave him."

"Ruth, I've only been butchering hogs for over thirty-five years. You might reckon I know how by now."

Tears of frustration came to her eyes as she helped Papa wrench the scalded animal back out of the vat and walk it over to an old wooden door he'd laid across two sawhorses to make a table. Then she said, "You don't think Chester's on my mind all the time, too? I'm worried to death about him getting killed. And when I'm not, I worry about what's going to happen when he gets home."

Her papa began to scrape the hair from the hog's carcass with a sharpened piece of metal, one edge fastened to a handmade wooden handle. "A better man would have the decency to make up his mind. Not leave you hanging."

"Papa. A more decent man wouldn't have made it necessary for me to hang."

"That's the God's truth. Now give me a hand here."

Ruth picked up a broken-handled butcher knife Papa had sharpened and began scraping at the hair, leaving patches of the skin, whitened by

CHAPTER 22 ◆ RUTH

the scalding water, lying exposed. "I know you rightly feel that way about Chester, but I hope you can spare saying anything around Charlie."

Her papa scraped harder, almost hard enough to cut through the pig's skin, but said nothing until they finished, and the white, hairless carcass lay between them. "You need a daddy for that boy, and Chester just ought to be here."

Ruth nodded. "That's so."

"It's the gospel truth. There's something else, too." He turned to her, and the narrowing of his eyes made her pulse quicken. "I know that you've been visiting a lot with Joe Williams on his front porch. But I heard in town from Jack Lawson that when he was over in Rocky a few days ago, he saw you two having lunch together. I don't think you ought to be doing things like that."

Ruth threw down her scraper and stumbled backwards, almost tripping on the bucket of blood. "Yes, I've gone down to walk home with Charlie because that Corky Alred made his life miserable after school if I didn't. And sometimes I stop in and visit with Joe while Charlie and Sarah play together for a bit. And that busybody who told you about me being over in Rocky with Joe can just go jump in the lake and drown as far as I'm concerned. Joe and I are just friends."

Her papa picked up a heavy butcher knife and began a cut that would sever the hams from the body. "Given what Charlie would think, I can't believe you would chance gossip like that."

Ruth's face burned, and she wanted to scream at Papa, taunt him that, yes, she had lunch with Joe, and would do it again if she got the chance. Wanted to say it was none of his or other people's business. Particularly those inclined to gossip. Instead, she turned toward the house and, gritting her teeth, threw angry words back over her shoulder—threw them hard as she could. "I'm going to the house. Call me down here when you're ready with that other hog."

"Don't you go off anywhere, now. I'll need you soon," he yelled out, but she closed her mind to him.

At the wash house, she paused a moment and looked at two distant buildings, Joe's house and the schoolhouse, both gleaming white in the clear morning air. Joe was likely sitting at the breakfast table having a cup of coffee and Charlie sitting at his desk next to Sarah. *I'd rather be in one of those two places instead of here*, she thought. *I'm just growing unhappier with every day that passes living with Papa and Mother.* To leave, she needed to find a job, and that prospect discouraged her. Never having worked outside the home, except in the field, she had no idea how she could support herself and Charlie if she left.

Lowering her eyes from the distant buildings, she pushed her way through the wash house door and inspected the crockery vats, where the meat would be salted. She'd made sure they were all scoured clean, that their brown glaze shined almost bright enough to give back her reflection. Her papa would have the hog cut up soon, bring the meat here to pack in the salt brine, and then come into the house with buckets of the fat. Going back outside, she glanced again in the direction of the schoolhouse. She hoped Charlie made something of himself. Not have to become a farmer living hand-to-mouth all his life. Chester had been a hard man to live with, but at least he'd got himself off the farm. No one else in the family had. Except maybe for her brother, who'd had to enlist in the army to do it. If Winston had stayed on at the farm, they wouldn't have drafted him. He could have just been miserable rather than shot at. To him, the choice he made was the lesser of two evils.

Winston had been a little like Charlie, picked on at school. Once, he'd had sneaked away from school and spent the day hitchhiking into Hobart and back. Her papa was so mad he'd thrown a bucket at Winston when he showed up after sundown. Winston had ducked just in time, but to this day there was a dent in the door where the edge of the bucket had caught it.

"You could've killed that boy," her mother had yelled. "Ain't you going to be satisfied until you kill both my boys?"

CHAPTER 22 • RUTH

Winston had left and not come back until it was time to do chores next morning. Her papa might mistreat a son or grandson, but he never mistreated his animals. Only slaughtered them when he had to.

She saw her Papa carrying a three-gallon bucket of hog fat toward the house and heard her mother, say, "Let me have that, Bob. I'll let Ruth carry the next one."

Papa's denial was harsh and accusing. "With that heart of yours, you got no business even thinking about carrying things this heavy. I'll bring it in."

Ruth came out of the washhouse and called, "Give me that bucket." Reaching Papa, the sight of the quivering mass of fat made her stomach turn, and she looked away; breathing deeply and closing her nose to the raw smell, she took the bucket and started for the house. Her mother held the screen door for Ruth as she entered the kitchen and then set the bucket on the counter.

"What's making your Papa so snippy with you, Ruth? I was looking out the window at you two, and I could see you weren't getting along too well. I know he's upset about the hogs, but . . ."

"He's probably told you about me having lunch with Joe Williams. He was aggravating me about that."

"Well, yes he did. You're not doing yourself any favors carrying on like that."

"Please don't you start on me, Mother. Papa already said everything I need or want to hear."

Her mother's mouth quirked to one side with disapproval as her shoulder shrugged up in a way that Ruth knew meant, *Okay, it's your funeral.* "Here, you set up the fat press while I cut up what's in that bucket," her mother said. She reached in to drag out strips of hog fat and began cutting them into smaller chunks.

Ruth turned away, guilt and anger bringing heat to her face. She reached for the press sitting on the kitchen counter. A metal contraption with a wheel and screw at the top that lowered a plunger, it seemed to weigh a ton as Ruth lifted it onto the table, cushioned the metal screw with a dish towel, and fastened the press to the table's edge. She then took a large crock and placed it on a stool under the press's spout, readying the container for the liquid fat that would come from the press.

Her mother put the pieces she'd cut up into the top of the press and then Ruth turned the wheel, lowering the plunger further and further down. Her arm muscles bulged with the effort of forcing the liquid pork fat to spew and sputter out of the spigot and into the crock. Finished, she placed what was left in the press into a large iron skillet.

Wanting to cool things down between the two of them, Ruth said, "Charlie would say that turning this wheel is just like steering Papa's car in a big circle."

"I remember Brian saying something like that once. Your papa had a Model T back then."

"That little brother of mine loved to help, never stinted on his jobs," Ruth said.

They finished with the first bucket just as her papa brought in another, set it on the counter, and left without saying anything but, "Ruth, I'll need you down at the barn in a few minutes."

Ruth flinched when the second shot of the morning echoed up from the barn. She tightened her jaw and kept turning the press until it reached bottom again, cranked the plunger back up and lifted it off. She again removed what remained inside the press and added it to the iron skillet which she lifted onto the stove. Soon it began to pop and sizzle and a rich smell like bacon filled the kitchen as it cooked down into cracklings. "I hope you're making crackling cornbread tonight for supper, Mother."

"I plan to."

"Don't forget to let me lift that pan off the stove when you finish frying the cracklings. You try and do it, weak as you are, you might drop it and spill that hot grease on yourself." Ruth wiped sweat from her face with a clean cloth. "Joan was two years getting over that burn she got from hot grease."

"I wasn't born yesterday, Ruth. I know better than to lift something too heavy."

"Well, you don't act like it sometimes." Ruth regretted saying that the minute it was out of her mouth. *I'm angry at Papa but shouldn't take it out on my mother*, she thought, and then refilled the press and went back to turning the wheel, once more forcing the cylinder downward, squeezing the hog fat, sending a steady stream of liquid grease into a crock.

Silenced by Ruth's remark, her mother began to chop more of the strips of hog fat into pieces.

"I know I'm being snippy. I'm worse than when I was at fifteen and pregnant. I'm sorry, mother," she said and turned the wheel one more time. "This thing with Chester and Alice—then the scolding Papa gave me for visiting with Joe and Sarah—has soured me something terrible. I don't know what to do. Or what more to say to Charlie about his daddy."

"Don't apologize. I know what you're going through. Just be careful not to make things worse. You're done here for now, so go help your papa."

Ruth wiped her hands on a dish towel, left the kitchen, and, as she walked to the barn, looked toward the school, where Charlie was sitting, most likely with his head in his hands, hurt, and near crying; he'd grown to think of those two hogs as friends.

CHAPTER 23

Chester

⤙ ✦ ⤚

In the murky half-light of dawn, Chester stared at the distant tropical shore but could see little of the invasion beach. Finschhafen Island lay directly ahead of them. The flat-bellied tank lighter approached the sandy beach of Langamac Bay at full speed. Waves battered the heavy boat as its motor revved and pushed toward East Beach. The heavy surf sent saltwater pouring in from both sides, splashing over them. Rifle bullets pinged off the sides of the craft. Chester shouted to any and all, "God damn those yellow bastards." Then, tight-lipped, he braced himself and stopped watching the palm-fringed island edge nearer. On Kiriwina, where he'd help construct two taxiways, there had been no Jap troops or air raids. Now he was going into a shooting war. He'd never felt so scared.

CHAPTER 23 • CHESTER

As they approached the shore, more small-arms fire centered on the lighters' coxswains. The high-pitched whine of the Japanese bullets cut through the noise of the lighter's motor and pinged as they ricocheted off the bow. Chester swore as he crouched down and clenched his fists till his fingers cramped. *"Jesus,"* he thought, *"I'm damned glad I'm not the one standing in the open and having to steer this son-of-a-bitch."* An explosion of return fire erupted from the marines' ranks as they stormed ashore. He hoped they'd kill every last one of the Japs shooting at him. "I should have stayed back in the States, Hough," Chester yelled.

Hough, work-hardened from his days on an oil rig and the work they'd done on Kiriwina, spit into the water sloshing at their feet and shouted, "If it weren't so clouded over, the Jap planes would have already been on top of us. They arrive, that's when we're really in the shit."

"Tell me something I don't already know." Chester glanced at the sky, overcast and threatening rain. He'd heard that, on a clear day, the strafing could be even worse than hell. On Kiriwina, they'd all cheered when the first allied planes landed and again when they took off for a major raid against Rabaul. A week later, they completed the second taxiway and shipped out for this hellhole. In his shirt pocket, he felt another of Charlie's letter resting there and hoped it would help give him courage to face what lay ahead on this God forsaken island. If he got through this, he'd someday give Charlie a big hug for sending the letter.

"OK. Let's get ready to go." Loud as an overloaded jackass, the lieutenant, old enough to be Chester's papa, brayed out his commands.

Chester took a deep breath and held it, his heart galloping inside of his chest. He hoped the Marines had cleared the jungle beyond the beaches enough that a sniper wouldn't put a bullet in him when he charged ashore.

The lighter beached, and the ramp in the bow crashed down, sending a spray of water over the beach's sand. The platoon leader charged ashore screaming out at the men, "Come on, you bastards, let's move. Go. Go. Go. Move it. Move it."

With the ramp down, Chester now had a full view of the beach and caught sight of Marines entering the edge of the jungle, crouching low and firing as they advanced. Some fell before others disappeared into the maze of palms. A sniper's rifle sent a bullet into one of the Sea Bees as he stood ready to jump ashore. He screamed, twisted to one side, fell into the water, and went under. Hough and Johnny Polk, who were right behind the man, jumped in, grabbed him under the arms and pulled him on to the beach, both shouting, "Medic. Medic." Chester picked up a load of mesh, and as he staggered onto the beach and threw down the load, a volley of rifle fire shredded the foliage of a tall palm and a single figure lurch out and down, halting as its harness tightened. The sniper jerked a couple of times and then dangled like a marionette. Chester ran back onto the lighter and grabbed another load of mesh, hoping any Japanese left alive were being forced back farther into the groves. He glanced up into the palm tree where the dead sniper hung from his harness, his arms splayed, as if he were ready to take flight. Between him and the dead man, the beach was littered with dead and wounded Marines and Japs. Chester threw down his load and turned to run back to the lighter but stopped at the sight of a Marine sprawled dead at the edge of the water next to one of the lighters. His body was savagely heaved farther onto the sand by the violent wash from the incoming lighters. On the beaches of California, Chester had watched the surf playing with dead fish and driftwood. But never with a human body. Bile rose in the back of his throat, and he looked away and saw a couple of medics tending to the wounded Sea Bee that Hough and Polk had dragged ashore. He heard the pop-pop-pop of automatic weapons and, turning to look, saw Aussie patrols plunge into the jungle. Turning back, he saw scores of landing craft hitting the beach and spilling more Sea Bees and Marines.

    Chester bent his back to unloading more mesh as other Sea Bees began laying it down for the heavy vehicles to drive inland. The leaden clouds that had kept the Jap fighters at bay began pouring down gallons

CHAPTER 23 ♦ CHESTER

of water on Chester and the others. Commander Nelson, a USNR civil engineer from Tulsa, a pint-sized son-of-a-bitch Chester had come to know, had the energy of a jackhammer, moved up and down the rain-drenched beach, prodding them on like a slave master. Under his breath, Chester muttered, "God damn Nelson, the Japs, and this cotton-pickin' rain." It seemed to him that he'd been working for hours getting the damned supplies ashore, and, from a glance at the steady arrival of lighters, there were hours more of back-breaking work ahead of him.

Trucks, heavy guns, ammunition, and other supplies now littered the beach, a perfect place, Chester thought, for bombing and strafing practice by the Japs. When the weather cleared, they were sitting ducks, so he stopped cursing the rain.

"Hey, Scarsdale," Hough yelled, "do you remember all those weeks in service school we learned military tactics—how to drill, how to salute, how to shoot a pistol and rifle, and how a machine gun works? What and what not to do with hand grenades?" Hough leaned against a crate he'd wrestled off a lighter and lit a cigarette.

"Yeah, and in a banzai charge a bayonet is as good for defending ourselves as shooting a gun. So, what about it?"

"I really didn't think we'd ever need all that information. Now I'm not so sure. There are God knows how many Japs less than a mile from here. They could overrun our Marines and be on us."

"So, keep your rifle handy," Chester said, "Or you might not see another birthday." Chester thought about next his birthday. He would be thirty-seven years old. Men his age just shouldn't have to go into battle. But here he was in the very guts of a major offensive.

He reached up again and patted the soggy letter of Charlie's. He'd written in his schoolboy hand about getting money from old man Buchanan and buying two war bonds. "So you can get home sooner." Chester sure as hell wanted to be home right now and would almost put up with living with the Choats to get out of this hell-hole.

In the late afternoon, the rain turned to a light mist, and Chester could see a break in the clouds off near the horizon. He prayed for darkness to descend. Dumping in place a section of mesh he was carrying, Chester paused and sipped from his canteen. Standing there, water soaked and muddy, the memory came again of Ruth and him rolling around in the mud the first time he'd taken her on a buggy ride. The thought warmed him but then stabbed him in the heart. He wanted to forget all he and Ruth had gone through together, the good times anyway, and leave it behind him so he could turn his attention to Alice and their new child when it came. But times like now, thinking of that hilarious day rolling around in the mud, he missed Ruth. That muddy day was the beginning of their courtship that had led to marriage a year and a half later. And there was Charlie as well. When he'd received another of Charlie's letters two days before he'd set out for this invasion, he'd changed his mind about abandoning them. Decided to let Alice fend for herself. But then he'd opened Alice's letter, and it had somehow gladdened his heart to read it. He'd decided to stick with her. Shaking the thoughts away, he shouldered another load and started toward the tree line. There was a Goddamn war to win before he needed to worry over this.

An hour later, burdened with a section of mesh, he slogged further into the trees and almost gagged at the sight of five dead Japs lying on the jungle floor. Hell of a lot of protection they'd gotten from the trees. He walked close to the bodies; they looked shriveled and small, like children who'd been playing at war with loaded guns. As he stared, one of the Japanese soldier's legs twitched. Chester jerked the rifle from off his shoulder, clicked the safety off, and pointed it at the Jap.

"Careful there, Chester. Don't shoot yourself in the foot."

"Damn Jap moved, Hough."

"Them's death twitches. Now, let's get a move on, little buddy. There's more to do back at the lighters."

CHAPTER 23 ✦ CHESTER

Chester helped unload six ships by sundown, but there were still more steaming in. It was near midnight when he threw down his last load and looked about for a place to lie down.

In among the palm trees and tangled tropical vegetation, Chester, Hough, and others in his platoon scooped shallow depressions in the soil. Any deeper and they became a mudhole. Countless other Sea Bees followed suit and started digging their own foxholes. "Dammit, Hough, you sure as hell couldn't mistake this for a foxhole."

"A stray bullet passes over; it'd only take a little skin off. So, feel yourself lucky to have any hole at all," Johnny Polk said.

"Hell right. We're so damn lucky, aren't we?" Hough said.

Chester spread a rough canvas ground cloth on the dank, tropical soil that smelled of wet leaves and decaying vegetation. He lowered himself onto the ground cover and pulled his poncho over himself, hoping he could remain halfway free of the millions of bugs that came out in the night to dine on him. As a kid, he'd dug holes in the moist red clay of Oklahoma, covered them with flat boards, heaped dirt on top, crawled inside and imagined himself in a cave, a hideout that made him feel safe from what he no longer remembered. He wondered if Charlie was doing something like that on Bob Choat's farm. He'd told Charlie once about crawling inside his cave when one of the barn cats hissed at him and dashed past so close that one of its claws scratched his hand. "Scared me to death," he'd said. Charlie had laughed himself silly when Chester added, "I damn near wet my pants." That cave was a hell of a lot deeper and safer than this shallow ditch he was lying in.

Sleep wouldn't come right away, and he turned from side to side trying to get comfortable. He'd been told there were six kinds of rats, seven of bats and eighteen of reptiles on this damned island, and he prayed none of them would get interested in joining him inside this poncho-covered depression. Unable to sleep, his thoughts turned to Oklahoma. In his backpack were the last letters he'd received from Alice, who said she was doing okay with the pregnancy, only had a month more to go before she delivered. She told him that there was talk about Ruth and Joe Williams spending time together, something that he wished he didn't have to know. The ones from Ruth always told him how heartbroken she felt at the thought of losing him. From Alice's letter it sounded like she was running around having a good time. He felt a wave of anger and jealousy sweep over him at the thought of Joe and Ruth spending time together..

He tossed and turned with thoughts of Alice, Ruth, Charlie, and next day's tasks, ferrying materials to the airfield, working his ass off all day and half the night, and dodging Jap bombs before the sun went down. *Christmas is coming,* Chester thought, *and I damn well think there won't be any sign of Santa Claus out here in this miserable hellhole. I'm too damn tired to worry about all that anyway. But damned if I can go to sleep.*

CHAPTER 24

Ruth

⇢ ✽ ⇠

Six days before Christmas Eve, Ruth watched Papa climb heavily out of his car and wade to the porch through two inches of new snow. Stepping onto the porch, he stomped his rubber boots, sending a spray of new snow and slush splashing to the side. He slipped his shoes out of his rubber pullover boots, looked up, and caught Ruth's eye. A frown creased his brow, and he shook his head before he opened the door and stepped inside.

"What's wrong, Papa?"

He took a deep breath and said, "Let me get a cup of that coffee, and then let's go sit for a minute."

"What is it, Bob? You sound awful serious," Mother said. The crocheting needle and the doily she was working on dropped into her lap.

Papa brought his coffee with him, sat down in his rocking chair, and took another deep breath. "I hate to be the one to tell you, Ruth, but I heard in the domino parlor today that Alice had a baby girl yesterday. Everybody seems to know it belongs to Chester. Alice isn't making any secret of it."

The news hit her hard, like a blow to her solar plexus, and a moan escaped her lips. Even though she knew about Alice's pregnancy, the arrival of the baby made it all too real. She began to shake her head as if to say "No!" to the news. Tears welled up in her eyes and rolled down her cheeks. Angry she was crying, she swiped at them, sending them flying toward the floor.

"I'm so sorry, Ruth," her mother said as she stood, put her arms about Ruth, and held her tight.

Papa spat out, "You need to divorce that no-account, Ruth."

"But he wrote me that he's not sure he's going to leave Charlie and me."

"Well, you're going to have a talk about Alice's baby with Charlie now, for sure," Papa said. "Maybe when he gets home from school today."

Ruth felt a fresh wave of tears scald her cheeks at the thought. "I just don't know how I can do that, Papa."

"He needs to know. And it's too bad Chester isn't here to explain things to him."

Ruth stood and, swiping at her eyes again, said, "I'm going to my room. See if I can get control of myself."

With the door closed, she threw herself face down onto the bed. Sobs racked her until all the hurt seemed to have drained out onto the pillow along with her tears. She had allowed herself to live in a fantasy world these past few months, pushing thoughts of Alice's baby to the back of her mind. *God forgive me*, she thought, *but I wished for that woman to have a miscarriage when I heard about her pregnancy. But I couldn't keep that awful thought in my mind.*

Over the next two days, as she told Pearl and Joan about it, she cried again. If it hadn't been for those two sisters, who consoled her without saying they knew what was best for her, she wasn't sure how she could have gotten through those days. They had encouraged her decision that, with Christmas only days away, she wouldn't tell Charlie he had a new half-sister. The good Lord knows how that would ruin the holiday for him. Bad enough it was ruining hers.

*

Late on Christmas Eve, Ruth placed under the tree a gift she'd bought for Charlie, setting it next to the package Sarah had placed there earlier.

Before Charlie had crawled, sleepy and exhausted, into bed an hour after his bedtime, he'd gone back countless times to shake Joe and Sarah's present to try to guess what lay hidden beneath the cheery wrapping with all its tiny smiling Santa Clauses.

Ruth stuffed an apple, orange, and some candy into one of the socks he'd left for Santa. Sitting down in one of the chairs facing the tree, she gazed at the homemade decorations that Charlie and Sarah had spent an afternoon making the day Papa brought the tree into the house and set it up. They'd cut out stars and round "ornaments" from construction paper and then colored in designs with Crayolas. The smell of popcorn had filled the air when she popped it for them to string. Some fluffy white puffs of corn, that which the two of them hadn't eaten, were draped over the branches of the tree. If there had been electricity in the house, she would have put up twinkling lights. Still, the soft, flickering glow of the coal oil lamp made the decorations almost seem to dance. And the half dozen treasured Christmas ornaments of Mother's did faintly twinkle in the lamp's glow.

Everyone else now asleep in bed, she sat alone, thinking of Joe. Then Chester. Then Joe. Since having lunch with Joe, she'd been unable to think straight about him. Or Chester. Neither of them would escape from her mind for long. Guilt. Longing. Daydreams of being with one or the other.

She could barely concentrate on what she was doing. Shaking her head as if to drive out her thoughts, she went to bed.

Ruth awoke to the sound of Charlie sobbing.

She hated that Charlie had to awake crying on Christmas Day. When she went to him, he was sitting on the floor near the tree. "What's wrong, Charlie?"

"I miss my daddy. I wish he was here. Remember last Christmas? I got a top. And pick-up sticks. And my erector set. I think all I got under the tree are clothes."

And somehow, all but the erector set had been lost over this past year, with all the moving around, she thought. "I know, son. I wish he was here, too. But he's away for a very good reason. He's helping keep us all safe." He quieted then but sat with a glum face during breakfast and then, again, as they waited for the rest of the Choat family to arrive.

An hour later, Ruth and the family gathered in the living room. The sad look on Charlie's face made her want to cry. He'd perked up a little when Pearl's and Joan's family arrived with gifts and laid them under the tree with those Mother and Papa had placed alongside Ruth's. Everyone found a seat; the adults on chairs and the divan and all the children, except for Joan's youngest, Bertha, sprawled haphazardly on the floor. Charlie scrunched into the corner next to Joan's chair.

After everyone was settled, Bill, Ruth's brother-in-law asked, "Who's going to play Santa Claus?" A chorus of, "I will, I will," erupted from Will, Carl, and Elizabeth.

Ruth looked at Charlie, surprised not to hear him speak up. She said, "How about you, Charlie?"

"Naw, let Elizabeth."

Not waiting to be challenged, Elizabeth jumped to her feet, grabbed a present, and then sang out, "Aunt Pearl."

Everyone watched Pearl unwrap a blouse and then walk over to Joan and kiss her on the cheek. Ruth's spirits dropped when she saw how nice

CHAPTER 24 ◆ RUTH

Joan's present to Pearl was; she hadn't enough money to buy much for anyone there today. But as Bertha squealed in delight at the small baby-doll Ruth gave her, she began to feel happier. Her mood didn't last.

The first gift Charlie opened was a pair of pajamas from Bill and Pearl, and she saw the disappointment he did not try to hide even as he mumbled, "Thank you." Everyone took turns opening their gifts, and, each time it was Charlie's turn, Ruth could once more see disappointment bloom on his face. First a wool hat, next a pair of gloves, and then a wool shirt. When he opened the coat Ruth had bought him, he looked ready to cry. Ruth knew that the family was trying to help her out by getting Charlie things he needed, but right then, she would have preferred they had cared more for what Charlie wanted.

There were only three presents left under the tree when Charlie's name was called, and Elizabeth said, "To Charlie from Joe and Sarah. Have a bang-up Christmas."

When she'd asked Joe what she should get Sarah for Christmas, he'd suggested a nightgown, a blue one—her favorite color—and she'd suggested a shirt for Charlie. She was first surprised and then upset when Charlie unwrapped the box. That turned to relief and gratefulness when his face lit up like the Christmas bulbs in Hobart's Five and Dime window display.

From the box, he pulled out a toy gun. He waved it around his head pulling the trigger over and over again, yelling, "I got a gun. I got a gun."

Her brother-in-law George picked up the discarded box and pulled out a half-inch-wide roll of paper. "Bring that over here, Charlie," George said. "I'll bet it'll pop louder if we put this ammunition in it." Taking the gun from Charlie, he opened a panel on the side of the gun, placed the small roll of paper inside, and fed the loose end through an opening in front of the hammer head. "Try it now, Charlie." Charlie pulled the trigger, which cocked the hammer back, and then released it. The loud pop that followed when the hammer hit the paper and punched out a confetti-sized piece of it, made Charlie laugh out loud. He pulled the trigger again and again, each time advancing the paper in position for another shot that forcefully ejected small pieces of white paper that floated gently to the floor. Charlie's Uncle Bill laughed out loud and said, "You'd think it's Christmas with all this paper snow falling."

"Let me try. Let me try," all four cousins pleaded, but Charlie only pointed the gun at the ceiling, at the walls, and at the floor, pop, pop, popping the gun and sending confetti flying in all directions. The glum face he'd brought to the gift-laden room had disappeared, his unhappiness lost in the furious gunfire.

When the first roll of paper was exhausted, George loaded it with another, but before Charlie could start shooting again, his grandmother commanded, "Take that outside right now," though there was a half-smile on her usually grim face.

Charlie and all four cousins charged out the door with shouts of, "Let me try. Give me a turn. Don't be stingy."

Joe knew she didn't like the idea of Charlie having a gun, even a play one. But he'd made his point several weeks before when he'd said to her, "Guns are something every boy wants, and if you don't let 'em have one, then it makes them want them all the more. And besides, he can always use his finger to shoot with. It's just more fun with a toy." And he had given one to Charlie. *Thank goodness he had*, Ruth thought, *or Charlie's Christmas would have been a total disappointment.*

The gun popped almost every minute of the next day or two as Charlie, slogging through the snow, shot at Japs sneaking around the back corners of the house, or hiding behind the wash house waiting for one of the family to arrive there to separate the milk, or even waiting in the outhouse where, he said, "A Jap might shoot you while you're doing your business." The constant fire fight almost drove her to distraction. To defend herself, Ruth sent him to the barn, saying, "I think it's likely there's a lot more Japs hiding out there. Go see if you can shoot them before they steal the eggs of that old hen that's been laying them up in the hayloft." *Thank the*

Lord, she said aloud when he'd charged off the porch and made a beeline for the barn, killing more Japs as he kicked up plumes of snow.

*

New Year's Eve came and went with very little said about the holiday in the Choat family. Ruth made no resolutions but managed to wish everyone Happy New Year and let it go at that. January was ushered in with bitter cold, and the long days crept by so slowly Ruth thought they would never end. Her mood was cold and despairing as the weather outside, and she couldn't stop dwelling on the memory of a year ago, when Chester was arrested for fighting and had to enlist. Memories of that awful day he was arrested and then what followed, plagued her, particularly in her dreams. Or were they nightmares? She believed she would go crazy if she didn't leave the house to pick up Charlie from school. She made a point of also picking up Sarah, so she had an excuse to stop and visit with Joe. With him, she felt her unhappiness fade into the background. She loved watching Joe be with Charlie. He was so much more patient and helpful than Chester ever was. He fixed Charlie's pop-gun when it stopped working right. He helped him with a math problem that Sarah wasn't able to solve, either.

She grew to love Sarah—and wished she were the daughter Ruth had wanted but not had. She helped Sarah make up a box supper, and, when she, Charlie, and all the people living within five or so miles of the Babbs School gathered for the auction, she encouraged Charlie to bid on it. They were all four happy when he won the bidding and paid with some of the money he'd made pulling bolls; he outbid two of her other admirers. Made her think of the time Chester had outbid Papa. She, or more likely Joe, would have loaned him more if he'd needed it to outbid the others, though they didn't tell him so. She and Joe had decided ahead of time it might not be seemly for Joe to bid on her box, though she really wanted him to. She barely knew the two men who bid on hers, one an old bachelor and the other a widower and the one who won the bid for her box super. He was a quiet man, who, like Joe, had lost his wife to cancer and took the opportunity to tell her about it. It was sad. Sad, too, for his two adolescent sons, though they both looked satisfied with the young women whose boxes they had won. She wondered if he'd heard the rumors about her and Joe. If he had, there was no hint of it from him.

On a freezing-cold day in the second week of February, three days before Valentine's Day, and a few days after the box supper, Ruth sat in Joe's kitchen drinking hot chocolate with him when Charlie and Sarah came stomping into the room, snow still clinging to their hair and coats. They were red in the face from trudging the quarter of a mile from the school.

"Hot chocolate," yelled Charlie.

"Can we have some, Daddy?"

Ten minutes later, between sips of hot chocolate, the two sat by the iron stove in the setting room drawing and discarding Old Maid cards while Ruth tried to keep a neutral conversation going with Joe. Make small talk.

"One of those cock-eyed calves of mine managed to get tangled up in my barbed wire fence," Joe said. "I almost froze to death trying to cut it loose."

"Would you believe a coyote came near Papa's barn?" she asked. "The cold weather's making it bad for all those poor outdoor animals."

Yes, small talk. The two children playing nearby made her feel awkward. Both of them were too apt to pick up on her growing feeling of comfort being with Joe. And likely what he was feeling as well.

Joe picked up the *Hobart Star* lying in a chair sitting by the table. She thought he might have read about someone they knew being in the hospital, having a relative come in from the city to visit, a marriage, an engagement, or a birth like that of Alice's. Instead, he spoke of the war,

CHAPTER 24 • RUTH

"Looks like the Germans captured Anzio beachhead. They're throwing everything they have at it."

"Is there anything about us fighting the Japs in the paper?" Charlie called out.

Ruth had hoped he hadn't heard Joe's remark. When the war was mentioned in Charlie's presence, he always asked about the South Pacific. Ruth didn't like it that Chester now crept into the room and sat with her, Joe, and the kids. She reached, took the paper from Joe, and said, "No, it's about the Germans." *Only a small, very white lie*, she told herself.

"Sarah wants to show me the new kittens in the barn. Can I go see?"

"Okay. Take off. But we have to leave in a few minutes. I have to help Mother with supper."

The two friends flew back out into the cold, not bothering to button up their coats. Ruth smiled and turned her gaze on Joe, ready to say something about the kittens but stopped on seeing that his face had grown sober, and his eyes thoughtful. He held her gaze for what seemed forever before speaking.

"You know, Ruth. I've been thinking. I'd like to take you to dinner for Valentine's Day." The shocked look on her face must have given him a second thought. While she tried to sputter out an answer, he began to backpedal. "It doesn't have to be on Valentine's Day, Ruth. It's just—I'd like to do something nice for you." He shook his head. "I'm not handling this very well."

Ruth felt a rush of guilt—and longing. Then more guilt for the longing. She should say "No," but she said nothing as Joe sat there, his face growing red with embarrassment.

"Are you going to say anything, Ruth?"

She had to clear her throat before she answered, "I'd love to go, but I don't know how we could get away without causing a storm. Somebody is sure to see us again. Papa's getting awful testy about us. And if he hears I went to dinner with you, he'll blow his top."

"True. But look at it this way. We're friends. Have known each other since we were kids. Went out for a few times before you fell for Chester. We're two adults."

"All true. But people living around here, and our parents, don't look at it that way. They just see a married woman hanging around a widower. Cheating on her husband. Her husband who is overseas risking his life to help protect this country."

"I know that. But Chester left a woman in this community with a baby girl. They could think he ran off to the war to get away from that."

"Rules are different for men than women, Joe. You can get away with running around with me. I can't get away being seen with you."

Followed by freezing arctic cold, Charlie and Sarah burst into the room, and then, with noisy energy, Sarah shouted. "Guess what, daddy? The kittens have their eyes open."

"I hope you didn't handle them too much. That old barn cat might just abandon them if you did," Joe cautioned.

"We didn't even touch them," Charlie said.

"Good for you. How was school, today?" Joe ruffled Charlie's hair. "Did you two learn anything? Stay out of trouble?"

Before Charlie could answer, Sarah spoke up, and the excitement in her eyes seemed to sparkle. "Aunt Ruth! Corky got his two friends to help him beat up Charlie after school, but Carl and Will, Jr. wouldn't let 'em. Corky wouldn't fight Charlie. The big fat coward ran off with his two friends!"

Joe grinned and started to say something but remained quiet when Ruth looked at him, pleading with her eyes not to encourage Charlie any more than smiling at him. He lost the smile and said nothing more.

"I'm glad your two cousins stepped in," Ruth said. "And that you didn't get into a fight, Charlie." Charlie stayed quiet—happy, she was sure, that he hadn't been scolded.

"Why don't you two go on in the other room and play some more Old Maid," Joe said. "Ruth and I have some things to talk over."

CHAPTER 24 ✦ RUTH

Ruth felt her stomach tighten. She did not want to finish the conversation with Joe. Standing up, she said, "We've got to go now, Joe. Charlie, get your coat back on."

"Do I have to?" Charlie whined.

"Does he have to?" Sarah repeated, her pretty face losing its glow of excitement.

"Yes."

"Could Sarah come with us and have supper?" Charlie pleaded.

Ruth paused, not sure how her folks would feel about her bringing Sarah to supper. "I'm not sure," she said. Your grandpa might not want me to use the car again today."

"I'll drive down and pick her up after supper," Joe promised.

Feeling trapped, but not wanting to deal with the two children's disappointment, Ruth said, "Okay then, Sarah. Charlie. Let's go."

They pulled their coats on, burst out the door together, and piled into the back seat of the car.

Joe walked her to the door, and they stood together for a heartbeat, as Joe said, "Please think about Valentine's Day dinner, Ruth."

She gazed up at him but had to look away, certain that the passion and desire in his eyes might weaken her resolve. Had the children not called to her, "Hurry up. Hurry up. It's cold out here," she might have given in and told him she would go to dinner.

Her mind roiling with desire, guilt, and rebellion—and a car full of youthful chatter and excitement—Ruth drove to her folks' home.

When they arrived at the front porch, stomping snow from their boots, Papa opened the door and glared at her. "Took you long enough to go get Charlie," he said.

"Sarah and Charlie were playing, and so I invited Sarah for dinner."

Papa held the door open for them without another word, a scowl darkening his face. Though chilled from the frigid night, Ruth boiled with humiliation and guilt. She hated that Papa's sour expression deprived her of pleasure and left only the shame. She wished she could dismiss his disapproval and shake it off like she had the snow from her boots.

*

The next day, Ruth moped about, and, when it was time to pick up Charlie from school, she resisted leaving early and stopping to visit with Joe. There was a devil sitting on one of her shoulders and an angel on the other, arguing incessantly. "You should go," the tempter would say. "No," her conscience would say, "It's wrong of you." She wasn't sure how long this debate would go on but hoped that her sisters Joan and Pearl would help quiet one or the other.

On Saturday, while Charlie was trudging the snowy streets of Hobart selling his stamps, Mother was with her own mother, and Papa was at the domino parlor, Ruth joined her two sisters in Joan's living room. She and Pearl fussed over Joan's daughters, Elizabeth and Bertha, and, then, after final hugs by Ruth and sister Pearl, the two girls were led to their bedroom for a nap. Ruth loved her little nieces, but, today, seeing how cute and lovable they were, she thought of Alice's and Chester's new daughter. It made her want to cry. Agitated, she paced the room.

"Can't you sit still for a minute, Ruth?" Pearl patted the couch seat and held out her hand.

"I've a lot on my mind, and I can't seem to set still." Opening up to Pearl wasn't something Ruth wanted to do until Joan came back out from the girls' bedroom.

As soon as Joan stepped back into the room and quietly closed the door to the children's room, she walked over, took Ruth's hand, and led her to the couch. Ruth felt like she was five years old and ready to cry.

"Okay, Ruth, what is it you need to talk to us about? You've been skittish as a young mare ever since you walked in the door and said you had something to ask us."

CHAPTER 24 ✦ RUTH

"I'm guessing it's more about Chester. Or Joe Williams," Pearl said, the stern line of her mouth reminding Ruth of their mother.

Feeling the rising heat in her face as she spoke, Ruth blurted out, "Joe asked me to go to dinner with him to celebrate Valentine's Day."

Pearl's eyebrows rose, and she was quick to say, "I hope you didn't say, 'Yes.'"

"Well, I hope she did," Joan said, smiling from ear to ear.

Ruth straightened one of the crocheted doilies on the arm of the couch and shook her head, wanting to deny the dueling impulses within her. Deny the turmoil her desire for keeping company with Joe had dragged her into.

"Can you imagine the stink that would cause?" Pearl asked, frowning.

"Look, you two. I didn't say 'Yes.' Don't you realize I know how it would appear to anyone who saw us together? Papa already thinks I'm spending too much time at Joe's house letting the kids play."

"Well, I still think you should say, 'Yes,'" Joan said, frowning back at Pearl.

Both her sisters continued to frown but said nothing. A nervous stillness flooded the room, but Ruth couldn't stand the quietness or the tension that was choking her. She took a deep breath and said, "I really care for Joe. He's been so decent to me and helpful with Charlie."

"There's more decency in his little finger than in Chester's whole body," Joan said.

Pearl began to look around the room as if she had lost something, and then she said, "You know, I've been mad at Joe ever since he threw me over. I was so taken by him when I was young. Maybe I'm just a little jealous, Ruth. Chester is no-account, but I'd still worry about what will happen if you keep this up with Joe."

"Please don't say anything more about Chester. With all his faults, I still love the man. And he is Charlie's father."

"And he's having a baby with Alice Jenson," Joan curled her lip as she spat that out.

The room grew quiet then as her sisters sat with eyes cast down, surely, Ruth thought, mulling over what had just been said. Joan's last comment had driven the naked truth home to her. Chester was likely to abandon her and Charlie. Alice was ten years younger than her. Was a good-time girl, from all she'd heard about her. Alice liked to go out dancing and drinking, two things Chester insisted on doing, and which Ruth detested. Joe really liked her. Was courting her. Was a homebody just like her and who would put her first. Not carouse with every female that took his fancy. Taking another deep breath and looking up at her sisters, Ruth said, "All things being said and done, I want to go to dinner with Joe. Get away from all my worry and sweat from living with Papa and Mother. Stop thinking about Chester, Alice, and their baby. I just don't feel right about it." She took a deep breath, slowly let it out, and then said, "But I want to do it."

She stood and reached for Joan's hand and then Pearl's. "I really want to get away for the evening with Joe. Would you two help me?"

Pearl looked as though she was about to cry, her eyes bright and her face flushed red. Ruth knew Pearl well enough to guess she was not happy being asked for help with Joe.

"How?" asked Joan, without any hesitation.

"Just help me get away from Charlie, Mother, and Papa for an evening. Not let them know the real reason. I'm not sure I could stand living another day with them if they knew. Mother would wear disapproval on her face from sunup to sundown, and Papa wouldn't stop carping at me."

"I don't know how we could exactly do that," said Pearl. "You'd have to have a good reason to leave Charlie behind or he'll throw a wall-eyed fit. And they'll all three pester you to death about what you'd be doing."

A growing pressure, like a tight fist clutching at her heart, made her want to cry. Hopelessness of arranging to have dinner with Joe overwhelmed her, and she began to cry.

CHAPTER 24 • RUTH

Pearl started shedding tears as well, and then, squeezing Ruth's hand, said "I don't feel exactly right about this, Ruth, but I'll help figure something out."

"This is a no-brainer," said Joan. "We're sitting right here together, and nobody knows or cares what we're doing. Why can't we do the same thing? Minus you, of course, Ruth."

Ruth didn't immediately get what Joan was saying; she was too wrapped up in her misery to think straight. When it dawned on her, she wiped at her tears, and the fist gripping her heart relaxed its grip. "Bless you, Joan. You will go along with this, Pearl?"

"I'm not going to go telling fibs to Mother and Papa," Pearl said, her face hardening into a frown.

"You wouldn't have to say anything to them, Pearl," Joan said. "Just say you're going into town to visit me and you're dropping by to pick Ruth up. They don't have to know you'll be dropping her off at Joe's place and picking her up on the way back home. You can do that, can't you?"

Ruth's heart was beating so hard she could feel it in her throat as she waited for Pearl to answer the question.

It seemed like a lifetime before Pearl's stony face began to relax and for her to say, "I can do that. But I still don't like it."

Ruth threw her arms around Pearl's neck, pulled her into a hard embrace, and whispered, "Thank you, Thank you. Thank you."

"You've got to go someplace where it's not likely anyone you know will see you," Joan said.

"Of course, sister. We'll do that." The tears coming to Ruth's eyes were tears of relief. "I can't wait to tell Joe what we've hatched up."

CHAPTER 25

Ruth

⇢ ❋ ⇠

*J*oe grinned ear-to-ear when Ruth outlined Joan's, Pearl's, and her plan. They decided the middle of the week would work best and settled on Tuesday night, the day after Valentine's Day. "I'll leave Sarah with her grandparents and pick her up early the next morning to get her to school. Her grandparents are always delighted to have her for an evening. Sarah will be happy, too. And I can only be hopeful none of the three will be too curious."

On Tuesday, seated at the small vanity in her room, Ruth carefully applied a touch of rouge to her cheeks and applied a new lipstick. Done, she gazed at the image looking back at her from the mirror. She remembered looking in this same mirror years ago and seeing a pretty woman in her teens who was slim and whose soft, brown eyes did not have lines at their corners. Her once-slim young body had thickened, and she'd put

CHAPTER 25 • RUTH

on twenty or so pounds. She wasn't fat but...? She was on her way. She bared her teeth at the mirror in a false smile that showed a mouthful of ivory white teeth. *At least my teeth are even and white*, she thought, *and I still have most of them.* She knew women who at her age already had false teeth. *Thirty-five*, she thought. *How did I get to be thirty-five?*

The sound of car tires crunching on the drive signaled Pearl's arrival. Standing quickly and grabbing her coat, she cleared the lump that had clutched at her throat and headed for the door. *If only I can get out of here without Mother and Papa making a fuss or asking too many questions*, she thought. Papa had gone down to do evening chores, and her mother was busy in the wash house. Pearl had wisely arranged for Charlie to come to her house after school and spend the night with his two cousins. Ruth had told Mama and Papa the little white lie that she and her sisters had cooked up. Half running to the car, she piled in with Pearl, and they were out on the road in seconds. All the snow had melted, leaving a landscape of barren cotton stalks. Ruth thought, *A night like this deserves springtime and a green earth.* But the thought was banished, and her tension mounted as they neared Joe's farm. When she spoke to Pearl, it sounded to her a little like a frog's croak. "I'm afraid I'm losing my voice."

"Just nerves, Ruth. You'll be all right as soon as you and Joe are together for a few minutes."

When she saw Joe waiting for her in the gathering twilight, standing on his side porch, leaning against one of the posts that held up the roof, she thought her heart would burst out of her chest. Instead, it lodged in her throat.

As she scooted out of the car, Joe stepped down off the porch, walked over, placed his hand on top of the car, bent down, and said, "Howdy, Pearl. I appreciate you helping us out like this. Thank you."

"You better wait to thank me, Joe. Papa hears about this, you may find out I didn't help at all," Pearl said, and then turned the car about and drove away toward Hobart without another word.

Straightening up, Joe turned to Ruth and said, "I'm so glad to see you." He half-smiled, and, like a teenager unsure of what to do next, stood scuffling his feet on the graveled driveway. "I'm so glad this worked out."

"I'm glad too, Joe," Ruth said. Then, her throat constricted, and she couldn't force another word from out of her mouth. Neither of them were able to break the awkward silence that followed. Ruth had the irrational thought that she should turn, run to the road, and hightail it all the way back to her parents' house. But then, Joe stepped closer, took her elbow, and guided her to his car, where, smiling broadly, he opened the passenger door. As she climbed inside, her spine stiffened, and her hands trembled. She could still think of nothing to say as Joe fired up the car and started it rolling toward the road.

"I'm not sure why things are so awkward for me," Joe said. "I was fine until about ten minutes ago. Then all my courage just up and vanished out the front door."

"I lost mine when I got out of bed this morning. Having a date is a lot different than that spur-of-the-moment lunch we had. Or when we are visiting with Sarah and Charlie around. It's scared me to death."

Joe laughed. "I wish it didn't. But it does me, too."

"Since I married Chester, I've never done anything like this. It feels so strange. And scary."

"Yes, it does. Same with me and Theresa. And ever since she passed, I haven't dated, either. Unless you count us sitting at my kitchen table or on my front porch."

"Or maybe that lunch we had?"

Joe shrugged but said nothing more, and they rode without speaking for a few minutes, nothing breaking the silence but the sound of gravel occasionally kicking up against the underside of the car. Ruth was glad it was Joe who broke the silence.

"Any trouble getting away from Charlie and your parents?"

CHAPTER 25 ♦ RUTH

"No. Papa didn't say anything. I think Mother was just short of asking to come along with Pearl and me. That would have sure put a damper on our plans. Thank goodness she tired herself out today and wanted to stay home. Charlie got to go spend the night at Pearl's. What about Sarah?"

"I drove her into her grandparents after school. No problem there." After another awkward silence, Joe continued, "Speaking of Sarah, I have to admit that I was thinking about her mother earlier today and started feeling a little guilty. After Theresa passed away, I couldn't get interested in anyone else. You're the first woman I really wanted to spend time with. But I guess, right now, I'm wondering what she'd say about you and me being out together."

Ruth laughed, thinking she must come across like a thirteen-year-old on her first date.

Young. Nervous. Naive. "I'm sorry. I didn't mean to laugh, but I do that sometimes when I'm scared. I had the same kind of thoughts about Chester. What would he say? I don't think it would be very pleasant. He'd fly off the handle."

"I can tell you what Theresa told me when she was real sick and knew she was dying. She wanted me to find someone else after she was gone. Someone to be a mother to Sarah."

"You think she wanted that someone else to be a married woman?"

He didn't answer her. They reached Babbs School and turned south onto the blacktop. Then the only sound was the gentle swishing of the tires on the smooth road. Ruth was thankful that they'd left the awful racket of the gravel hitting up under the car.

Joe was quiet for a few minutes more and then said, "I kind of hoped Theresa and Chester wouldn't ride along with us tonight, but I guess that's too much to hope for."

"That is hoping a lot." Ruth said, wondering if the two of them would ever get over the feeling that Chester and Theresa were shadowing them. There had been times when she and Joe were sitting in his kitchen, waiting for the kids, when she had forgotten Chester and Theresa for a bit. She hoped that would happen tonight. "Where are we going? I hope it isn't too far. I can't be out late."

"Cooperton. There's a nice little restaurant there. Not too fancy, but the steaks and pork chops are good. And I really like their chicken fried steak. More important, it's twenty miles away, and I don't think anyone from around Hobart is likely to be there. And I think we can get you back in plenty of time."

"Having a curfew makes me feel like a kid again."

"If we were back when we were kids, we'd be riding in a buggy. Twenty miles would've taken us three or four hours and the same getting back. Instead of coming to Cooperton, my old horse would have just trotted us off to the mountains, where we'd go picnicking. Well, not in this weather. I'm happy we're going to a restaurant tonight."

"That's so," Ruth said. But the mention of the horse and buggy brought back the story she had told Charlie back a few months ago. A picture of her and Chester rolling around in the mud flashed across her consciousness, and her whole body went rigid again. Taking a deep breath, she pressed her back hard against the seat, wishing her tension would drain away.

Joe kept to the enforced speed limit, and it seemed to Ruth that it took forever to reach Cooperton, even though they weren't riding in a buggy. There was a long silence then—neither she nor Joe finding the words to express the mix of feelings and memories stirring in them. Her throat was so tight, she wasn't sure she'd be able to swallow anything after they got to the restaurant. Joe's stomach growled once, and she thought, *That's not from hunger. He's as uptight as I am.*

Breaking the silence, Joe said, "I wanted to give you a Valentine, but I figured that was not such a good idea. I hope you see dinner tonight as my Valentine."

"Yes. But I don't have one to give you."

"Just being with me is a great Valentine, Ruth."

CHAPTER 25 • RUTH

Before she could think of something to say to that, they turned off the highway onto the gravel road leading to Cooperton, and it wasn't long until they entered the outskirts of town. Ruth read a small sign beside the road: Cooperton, population 193. They passed a cotton mill and then a cigar factory, and, as they drove past a large rock building, Joe said, "That's the Cooperton Valley High School and gymnasium. I've driven over a couple of times to watch Hobart play basketball." After passing four churches and entering downtown, they parked in front of a store with a sign across the front announcing, "Huber's Drugstore." As they walked past a small building that housed Eberhard's General Store and a post office, Joe took her arm as they walked across the street. He held it as they approached the restaurant that huddled between a bank with a cornerstone boasting the building was built in 1925, and the Jefferson Hotel, with a sign in the window that advertised rooms for rent. She blushed when the thought occurred to her that, if anyone saw them, they might think they were staying overnight in the hotel. Her face grew warm with the thought. *I'm glad Joe is not looking at me. Or reading my mind.*

As they entered the almost-empty restaurant, the few people there turned to see who the arrivals were. That happened, Ruth knew, when strangers entered a small downtown restaurant where everybody knew each other. Still, she was relieved when, as one, they all turned away, satisfied that she and Joe were not one of their neighbors, relatives, or friends. The warm inviting smell of chicken fried steak filled the air, and, despite the anxiety roiling her insides, Ruth felt pangs of hunger.

The restaurant was a nicer one than they'd gone to for lunch in Rocky. It was newly painted, and though the tables and chairs were worn, the upholstery of the booth they sat in looked shiny new. The oak flooring was scrubbed clean. One wall was decorated with photographs of the early days of Cooperton, and, on another, there was a large scene of a creek-side stand of trees as background for a cotton field dotted with people bending to pull bolls. It was pretty but too much a reminder of the days this past summer when she'd bent to the work. They took seats as far from the others as possible. The booth was next to a window looking out over the street and across the way a building with a large sign proclaimed *The Banner*.

A woman of indeterminable age, dressed in a worn blue cotton dress, was standing behind a counter reading a copy of *The Banner*. Ruth saw a large, front-page picture of some war scene, a reminder of Chester she didn't want. She pushed it out of her mind when the waitress laid down the paper, came to their booth, and poured them ice water. The bib of the white apron she was wearing was decorated with embroidered blue daisies and several small coffee stains. Her hands were knotted with arthritis, but she easily wielded the lead pencil as she took their orders.

Ruth wasn't surprised when Joe ordered the chicken fried steak he'd praised on their drive over. Her stomach was so fluttery now that the thought of steak made her feel queasy. "Just give me the baked chicken and mashed potatoes," she said to the waitress.

While they waited for their food, Ruth's mind kept returning to thoughts of Chester that *The Banner* had stirred up. She tried to push them away and concentrate on Joe talking about his parents giving him their four-hundred-and-eighty acres to farm when they'd moved to town four years earlier—small talk. Something for them to do while they waited.

When the food came, she forked a piece of chicken but then laid it down and looked out the window at a passing car. *Am I making a big mistake?* she wondered.

Joe put down his fork, a generous piece of chicken fried steak still attached to it, and asked, "Is something wrong, Ruth?" He reached across the table and took her hand.

Joe's touch felt hot, like something that could burn her if she let his hand stay on hers. But then chills and goosebumps crowded her arms, and the heat fled. She pulled her hand away. "I'm sorry, Joe. It's just that I wonder if this is the right thing to do. Those thoughts turned my appetite

CHAPTER 25 ✦ RUTH

off." She picked up her fork and again pushed the food about on her plate. "I wish those thoughts would all go away. That all the thoughts about Chester and Alice would also just go away."

"Well, I sure can understand that."

"Here I am with you in a town where nobody knows us, and she's living in a community with everyone knowing she was with Chester. And is pregnant by him. How could they have been so careless? And if Chester abandons her and the baby, what then? What will people think?"

Joe sat still, his brow wrinkled and, for a moment, his eyes closed, as if he didn't want to see what she was worried so much about. "You've got a lot on your mind, Ruth. I'm sorry if this wasn't a good idea."

"It was a good idea. But I feel like a bad person to be here with you." She put her hands in her lap.

"I have to admit that I feel a little guilty myself what with Chester being overseas fighting the Japs while I sit here all safe and sound with you. Do you want to go?"

She didn't want to go. She wanted to stop thinking about Alice and her baby and about being a cheating wife. She wanted to feel sure of herself and enjoy a meal with Joe. Enjoy Joe. She looked across at him and saw his brow furrowed in . . . what? Doubt? Hurt? She felt a rush of pity for him—and for herself. Taking a deep breath, she reached for his hand, took it in both of hers, and said, "No, I want to just sit for a moment and pull myself together. I really want to be with you. To sit here and enjoy this good-smelling food. To see you smile again."

He nodded and the ghost of a smile flitted across his face. "So, let's see if we can do that."

*

"Joe, we're going to be late. We should have started back sooner. I'm afraid Pearl will have given up on me and gone on home."

Joe sped up past the thirty-mile-per-hour speed limit, but, as each mile seemed to crawl by, the pulse in her neck quickened, and her throat grew tighter. When they sped past Babbs Switch and a red light flashed behind them, she almost wept.

"And I thought I was buying us time," Joe said, shaking his head as he pulled to the side of the road, stopped, and cranked down his side window.

Turning in her seat, Ruth watched the uniformed highway patrol officer slowly unbend himself from the black-and-white cruiser and saunter up to the window.

"May I see your driver's license, please?" he said to Joe. Then, shining his flashlight on the license and then on Joe's face, he said, "You realize, Mr. Williams, that you were going fifteen miles over the speed limit?"

Joe shook his head as he replied, "Yes, officer. Guess I got in too big a hurry to get home."

"Wait here while I go back to my car," the officer said, and then he turned and sauntered back to the cruiser.

The minutes passing seemed hours to Ruth. Every second ticking by was one too many. *Pearl will have given up and gone on home by now.* "I'm so sorry I didn't tell you to slow down, Joe. This is taking longer than if we'd kept under the speed limit."

"You're not to blame. It was me who decided to speed."

The officer returned and handed Joe a ticket. "There's a good reason the speed limit is thirty miles per hour, Mr. Williams. There's a war going on. Our boys overseas need gas."

"Yes, sir, officer. I agree. It won't happen again."

The officer nodded and returned to his cruiser as Joe pulled slowly back onto the highway and drove thirty miles an hour all the way to his house.

As they pulled into his farmyard and stopped, the headlights lit up the front porch where she and Joe had sat so many times before, waiting for school to be out and the two kids to come running into the yard. Joe's barn lurked in the background, its dark shadow outlined against the sky.

CHAPTER 25 ✦ RUTH

Pearl's car was nowhere to be seen. "You'll have to drive me on down to Papa's, Joe, and I'll have to hope he and Mother are sound asleep."

"Since we're already late," Joe said, "we might as well sit for a spell. I'll leave the heater on." He reached down, switched off the lights, and leaned back in the seat.

CHAPTER 26

Chester

As the rain sheeted down on his tent with no letup, Chester pulled himself awake from a fitful night's sleep. His clothes were soaked with his own sweat; he might as well have been sleeping outside in the rain. *Hell,* he thought, *if I were back home, it would be a welcome thirty-, forty-, fifty-, or sixty-degree day, and maybe there'd be some snowdrifts that hadn't melted away. That wasn't unusual in February. It sure as hell wouldn't be raining cats and dogs.* Drawn by the smell of coffee, he dressed, put on a slicker, sloshed through the puddles and mud to the mess hall, grabbed some coffee, and found an empty table. Breathing deeply, he drew in the rich fumes of the coffee, hoping it would clear the cobwebs from his mind. Alice's letter telling him she'd had a baby girl ruined his sleep. All night long, he awoke again and again to dreams of Alice, or Ruth, or Charlie.

CHAPTER 26 ♦ CHESTER

For God's sake, he thought, *I can't have a two-month-old little bastard named Bethany.* But he did.

During the day, working his tail off, sweating and cursing, he could forget all that. But it came to him in the middle of the night. Hell, it came to him all night long, sometimes as a nightmare. There would be Alice, Bethany, Ruth, and Charlie all together with him in a room. Or sometimes they would be standing on either side of a road through this goddamn jungle with Jap bombs falling or Jap planes screaming in low to strafe while he tried to get them all to safety. Sometimes trying to save them all, sometimes only Ruth and Charlie, and sometimes only Alice and Bethany. Then he'd awaken slick with guilty sweat and not be able to go back to sleep for what seemed hours.

He sipped at the hot water they'd dropped a few coffee beans in and called coffee. The promise given by its smell was bullshit. Draining the cup, he sat staring into a knothole in the wood-plank table, trying unsuccessfully to make his mind blank. Hunger pangs refused to give him solitude, so he returned to the food station, served himself more coffee and something he couldn't identify, though he suspected it was a substitute for scrambled eggs. He wolfed it down and then went back to staring into his empty cup.

Hough slapped him on the back and said, "Get your butt up, and go to work. That damn airfield isn't built soon, the Japs will be all over us."

"Damn you, Hough," he shouted. "Don't do that."

"I won't. Not till next time."

Shaking his head as if to rid himself of his irritation, Chester stood and trudged off after Hough. On the beach, he began the endless task of helping unload incoming boats or making short trips in his truck to ferry supplies to the edge of the jungle. Later in the morning, he was drafted to help hand-carry supplies farther into the jungle and onto the airstrip the Sea Bees were repairing. He was glad the Japs had begun building the field before the Marines landed, so now he and the others had less work finishing it. He grew sick of carrying Marston matting and laying it in place so planes could land without sinking up to their fuselage in mud. But, he thought, it would be finished none too soon; he wanted the air cover. It was a welcome relief when he was put to work driving a captured Japanese bulldozer to lengthen and widen the field.

Halfway through the day, he barely heard the distant roar of airplane engines when someone yelled, "Run for cover!" Jumping off the bulldozer, he took off for the foxholes hidden beneath the trees.

Looking back over his shoulder as he ran, Chester saw Polk, who had been working fifty feet farther from the trees. Polk was running to head off a bulldozer lumbering toward the ocean shore. He was waving his arms and screaming at the driver, "Jack, get the hell out of there. Run for cover!" But not hearing over the racket of the dozer's engine, Jack kept driving on the open sand toward the ocean where the lighters were unloading.

Diving into his foxhole, Chester peered through the trees and saw Polk give up getting Jack's attention and run for the foxholes. He was almost off the beach when the earth heaved and the blast sent Polk rolling across the sand. A bomb landed near another big machine, and it reared up before landing on one of the Sea Bees. Another bomb landed near a Marine running for cover, and Chester saw the man's arms land twenty feet away. Further back in the jungle, a fuel dump suddenly erupted in flames, but the force and heat of the explosions rolled harmlessly over Chester, who now lay sprawled in the bottom of his foxhole. The engine noise of the bombers grew fainter as they flew away. Chester again looked over the edge of his foxhole and saw that Jack's bulldozer lay pulverized, parts of it scattered down the beach.

He then saw Jap fighters approaching, coming in low, strafing the open beach where scores of men were still lying. He ducked back into his foxhole as bullets kicked up sand all along the tree line. A cache of ammunition went off nearby, the noise exploding into his left eardrum, deafening him. When the fighters had roared by, he looked out again

CHAPTER 26 ♦ CHESTER

and saw Polk still alive on the beach but staggering around, falling, and then struggling to pull himself to his feet. Giving up, he used his arms to drag himself toward the foxholes. He moved forward only a few feet before he slumped face-down on the sand.

"Jesus, God Almighty," Chester yelled as he saw the Jap fighter planes making a steep turn to come in for another pass. He scrambled out of the foxhole and ran to Polk, grabbed his shoulder, and shook him. "Polk," he yelled and grabbed the man under the arms and tried to help him stand.

Polk's face and hands were slick with sweat and his own blood. He looked up at Chester and said, "Shit, man. What're you doing?" The words came out like they were bubbling through water, and his confused eyes held hostile recognition as he rolled over onto his back.

"Trying to help get you off the beach, you sorry son-of-a-bitch," Chester yelled, grabbing the man under his armpits.

The rattle of Jap planes' machine guns from farther down the beach seemed to penetrate Polk's confusion, and, with Chester's help, he lurched to his feet. Chester half-carried, half-dragged him into the cover of the trees, pushed him into a foxhole, and tumbled in after. The deafening roar of Jap fighter planes deafened Chester, and the rapid fire of their machine guns tore at the beach where he and Polk had been seconds ago. He lay back and held his hands over his ears as more detonating bombs peppered the machines still sitting in the lighters offshore. The soggy earth quivered like jelly with each bomb blast. Polk's eyes closed, and Chester thought he had had died. Then he heard screams of pain coming from the beach.

Chester glanced out over the edge of the foxhole and saw another Sea Bee trying to crawl to the shelter of the trees and foxholes. For a second, Chester wondered how in the hell the man had lived through all the strafing and bombing. "The poor son-of-a-bitch isn't going to live through another pass by the Jap planes," Chester muttered and then ran out onto the beach. Helping the injured man onto his knees, Chester pulled a bloody left arm around his neck, encircled the body with his other arm, and dragged the wounded Sea Bee back to the foxhole. As he laid him alongside Polk, all hell broke loose on the beach. Chester held both arms over his head and started breathing hard. His guts were roiling, he was light-headed, and his heart was pounding.

When the noise of the guns and bombs stopped, Chester sat up and saw Polk's dark eyes staring at him. "You okay, Polk?"

"Hell, no. I can't think straight."

Chester then turned and looked at the blood oozing from the other injured man's leg wound and yelled, "Medic." No one came. "Damn. I think they're all dead." Chester tore the man's belt from around his waist, wrapped it around the upper thigh and pulled it tight, stopping the deep welling up of blood from the man's shattered shin bone.

With what sounded like the whining motors of a thousand aircraft, the sky came alive. Looking up, he saw American fighter planes finally engaged with the Jap fighters.

"What the hell's happening?" Polk said, his words thick as molasses and barely audible in the screaming whine of aircraft motors and rat-a-tat of machine guns.

"You damn near bought it out there on the beach, is what happened," Chester yelled. "I had to drag your ass to the foxhole here before it was shot to hell by the Japs."

The sky quieted as the Zeros turned tail with the Americans hot after them. "Knowing you, I figure you'd leave me out there," Polk said, shaking his head as if in disbelief of Chester saving him.

"When I saw you lying out there in the open, I considered it for a second," Chester said. "But then I thought, we need every man we got to clean up the goddamn mess the Japs are making."

Still dazed, Polk sat up and began shaking his head as if to clear away the fog swirling at the edges of his mind. "I shouldn't have taken time to run to that damn bulldozer. Should have known that'd be the

CHAPTER 26 ✦ CHESTER

first damn thing those bombers'd aim for. I wanted to warn Jack. Poor bastard's probably blown into a million pieces. Won't be anything left of him to bury."

"What about Hough? You see him out there anywhere?" Chester asked.

"No, they sent him in the truck to the airfield with another load of matting."

"Jesus Christ, I hope he's okay," Chester said and then took Polk's arm, helped him to his feet, and led him to a nearby palm tree.

Polk leaned heavily against the tree and shook his head. "Those bastards'll be back as soon as they refuel and arm," he said.

"They must have already bombed the shit out of the airfield," Chester said. "Why in hell come back?"

"Because, by God, they haven't killed us all yet," Polk said.

"Just be glad we've got some planes up there now," Chester said. "You able to walk?" His own head had begun to clear, and he could hear better out of one ear. When he walked, his right leg hurt, though when he looked down, there was no blood. He took a couple of steps, gritted his teeth, and began to walk to the beach to help tend to some of the men who were lying there hurt. Or dying.

Walking with him, Polk took hold of Chester's arm and said, "Thanks, Scarsdale. I owe you one, man."

Chester stopped and glowered at Polk. "I should have left you out there, Polk."

Polk laughed. "That's more like you, Scarsdale. I don't know what I'd do if we had to be nice to each other."

Walking on, Chester said, "Let's help give those poor sons-of-a-bitch still on the beach some help."

*

Hours later, Chester followed Polk and Hough to the ocean's edge and rinsed the sweat and blood from his face and hands. Then he reached for a barrel that was rolled to him from off a lighter that had just landed. The dizziness and ringing in his ears had almost stopped. He rolled the barrel farther onto the beach, toward the palm trees. Hough and Polk, each with their own barrel, kept pace with him. They passed a Sea Bee sitting on the sand, staring, frozen in place, as though he were playing one of those childhood games Chester had joined in where he had to stand like a statue until unfrozen, or not, by a friend. When they reached the jungle's edge, Chester looked back and saw a medic lead the man off toward a first-aid station at the jungle's edge.

"The war's probably all over for that man," Chester said.

"But not for the rest of us," said Polk.

"Yeah, but I wonder sometimes if I'll be like that before all this is over," said Hough.

"More likely, we'll end up like Jack. Blown to bits by a Jap bomb," said Polk.

"What in God's name would I do without you two here cheering me up?" Chester said.

*

When night fell, Chester wrapped himself in his poncho and leaned against a fallen palm tree. All he'd had to eat was some cold C-rations. His stomach growled its unhappiness. He lit up three cigarettes and passed one to Hough and one to Polk.

"Thanks, Scarsdale. Hough, you hear how this asshole was so worried I was going to get a load of bullets up my ass that he came and pulled me off the goddamn Jap bombing range?"

"I'd have thought you'd leave him out there, Chester," Hough said.

CHAPTER 26 ♦ CHESTER

"He's a bastard. But he works like a son-of-a-bitch. I wanted to save his ass so he could work it off. I'll try to keep him safe till we all get out of this damn war and back home. Then, if I see him lying in a gutter somewhere, I'll let him stay there. Or piss on him."

"Thanks, asshole," Polk said. "But asshole or not, what you did out there for me today deserves a medal."

"You'd have done the same, Polk," Chester said.

"Maybe. But I'm not so sure I would have. There was a damn good chance we'd both get shot to hell when you came out there. Not just me."

"Forget it," Chester said and took a deep drag on his cigarette, letting the smoke slowly dribble out his nose, as if he could parcel it out till the end of the war, keep his sanity, and not get killed. He didn't see himself as a hero; he was too damned scared when he was dragging Polk off the beach to think of himself as that. Wanting to change the subject, he said, "I had a choice now, I'd join the regular Navy."

"Hell, yes," said Hough. "Them Navy boys aboard ship don't have to roll in the dirt and mud like us Sea Bees. They take a shower, wash down with antiseptic soap, and put on clean clothes before a fight. And after one."

"If a Jap sub don't send them to Davy Jones' locker first," said Chester.

Polk said, "I'd join the Air Force. You can have a bath before taking off in one of those fancy planes. You get shot and survive, you get flown to a nice hospital. Eat regular food. Not this dog food in a can they give us."

"And sleep between clean sheets. And have those pretty nurses take care of them, when all we get are these male nurses and medics," Chester said.

"Hell, we get shot, we get to lie in the sand, mud, or muck," Hough said.

"When we die, we die in the goddamn sand, mud, or muck," Polk said.

"When you die, you die. Clean or dirty."

"Jesus H. Christ, Hough, you said I was a sour son-of-a-bitch. But you're one, too," Chester said.

Hough pinched off the glowing end of his half-smoked cigarette, laid it within reach, turned away from Chester and Polk, and laid his head on a slicker he'd rolled into a pillow.

Polk laid his head back on his slicker and let out a deep sigh. "Damned if we didn't live another day," he said.

Chester lay back, too. "We're just three peas in a pod," he said. "Let's just hope the damn insects won't try to finish the job the Japs weren't able to. Bastards will probably eat us alive."

CHAPTER 27

Ruth

⤞ ✽ ⤝

Ruth wanted to say "Let's go," to Joe. Have him drive her to the folks' house and face the music if there was music to be faced. A stronger urge to keep quiet battled that wish and won out, so she said nothing. Instead, she leaned against her door and watched Joe staring out over the darkened field where his cotton had for years sprung forth, coloring the earth green. His jaw moved up and down as if he were chewing something. Is it his thoughts, Ruth wondered?

He finally said, "I hope you're all right with sitting for a spell before I take you home." Without turning, he put his arm up along the back of the seat, his fingers lightly caressing the back of her neck before he let his hand drape across her shoulder.

As if his hand were gripping her throat, shutting off her air so she couldn't speak aloud, she whispered, "It's all right," and moved closer to him.

"My folks lived on this land a long time before they gave it up. Raised up my brother, sisters, and me. Now I'm the farmer. I love this place, but Theresa never wanted to live out here."

"I remember your folks. They were good to me when I was a girl passing here every weekday going to school and back. Your mother would invite me in for fresh-baked cinnamon rolls sometimes. And she taught me how to cross stitch." Ruth reached up and patted his hand. "And sometimes we played together if there weren't any other boys around to tease you." She paused a moment when he didn't respond and then said, "Your place is filled with lots of good memories."

"It is. But it gets lonely livin' by myself, Ruth. Ever since Theresa died, I wake up nights thinkin' she's there, and then I get this chill, like I'd seen a ghost." He reached up and slicked back his hair with his free hand and then turned to her. "It's good to be with you. Talk. Touch a woman again." He gently pulled her closer and let his hand slide further around her shoulder and lie just above her breast.

She melted then, leaned against him, reached for his other hand, and intertwined her fingers with his. She tensed some when he turned and put his lips against hers. Chester's were the only man's lips she'd felt in their eighteen years of marriage. When he started kissing her, Chester's lips were usually as tight and dry as a piece of linen she'd bring to her mouth to bite off a loose thread. But the lips Joe Williams pressed lightly to hers were soft, moist, and full.

She put her hand behind his head and pulled his face hard against hers; then she pulled back and looked at him in the dim light of the moon that had followed them here from Cooperton. She could see the strong curve of his jaw and an inner circle of light reflecting from one eye. It was a tiny reflection of the moon, she realized. He blinked and looked down, the inner light then replaced by shadow. She reached up and traced the

CHAPTER 27 ✦ RUTH

rough angle of his jaw. His heavy beard, like coarse sandpaper, had left her face prickling, as if all the nerves in her skin had come alive.

He licked his lips, pulled her closer, and pressed his mouth to hers once more. Her head began to spin and her fingertips to tingle. She began to feel closed in, as if trapped in a storm cellar, with dangerous clouds of passions spinning around her. Putting her hands to his chest, she pushed and turned her head away. Over his shoulder, the dark outline of the stark mulberry trees from which all the leaves had fallen left her and Joe exposed to the road and to any spying eyes that might glance their way as a car passed. "No. Please," she murmured.

He loosened his grip but did not let go. His chest began to rise and fall as if he'd just run a mile race. Ruth's hand, resting there on the broad muscle, moved with it. Gently pulling her to him once more, Joe pressed his lips against her forehead.

"Don't, please."

"Okay, Ruth. I don't want to push you."

They sat there, him holding her in a soft grip, and she began to relax against him. "I think you better take me home now." The words felt bitter hot, searing her lips as they passed. She thought of Chester's lips on hers the last time they had been together, her fearing it might be for the last time. Over the last year, there had been long, bitter nights when she'd lie in her bed, crying herself to sleep. And sometimes, in her dreams, she felt an awful emptiness and fear that she might never again be in his arms. She would awaken and flee to her papa's rocking chair or the porch swing and rock till morning's first light appeared. But now that Joe was holding her, she wasn't sure if she wanted his lips to take the place of Chester's. This was no time to decide, she thought, and again gently pushed him away. "I just can't get Chester out of my mind. If he decided to come back to me, how could I face him?"

Joe released her and sat back against the door. "I sure wouldn't want to be in your shoes right now, Ruth. It's different for me. It's been a year since I held a woman, Ruth, and all I'm thinking is that I want to hold you. I wish you could get Chester out of your mind, but that's asking a lot."

"I want you to hold me, though God knows, at this minute, I can't let you."

He reached out and stroked her hair; then he rested his cupped hand, large as a helmet, against her head. "I'm sorry, Ruth. I ought to have known better."

She began to sob and then moved close and put her head against his chest. Her tears soaked into his coat as he stroked her back and patted her like he would to comfort Sarah. "No. I'm the one who's sorry, Joe. It seems like the life's been sucked out of me the past few months, and I've cried till I thought I was all dried up inside. I'm like those dry, dusty fields we had back in the thirties. You could plant them, but they could give nothing back. I don't think I have anything to give you." But even as she said this, she realized that, with Joe, she felt so much better. Not parched and lonely. Though thoughts of Chester lurked about in the shadowy car, she was more at peace with this kind man sitting beside her than she'd been for a long time.

"Let's get you back to your folks' house, Ruth." Joe reached to switch on the engine.

She took hold of his hand and stopped him. "No," she said. "I want to stay here with you for a while yet. Be with you. Let's go into the house." Forcing away all her doubts, she moved closer to him.

Joe opened the car door, gently pulling her across the seat, and stepped into the chill wash of night air. She slid under the steering wheel and stepped out beside him; then she let him lead her to the front door and into the house. "I don't want to go into the bedroom, Joe. I'd feel Theresa's presence in there."

He took her hand, walked to the living room with her, and said, "Give me a minute, Ruth." Going to the cold iron stove, he laid a fire and lit it with a match from his pocket. He left for a moment to return

CHAPTER 27 ✦ RUTH

with three heavy, hand-quilted blankets that he spread out on the worn carpet in front of the stove. She had to smile seeing the careful and intricate stitching of the bright cotton quilt pieces of one blanket placed alongside her. Another, obviously made from pieces cut from old, retired woolen suits and dresses, was sewn with the same care. They had to have been stitched by careful hands—Joe's or Theresa's mother's or grandmother's.

Waiting for the room to warm, she and Joe stood side by side holding hands. The coal burned hotter, and the stove slowly began to radiate welcome heat.

When she was a little girl, on cold mornings she loved to stand near their big heating-stove waiting for the room to heat so she could get dressed. The pleasant thought warmed her even more, and she sank down onto the warm comforters. Joe stood above her as if he had no idea what to do. Behind him she could see the moon and stars shining through a windowpane, a multitude of tiny pinpoints bathing the road and yard in faint light, making everything almost as visible as if it were early morning. She tried to push away thoughts of all those imagined busybodies who might pass by on the road, drive away thoughts of her parents' disapproval, and push the presence of Chester's and Theresa's ghosts out of the room, out of the house, out of this whole wide country.

"Are you sure about this, Ruth? I really can wait, you know."

Standing over her, his face lit by the dancing flames from the open stove door, his eyes were so kind that Ruth wanted nothing more than to hold him close, feel the touch of his skin. For an answer, she reached for his hand and pulled gently until he was kneeling in front of her, his head tipped down. She raised her lips to him. "You shouldn't have to wait any longer. We shouldn't."

He knelt beside her and fumbled in his pants pocket, pulled out a small square packet.

He came prepared, she thought and smiled. "You don't need that, Joe."

"I don't?" Confusion clouded his eyes, and he knitted his brow. "You don't want to get pregnant." There was no question in his statement.

"Chester brought something home to me soon after Charlie was born, and the doctors treated it as best they could. Got rid of it for me, but they said I'd never get pregnant again. Must have been true. It's been nine years now."

"Bastard," Joe muttered and laid the packet aside. Then he undressed her.

Fear and excitement beat against her chest until she was sure it would burst forth. Then she was in his arms and wanted to be nowhere else.

*

When Ruth opened her eyes, the stars outside the window took a moment to stop moving and resolve into individual points of light. The Williams' front porch shimmered and wavered before pulling back together and standing firmly anchored to its foundation. The moon rested serenely on the starlit blanket of heaven.

"Lord God above, Ruth. I never expected something like that." Joe turned toward her and propped himself on an elbow.

"Joe. I want you down here." She pulled him closer and held on, storing up memories of the feel of him. Her chest and belly were filled now, with nothing left of the deep emptiness she'd carried around inside for these past months. Into the silence of the moment came the far-off sound of a coyote calling to its mate. "That was wonderful," Ruth breathed. "Did you have what you wanted from me, Joe?"

"I got more'n I wanted, Ruth. But what about you?" Joe's breathing became deep, like he was pulling for breath and not able to take in enough.

"Yes. And yes. And yes."

He slipped his arm around her shoulders and pulled her even closer.

A night flight of bombers dashed overhead on their way to Altus Airforce base, showering them with noise. When they had passed, it seemed to Ruth that the night became even quieter than before, as if they were the only ones present in all the fallow land around them. But then, the noiseless darkness was shattered as Joe's nearest neighbor's wife called in a high soprano voice that carried the whole half of a mile distance, "You get in the house this minute. It's way past your bedtime."

Ruth laughed, and Joe chuckled, a deep-throated sound that started in his chest and rumbled out his mouth. "You think that's my mother calling me, Joe?" She sat up, put on her underwear, pulled her dress down over her head, and smoothed it down over her breasts, letting it spread out below, covering her. Through the window she scanned the horizon until she saw the steady glow of the neighbor's yard light.

"Could have been mine once upon a time." He sat up and began to pull on his clothes. "She had a fine voice, my mother. And sometimes a heavy hand."

Ruth chuckled as she rose. She stepped into her shoes and then waited as Joe dressed, admiring the play of muscles across his shoulders. Back in the car, driving the half mile to her parents' home, Joe deliberately set it jerking and swaying crazily, causing Ruth to finally shift closer to him before smoothing out the ride. She put her hand to her belly as if to steady the fullness there, not let it escape. "Joe? What will we do when Chester comes home?"

"You'll divorce that horse's rear-end, and by damn, marry me, that's what." He took his hand from the steering wheel and put his arm over her shoulders, pulling her in closer.

Beautiful as that thought was, it terrified her. Could she really do it? Did she really want to do it? As they turned into the yard and saw a lamp still burning on the dining-room table, that terror was replaced by the unhappy prospect of entering her parents' house and facing the hurt, disapproval, and anger that likely was waiting for her there.

CHAPTER 28

Ruth

→➤ ✼ ⊰←

The moon and stars had disappeared behind a bank of clouds that were moving in from the north, and, without their cold light, it was dark as pitch as Ruth walked onto the porch and stood at the door watching Joe turn onto the road and drive away. *I hope to God in heaven Papa and Mother are fast asleep*, she thought as she slowly opened the screen door, and, when a faint squeak erupted, wished she had oiled the hinges. She paused and listened for Papa to call out. Dreading the thought. Opening the door just as carefully as she could, she slipped inside and felt her way to the bedroom she shared with Charlie and thanking the stars he was spending the night at Pearl's. It took moments to undress, fold her clothes across a chair and climb in between the ice-cold sheets. She stopped shivering moments after pulling wool

CHAPTER 28 ♦ RUTH

blankets over herself and was warmed further by thoughts of Joe. Of herself and Joe.

A colder wind blew in from the north during the night, and Ruth's dreams and troubled sleep drove the warmth from her. She awakened to the sound of her papa stoking the fire and was so cold that the extra woolen covers she pulled close could not warm her. What chilled her was that she'd done something she never could have imagined letting herself do. Hearing her papa leave to do chores, she grabbed her robe and hurried to stand by the stove which now burned red hot. She vowed to not repeat what had happened the night before. It was a vow she was afraid she could not keep.

She made an effort to keep her vow the next day when Charlie and Sarah insisted they had to spend time together on a project Miss Zickenfoose had assigned them. They had to read and report on a subject from one of Joe's last week's newspapers. Joe walked out onto the porch when they drove up, his smile so welcoming that Ruth wanted to leap out of the car and run to him. Instead, she sent the children inside and called to Joe that she would be back later to pick Charlie up. As she made a U-turn and glanced at Joe, his smile faded. Still, he waved, and, in the rearview mirror, she saw him stand in the cold wind to watch her drive away.

It was the only time during the next month that she drove away without visiting with Joe while their two kids played or worked together. Only when the two would decide they had to run to the hayloft to play did they have time to hold each other for a moment or two, afraid they would otherwise be caught in an embrace. Charlie and Sarah were unpredictable, sometimes staying away for an hour and sometimes only minutes. Slowly, as spring approached, Ruth came more and more to accept that she could not stay away from Joe.

*

Early spring had crept into rural Oklahoma on a day when Ruth, for the first time, walked, rather than drove, to Joe's place. When she arrived, he was hand-pumping water from his cistern. He caught sight of her, set the bucket down, and walked to meet her.

Taking her hand, he gave it a squeeze and then said, "Let's walk down to the pond out of sight from any nosy busybody that might drive by."

As they strolled under the cottonwood tree that grew close to his large pond, he took hold of her hand once more. Ruth pulled her coat closer about her to ward off a cold puff of spring air coming in off the plowed and newly planted cotton fields and then felt Joe's arm drape around her shoulders and pull her close. They stood there looking out over the ripples sliding across the water as some creature, a turtle or a fish, or even a water moccasin, swam near the surface. Ruth had the uncomfortable thought then of Eve being tempted by the serpent. *I've given in to temptation*, she thought, but turned her back on the troubled waters of the pond and faced Joe. She let him encircle her with both arms and bend down to kiss her. As she raised her face to him beneath the sprouting new leaves of the cottonwood, the troubling biblical thoughts disappeared, and Ruth melted into the safety and warmth of his embrace.

"I love you, Ruth."

"And," *God forgive me*, she thought but said, "I love you, too, Joe." She had not, could not, come out and tell him the tortured truth that she also still loved Chester. She could only remind him she was married and that these moments might be all they had.

Their kiss was interrupted by the distant yells of children let loose from school for the day, so they started back to the house. As they reached the barnyard, Ruth saw Charlie and Sarah waving from the porch. She waved back. Reminded of the conference with Charlie's teacher that previous afternoon, she said, "Miss Zickenfoose told me Corky wasn't picking fights with Charlie anymore, and he seems afraid of Charlie."

Joe laughed, "Good for him. Now Charlie won't grow up believing he has to be bullied by anyone takes a notion to push him around."

CHAPTER 28 • RUTH

She stopped, looked up at him, and frowned. "He certainly can't let anyone push him around. I agree with you, but . . ." She paused. "His teacher said he's standing up to Corky's insults. And giving back his own; being smarter than Corky, his insults are worse. They sting Corky." Ruth took a deep breath and let it out to relieve the tension that had just filled her chest. "She told me that Corky called Charlie a 'horse's ass.' And Charlie had said, 'What are you, Corky, a horse's ass inspector?'"

Ruth lowered her eyebrows at Joe and tightened her mouth when he continued to smile broadly.

"I'm sorry, Joe, but I don't like that kind of behavior. And Miss Zickenfoose doesn't, either. She was so shocked she didn't stop them before Corky said, 'It takes one to know one,' and Charlie said, 'I guess you just admitted to being one.' The teacher made them both write 'I will not swear' fifty times before they could go to recess again. I don't want Charlie behaving like that."

Joe grinned. "I promise I'll have a talk with Charlie next time I get him alone. Encourage him to try to pull back a little on the insults."

"Please," Ruth pleaded.

Joe said. "But the kids are going to start asking questions about what we were doing out in the pasture. Let's get on up to the house." He hurried them back to the porch, where Charlie and Sarah stood waiting.

Sarah hugged Joe and Ruth; then she took Charlie's hand and pulled him toward the door. "We're going to play rummy," she announced as they disappeared into the house, leaving Joe and Ruth smiling.

"They enjoy each other so much," Ruth said. "I'm so happy for Charlie that he has Sarah as a friend."

Joe grinned and whispered, "And I'm glad I have his mother as a friend."

"Shhhh. They'll hear you."

Joe said, "Walk with me over to the fence, away from where they can hear us." As they stood at the edge of the cotton field, Joe said, "I've been wanting to ask you something. Meant to when we were down at the pond but lost my chance when we heard the kids." He paused before going on. "Ruth, do you think there's any way we could manage to get away together for a couple of days? Maybe visit the Alabaster Caverns up near Freedom? Just spend a couple of days and nights together?"

"Oh, Joe. I can't do that. You know I can't." Tears sprang to her eyes. There was nothing on Earth she'd rather do, but there was no way she could leave Charlie for two days without him and her parents throwing fits. And if Papa and Mother got wind of her going away with Joe, they'd likely throw her out of the house. Or make life miserable in some way or another.

"I know. But I thought you might get your sisters to help us again."

"It was one thing to help me get away for a few hours. But two days? Pearl wasn't big on helping me, and she would balk for sure at two days and nights."

Joe's shoulders sagged as he took a big breath and let it out slowly. "I understand. I don't like it, but I understand."

*

A week later, her heart in her throat, Ruth took a deep breath and opened her mouth to tell Charlie and Mother that she was going away for a couple of days to visit a friend in Cordell, but before she could get the words out, her mother spoke sharply to Charlie, saying, "Go call your grandpa to breakfast," and then peered into the oven. "Tell him he's got five minutes to get here before the biscuits start getting cold." Charlie jumped up from the kitchen table and bolted out the door, letting it slam behind him.

"I swear I've told him a hundred times not to let that door slam behind him," Mother said as she sat down across from Ruth, took off her glasses, and began wiping them on a handkerchief.

"I've probably added another hundred times to that," Ruth said. "I sometimes think there's nothing but air between his ears and my

CHAPTER 28 • RUTH

words just go in one ear and out the other." *That won't be the case*, she thought, *when I tell him about leaving for two days*. She'd wanted to tell him and Mother while Papa was still doing morning chores, but she hadn't gotten up the nerve till it was too late. It had been over a week since Joe had asked her to go away with him for a couple of days. She'd spoken to both her sisters and agonized over her decision, but with Joan's encouragement had decided to go. She'd thought that had been hard until she sat down to tell Charlie and her folks.

"You mind starting the bacon frying, Ruth? And the eggs? I need to sit a minute."

As Ruth peeled off slices of bacon and put them to sizzling in a skillet, she felt lightheaded with fright at the thought of dealing with all three of them and lying about visiting a friend. Over the past weekend, she'd schemed with Joan and come up with a plan to get away with Joe for the two days. When she first confided in Joan, her sister had insisted she figure out a way to make it happen. Pearl had flat-out refused to help at first, but then grudgingly given in to Ruth's and Joan's appeals for help.

Ruth'd finished frying the bacon and stirring flour and milk into the hot grease to make gravy when Charlie burst back into the kitchen and scooted into a chair across from his grandmother. "Grandpa says he'll be here in a minute."

Ruth placed the bacon and gravy on the table, sat down with her mother and Charlie, and said, "I'm going to Cordell for just a couple of days to visit Julie Goforth, a girlhood friend of mine."

"Does that mean I get to skip school?" Charlie's eyes brightened, and he bounced in his chair.

It was hard for her to go on, but she said, "No, you'll stay in school. You can't go with me or you'll get behind in your schoolwork."

Charlie glared at her, his face turning red as he shouted, "That's not fair." Tears started coursing down his cheeks.

"Fair or not, it's going to happen," she barked and then wished she'd not given such a sharp response to his disappointment.

Her mother said nothing, and Ruth saw no disapproval in her eyes before she stood, went to the stove, pulled out the biscuits, placed them in a bowl, and set them on the table. Ruth and her mother each took one; Charlie grabbed another and splashed gravy over it, anger sparking from his eyes.

A few minutes later the door squeaked open, and Papa came in but stopped before sitting down at the table and stood looking from red-faced, tearful Charlie back to Ruth. "What's going on?" he asked.

Her mother snapped, "Nothing. We were waiting for you to show up for breakfast."

"Like one hog waits on another?"

"That doesn't deserve an answer," her mother said.

"I was carrying water to the wash house to fill the tubs like you asked last night. I left one on the stove to heat while we had breakfast."

Before Ruth's mother could respond, Charlie stood, shoved back his chair, and pointed at Ruth. "Mama's going away without me. Gonna be gone two whole days."

"First I heard of it," her papa said.

"I don't like it," Charlie whined, his glare hot enough to burn a hole through her.

"I'm just going to visit a friend in Cordell." Ashamed that she was lying, she looked down at the floor, wanting to bury herself under the edge of the timeworn linoleum. "And I'll be back before any of you hardly know I'm gone." Charlie tightened his mouth and wrinkled his forehead, scowling in a way that her papa had come to call, *that Chester Scarsdale scowl*. "Why can't I go?"

"You've got school. That's why. And I'll only be thirty miles away, and I'll call you every night."

"You ain't never, ever been gone all night, before," Charlie sobbed.

CHAPTER 28 ✦ RUTH

Ruth's mother stood up, signaling that she was through listening to the argument, and started clearing the dishes "You're going to be just fine here with us, Charlie."

"Charlie's right. Don't seem right to go off and leave him," Papa said. "Your mother's health isn't all that good. Or did you forget?"

"Don't you start up, Bob." Mother said. "I think Ruth deserves a day away for herself once in a while. And like I keep telling you, I'm not an invalid."

A rush of gratitude filled Ruth's chest. *At least there's one person in this room who's on my side.* She wondered then if her mother suspected who she was really going to spend time with and had accepted it. Maybe even approved.

"I won't nag. I won't eat too much. And I promise not to get in the way," Charlie pleaded.

"I wish you hadn't sprung this on us at the last minute, Ruth. You've really upset Charlie," her papa said.

"I'm sorry if I'm upsetting everybody, but I've made up my mind." Finished with breakfast, Ruth stood, tied an apron around her dress and began washing the dishes. "Charlie, it's time for you to start walking to school."

"It's not fair," Charlie said and then stomped out of the kitchen to get his homework; then he slammed out the door without telling anyone goodbye.

"When you leavin'?" Papa asked.

"Tomorrow."

Her papa shook his head. The room was silent except for the clack of his fork against the plate or of dishes clinking together in the dishpan as Ruth rinsed and placed them on the drainboard for her mother to dry. Papa, the last to finish his breakfast, left his dirty dishes on the table for Ruth or her mother to clear. Going into the setting room, he settled down in his oak rocker at the radio and turned on to the latest news. Ruth shuddered when the announcer solemnly told of Japanese bombing raids, allied advances, and casualties in the Pacific theater. She did not want to think of anything to do with Chester right now. She was beginning to feel a deep ache in her stomach from the lie she'd told and about going away for two days with Joe while Chester was in the middle of those bombings and advances.

Finished with the dishes, Ruth left the kitchen and walked to the wash house, carrying a basket of dirty clothes and bedding with her. When she entered the small, one-room house, the smell of laundry detergent mingled with the stale odor of the laundry she carried. Not unpleasant, but nothing she would choose to linger in if she had a choice. She poured the water heating on the kerosene stove into a washtub and, in its place, set more water to heat for rinsing. Putting laundry soap and the whites, sheets, and pillowcases, in the tub, she set the scrub board in it and began scrubbing hard against its ribbed surface. *If I have to do this many more months,* she thought, *my hands will look as rough and knotted with arthritis as Mother's.*

Done with the whites, she wrung them out, pitched them in another tub and poured the heated rinse water from the stove over them. Then she started washing the coloreds—blouses, shirts, and skirts. She cycled through all the wash in this way—whites, coloreds, underwear, and socks, and then Papa's soiled work overalls and Charlie's equally dirty school overalls. By the time she finished cycling through to the end, the first tub of water was filthy and the other a sickly grey. It wasn't any different when all four of them shared the same bath water, Mother first, her second, Papa third, and Charlie last. That was one of the prices paid by farm families living out here, where the ground water was so hard that soap wouldn't lather, and they had to make do with the water that drained off the roof and collected in cisterns. Couldn't drink ground water, either.

She'd spent a lot of time from age six to sixteen carrying cistern water to the wash house and then being up to her elbows in soapy wash-water.

CHAPTER 28 ✦ RUTH

Had hoped never to do it again after she and Chester moved off the farm into town, where pure, fresh water came out of a faucet and not out of a cistern filled with runoff from the roof.

That thought of moving into town with Chester brought a fresh wave of anxiety and guilt washing over her. That snippet of news she'd heard on the radio before coming out to the wash house was like a slap in the face. Here she was, safe and sound, planning a wonderful two-day trip with another man, a man she was beginning to love as much, and certainly respect more, than she did Chester. Didn't seem fair to Chester. Or to Charlie. And what would it be like married to Joe? A life spent doing laundry by hand rather than at a Wash-a-teria. At least Joe had a wringer washer his mother had used since the early twenties. If Chester divorced her, and she stayed with Joe, at least wash-day would be only half as tiresome as it was today.

Feeling as wrung out with strain from her feelings as the clothes she had twisted the rinse water from, she walked to the side-yard and began hanging the sheets over the clothesline. A brisk gust of wind set them flapping and dancing like live things. Or maybe ghosts. She heard a door slam shut and, looking toward the house, saw Papa glaring at her from the porch. Her little adventure might cost her if Papa figured out she'd fibbed to them.

CHAPTER 29

Bob

Bob peered out the window and scowled as he saw Pearl's car turn into the yard, a fog of exhaust following it in from the road. "Ida, it's Pearl turning in."

"She's giving Ruth a ride into town," Ida said and then went out to the car to greet Pearl before starting down the path toward the chicken house."

Ruth walked into the kitchen, and, when Bob saw her eyes filled with rebellion, his voice rose. "You sure you want to do this, Ruth?"

"Yes, Papa. I know you and Charlie are dead set against it. But Mother is all right with it, so I'm going."

"Can't say as I blame Charlie for being a mite upset, Ruth," he said.

CHAPTER 29 • BOB

Ruth turned away and went into the bedroom. When she returned carrying a suitcase, he saw her silky nightgown poking out of one corner. A thread trailed from its hem.

He felt a cold anger at the sight of it. Ruth had told him once how Chester would throw things into a suitcase, leave, and not come home for days. Fooling around, most likely. He had an inkling it wasn't somebody in Cordell Ruth was visiting. If it was Joe, would that be any different than what Chester did? No. No. And it wasn't right for either of them to behave that way. He followed Ruth out the door, waved at Pearl, and stood on the porch, wanting to say more to Ruth, but afraid he'd haul off and say something that would make things even worse. Sure as God made green persimmons, Pearl and Ruth were up to no good. Charlie came running from the barn, old Hitler the dog at his heels. Glowering up at his mama and wiping angrily at the tears in his eyes, he shouted, "Going away and leaving me here isn't fair."

Pearl, who'd stepped out of the car, stood rubbing her hands together, like they were part of a perpetual-motion machine that Bob'd heard tell about on the radio. She said, "I tell you what—why don't I pick you up later, and you can stay the night with us."

"No. I want to go with mama."

"You drivin' your sister all the way to Cordell, Pearl?" Bob called.

"No. Just to Hobart." Pearl didn't look at him, just kept wringing her hands, a nervous habit when she was up to no good. Had that habit ever since she was old enough to make trouble. Or lie.

Ruth reached down and hugged Charlie, but he kept his arms stiff at his side. "I tell you what, Charlie, I'll bring you a present when I come back."

"I'd rather go than have a present."

"You be nice now." Ruth threw her suitcase into the back seat. "Look. I'll be back lickity-split. You won't even have time to miss me. But I'll miss you." She lowered herself into the car and closed the door. Charlie turned, ran to the porch and then on through the kitchen door, slamming it behind him so hard Bob was afraid the glass might break. Hitler followed Charlie but stopped at the porch and turned to Bob, who gave him a pat on the head. He wanted to yell at his conniving daughters, both thinking they were getting away with something. The engine growled to life, and Pearl put it in gear. Bob heard the loud clucking of his chickens and turned to see Ida, who stood in the midst of their scrabbling flock of old hens and the one rooster. She raised her hand and waved setting the chickens to clucking and running about looking for the grain they must have thought she was throwing to them.

He turned back and watched as Pearl's car turned into the road and disappeared; then he went back into the kitchen, poured a cup of coffee, and lowered himself into his favorite rocker. When Ida came in a few minutes later to join him, he said, "If them two have cooked up something to help Ruth go somewhere with you know who, the whole damn town's going to be flapping their tongues about this," he said.

"She's just going to see a friend, Bob. And, besides, Ruth's a grown woman. We can't tell her how to live her life."

"I could darn well throw her out of the house and see how independent she'd be then."

From his bedroom Bob heard Charlie stomp the floor and yell, "Mama's being mean to me."

"You should watch your tongue, Bob Choat. That boy don't need to hear that kind of talk." Ida stood glowering at him, angry lines wrinkling her forehead. She pushed her glasses higher on her nose as if to magnify the anger burning in her eyes. Charlie appeared in his bedroom door glowered at his grandmother and then at Bob. "I hate her."

"Charlie! Don't talk that way. It's not nice." Ida reached out to take his arm to shake him, but he turned and ran.

"Mama's not nice. Why should I be?" Charlie yelled back over his shoulder as he grabbed his books and raced out the door.

CHAPTER 29 ♦ BOB

"Can't say as how I'd disagree with that," Bob said and then turned his back on Ida's glare.

*

"You sit there like that, and it'll take an hour for each minute to pass," Bob said. Charlie shrugged his shoulders and didn't move. It was only seven in the morning, and he was sitting in front of the old green alarm clock, watching the minute hand crawl around.

Two days had passed, and Bob would be almost as glad as Charlie to see Pearl drive up with Ruth in the front seat with her. The boy had done nothing but mope around ever since his mother left. And Ida was wearing herself out with no one here to help with the housework.

"You get on in to breakfast, Charlie. It's going to be this afternoon before your mama comes back." Ida gave him a friendly whack on his backside with a folded newspaper. Charlie sulked into the kitchen for a breakfast of cold cornbread and milk. Ida followed him to the kitchen table and began crumbling last night's left-over cornbread into her bowl.

Bob laid down his paper and joined them. He was just as happy that no one had anything to say more than, "Pass me the milk," or, "Hand me another piece of cornbread. Afterwards Bob sat down beside the radio to listen to the eight o'clock news while Ida did the dishes and Charlie sat on the side porch staring down the road that would bring his mother back. The news over, he stepped out onto the porch and watched Charlie, now grown tired of waiting, race to the barn with the old hound outrunning him and then both tumbling in the dirt and wrestling. Charlie then threw dirt clods at a tin can he'd set on the top of a fencepost.

When Bob heard Pearl's car drive into the yard a little after noon, he stood up from his chair and walked outside to the edge of the porch. She would be staying around helping her mother till she drove into town to get Ruth. *It's a good thing we have a girl living so close*, Bob thought, *even if she is a conniver.*

Pearl climbed out of the car, opened the trunk, and took out a sack of potatoes she'd bought for them. She trudged toward the porch, carrying the sack and one too many secret schemes with Ruth for his liking. He forced the thought down, guilty to have such critical ideas about the sweetest of his three girls.

In the kitchen, Ida reached to take the potatoes and put them away, but Pearl held them away, saying, "You oughtn't to carry around any heavy things, Mother. Let one of us do it."

"You worry too much, Pearl," Ida said as Pearl laid the sack beneath the kitchen sink, but she walked into the family room and dropped into a chair with a heavy sigh.

I've never seen Ida looking so peaked, Bob thought as he pulled one of the dining-room chairs around to face Ida. "You ought to listen to your daughter, Ida."

"Now I got to put up with both of you hollering at me."

Pearl relaxed back into the other rocking chair. "Today's so chilly I'm thinking of moving to south Texas. And look at that boy out there, lying on top of that chicken house like it was a summer day."

"In case you hadn't noticed, Pearl, it is getting close to summer," Ida said.

"Ruth's supposed to get back today. You're going into town to pick her up, I understand," Bob said.

Pearl's chin trembled, and her face darkened, but before she could respond, Charlie burst through the screen door, yelling at the top of his lungs, "They're bombing Babbs Switch," over and over again, as if no one heard him the first time.

Pearl stood, took hold of Charlie's shoulders, and said, "Just slow down a minute. What are you talking about?"

"The Japs or Nazis. They're bombing Babbs Switch."

CHAPTER 29 ♦ BOB

"Hold on, now. You're not making this up, are you?" Bob rose from his chair, feeling anxious, even though he knew that neither of the Axis would bother with a service station and a wheat elevator.

Charlie shook his head violently. "No. I did. I did. Three explosions. Big old balls of fire shooting up into the sky. Just like on the newsreels at the picture show." He danced from foot to foot as if he was holding back a full bladder.

"I thought I heard thunder a moment ago," Ida said. Pushing herself up out of the chair, she went to the kitchen window and peered out. "Lord-a-mercy, Bob. There is a lot of smoke." She turned from the window and began to untie her apron.

Pearl, looking pale, said, "If there's any chance they're bombing Babbs, they might start shooting at us next. Let's go to the cellar."

Bob joined her at the window and looked out, "Darned if there isn't something burning over there, but no need for us to go to the cellar. There's no Krauts or Japs going to bother with a wheat elevator. We better get over there and see what's goin' on. Might be somebody needs help."

"You go on. I've got to stay here and mind my heart. It's beating a mile a minute." Ida turned from the window, her body stiff with fright.

"I'm staying with mother. You two can go," Pearl said, her look of concern making him pause.

Ida motioned at him as if shooing flies. "Go on now. Pearl can help me if I need it. Take that boy with you, though. He'll just be a worrywart if you leave him here."

He and Charlie piled into the car, and Bob drove fast toward the smoke. The road tunneled through fields that would be awash in high cotton when fall came. The excitement gave him something of a sour stomach, even though he knew there was no way a Jap or Kraut bomber could have flown this far inland. Still, he wondered what other awful thing might have happened. Most likely one of the gas storage tanks had blown up.

When Bob turned onto the pavement and approached the service station, Charlie leaned forward and pointed. "Looky there. They hit a truck."

Through the thick smoke pouring from the still-burning tires, Bob could make out the charred cab. A grass fire was spreading across the ditch to the pastureland across the fence.

"You stay in the car till I see what's going on," Bob said.

"No. I want to see. I'm the one who told you about it."

"Hush now, and do what I say." Bob pulled to the side of the road and parked. Charlie bolted out his side of the car and ran toward a knot of people standing in the drive of the service station. *Damn kid doesn't listen any better than his mamma*, Bob thought, as he followed Charlie. They both stood listening to old man Hines, the owner, jabber excitedly to someone in the crowd.

"Jack drove that damn burning gasoline truck out of this here drive to where it sits. Saved the service station and with me in it." Hines pointed to a man leaning against the side of the station as if to hold himself up, his clothes looking as if he'd rolled around in ashes.

The man, pale as a ghost and sweating, turned and stared, his eyes slightly out of focus. "Crazy son-bitch, ain't I?"

One of the bystanders, a tall, lean man dressed in jeans and a straw hat, sniggered and slapped his knee. "We got us a real hero here," he said.

"My daddy's a hero, too. Fighting the Japs." Charlie looked from Hines to the man as if waiting for them to agree.

Hines shook his head and said, "It's hard to believe that of Chester, boy."

Charlie's eyes narrowed, and his mouth drew down at the corners. "No, it's not. He rescued two Sea Bees from getting shot by the Japs."

To keep Charlie from any further back-talking, Bob took hold his arm. "That's enough, Charlie." Turning to Hines, he glared. "You got no right to say that about his daddy." *Even if it's true*, he thought to himself. Anyone not family had no business bad-mouthing Chester to the boy's face.

CHAPTER 29 ✦ BOB

With a grunt of dismissal, Hines turned to the truck driver, who seemed to have regained some color. "Come on inside, Jack. You need to sit down and get yourself something to drink." Hines stalked away to his station door with his hero and disappeared inside. The crowd began to drift into the station or break up into small knots to stare and talk among themselves as they watched the fire.

"Come on, Charlie, let's get back to the house," Bob said. "Your grandmother and aunt are sitting on pins and needles wondering what's happened."

As Charlie turned to go, a Hobart fire engine came to a screeching halt on the other side of the blaze and disgorged red-hatted fireman who unreeled hoses, hooked them to a tank in the truck and aimed them at the small grass fire that had ignited. Water gushed out, dousing the spreading grass fire, and the firemen then turned it on the still-smoldering truck. Beyond them, cars had come to a stop and emptied their passengers, who stood gaping at the fire.

"Can I stay and watch them put out the fire?" Charlie squirmed out of his grasp. "I'll walk back home in a little while."

"Let's both go look," Bob said.

Charlie took off at a dead run, only stopping when a puff of wind sent black smoke writhing around him.

"Charlie, don't get that close," Bob yelled as he hurried toward the smoking truck. Taking a deep breath, he stood with Charlie and watched as the firemen bathed the area around the truck with a hard stream of water.

When another sharp gust of wind sent the smoke spiraling away into the pasture, he saw two people turn away from the scene and walk to a familiar pickup truck and crawl inside.

Neither Ruth nor Joe appeared to see Charlie's waving at them as they drove away.

*

Back at the house, Bob found Ida lying on the couch while Pearl sat nearby, a worried frown on her face.

"We saw Mama at the fire," Charlie blurted out. "Standing with Joe."

Pearl frowned and said, "I'm sure you must be mistaken."

Bob shook his head. "No, he's right. They were on the other side of the fire. We saw them climb in Joe's pickup and drive away. Headed for his place, I suspect."

"I waved to them, but they didn't see me," Charlie said.

And you've been in on it from the first. Helped her try to fool us. You ought to be ashamed, Pearl, Bob thought, holding back his anger so he wouldn't spout off in front of Charlie.

Pearl stood, her mouth twisted in something almost akin to a snarl—a look of defiance Bob'd also seen off and on ever since she was three years old—and said, "I've got to drive to Joe's and pick up Ruth. Bring her back here." Turning on her heel, she slammed out of the house.

*

His two girls arrived at the house thirty minutes later, and Bob watched as Ruth crawled out of the car, took her suitcase from the back seat, and walked with Pearl up to the porch, where he was standing. He opened his mouth to tell Ruth how aggravated he was about her lying to them all, but she cut him off.

"Papa. Just don't say a word," Ruth walked past him into the house. As she passed, she said, "Pearl told me that you and Charlie saw Joe and me at the fire."

Bob followed her into the living room, where Ida sat upright in her chair stiff as a fencepost. Again, he opened his mouth to say something, but then Charlie rushed up to Ruth and threw his arms around her waist.

"I missed you so much," he cried and hugged her so tight she grunted.

CHAPTER 29 • BOB

"And I missed you, too," she said, putting her arms around him, hugging him to her.

He pushed away then, and, with his eyes wide and excited, said, "You were with Joe. I saw you at the fire."

"I didn't see you," Ruth said.

"With the two of you standing out there at that fire with half the county watching, we couldn't have missed seeing you," Bob said.

"I thought you were going to visit your friend," Charlie interrupted. "Did Joe drive you back?"

"Yes Charlie. Part way."

"Did you bring me a present?"

Ruth shook her head. "I just didn't see anything I thought you'd like, Charlie." Charlie's face clouded over and he yelled, "You promised."

"You're settin' a poor example for Charlie here," Bob said, raising his voice.

"Papa, that's enough. It's none of your business."

The venom in Ruth's words stung, and Bob growled, "Damned if it's not."

Ida, till then rooted in place and silent, stared a hole through him and said, "You haven't the sense God gave a goose. "Talking like that in front of Charlie. And you stop cursing in front of us." She rose, said to Charlie, "You come with me. And no back talk," and disappeared into the kitchen, where Bob could hear her banging pots as she set them in the sink. Charlie, who had followed her, slammed the door as he ran out of the house.

Ruth, face reddened and with her eyes burning and tearful, said, "Mama's right. You got no business talking to me that way in front of Charlie." She collapsed onto the divan and sat holding herself and rocking. "You're kinder to your dumb animals than you are to me, Papa. God, I wish you knew how much this hurts me."

Pearl sat beside Ruth, put an arm around her, and the two of them rocked, ignoring him.

Ida came to the door and stood a moment, shook her head at him, and then sat opposite her two daughters. "Your papa can be a harsh man."

It was as if he wasn't present, as if the three of them had dismissed him, left him to stew. He stalked away to his bedroom and flopped down on the bed. Outside in the pasture, Isabelle lowed an answer to the Furgesons' bull's resonant bellow. It gave back a deep-throated answer. *Animals are a lot more predictable than humans*, he thought. *That's why I get along with them.* And he couldn't have predicted a few months ago that his daughter would go and do something like this.

CHAPTER 30

Chester

→→ ✤ ←←

"Dammit, Hough," Chester pounded the steering wheel of the truck as if it were the cause of his trouble. "I was feeling lucky this goddamn truck hasn't already been swallowed up whole in this cotton-pickin' swamp. And now it's ass deep in the mud." He glanced through the back window at the huge gun they were hauling to the front. The six marines who were along to help guard it had tried to push him out of the mud. Now they stood around blowing cigarette smoke into the hot and muggy air.

Hough shrugged and said, "Quit your bitching, and let's one of us walk back and get a Cat to pull us out."

"Hough, I'm sick of walking through this muck. And drivin' in it."

"Yeah, but we need to get these damn guns in place. Otherwise, those Jap planes are going to put more than your ass in the mud."

Chester looked back again at the 90mm M1 anti-aircraft gun they were pulling to the airstrip. "I was hoping to hell that we'd get this to the airstrip before some goddamn Jap bombers paid us a visit."

"Yeah. Me, too. This baby on the back of our truck sure as hell will keep the bastards higher and make it harder for them to lay a blockbuster on anything—like our truck here, for instance," said Hough.

Chester turned his gaze on the sea of palm-tree stumps on either side of his truck and thought of the days he'd spent swinging an axe at one palm tree after another until they fell. He'd then helped cut them into twelve-foot lengths to corrugate this road so traction-treaded bulldozers and big trucks wouldn't bog down. But today, pulling the extra weight of the heavy gun, his truck's wheels had hit a soft spot, sent logs flying, and buried those wheels up to the axle. Now it would take a big Cat to pull him out.

One of the six Marine escorts peered in the passenger side window. "What're you going to do now? We may have a bunch of Jap infantry somewhere close by. They've been making banzai charges, and, if they get wind of us sitting here, they'll sure as hell want this gun destroyed. And us, too."

"We have to go for a Cat to pull us out," said Hough. "You want to go, Scarsdale? Or should I go?"

Chester did not want to go trekking through the Jap-infested jungle, and he knew Hough wouldn't, either. "Let's flip a coin," he said.

Hough snorted, "We don't have time for that kind of nonsense, Scarsdale. I'll go."

"Take one of those Marines with you. I'll take a quick nap."

"Screw you, Scarsdale." Taking his gun, Hough climbed down out of the truck, asked the sergeant to give him a man to go with him, and took off at a fast walk. One of the marines threw his cigarette butt down and ran to catch up.

Chester climbed out of the truck just as small-arms fire started up somewhere nearby, but not from the direction Hough had taken. Reaching

CHAPTER 30 • CHESTER

back in the cab, Chester took his rifle and joined the five Marines who'd hit the ground the minute they heard the shots. As he crawled close to one of the Marines, he heard the whine of bullets and the tear of metal as a round went into the truck bed.

"Those bastards broke through again," a Marine said. "They sure as hell don't want to give up that airfield."

Chester could hear men screaming and shouting words he could not understand and others shouting in what he thought was English, though it was coming from too far away to know for sure what was said. The chatter of a machine gun broke through the trees, and as quickly as the noise had begun, it stopped, and there was an eerie silence broken only by the angry cry of a jungle bird. As he scanned the far edge of the clearing he'd helped make when the trees for the roadbed were cut down, he saw a lone Jap soldier stepping from the jungle.

"Look alive," the sergeant yelled, and the Marines who were fanned out along the road behind stumps, began firing their guns.

The lone man screamed as he fell. Eight other Jap soldiers then erupted from the jungle and opened fire. One of the Marines screamed as a bullet sliced through his shoulder. The screaming Japs charged then firing as they came.

Petrified for a moment only, Chester aimed his rifle at one of the charging men. He'd shot rabbits, squirrels, birds, hogs and steers, but aiming his rifle at a man almost made him freeze. *Buck fever*, he thought, and then pulled the trigger. The man he'd put in his sights fell. They all kept firing until only one man was still charging at them. As the lone Jap drew back his arm to throw a grenade, Chester fired. He wasn't sure if he'd hit the Jap or bullets from the other Marines had cut the man down.

Chester ducked his head just before the grenade, which lay next to the dead Jap, exploded sending shrapnel pinging into the truck. It was quiet then but for the moans of the injured Marine and the reassuring words of the sergeant binding the man's wound. Chester's hands began to shake, and he felt heat rush to his neck and face. A wave of remorse swept through him, followed by elation, pity, joy, relief, shame. Then he felt numb. The Japs looked like small broken toys, their bullet-ridden bodies twisted in and around and over the stumps. The blast area of the grenade had done things to the Jap's body he didn't want to look at.

"Good going," one of the Marines said to Chester, and slapped him on the shoulder. Chester nodded but couldn't speak. The rumbling noise of a big Cat's treads moving over the log road as it approached flooded him with relief. Hough was coming.

*

"How long am I going to have these nightmares, Hough? It's been damn near a week since I shot at those Japs, and I'm still waking up seeing them lying there dead. Or charging at me with those damn rifles blazing. It was a goddamn suicide charge."

"I don't know, Scarsdale. I never shot anybody myself. If I did, I suspect it would take me a while to get over it, too. But you did what you had to do. Bastards would have killed you if they could've."

"They may yet. They keep trying to take back the ground they've lost."

"Yeah, but each time they do, we drive 'em back. Those damn Marines are a tough bunch of bastards—I'll say that for them."

"Yeah. But I'll be thankful if I don't find myself with them in the midst of a damn firefight again."

"Get your sorry ass up, and let's go to breakfast."

"I'm so damned tired I don't want to move."

"Tired or not, we have to snake more of those big 90mm M1s through two miles of this God-damn muddy jungle."

*

CHAPTER 30 ✦ CHESTER

As the day waned, Chester rode with Hough back toward the beachhead. They had delivered the last of the big guns, and most of the ones already there were in place to fire. As they pulled up to park at the jungle's edge, Chester heard the drone of Jap bombers. "Get the hell to cover, Hough," he yelled as he jumped from the cab and ran for a foxhole with Hough right on his heels. The others driving trucks and bulldozers were running and diving into foxholes as well. Chester was sure the attacking Jap fighter planes would not miss the chance to strafe any men or trucks on or near the beach. As he lay flat in the foxhole, he heard the Marines open fire with the big 90mm M1s. Peering at the sky, he saw Jap bombers begin to explode, sending great gobs of fire and smoke into the sea. The sight and sound were music to Chester's ears, and he joined in with Hough and all the other cheering men. Only three bombers made it to the beach and unloaded their bomb as Chester lay flat in his foxhole and covered his head with his arms.

When the bomb blasts and explosion of Jap planes torn to shreds by the big guns faded away, Chester crawled out of his foxhole and, with Hough, went back to work loading their truck with ammunition for the M1s.

When they reached the airfield and climbed out of their truck, Chester saw the guns pointed not at the sky but into the forests. "They've turned those guns into artillery weapons, Hough."

"Hell, yes. They'll push those damn Japs right back to the other end of the island."

The zing of a rifle bullet whizzing past him and dinging into the truck sent Chester and Hough diving behind the wheels. "Damn—those bastards are still close," Chester yelled. One of the big guns opened fire then, and huge gouts of earth and dismembered trees blew up into the air. Marines then charged into the smoke and laid down a barrage of small-arms fire. The sound of fighting grew fainter then, as the enemy soldiers were driven back further from the airfield.

On the return trip to the beach with Hough driving, Chester kept his rifle propped on the floor in front of him. They drove on to the beach and parked the truck under the protection of the trees and pitched in with Polk to help build a new road to a storage area some distance back into the jungle. That done, Chester, Hough, and Polk, and dozens of other Sea Bees worked desperately to haul more supplies off the open beach and into camouflaged storage. Chester constantly glanced at the sky and strained his ears for the sound of more approaching aircraft, afraid a new wave of Jap planes would catch him in the open.

"If you don't stop staring up at the sky, you're going to get a crick in your neck," Polk said.

"Screw you, Polk. I'm just making sure if I hear them coming that I get you off the beach so I don't have to haul your sorry ass into the jungle again."

"Dammit, Chester—Hough, if I find myself flat on the beach again lying between those gasoline drums or powder barrels when those bastards come back, it won't make any difference. I'd get blown to kingdom come."

"Yep, blow a fella into a thousand pieces," Hough agreed.

"This goddamn beach and storage unit are like unlit dynamite just waiting for a Jap's match."

"Don't have to tell me that, Polk. I damn well know it." Chester sat down on the sand and lit a cigarette.

"Hey," an officer yelled. "Everybody get over here in line and help wrestle those gas drums and powder out of sight."

Too tired to bitch, Chester rose from the ground, took one last drag on his cigarette before stomping it into the mud and then stood in line with Hough, Polk, and ten other men to form a brigade. For the next two hours, he heaved supplies back into the camouflaged area, sinking deeper into the mud each time he was handed one.

"We been workin' at this for days with damn little sleep," Hough complained. "I don't know how much more I can do."

CHAPTER 30 • CHESTER

"Me and a lot of the other guys are running a temperature," said Polk. "We been working all those days in this damn mud, water, and sand while these damn insects eat us alive."

Chester straightened to his full height and stretched his back. "I'd rather be bit by the damn bugs than any one of those Jap bullets."

*

That night there were only enough tents and cots for the expanding sick quarters. Chester wrapped himself in his poncho and hoped to sleep through the drizzling rain and the night insects buzzing his ears.

Hough, who lay nearby, spoke up and asked, "How're you doin', old man?"

"When you're past thirty-six and working your tail off and then try to get any rest in this damn rain and muck, you have one helluva time going to sleep. And I'll have a worse time getting up in the morning. This is hard on an old man."

"Hell," said Hough, "there isn't a Sea Bee here any younger than thirty-five. But the damn war machine would get stuck up to its axles in this shit if it weren't for us."

"I hate that goddamn Bell, though," Chester said. "He and the rest of our unit are cooling their heels back in Australia by now while we work our butts off—or get them shot off by the Japs."

"Well, now, that's what you get for pissing the asshole off. And what I get for being your goddamn friend."

"Yeah," Polk bitched, "And me for not beatin' the shit out of you, Scarsdale. Lettin' you get away with coldcocking him. He never forgave me for that."

*

The next morning Chester awakened to the sound of Zeros strafing the incoming lighters bringing more troops and supplies in. He rolled from his damp bed to the loud braying of an officer.

"Get your skinny asses ready to go down to the beach," he screamed. "We've got to get some of those intact supplies inland as soon as this raid's over."

Chester huddled where he sat and waited with the others till the American planes engaged and shot down or drove the attacking planes away. Still half asleep, he stumbled with the rest of his group to the mess tent, grabbed a cup of coffee and then slogged through the water-soaked jungle and wet sand till he reached the lighters, some half sunk and others blown to smithereens. Medics were helping the wounded whose bodies the Zeros' heavy caliber machine guns had ripped through. Hurrying up the ramp of one of the undamaged lighters, Chester helped load boxes of ammunition onto the bed of a battered truck.

A noncom yelled at him, "Scarsdale, take Hough and get that truck to the airfield. The Japs are making another big push right now. They need that ammunition yesterday."

Chester jumped into the truck cab, shifted down into low and started for the jungle, some of the new Marines following behind. It seemed hours before he drove up to the big guns and started helping unload. Several hundred feet away, he saw a fresh wave of Japanese soldiers come screaming out of the trees. "God in heaven," Hough shouted, "I hope those bastards don't break the Marines' lines."

"They capture these guns, and we'll lose the airfield," Chester shouted back. Finished unloading, Chester jumped back in the truck's cab and had it rolling back toward the beach before Hough swung in beside him.

"You lousy son-of-a-bitch. You trying to leave me behind?"

Chester took a deep breath but said nothing. He peered in the rearview mirror and saw what looked like hundreds of Jap soldiers charging out of the trees as the concussion blasts of the big guns shook the truck. Leaving

CHAPTER 30 ✦ CHESTER

the front lines behind, he reached and turned on the windshield wipers as sheets of heavy rain began lashing the windshield.

When he pulled to a stop at the edge of the beach, he saw Jap fighter planes hightailing it back to their airstrips after coming in low and strafing the landing craft, Sea Bees, and fighting troops farther down the way.

Driving to the water's edge, Chester and Hough picked up another load of ammo for the big guns and headed back to the airstrip.

"I hope to God the marines still hold it," Hough said. Chester nodded and gunned the motor as they hit the edge of the trees. When they approached the near edge of the field, Chester was spooked by the eerie quiet that greeted them. The big guns were still, and the runway at the far end had been blown to bits along with what must have been hundreds of Jap soldiers. Medics were rushing about tending the wounded, Japs and Americans both. "Those tough sons-a-bitchin' Marines sent a lot of Japs to hell today, Hough."

"Yeah. But the Japs just keep coming. So let's get this truck unloaded and get the hell back into the jungle."

Back and forth all day, it seemed to Chester that relief would never come. Night came without relief, and he kept the truck rolling till he had to slap his face to keep awake.

Hours after night fell, Chester rolled up in his poncho just inside the jungle's edge. Hough and half a dozen other Sea Bees grunted and sighed as they settled in around him. Sleep wouldn't come to Chester. He tried pushing away thoughts of all that blood and guts he'd seen, and then he'd think of Charlie out selling savings stamps so he could, "help you come home sooner, daddy." He hoped to God he would get home—sooner or later. Thoughts of bombs exploding blew those thoughts away. Then he tried to think of her. He remembered those times in California when he'd spent nights with Alice. One of those nights had been a hell of a night. They'd gone drinking and dancing, and then stumbled home, and that's probably when she got pregnant. He could never have that kind of fun with Ruth. She hated dancing and drinking. Too damn much like her mother and papa. Those two wanted to see Ruth and themselves as respectable and upright. Like hell. The memory flashed in his mind of the time he'd screwed Ida. She wasn't so high and mighty then. He heard Hough lying next to him grumble, "Damn Japs." Wanting to get away from those thoughts of home, he whispered, "Hough? You're awake. I can't sleep, either."

"You start yapping at me, and I won't go to sleep."

"I keep trying to get thoughts about what we saw today out of my mind."

"Yeah. Those goddamn Japs did a lot of damage today. And damn them, they killed Abbot. Pete is missing—probably blown into a thousand pieces—and Jeffers has a wounded leg. And if that isn't bad enough, there were some of our guys died of some damn jungle rot. That's not to mention the ones who got shell shocked and had to be evacuated."

"If those shit-eating Japs drop many more bombs, I think I'm going to have a nervous breakdown myself," Chester said and then wrapped himself tighter in his poncho. He heard the big guns open up then, pouring shells into the night sky as they hammered incoming Jap bombers. "Those guns are playing music to my ears," Chester said. Then he was silent as bombs from some of the planes making it past the guns began exploding on the airfield they were rebuilding, likely tearing huge craters that would have to be filled before the rest of the runway was finished and their own bombers could land.

When it became quiet again, Hough said, "Way things are going, we'll finish with the airfield in a week. Then it won't be long till we load up and ship out."

"What? No shore leave first?"

"Hell, yes, there is. But it's another goddamn Jap-infested shore." Hough chuckled at his own humor, ignoring boos and groans from some men around him still awake.

CHAPTER 30 ✦ CHESTER

"What the hell, you all can't sleep anyway," Chester growled.

*

A week later, long before dawn, Chester, along with Hough and Polk, boarded a lighter and, for eight hours rode frothing, thrashing waves across to another island that had not yet been named. As they neared the shore, Chester saw thousands of troops splashing ashore, and, by late morning, a beachhead had been established. He began unloading supplies or hauling 155s and their ammunition through the mud to emplacements. Sweating from work and fear, he watched as American planes from the airfield he'd just helped finish swoop in to engage incoming Jap aircraft. The 155s he helped put in place began belching flame and shells that targeted any of the Japanese bombers or fighter planes that got past the U.S. air defense.

A dozen Zeros came in low from another direction and began strafing the beach, sending Chester diving into a muddy foxhole. From his horizontal grandstand seat, he counted at least half a dozen falling Japanese aircraft. Each time a Zero burst into flames, Chester and the other mud-covered men watching cheered.

During the day, Chester watched three more air battles fought offshore, but no Jap plane reached close enough to either bomb or strafe his position. That night the Japanese came over four more times, forcing Chester to cringe in his foxhole. *Damn*, he thought, *those bastards aren't goin' to let me get a wink of sleep.*

Just before dawn the crackle of gunfire and explosions of grenades woke him from the little sleep he'd enjoyed.

"Those bastards are trying to take back this beach," Hough croaked.

"Not a chance in hell," said Chester, hoping he spoke the truth. The noise of the guns stopped almost as abruptly as they'd begun, and Chester rolled out of his foxhole and began his day.

He had to hit a foxhole three times during the day when the remaining Japs on the island made suicide charges and were cut to ribbons by the Marines.

As the week progressed and all the Japs were captured or shot, Chester's morale improved. He even smiled when he heard that the Sea Bees' cooks had managed to borrow three stoves from the Army and Marines and began providing hot food. He wasn't smiling quite so much when he had to help clean the dead Japs out of the elaborate tunnel systems they'd dug in the coral. *God damn,* he thought. *It had to be a horrible way to die. Sent to hell by a flame thrower.* He was smiling again when he helped convert one of the tunnels into a bunker for himself, Polk, and Hough. The first night in it, lying back with his head cradled in his hands, he said, "This is the first time in months we've slept in a dry bed without those buzzing little bastards dive bombing us all through the night."

"You talking about the Japs or the mosquitoes?" Hough asked.

"Hell. Now you mention it, both."

Chester relaxed his head back onto his pallet and said, "Damnation, but this is the life."

"Shame it just won't last," Polk groused.

Chester snorted, "Always look on the bright side, don't you, Polk? That's what I love about you."

"You two quit flapping your gums so I can go to sleep?" Hough growled.

Chester took a deep breath, let it out slowly, and, feeling safer than he had in weeks, allowed himself to drift into sleep.

CHAPTER 31

Ruth

⇥ ✤ ⇤

*I*n the warmth of a late-April morning, Ruth sat in the swing on the front porch waiting for her sisters and their families to arrive. With the toe of one foot, she pushed herself back and forth, hoping the gentle movement would soothe her and release a knot in the middle of her stomach. It was a knot of worry and something else she didn't want to admit to herself. She had to get her sister Joan alone today, talk with her, and share the secret that was twisting her insides. Today the family was gathering for a one o'clock dinner. Since being caught out in the lie about spending two days away with Joe, the pressure in the house had kept her on edge. Now a new reason for tension to heat up, maybe boil over, made her want to run to the thicket and hide somewhere among the new leaves. Charlie had not fully forgiven her for being away and not bringing him a present. Thank goodness he hadn't figured out that she'd been away with Joe for those two days. Papa stalked about with a scowl on his face. Mother was distant. Ruth wanted more than anything to get away from her parents, but that was not possible. She wanted to be with Joe. That wasn't possible right now, either.

Today was a family day, and she and Charlie, her sisters, her brothers-in-law, nephews, and nieces would all spend hours together here with Mother and Papa. Pretend all was normal. Keep hidden as much as possible all the tension and aggravation she had brought into the family.

The newspaper lay on her lap unread. She knew all she wanted to about the progress of the war—even though, of late, the news was encouraging. The Allies had begun to take back land conquered by the Japanese, whose hold on the Pacific Islands was slowly being broken. The war could be over soon. Chester would come home. Every time that fact forced its way into her thoughts, she wanted to run somewhere and hide.

As one o'clock neared, first the Perrys and then the Dennisons turned into the driveway, bringing their contributions to the dinner. She was surprised when tears came to her eyes and she wiped at them, hoping no one saw. She swallowed several times, forcing down her gorge before joining her sisters and mother to get the food ready.

The children rushed about in the yard, hollering and playing tag, and the men stood on the porch, talking about the cotton crop. The rich smell of roast beef Joan brought made Ruth's mouth water, though she knew that when she sat down to eat, her appetite would flee. She'd felt nauseous earlier that morning as she helped Mother prepare the mashed potatoes, green beans, and hot rolls. Earlier, Ruth had set the dining-room table for the adults and the card table for the children, while Papa sat in his chair reading and occasionally glancing up at her, his brow knitted and with a sour twist to his mouth. It was all she could do to bear it.

Throughout the meal, most all the talk was about the war, and Ruth sat silent though most of it. She had on her mind the split between two

CHAPTER 31 • RUTH

realities: Joe and Chester. And a third reality forced on her that she wanted to talk about with Joan. She would like to share with Pearl but knew she would be more upset and judgmental than Joan.

Pearl had brought a mouthwatering Devil's food cake which Ruth was able to take few bites of. Finished, she sat impatiently as the others forked the last crumbs of chocolate cake from off the good dishes Mother reserved for Sunday and holiday use. She was exhausted from tension, not sleeping well, worrying over what would happen with Chester and Alice, with her and Joe. Sarah had grown so close to her in the past two months that Ruth was beginning to think of her as a daughter. But it was this newest reality that had given her a stomachache, and she wanted to hide in the bedroom with a pillow over her head and squeeze out the pain. But instead, she helped clear the table, wash the dishes, and put away the leftovers. Thank goodness no one could read her mind, depressed, scared, confused, and worried as her thoughts were.

When her papa and brothers-in-law, Bill and George, finished eating, they strolled down to the barn to take a look at one of Papa's ailing calves. From the kitchen window, Ruth watched as Bill and George sent clouds of pipe and cigarette smoke billowing up to then disappear in the warm, dry air.

Papa was becoming more and more impossible. He had snarled at her this morning when she was gathering eggs, all but called her a loose woman for continuing to go out with Joe. She'd almost dropped the basket of eggs. She wasn't sure how much longer she could remain in Papa's house. The sound of Carl dumping a set of his grandfather's dominoes on to the table brought her out of her funk.

Turning away from the window, she saw her nephew, Will Junior, looking every bit the carbon copy of his daddy, sitting at the card table with his brother, Carl. The two of them were trying to coax Charlie out of the bedroom, where he'd retreated after being denied a second piece of cake. They wanted him to play dominoes with them. When he came out, he was wearing that long face the likes of which Ruth had seen so many times on his daddy's face. He sat down at the card table without a word and started turning the dominoes facedown, showing the snarling dragons imprinted on their backs. *Those dragons fit his mood*, Ruth thought. Carl, cute in a twelve-year-old, pug-nosed way, swirled the dominoes about, setting them to clicking and thwacking against each other. "I'm going to whip your-alls' butts," he bragged. Catching Ruth's eyes on him, he gave her one of his lopsided grins that had always captured her heart. She had to smile when he then tried to hold his seven dominoes in one hand like Papa could. But one and then another dropped face up on the floor.

"Show any more of them dominoes, Carl, and Will Junior or I will be whipping your butt instead," Charlie crowed.

"Don't use that language." Ruth walked over to the table and squeezed Charlie's shoulder hard; making him squeal and squirm away. "And keep your voice down, Aunt Joan is trying to get the girls down for a nap. Elizabeth hears you, she won't take a nap for sure. And Bertha wakes up, your aunt Joan will skin you alive."

They began playing, and, by the time Ruth had watched each of them lay down all but two of their dominoes, Charlie played and said, "I'll have to give you a nickel, Will, but Carl can't play, so, I'll take a dime and domino."

"Darn you, Cuz, you're worse than Grandpa. I swear the two of you can see through my dominoes," Will complained.

That really was so like her Papa, thought Ruth. Charlie was ahead of both cousins. Only in fourth grade, he did math problems that even Will Junior found hard, leading his older cousin to sometimes be downright nasty, calling Charlie an egghead or a know-it-all. Though smart, thank goodness he was innocent enough not to know what was going on between her and Joe.

From somewhere down by the barn, Ruth heard Bill laugh and Papa yell, "Good dog, Hitler." Ruth wondered what the old hound had done

CHAPTER 31 ♦ RUTH

but then turned her thoughts to the three men. Their worlds were so narrow. Papa loved his animals and his dominoes and acted as if the rest of the world was a burden he had to bear; George and Bill were good husbands but, Bill, like Papa, centered his life on cotton, his livestock, and dominoes. George, an assistant fire chief, centered his on putting out fires and playing dominoes. They both loved their families. Didn't run around on her sisters like Chester did her. But Chester had managed to get off the farm and then out of small towns. Had taken her with him. But did he love her now? Or Alice? She wondered if Papa had ever loved his family, or if he'd seen each child born to him and Ida as just another burden to bear, another mouth to feed. And now he'd had her and Charlie's mouths to feed.

She had to get away. But to where? When? And who with? Joe? Chester? Neither?

Maybe she could learn to love Joe as much as she had Chester, even though he was a farmer, like her brothers-in-law. If married to him, she would live out her life on a farm. Joe would certainly give her and Charlie a more stable life than Chester ever would. The problem was, she couldn't get over feeling Chester was the one she loved most. He was different from those three down by the barn. He never could have been a farmer. He had ambition to do more even though he ended up driving a bulldozer. He'd never liked plowing and planting and then waiting on lady luck to bring the rain when it was needed, or to keep it away when it wasn't. Joe would always be a farmer.

She was married to a man who didn't know what he wanted. Chester was married to a woman who now had no idea what she wanted when he returned. And had a child with Alice. Her thoughts of Chester were shot through with anger and hurt, but if he came in the door this minute and asked her to take him back, she wasn't sure but that she would. No matter how much she cared for Joe. She shivered at the thought of what she was going to tell Joan when they had a minute to themselves.

"Domino," yelled Carl, startling Ruth out of her thoughts. "Put that in your pipe and smoke it, Charlie."

"Just dumb luck," Charlie shot back.

"Be a good sport, now, Charlie," Ruth scolded. She left the domino players and joined the women in the kitchen, going to the sink and taking a soapy dishrag from her mother's reddened hands. "You go on in to rest, Mother, and let Pearl and me finish up in here."

"There's no rest for the weary," her mother said, but she moved away from the dishpan to sit at the porcelain-topped table and rub at the knuckles of one hand. A fly buzzed her ear, and she waved it away. When the fly lit on the edge of the table and sat a moment, combing at the back of its head with two front legs, she hit it with a swatter and then gave a short, satisfied sigh. "If Bob don't get that screen door fixed soon, I swear I'll move to the barn. There's got to be fewer of these pests out there than there is in here." She stood and left the room to the flies.

Pearl moved closer to Ruth and whispered, "I worry about Mother. With all the aggravation around here lately I'm afraid she's going to have another spell with her heart."

Ruth felt stung knowing that Pearl included her as more the aggravator than Papa or Charlie. "I don't know what to say to that, Pearl."

"I'm sorry. I shouldn't have said that." Pearl walked into the sitting room, where Mother was fanning herself with a paper fan Pearl had brought her from the Roosevelt Baptist Church. A picture of Jesus's praying hands decorated one side, and the other had the address of the church. Ruth, Joan, and their folks attended church only for weddings and funerals, but Pearl and her family were regular members. Ruth believed Pearl's less-forgiving nature was fueled by her churchgoing. She would not be a person to share the concern that troubled Ruth. It had to be Joan.

In the other room, a domino slapped down hard on the table, and Charlie yelled, "Domino! I beat you-all again."

CHAPTER 31 • RUTH

Pearl stepped into the room, snapped her fingers, and said, "You all go on outside. We women need some peace and quiet. And you're apt to wake Joan's girls."

They all trooped out the kitchen door and around to the front porch, where Ruth could hear them playing rock-scissors-paper. Will chanted, "rock breaks scissors, scissors cut paper, paper covers rock."

Ruth walked into the living room and stood in the doorway watching them. She'd played this game with Chester when they were going out together. When she chose wrong and her scissors got broke, or paper got cut, or the rock was covered up, Chester would give her a stinging, two-fingered blow to her forearm. She stepped onto the porch and watched the three boys take turns, the winner slapping the loser. Charlie's eyes teared up with one hard blow from Will, but he forced the tears back.

Chester had once hit her so hard, she'd cried and left him sitting on the porch, calling out how sorry he was. Ruth wanted to cry now from the turmoil in her heart and the memories of Chester.

"Ruth, are you going to stay there and watch those boys play that game till everyone else has gone home?" Joan said. "Come on in here, and have this lemonade."

"Lemonade," shouted Charlie as he pushed out of the swing, leaving it to gently rock back and forth as he ran back around the house to the kitchen door. His two cousins followed, but strolled with their adolescent long-limbed slouch.

"You've got tears in your eyes, Ruth."

"I was just thinking of playing rock-scissors-paper with Chester when he slapped my arm hard."

"I've said it before, and I'll say it again..."

"If I hear anyone else say it again, whatever it is, I'm going to scream."

Joan drew her mouth into a knotted pucker and let the screen door slam behind her as she sat in the swing with Ruth and handed her a lemonade. "I don't want to hear you scream, sister, so I won't say it."

Taking the glass, Ruth drank deeply, the sweet and lemony flavor washing away the bitter taste in her mouth. A flurry of wings announced the noisy arrival of the sparrows who frequented the eves of the porch where Joan and she now sat. The rhythmical creak of the swing as they gently set it in motion was usually soothing but not today. The hum of the telephone wires that snaked along the road seemed louder than usual.

A wave of nausea rolled up from Ruth's stomach, and she braced herself against the swing's chains. She leaned close to her sister and whispered, "I may have a problem, Joan."

Joan's face clouded over with concern. "Can I help? You want to tell me about it?"

Ruth nodded. "There's some big ears around here, though, Joan. Can we walk to the trees?"

Joan followed Ruth to the road, where three mulberry trees grew tall, their leaves rippling in the breeze. Papa's white dog came tearing around the corner of the house and joined them. "Now why aren't you down at the barn with Papa and the others." Joan reached down, patted his head, and then shooed him away. "What is it, Ruth?"

"I missed a period. I haven't done that in years." Her heart beat mercilessly fast as she added, "And I'm feeling sick to my stomach every morning."

"Lord help us. Does Joe know?"

"No. I don't want him to know. I'm still not sure I'm pregnant. I don't want to worry him. Besides, I still don't know what's going to happen when Chester gets back from overseas."

"You're not some silly young girl making out in the back seat of a car. Didn't Joe use some protection?"

"You know Joan, after Chester gave me that infection, a doctor told me I could never get pregnant again. And for the past eight years I haven't. I told Joe we didn't need protection."

"So much for that doctor's opinion. Oh, Sister, I'm so sorry. What are you going to do?"

CHAPTER 31 • RUTH

"I don't really know. Chester's my husband. And despite all he's done, I still love him. And God forgive me, I love Joe as much or more. I don't know who I want to be with."

"That might be something that Alice Jenson is going to help decide."

"I'm not so sure Chester is going to want to live with Alice, Joan. Oh, God, Sister, I don't know what to do."

"I hope you'll forgive me for saying it, but I'd hate to see you go back to Chester. You stay with him, and you'll be miserable. What's more, Charlie will grow up to be no different from that hell-raising daddy of his. Chester never grew up."

"I know."

"Joe did. And he settled down with a good woman and made something of himself. Grew into a responsible man. Took over his parents' farm and rents another. Makes a decent living. He hasn't moved but once in the twelve years he was married, while you and Chester moved so many times, I couldn't keep track."

"I just seem paralyzed, Joan. My mind goes from thinking I could never leave Chester if he chooses to come back to me and not Alice, to wanting more than anything to be with Joe."

"You don't decide and do something right soon, you'll start showing. It won't be a secret anymore."

"Please, don't mention this to anyone, you hear? Not even Pearl. You know how she is."

"I won't. But it'll do little good. That secret won't keep. When you start showing, it sure won't be a secret."

Mother and Pearl appeared at the door and waved to them, and Ruth returned a half-hearted flutter of her hand. Mother looked worn, standing there with her hair pulled back in a severe bun, one arthritic hand on Pearl's shoulder. Her heart might give out any day. If she heard that Ruth was pregnant, God knows it might kill her.

Joan put her arm through Ruth's. It felt good to have that loving arm supporting her. Bowing her head before she walked to the porch with Joan, Ruth lamented, "How much trouble have I brought down on Charlie and me?"

Joan only shook her head.

I've asked this question of myself I don't know how many times, Ruth thought, *but there's no happy answer.*

CHAPTER 32

Ruth

Ruth sat beside Charlie's bed, watching him under the lamplight. Even asleep, the ridges and furrows on his forehead had not yet smoothed out. He moved restlessly, mumbling something Ruth could not make out. *Bad dreams*, she thought, and reached out to push away a strand of hair trailing across his eyes. She wondered what unhappy images would visit her tonight if she could ever go to sleep. Her admission to Joan had been like a slap to the face; it had shaken her into fully admitting—and accepting—that she was more than likely pregnant. She asked the hundreds of roses curling about on the wallpaper, *How could those doctors have been so wrong?* The roses stayed silent.

She tried to push Chester out of her mind. But he wouldn't go. A moth started circling the glass lamp globe, bouncing against it and then circling up and hitting the ceiling. Its shadow flittered among the roses. A tear coursed down her cheeks.

She remembered that time in Tulsa when Chester ran off for a week, leaving her and Charlie without any money or food. They'd had to live on Quaker Oats for five days. She'd felt so helpless then, wondering if he'd ever show up. Now she wondered what would happen when he did show up. Her with Joe's baby. Alice with Chester's. She wondered if she could find someone to do an abortion but had no idea who to ask.

She tucked the cover up under Charlie's chin and picked up the lamp. The light bounced around the room and across Charlie so that his face appeared in motion, pulled one way, then pushed another. She turned quickly and left the room.

Her needle poised over a half-made doily, Mother looked up from crocheting as Ruth entered the room. "I thought you'd gone on to bed, you were in there so long." Her hook dipped and rose as she added row after endless row of stitches.

Ruth set her lamp close to her papa's chair, sat down heavily, and picked up a pillowcase she was embroidering. She'd never really had any patience for the fine work of crocheting or embroidering, hadn't done any since leaving home at fifteen, but lately, faced with long hours in the company of her mother, she had taken it up again. As a girl with her sisters, overseen by her mother, it had been a weary pastime to while away many a bitter, winter's cold or a summer's sweaty day or evening.

"I was wondering what you and Joan were up to, hiding out by the mulberry trees after dinner today."

If she really were pregnant, how long could she keep that secret from her mother? Not long. Ruth wondered if her mother had already guessed, and this question was her way of letting it be known.

"We were talking about whether I'd marry Joe if Chester gets a divorce. But I have to say, I really don't know what I'll do if Chester decides he wants to stay with Charlie and me. I might ought to, for Charlie's sake."

CHAPTER 32 ♦ RUTH

"Or not. That Joe Williams is a steady sort," her mother said. "Not a two-timing rascal like Chester." Mother laid her sewing in her lap and caught Ruth's eye. "And you'd be just down the road from us. Livin' close to Pearl, too. And Joan there in Hobart. Those two nieces of yours just love you, Ruth. They would be heartbroken to see you leave."

"Don't push me off on Joe," Ruth snapped.

Her mother took up the needlework from her lap and frowned. "My, aren't we touchy?"

"Sorry. I still think I love Chester, Mother, even though he got somebody else pregnant." She laid down her own sewing and looked at the darkness outside the window, deliberately not meeting her mother's eyes.

"Tell you the truth, dear, it don't surprise me any." Her mother dropped a stitch and mumbled something Ruth couldn't hear and then laid the work aside again; removing her glasses, she rubbed at the bridge of her nose. "I sure wouldn't wait around pining away for Chester if I were you. There are a lot of divorced and widowed women around here who would fall all over themselves to marry Joe. I have to say you're lucky he's taken such a shine to you."

"Mother," Ruth scolded, though it seemed to Ruth strange that she was shocked by her mother's remark.

"What I say is true. Joe's the best catch in this county."

"Maybe Joe just wants me to help him stop being lonely right now. I don't really know if he wants to marry me"

"What do you expect? Man lost his wife. He's got a little girl to raise. So, is wanting to marry you such a bad thing?" She leaned back, closed her eyes, and rocked back and forth, the old rocker giving off a comforting creak like the one that Ruth remembered had put her to sleep when she was a little girl. "Come to think of it, your papa and I weren't all that much in love when we got married. He was a mama's boy, really. Wanted me to mother him. And I wasn't head over heels in love with him, either.

I just needed to get out of that house full of brothers and sisters. Never a moment's peace there."

Ruth felt the color rising in her face. Her mother didn't ordinarily speak of these things to her. Why was she now?

Mother settled back, closed her eyes, and knit her brow. "Your papa had just lost your grandmother Choat, three weeks before we met. There was something sorrowful about him that attracted me, I guess. It appealed to a lot of women over the next few years." The bitterness in her voice settled heavily over the room, and, almost in answer to her criticism, the harsh snores of her papa drifted through the closed door of his bedroom.

"Man could raise the dead," Mother snorted, but did not open her eyes. "Bob stuck to me like a bee to honey. At sixteen, I didn't realize that settling down to a marriage, doing farmwork, and keeping a house was a far cry from getting away. I just repeated what my mama had done. Including having all you kids."

"You really didn't love each other when you married?" Ruth felt a hollow growing in her stomach. She knew that there was no love between them now, but she wanted to have a picture in her mind of them once being in love. She'd thought that misunderstanding, deceit, and the death of her brother Brian were what had whittled away at the love they once felt.

"Oh, I can't say I didn't love him. I guess I did a little. Talked myself into thinking I did. I don't rightly know now. I think I just felt sorry for him." She started rocking back and forth again but the squeak of the chair was no longer comforting.

Ruth laid her needle aside and went to the water bucket. Taking the dipper, she filled it and then drank in huge gulps. Water filled her nose, and she sneezed, spilling water down her front. Dropping the dipper back into the water, she gripped the sink with both hands and held on as if she were about to fall. She tried to picture some token of affection given or received by her parents, but nothing would come to mind. They worked hard. They lived together. But she knew they took

CHAPTER 32 ♦ RUTH

little or no joy in one another. And now she'd learned that they had never loved each other.

Ruth turned. Through the doorway, she could see her mother had taken up her needle again and was making quick, darting movements with it. She asked, "Why did you stay with Papa? If you never loved him?"

Her mother flicked a strand of hair that had fallen across her eyes, interfering with her fast-moving hands. "What would you have me do, Ruth? I had four or five kids before I could hardly turn around. Then it was too late. And now what would I do? I've got no money. I've got no job skills. I'm past fifty. Do you know how many down-and-out women there are out there past fifty, single or widowed? And living hand to mouth?" Her mother stood and walked out to the front porch.

Ruth followed, stepped out beside her mother, who was now sitting in the swing, pushing it slowly back and forth. Ruth took hold of a porch roof support and leaned her hip against it. She heard a coyote howl from off in the thicket. It was answered by another cry far over by the creek. The cicadas quieted and then increased their rhythmic hum. A bat swished nearby, chasing cicadas most likely.

"Well, Ruth, answer me. What could I have done?"

Looking up, Ruth could see a three-quarter moon forcing its way through a thin overcast. It cast a light so dim that her mother's face wouldn't come into focus. There were few stars shining through. "I don't know Mother, probably nothing. I may be one of those women you spoke of myself, all of thirty-five, no skills, little enough education. I have only Charlie to raise, not five kids, but it would still be a challenge."

"I never went hungry since the day I married your papa. None of you kids ever went hungry, either. That's more than you can say about you and Chester Scarsdale. And you still hang on to him like he was priceless."

"Yes, I do. I've loved Chester. Through it all—his absences, his selfishness, his other women, not being sure where the next meal would come from. I guess I still love him, even though I love Joe, too and know he's best for me and Charlie."

"I know a little of why you love Chester. He's personable. And he can turn on the charm when he wants to. Hide behind it."

Her mother's voice didn't sound right to Ruth. It held something that was troubling. But what? The moon came from behind the clouds and showed her mother's face relaxed and serene for a moment before disappearing again as clouds obscured the universe once more. A chill invaded Ruth that spread to every exposed pain and uncertainty standing there with her. Why would her mother seem so relaxed talking about Chester? She recalled that one time, in a fit of rage at her parents, Chester hinted that he'd slept with her mother, but when he calmed down, denied it, said that he just wanted to bring those self-righteous Choats down a notch. Not hurt Ruth. But every now and then, the awful memory of what he said invaded her thoughts and, knowing Chester, there could be truth to it. She had never said anything to her mother because it was so awful of Chester to claim such a thing. Or for Ruth to give any credit to it.

"Mother? You had a soft spot for Chester, didn't you?"

"Well, like I said, he was charming when he wanted to be."

"Chester got mad at all of the Choats once and hinted that something went on with you and him back years ago. I just thought he was being mean. But could that be at all true?"

The calm tenor of her mother's voice changed to anger as she retorted, "How could you even ask such a thing, Ruth?"

She stood very still, waiting for her mother to say more, and, when she didn't, Ruth said, "I don't know. I'm sorry."

"Sorry is not enough. I don't know how I could raise a daughter who would believe such a bald-faced lie from a man whose morals are lower than one of those tomcats that sneak into your papa's barn sniffing around for one of the females he keeps around." Her mother stood, pushing the

CHAPTER 32 ♦ RUTH

old porch swing into motion as she shoved past Ruth, entered the house, and and let the screen door slam behind her.

Ruth stumbled to the swing and sat down, her whole body tingling with hurt, anger, and disbelief. She'd couldn't help noticing her mother's quiet calm when talking about Chester and then the outraged denial when asked about Chester's angry accusations. It left Ruth feeling hollowed out, like she'd felt those first few months after arriving at the farm before falling in love with Joe. Could mother's reaction be a stark, angry denial of God's truth? Ruth wanted to sink through the cement porch. No, even better, she had to take herself and Charlie out of this house. Leave. Even at the risk of being destitute.

If her mother and Chester did have a thing between them, Ruth didn't know who she'd hate most, her mother or Chester. What she did hate without doubt was how hard Papa had been on her about Joe. Papa was a hypocrite. He had done worse things than she ever had. And maybe Mother might have done even worse—lain with her own daughter's husband.

It was well past midnight before Ruth was ready to go to her bed. As she stood, trying to find enough energy to go inside, she heard another coyote howl, and, this time, it was answered by others from what seemed like every direction. The loneliness of the coyotes' cries, the emptiness of her mother's life and the stark reality of her own, closed in about her. The moon, which had cast a soft light through thin clouds totally disappeared behind another darker one. In her bedroom, blowing hard against a cupped hand she held close to the top of the lamp globe, she extinguished the soft glow of the light, found her way to bed in the dark, and took her tears into her dreams.

CHAPTER 33

Ruth

"Ow," Ruth yelled and dropped the large butcher knife she had been using to chop up the potatoes. A small drop of blood welled up from the finely sliced skin of her left middle finger.

Her mother's face screwed up in a severe scowl. "Bob sharpened that thing yesterday. I should have warned you."

"Small comfort, now," Ruth said. "You finish these potatoes while I find a Band Aid." Ruth put her finger in her mouth as she walked into her bedroom. The sharp taste of raw potato mixing with that of warm saliva and blood was unpleasant and she wrinkled her nose. In her dresser drawer, she rummaged with her free hand until she found a small cardboard box filled with Band-Aids. Blood oozed from the cut and smeared onto the Band Aid as she peeled it open.

CHAPTER 33 ✦ RUTH

Keeping her cut middle finger stuck straight out while she pasted the Band Aid on the cut, she was struck by how vulgar it looked. But vulgar was how she saw her mother since she got so testy about Chester. Ruth could barely stand being around her. Or Papa.

Back in the kitchen, she started setting plates on the table, not speaking to her mother, who sat quietly watching her.

"You keep that finger out of things, now, Ruth. I don't want you getting an infection."

Ruth winced. "I've got some sense, mother. Don't need a reminder to take care of myself."

"I was just being concerned, after all. You don't have to bite my head off."

The sting of being treated like a child had angered her. She wanted to give her mother and papa the news together, but now she didn't want to wait for Papa. She took a deep breath, put down the last plate, sat down across the table from her mother, and said, "Joe needs someone to help out with his parents in town. He'll pay ten dollars a week, and the Williamses will provide room and board for Charlie and me."

Her mother stood, walked to the stove, poured fried potatoes into a skillet and began stirring. Hot grease popped and sputtered as a warm, thick smell rose out of the pan. "You know, there's no real need for you to be moving. You're more than welcome here."

Ruth stood, took a handful of knives, forks, and spoons, and began setting the table, arranging silverware carefully. It soothed her to do something orderly that gave her a sense of control in her life, a life that had been turned on its head. Ruth wondered at the flatness in her mother's voice. Did she mean what she said? Could she admit to herself that she didn't? "I know. It's just that I feel I ought to start making my own way. You and Papa have been saddled with Charlie and me far too long. I can't go on living here the rest of my life." She could hardly bring herself to stay another night.

"Still, there's no cause to leave just yet," Ruth's mother said. "Now go call Charlie and Bob to dinner."

Ruth sighed, walked to the door, and called to her son, who was sitting astraddle the coal-oil barrel making dive-bomber noises. "Charlie, go down to the barn, and tell your grandpa to come and eat."

She watched as he ran to barn with old Hitler nipping at the flying, barefoot heels. Slamming open the door, Charlie yelled, "Dinner, Grandpa", then he came hurtling back and pushed past her and through the kitchen door. The flop-eared, spotted hound stopped at the door, grinning his doggy grin, panting from the run and drooling at the smell of fried ham. Charlie plopped down in a chair at the table. "You're more interested in ham, beans, and fried potatoes than that old hound," Ruth teased.

Hitler continued to stand at the screen sniffing and whining. He barked once, *but in vain*, Ruth thought. There would be no table scraps finding their way to him tonight. "Go on, Hitler," she said. "Go on to the pasture and find yourself one of those long-legged jackrabbits." On saying that, it galled Ruth that even an old hound could look after itself better than she could.

Her papa came in just as the last glass of cold milk was poured. He sat down without a word.

"How many times have I said I don't want you dragging the barnyard in here with you?" Her mother's voice was sharp and unfriendly, her face drawn up in an unpleasant scowl. "Now take those shoes off."

Her papa's eyes narrowed, and a resentful frown furrowed his brow as he rose, opened the screen door, and kicked his shoes off onto the porch. The old hound must have snuffled at them because of her papa's angry, "Get on away from those shoes, Hitler, or I'll take a hoe handle to you."

Ruth sat down at the far end of the kitchen table and placed her hands on the cool porcelain top, feeling the dull throb in her cut finger. When they were all seated, Ruth said, "Papa, Charlie, I've told Joe I'd move into town and help take care of his folks."

Charlie almost choked on a mouthful of cornbread. He grabbed his glass of milk, gulped it down, dragged the back of a hand across the

CHAPTER 33 ✦ RUTH

milk mustache, and then wiped his hand on the leg of his overalls. "You mean just you're going to move into town?" He bumped up and down in his chair, sending it scooting back from the table. "I'm not going to stay here." Tears had sprung to his eyes.

Ruth's mother put a hand on his shoulder. "Well, of course, she's going to take you. Now, how many times have I told you not to wipe your hands on your clothes?"

Ruth wanted to scream. She should be the one correcting her son, not her mother. And who cared right now that Charlie wiped his hands on his pants? She reached and patted her son's shoulder. "I'm never going to leave you, Charlie." Charlie settled back into his chair and picked up another piece of cornbread, the stricken look on his face softening. "When are we going?" he asked.

"I told them we'd move in next week."

"Why'd you go and get a job without telling us anything about it?" Her papa, laying down his fork, scowled at her, and it was hard to tell if it was because she and Charlie were going or pique that he had not been let in on it till now. "How's your mother going to manage with that heart of hers?"

"One of us girls will come out and help with the heavy work of washing the clothes and bedding. We'll scrub the floors at least once a week. All Mother has to do is dust, cook, and wash dishes. I've stayed around here with Charlie too long as it is. It's been too hard on you two having us here."

Papa looked at her, his scowl deepening, his lips moving as if he wanted to say something but couldn't get it out. Mother, tight-lipped, let her fork sit on her full plate. Charlie looked from one to the other, an anxious frown on his face. *He's still afraid I might just leave him behind,* she thought.

*

Charlie began pestering her with questions from the moment she'd told him and her parents at the dinner table. "Why are we moving out? Can I come visit Sarah? Where will I go to school? Why do we have to move? Why? Why? Why?"

She tried her best to reassure him. "We need to depend more on ourselves, not Grandpa and Grandmother. Of course, you can visit Sarah. There's a really nice school three blocks away from the Williams. No more walking half a mile to school in the freezing weather. Yes, we have to move. Because. Because. Because." The questions wouldn't stop, so, at one point, with no good answer to questions like, "Why can't I bring one of the barn kittens with us?" she snapped, "Because I said so."

"My folks are seventy-five, now," Joe had told her when he first brought up moving in with them. "They remember you from when you were that little girl running past our place on the way to school back in the early twenties. They were even talkin' about that time they caught you and me holding hands walking past on the way to your folks. Teased me about how far it was I had to walk a girl home. They've lived in town since Theresa, Sarah, and I moved to the farm four years ago. My mom don't get around too well. They need your help." Left unsaid but understood by both of them was that she would be out from under the roof of her parents. Ruth hoped that life was going be a lot easier for her now.

She hadn't fully believed it was going to happen until they walked with Joe up to Ed and Ethel Williams' front door with all their belongings. The Williamses met them there before Joe could open it. Ed's eyes twinkled as he greeted her with a huge smile. Ethel gave Ruth and then Charlie a big hug.

"I want you to know, Ruth, that I dearly love this boy. You've got a fine one here. He's been coming by for over a year to sell us savings stamps. We're so thankful our Joe isn't overseas like Chester, so we always bought one."

"And sometimes even three," Charlie said. "One for them, one for Joe, and one for Sarah. Mrs. Williams always has cookies for me. And

CHAPTER 33 ✦ RUTH

hot chocolate when it's cold outside. Mr. Williams always bets he can eat more cookies than I can, but I always win."

Ruth laughed, knowing that was likely very close to the truth.

"You cheat, though, Charlie. I didn't know you had a hollow leg till last time you were here playing with Sarah, and she ratted on you."

"Sarah wouldn't do that. You aren't tellin' the truth, Mr. Williams."

"Okay, you two. Ruth needs some time to get settled. And guess what, Charlie?"

"Cookies!" Charlie yelled and started toward the kitchen with Ethel in his wake.

"You wait up a minute, you two, and help Ruth and me get her settled," Joe called after them, but they kept going.

Joe shouldered her trunk, and Ed picked up one of her bags, leaving her with paper sacks she'd filled with what the suitcase wouldn't hold. She was led to the small spare bedroom she and Charlie would share.

"Sorry, but you'll be sleeping on a pallet, Charlie. Hope you don't mind too much," he apologized to Charlie, who'd appeared in the doorway with his mouth full of cookie. Ethel stood behind him with a hand on his shoulder.

"I sleep on a pallet at my grandpa's and grandmother's place," Charlie said. "I won't mind."

"Well, that's good, that's good," said Ethel. Now the two of you get out of here, and go play a game of checkers while I help Ruth here get things put away. Grab you some more cookies first."

As they turned to go, Ed teased, "I can't seem to beat you at checkers, either, Charlie. You sure you aren't cheating me at them, too?"

"I'm not either cheatin'. I win fair and square," Charlie said as he followed Ed out the bedroom door. "And I'll beat you this time, too."

"Maybe you will, and maybe you won't," Ed challenged.

"Sarah says you let her win sometimes, so she don't feel so bad losin'. You better not do that with me."

"Not in a million years." Ed's laughter was full throated, deep, and warm.

Ruth's heart melted at the sound of it. She shook her head and smiled at Ethel, who had a wide grin on her face.

"That boy. There's always something coming out of his mouth that makes me laugh, sometimes even though I shouldn't," Ethel confided.

Ruth almost couldn't believe the warmth and generosity coming from Joe's parents. It was so different from that of her own. No wonder Joe was such a sweet man and hadn't ended up as wild as Chester. And, unlike Chester, grew more mature with age. "I truly appreciate you letting us live here and working for you, Ethel."

"Now you hush, Ruth—it's you doin' us a favor to be here. Our Joe has let us know what's been going on in your life, and my boy and granddaughter have taken a real liking to you and Charlie. And that Sarah, bless her heart, told me right away that if her daddy ever got her a new mama, she hoped it was you or someone like you."

Ruth felt her face grow warm, and she wasn't sure if it was from the compliments or the fact that Ethel might have guessed a great deal more about her and Joe than either of them would want.

*

Ruth sat in the swing on the Williamses' front porch, gently pushing herself back and forth. A week had passed, and she knew beyond a doubt that coming to live with the Williamses was one of the better decisions she'd ever made. Not knowing at first what to expect, it soon became clear it was a blessing to be living here. She didn't mind the work. After thoroughly mopping the linoleum floors, scrubbing the living room rug, washing and drying all the throw rugs, and dusting the entire house, she started all over again. The house wasn't unclean; it was that she needed to keep busy, feel as if she were earning their keep and the ten dollars a week that Joe gave her. Ethel let her do most of the cooking and baking as well,

CHAPTER 33 • RUTH

though she liked to visit while Ruth did it. That first evening, Ethel said to her, "I love to see someone younger do things right. Just like I've done them all my life." Ed kept up with work in the yard and small garden at the back. She would have helped him, too, but he told her, "I miss farming, and, though this isn't like my 150 acres of cotton, it's still farming. I want to do it."

Joe's pickup ground to a stop in front of the house, and Ruth stood, a feeling of warmth and happiness spreading through her as she watched him unfold from the seat and walk toward her. Sarah jumped out of the other door and came running up, throwing her arms around Ruth.

"I wish you and Charlie lived with daddy and me out on the farm," Sarah said as she squeezed.

Ruth felt the color rise in her face. Then it deepened more when she realized Ed and Ethel had come to the door and, knowingly or not, were smiling an encouragement.

"I miss Charlie. I don't see him as much with him not living down the road from us. And I miss seeing you. You don't stop by to see daddy anymore." Charlie came tearing around from the back yard yelling, "Sarah. Joe. I was hopin' you-all would come by today. Mama said she was, too." He did not embrace Sarah or Joe, though Ruth suspected he wanted to. It just wasn't something a boy his age would do.

Ethel, likely seeing Ruth's embarrassment, said, "You two, go on and play now, while we grown-ups have some coffee."

"Grandpa, will you play monster with us first?"

Ed shook his head as if to say no but then hunched his shoulders and loomed over her, sending both children running back the way Charlie had come.

Joe, Ed, and Ethel went to the kitchen and sat down at the table while Ruth bustled about to fill the bottom of the metal percolator with water, add Folger's coffee, and set it on to perk. She set cream and sugar on the table and then sat down across from Joe.

"That should be my job, Ruth," Ethel said, "but you seem to think you have to do all the work around here." There was lightness to her tone and a twinkle in her eyes as she scolded.

"I told you she was a worker, Mama. You should see her pull bolls. Does it faster than a lot of the men."

"Well, for your information, Ruth shouldn't have to be out there in the field." There was no lightness to her tone or twinkle in her eye as she scolded her son. Color rose in Joe's cheeks, but he laughed. "See what I had to put up with while I was growing up?" He reached over and patted his mother's hand. "But I love you just the same."

"Go on with you."

"You only had to put up with her for eighteen years. I've had to live with her for almost fifty," Ed joked.

Before Ethel could respond to that loving jab at her, Sarah and Charlie burst in through the back door into the kitchen. "Grandpa, Grandpa. You were supposed to play monster with us," yelled Sarah. "We were hiding out back waitin' for you."

"I haven't had my coffee yet, you little rascal."

"Please?"

"Please, Mr. Williams?" Charlie chimed in.

"Oh. Okay. Don't you drink all the coffee, now. Save me a cup."

"Ed has played that with Sarah since we moved in here, and she can't get enough of it," Ethel said as Ed stood and disappeared into the dining room off the kitchen. "It's one of his and Sarah's favorite games."

There was a hall that ran the length of the house; the kitchen and living room were on one side, and a utility closet, bathroom and two bedrooms opened off the other. Ruth could hear Ed make his slow way around that circle following the two kids, making growling noises, and telling them he was going to catch them and gobble them up. They squealed with fright and excitement as they scampered ahead of him. Ruth watched as Ed stopped growling and quietly hid just out of sight in the kitchen, waiting

CHAPTER 33 • RUTH

for them. As Charlie and Sarah, breathlessly listening for him, sneaked through the door into the kitchen, he grabbed Sarah and started chewing on her neck, sending her and Charlie into hysterical giggles. Then the game resumed, only this time he must have grabbed Charlie because she heard her son squeal, "Let me go! Let me go!" and then, like Sarah, dissolve into giggles.

"That fool game will keep going until Ed is tuckered out," Ethel said, and then called, "You come on in the kitchen and sit yourself down with us grown-ups now, Ed. Ruth poured you a hot cup of coffee."

"It's so like Papa to play with the kids. That's one of the reasons Sarah loves visiting her grandparents," Joe said.

Ruth felt a sting of regret that her own papa was so unloving of his grandchildren. Of Charlie.

Huffing from the play, Ed plopped down in one of the chairs. "I may be getting a little old now to do that, but I say you never get too old to have a little fun with kids now and then."

"Well, I don't know which of you is the biggest kid, Ed—you, Charlie, or Sarah."

"Me, of course. I'm way into my second childhood, Ethel."

"Come on, Ed. You've always been a kid at heart. It isn't age makes you do it."

From the front of the house, where Ed had left them, Sarah and Charlie came rushing through the kitchen and charged out the back door.

"Now if I had that kind of energy, Ed, I might play as much as you," Ethel said.

Joe stood and picked up his straw hat. "Folks, Ruth, I've some errands to do. Got to pick up some feed for the chickens and run to the bank. Bill Farley's got a young heifer I'd like to buy. I'll be back to pick Sarah up when I'm done."

"You'll stay for dinner. That Ruth can cook up a passing good chicken fried steak," Ethel said.

"You talked me into it." Joe patted his dad on the shoulder and bent to hug his mama. He looked at Ruth, and she knew the longing in his eyes carried a desire to hug her as well, but he only nodded.

Ruth walked him to the front door and watched as he drove away. *Life is going to be so much better now*, she thought. But a heavy strain of guilt gripped her as she thought of her mother and papa. They were so miserable, and now they were all alone with that misery. She wondered, though, if they missed her or wished she was back with them. She would never go back except to help out. Living under the Williamses' roof was so right for her and Charlie. She was still unsure of what she would do when Chester came home, but, at times like this, she didn't want to live with Chester any more than she wanted to live with her folks. She wanted to be with Joe.

Ethel and Ed had disappeared before Ruth walked back into the kitchen, gone into their bedroom to nap. She went to the back door and looked out at the kids sitting on the back stoop, Charlie was whittling on a block of wood he was fashioning into a gun. She still refused to buy him one of those shiny new cast-iron six shooters that exploded caps. He'd defiantly said he'd buy one himself, and she'd told him it would be a waste of money because she'd throw it in the garbage. Charlie, who was handy with a knife, had then carved out of wood the likeness of four guns and polished them with black shoe polish. Now he was carving out one that he said looked something like the one Jelly Nash, the bandit, had carried. She could thank old man Buchanan for that, filling Charlie's head with stories of that gangster. Charlie'd found an old gun magazine out in the back alley, so he had lots of guns to choose from. Sarah thought it was a pretty smart idea and was sitting on the back step with Charlie, trying to carve one as well, but wouldn't come up with the same results as Charlie. Still, she had one of her daddy's old pocketknives and was working away at what Ruth suspected would be the gun handle.

Already like brother and sister, she thought. *Maybe I should be Sarah's new mother.*

CHAPTER 34

Ida

➤➤ ✻ ⫷⫷

It was mid-afternoon when Ida and Bob arrived home from visiting Pearl for the noon meal. It had been sunny when they drove out of the Dennison's yard, but now the sky was darkening. As she pushed out of the car, Ida looked toward the chicken house and saw no chickens scratching about. They had all gone to roost. She looked toward the western horizon, where darker clouds were advancing. "Looks like it's getting ready to storm, Bob. We better hurry and get the windows closed."

Bob nodded as he stepped onto the porch. Old Hitler, the hound, rose to his feet and accepted a rough scratching behind the ears by Bob. He then lifted his nose, sniffed the breeze, and ambled off toward his den underneath the floorboards of the wash house.

Standing together with Bob, Ida gazed at the black clouds roiling up from the southwest. Brilliant lightning stabbed earthward, and thunder rolled in, long and sustained. "Those animals have all gone for cover early. Must be a bad one coming up."

"If Ruth were here, she'd already be sitting in the cellar with Charlie," Bob said.

"That just might be a sensible thing to do, Bob. That's an awfully fast-moving storm. Won't take it long to get here."

"We better get inside and make sure all the windows are closed. I shut up the barn pretty tight before we left for Pearl's. Hay won't get wet. I see the livestock all down there in the far end of the pasture. They'll do okay."

Another crash of thunder, much nearer now, jarred them loose from the porch, and she hurried inside, Bob right behind her. Going through the house, she found nothing open but a window in her bedroom that was cracked open an inch or two.

"Ida, I've half a notion just to stay inside and read the paper."

She was almost inclined to agree, but a crash of thunder that made the house shudder changed her mind. "You can just sit in here and get yourself blown away if you want. I'm headed to the cellar. I need you to open the cellar door for me." She grabbed matches and rolled up an old newspaper.

He gave a heavy-enough sigh that it should have kept him in his chair, but he rose and followed her to the door, grumbling beneath his breath.

Ida didn't want to know what nonsense he was mumbling. And once outside, the wind blew his words all the way into the back pasture, where they belonged.

Before they reached the cellar door, the air became so still she had no trouble lighting the newspaper and burning the cobwebs out of the stairwell. At the bottom of the stairs, she called up, "Don't just stand up there. Either close the door for me, or get yourself down here out of harm's way."

CHAPTER 34 • IDA

She wasn't sure what decision he'd have made had a streak of lightning not hammered the earth somewhere nearby and a peal of thunder pounded down so hard it shook the dickens out of her, even though she was at the bottom of the cellar stairs. Shook Bob, too, she guessed, because he grabbed the cellar door, pulled it over the opening as he descended the stairs, and slammed it down over him. Hail began peppering the wooden door an instant later.

She set about lighting the kerosene lamp while Bob pulled two chairs to the center of the cramped little room. Light from the lamp reflected back from the fruit jars lining the walls, all now empty but last year, at the beginning of winter, filled with fruit and vegetables she, Ruth, and Pearl had canned. They'd all be full again by winter. Bob had helped dig this cellar not long after they moved here, and it had served them well ever since. She never liked coming down here, though. Too dark and damp. Too many spiders and bugs made it their home.

"I hope this cotton-pickin' hail don't keep up for long. I won't have any cotton left." Bob said and sank down into one of the chairs.

Ida sat in the other, but she was no sooner settled when she heard crashing and hammering. Something heavier than hail slammed down against the cellar door. "Lord have mercy," she screamed.

Bob leaped from his chair, knocking it over backwards. "I sure hope that wasn't one of the buildings going."

"Or God willing, not the house," Ida whispered.

They both stood and listened to the wind roaring, wood splintering, and a hammering against the cellar door so violently she was afraid it would break and let in the hateful things pounding at it. She stepped closer to Bob, who put his arm around her, and they both stood for what seemed an eternity as they imagined the world tearing apart above them. They held on to each other until the violent noise was replaced by the pattering on the door of a hard rain. Then, there was several minutes of silence. She wasn't sure how long she'd stood with Bob holding her and her holding on to him, but they both seemed to realize, at the same moment, that they needed to face what had happened. They moved apart, and Bob climbed to the top of the stairs. He pushed at the door. It didn't want to move.

"What's wrong, Bob?"

"Don't know, but I suspect something pretty heavy's lying across it."

Tears streamed down Ida's face as she steadied herself against the door jamb. "Are we stuck down here?"

He didn't answer but took another step up and putting his shoulder against the door, grunted as he used his legs and back, straining to force the door higher. Something clattered and bumped, and the door pushed open. Bob stuck his head out of the cellar entrance.

"Lord, Lord, Lord," was all he said, but Ida didn't need to hear anything more.

"I'm coming up," she said, and he moved on out, turned, and gave her a hand.

"Be careful, now—watch your feet."

Ida almost fainted when she stood on the last step of the cellar, looking at the spot where the house she'd lived in for thirty years should be standing. It was gone, flattened to the ground and spread over the whole south pasture along with the ruins of the barn. Only the chicken house was still standing. The sky had cleared, and an uncaring sun peered down at her and the wreck of their possessions. Everything gone, as if a bulldozer had rammed through the barn and just kept going to the house and then across the road into the neighbor's pasture. All her clothes, furniture, pictures, keepsakes, and whatnots, consumed, twisted into an unrecognizable mess of glass, cloth, wood, and metal. Her lips trembled, and tears coursed down her cheeks as she thought of her dear departed first son's picture that was somewhere out there, the frame broken, the glass in a thousand pieces, and the picture, drenched from the downpour, now a sodden mess. Marbles of hail on the ground sparkled like large diamonds. Not pretty to her. Not now. They'd taken part in the destruction.

CHAPTER 34 • IDA

While she stood, taking deep, anguished breaths, Bob went into the cellar and brought out a chair for her. He led her to the cement slab at the front of the house and had her sit while he inspected the car which sat almost untouched but surrounded by pieces of the destroyed house and barn. He shook his head and came back to her. "Can't drive even if the car starts; too many boards lying around with nails sticking out of them. I'd flatten all four tires." He took a deep breath and said, "You sit here and rest while I walk over to Pearl's and fetch Bill and the boys. Get one of them to drive you over to their place."

As he trudged away, the old hound dog came loping up from under the wash-house foundation and fell in behind him. Ida felt numb, her mind emptied of thought, though cottony tendrils of grief had managed to force their way in. *What will become of me now?* was the first one that registered. Then others forced themselves through. *Where will I live? Can I stand to live anywhere but here? God help me—I'm not sure I want to live!*

*

Fifteen minutes after the storm had struck, Bob and the Dennisons drove up. Pearl hugged Ida while more tears fell, and then her daughter walked Ida to the car. Ida saw Bob and Bill making their way through the wreckage toward what was left of the barn, Old Hitler at their heels. Then she heard the high-pitched squeal of those two hogs. Those two old workhorses had wandered up from somewhere in the pasture and stood with their heads hanging over the cow lot gate The jersey cow stood near them, cropping at the grass. As she rode away, leaving the men and boys to see what could be salvaged, Ida could not bring herself to look back.

When they turned into the drive, Ida could see that Dennisons' house and farm buildings had mercifully been spared. *At least I can be thankful for that*, Ida thought.

In the days that followed, Ida felt drained of purpose and could do little else but help out with the cooking. She did not return to the trash-strewn yard, where all her possessions had been shattered and torn to pieces by the twister. She could not have stood the sight of her daughters, sons-in-law, neighbors, and grandchildren picking through the wreckage that lay scattered across the pasture. They were salvaging what they could. Bob told her most things had been ripped to pieces, cracked, twisted, or smashed into a thousand pieces.

"I looked for Brian's picture," Bob told her. "But I could find hide nor hair of it."

It had gone missing, forever. She could not stop the tears.

Relatives, neighbors, and friends stopped by Pearl's house to bring food and their attempts at comfort. One of Ida's sisters said, "Thank the Lord you were hunkered down in the cellar when the tornado came through." Ida didn't say it but thought, *I'd have a lot more to thank the God Almighty for if He'd spared my home. Or the barn. Even the washhouse.* But they were all gone, smashed to pieces and sent flying. She thanked those who tried to comfort her, even though she couldn't put much heart into her thanks.

A week passed before she could bring herself to ride into town with Joan and look at a house her daughter had found that was for rent.

"I'm not sure I can do this, Joan," She said as they walked into the second of two small bedrooms. "Four tiny rooms and a bath?"

"I know, Mother. But Papa says it's driving him crazy to be cooped up with Pearl and her family. This is the only house for rent in this whole town that don't cost an arm and a leg."

Ida took a deep breath, peeked into the bathroom that opened into both bedrooms, and said, "At least we'll have an indoor toilet. That'll cover a lot of sins, I guess." She walked back into the small living room/dining room and on into the kitchen. "And Lord a-mercy, a gas cooking stove." She flipped a switch at the door, and light flooded the kitchen. "And no more coal-oil lamps." She was surprised that some of the deadness she'd

CHAPTER 34 ♦ IDA

been feeling lifted slightly. *This won't be so bad after all*, she thought. "If your papa signs off on this, I'll try and manage," Ida said.

Three days later she was standing at the stove of the tiny house stirring a pot of black-eyed peas. Bob had brought what few things they now owned and stored them in the small closet, the two chests Bob had bought at a farm sale, or under the two beds he bought from the children of an old woman in town who had just passed. The same friends, former neighbors and relatives who had stopped by Pearl's bringing food and solace, now brought quilts, blankets, sheets, and pillowcases they weren't using anymore. Pearl and Bill brought two kitchen chairs and an oak kitchen table they'd stored in their barn. Relics of Bill's grandparents. One of her sisters gave Ida some well-used kitchenware.

She now lived with no pictures on the wall, no piano, and not a stick of their former household furniture—little or nothing of anything familiar. Only four of her figurines were found lying unbroken beneath a pile of shingles, and they now sat on a shelf in the living room, where Bob sat reading the paper while she set about fixing supper. There was nothing much in this place but secondhand furniture and hand-me-downs. Nothing new or familiar but the black-eyed peas on the stove, the potatoes in the skillet, and cornbread in the oven. God help her, Bob loved the cornbread and black-eyed peas more than he'd ever loved her. But she was finally beginning to be thankful she and Bob could still have more suppers like this one. Lord knows if either would have survived that twister if they hadn't got to the cellar when they did.

When the food was done cooking, she called Bob, who sat down at the table and eyed the bowls of potatoes and black-eyed peas, a platter of fried ham she'd heated when the potatoes were done, and a plate of cornbread. He had a peaceful smile on his face as he ate in silence for fifteen minutes, saying nothing. Bob's moods were as cramped as this small three-room house they'd rented.

She looked at him shoveling the food into his mouth and wondered if the only thing he'd ever really liked about her was that she could cook up a good pot of black-eyed peas and a tasty pan of cornbread. She'd long ago accepted that staying with him was the only way she could get by. And now that the house had been blown to kingdom come along with everything she cherished, she had to make do living here in this cracker box. *I've lived fifty-one years*, she mused. *And for what?* She wanted to say it out loud to Bob, but she knew he would be of no help, so why bother to say it to him? Still, since that moment he put his arm around her during the storm, she hadn't felt as hateful toward him.

Thank God my girls are nearby, she thought. *And that I'll have Winston, if he comes back whole from the war.* There were her sisters and brothers, that was true, and some of them meant a lot to her. Had even come by bringing things she needed, gave her comforting words. But they had their own lives and lived just far enough away over by Rocky to not come see her often. Or her to go see them. She was thankful her mother still lived here in town—for a few more years, anyway. Mother was getting old. And for that matter, so was she.

Her mind turned to Ruth and what had come between them. It made tears come to her eyes. She'd been so caught off guard when Ruth asked her about Chester. She'd had to lie. But it was a weak lie, and a part of Ruth knew that. Probably wouldn't have been so quick to move out, otherwise. Ida'd been such a fool with Chester back then, but, at the time, she was mad at Bob for running around on her, and frustrated. In her mind's eye, she could see Ruth eight months along and Chester lying around the house, out of work, both living with her and Bob for a time because Chester got fired from the bowling alley. She was upset, too, about Ruth, who had started spotting. She insisted Bob take her in to see the doctor. Chester should been there to take her, but he was off somewhere riding the old piebald mare Bob owned. Her other two girls were in school, so when Chester rode back from wherever he'd been and

CHAPTER 34 ✦ IDA

pushed into the house with half the cold wind in Kiowa County following him in before he got the door closed, they were alone together. Chester was so charming to her that day, but she should have realized why and sent him out to ride that mare into town to be with Ruth. Anything but stay alone with him, feeling so down that she couldn't resist all that false charm he turned on her. The house was cold as sin, and they were both huddled around the stove trying to thaw out when he moved close, put his arm around her, smiled, and kissed her. She pushed those memories away. Ashamed. Sad. Excited in a way that surprised and shamed her. Hurting Ruth was the last thing on Earth that she'd ever wanted to do. At the time, back then, she wasn't even thinking of Ruth. Sitting close to Chester and feeling a raw desire for him as her bruised heart stirred with hate for Bob, she gave in. What was happening between them was all that mattered for that short moment.

God forgive me, she thought. *I'm not sure Ruth ever will.*

CHAPTER 35

Chester

→ ❁ ←

"I hate this godforsaken place," Chester grumbled. He gunned the truck's engine as he hit another of the jungle's quagmires.

"Don't you dare get this damn wreck stuck. I don't want to walk back," Hough growled.

Giant green fronds beat against the sides of the truck, sending up clouds of disease-carrying mosquitoes, pests that Chester figured were the second worst plague visited on him here in this plant-choked hell. The Japs were the worst. "We get anywhere nearer the front lines, and you may not be able to walk back. I'll have to carry you piggyback."

"That'll be the day, Scarsdale. You haven't looked in a mirror for a while. You're so damn skinny I'd be surprised if your ugly carcass showed up in a mirror."

CHAPTER 35 ✦ CHESTER

Chester knew it was true. Like most of the men here, he suffered from dysentery and from malaria that he barely controlled with the Atabrine he took. Religiously. It had turned his complexion yellow, but unlike some of the men who believed it robbed them of their manhood and so refused to take it until they were flat on their backs, he persisted. He hadn't lost his manhood yet. But he had lost twenty pounds since joining this man's Navy.

"Wasn't for that bastard Bell, we'd be somewhere a hell of a lot safer than here," Chester groused.

"Let me remind you for the umpteenth time that wasn't for you knocking him senseless that time, he wouldn't have made sure that your ass was still in a major war zone," Hough said. "And because I made the stupid mistake of being your buddy, I'm here, too."

"Screw you, Hough," said Chester as he guided the truck out of the tangled jungle into a clearing. "You sound like a broken record every time you say that."

Barely into the clearing, Chester heard the roar of approaching aircraft and, looking to the horizon saw a Zero come roaring in low, over the treetops. Shoving the gears into reverse, he gunned the motor and sent the truck shooting backward toward the cover of the trees. The Zero opened fire just before Chester and Hough reached the safety of the trees. The earth in front of the truck hiccupped from the spray of bullets, and the skin of the hood dimpled from multiple hits. The motor died. Chester sat blinking, shocked and scared, not believing the cab with them in it had been spared.

"Shit," yelled Hough as he piled out of the passenger seat and ran into the trees. "Get your ass out of the truck, Scarsdale. That bastard'll be back."

Chester jumped from the cab, ran into the underbrush, tripped, and fell hard. Face down, he covered the back of his head with his hands. The raw earth he lay in smelled of rotting vegetation and swamp water.

Hough scrambled back through the underbrush closer to Chester. "Goddamn if that's going to stop a bullet to your thick skull, Scarsdale," he yelled. "Get further away from that damn truck."

As Chester scrambled to his feet and ran with Hough further into the jungle, he heard the shriek of bullets peppering metal as the Japs passed over once more. It sounded to Chester like the drumming of hail on his pa's tin-roofed barn. Glancing back, he saw gouts of torn-up earth and shattered bushes spouting up from where he first lay covering his head. Then the roar of the plane's engine grew fainter. "I think he's gone," Chester said, but, then, the noise of approaching planes grew louder.

"There's more of those bastards coming back," Chester yelled, and he imagined that twice the number of Zeros were swooping in to finish them off. He heard a burst of gunfire and felt the *whoomph* of an explosion high above.

"Damn," said Hough, "It looks like those are our planes. I think they just shot the bastard out of the sky."

They both crawled to the edge of the jungle and peered out at spiraling smoke that ended in an explosion a few hundred feet away. The jungle belched a black cloud of smoke. "Good goddamn riddance," Chester said as he saw two more Zeros turn and speed away, six American planes hot on the son-of-a-bitches' tails.

"I'd sleep better tonight if every damn one of them took a nosedive into the ocean." Hough started walking toward the truck, and Chester followed.

Climbing into the bullet-riddled cab, Chester turned the key. Nothing happened. "Damn thing won't start."

"Hough yanked at the hood until it raised up enough to see the motor. "They shot the hell out of this engine, Scarsdale. We have to hoof it back to base and get another truck to unload this cargo onto. And I hope to hell it's quiet all the way there and back."

CHAPTER 35 ✦ CHESTER

*

Two hours later, Chester drove into the edge of the clearing, pulled alongside the damaged truck, and helped Hough offload the ammo onto the one he'd driven back. As he sweated and cursed the Japs, he kept an eye on the horizon and his ears alert to sounds. All he heard was the call of jungle birds and the distant boom of cannons. As they started on and rolled closer to the front lines, Chester began hearing distant machine-gun chatter and the concussion of cannon shells. "God damn—I hate to drive any closer," he said but kept driving.

"Somebody has to do it," Hough said.

"You trying to tell me to man up," Hough? Well, go to hell." When Chester pulled into the forward position and crawled out of the truck, he felt his legs almost give way. "You may have to unload this damn truck yourself, Hough. I've been shot at, walked four miles to get another truck, and helped you reload this ammunition. I'm dog-tired and don't have the energy to unload this goddamn truck."

Hough called out to a harried sergeant, "Can we get some help?"

The sergeant pointed toward a group of fifteen or twenty Marines sitting on logs with their rifles at their sides or stretched out on the damp ground. "They're heading to the front in a few minutes, but get some of them to help you."

Unlucky bastards, Chester thought as he crawled into the back of the truck, ready to hand down the boxes. Three of the seated Marines pulled themselves up off the ground where they were sitting and began helping. In five minutes, all the cases of ammunition were on the ground. With every tired muscle in him complaining, Chester found the energy to say "Thanks," jumped down from the truck bed, and started for the cab. As he stepped onto the running board, he heard artillery shells whistling toward them.

"Incoming!" yelled one of the Marines as he rolled into a nearby trench.

Hough ran toward another trench, and Chester, his heart in his throat, took off after him. Hough threw himself into the trench, but as Chester made ready to launch himself in after Hough, there was a deafening blast behind him, and he found himself picked up and tossed like a discarded toy doll and thrown into the trench. When he landed, the back of his head felt like he'd been kicked by a mule. White-hot, searing pain stabbed at his left arm, shoulder, and leg.

He screamed as he lay next to Hough, who held him to the ground as more explosions erupted around them. Then it was quiet, and he felt himself being dragged along the ground, his feet trailing through brush and water and more brush. Hough was yelling, "Medic. Medic," but the words came from a long way away, muted—lost in the surrounding jungle. He knew he was dying.

He felt someone's hands on him and heard shouting, but his own screams and groans drowned out everything. He felt surprised, then, when he drifted into a fog, and the pain floated lazily away. Something was being wrapped around his leg and then about his arm, but there was no pain. He was lifted onto a stretcher and a strap was pulled tight against his forehead, trapping his head to something hard. Though the pain was gone, he gritted his teeth as he was half-carried, half-dragged farther away from the front lines. Blackness began descending on him then, and he floated away.

He was pulled back to awareness as his leg and arm were shifted from side to side and up and down, and his shirt and pants were cut away; then he drifted away again. He had no idea how much later it was, but, when he woke up, he felt tight bandages encasing his left leg and arm. And he couldn't move his head; it was strapped to a board. "What in hell is going on?" he shouted, though it came out as a croak. Hough and a young doctor appeared at his side, both peering down on him.

"Take it easy there, hot-dog. They've patched you up. They're getting ready to send you away from this hellhole," Hough said.

CHAPTER 35 ✦ CHESTER

The doctor then spoke up. "You have shrapnel wounds to your right arm and leg. We think that you've also sustained a neck injury. May have fractured some vertebrae, but so far it seems that there's nothing pressing on the spinal cord. We strapped you down because we don't want you injuring yourself further by moving your head."

The doctor and Hough disappeared from view, and Chester felt himself lifted and placed onto the rough surface of a canvas litter, loaded into a jeep, and strapped down. He was dimly aware of the groaning, moaning and cursing from men lying beside and above him and of his own muttered groans. He heard people shouting, but the words directed to him sounded as if they came from dream figures, and he couldn't bring himself to answer. Hough, who rode in the jeep and kept talking to him, floated in and out of Chester's awareness. As they drove through the swampy forest, the jeep's tires bumped over rough surfaces, jiggling and shaking him. He didn't know how much time had passed when the bumpy ride began to make his arm and leg feel like they were breaking in two. One deep rut shook him so hard he screamed; then he felt a needle pushed into his arm. Blessed relief sent him drifting toward sleep. A sharp stabbing fear startled him awake from a dream.

He was in the cotton patch with Ruth, who was gathering flowers from the plants and placing them in her hair. He called out to her. "Stop. Those will grow into cotton bolls." But she paid him no mind and kept filling her hair with the white blossoms. Then Charlie and Alice came running toward him, and he felt panicked and dove into a foxhole.

On awakening, rough hands lifted him from the jeep litter, and he could hear the wash of the sea as it broke on the beach. Whatever they had given him was wearing off again, and his left leg and arm were clamped in the mouth of an alligator, its jaws bearing down harder and harder.

Hough yelled, "Medic," again and something was almost immediately plunged into his right arm. As he was drifting once more into the fog, Hough gripped his hand and said, "Hang in there, Scarsdale. In case you're thinking otherwise, you're one lucky son-of-a-bitch. There's a transport ship in the harbor right now that'll take you out of this rotten mess. Maybe even to the States." Hough let go his hand. "I've got to get back to our unit. Good luck, Buddy."

On board the lighter, he could feel the rise and fall of waves as they lifted and then let the lighter down again as it made its way to a hospital ship that, in his drug-fogged thoughts, he hoped would take him as far as possible from all the shit he'd been wallowing in the past two years.

CHAPTER 36

Chester

Once more he felt himself lifted, carried somewhere, and deposited gently onto a hard berth. The vibration of enormous engines revved up and he realized he was on a ship that was getting underway. Soon, it must have left the harbor and entered the open sea because it began to rock back and forth and up and down. It relaxed him but for what seemed only minutes before he felt like red-hot pokers were being shoved into his neck, leg, and shoulder. "Medic," he yelled, and a young man who had the smooth, pimply face of a teenager came to his side. "I need something to stop this goddamn pain," he shouted. The effort cost him more pain.

Moments later he felt a pinprick in his right arm, and the beautiful rush of narcotic bliss began dousing the burning pain. "Where the hell am I?!" Chester demanded of the young medic.

"You're on a hospital ship headed for Brisbane."

"Jesus H. Christ but I hurt. Why the hell am I going to Brisbane?"

"You'll feel better in a minute. You were pretty badly hurt, and they couldn't provide what you need at the base hospital. Brisbane is a good place, I hear. Now, you get some rest."

A hazy memory then came to him of running for cover when a marine yelled, "Incoming." But that was the last thing he could remember. God, he thought, *I wonder how that lucky bastard Hough made it through that.* But then he drifted off.

He awoke in pain, thinking; *I hope a damn Jap boat or sub doesn't find me.* At the island's base hospital, they'd put him into a traction neck brace. It was maddening to wake up to his pain and feeling like what he imagined a frying chicken must feel when its neck was stretched just before the head was wrung from its body. He swore never to wring a chicken's neck again if he lived to be a hundred.

After another pinprick to his arm, he was vaguely aware of the lift and fall of the ship, and thoughts of enemy subs faded. In a fog of indifference to pain or what was going on about him, a memory came to him of the first time he took a good look at Ruth, when he was fourteen. He and his brothers were in Bob Choat's cotton patch hoeing away at the weeds one summer when Ruth came to the field. She was standing at the water bucket drinking from the dipper and dripped some down the front of her dress. She'd jumped back, sloshing more of the water onto her dress and then stood there with her brow knit and pretty mouth pinched in aggravation. He was charmed. He'd known her since they were in first grade, but all he'd ever done was devil her in one way or the other. But when she stood there at the water bucket with her pretty mouth pinched down and the dress over her left breast soaked with water, it seemed to him that she had totally changed; she looked pretty as a picture. Her breasts looked larger than he remembered, too, even though he'd stared at them only a month earlier when they were both in the schoolyard. He stared at them now until she looked up at him.

CHAPTER 36 ♦ CHESTER

Noticing her flushed cheeks under the bonnet had reminded him of cotton flowers after they'd turned from white to pink. He'd made the silly comment, "Hey there, cotton flower, you going to let me have a drink of that water?" Her face turned the deep red of an eight-day-old cotton flower just before it dropped off and left behind the tiny cotton boll. She dropped the dipper back into the bucket, fled to her cotton sack, and begun pulling bolls like mad. He watched her scamper away and then bend to her task, her well-developed backside unmistakably sexy despite the long skirt she wore. After that day he'd often called her "Cotton Flower." And she always turned pink when he did.

They'd been married two years later.

His mind wandered then to thoughts of Alice and the good times they'd had together. The time they'd driven down into Tijuana with Hough and his girlfriend and started raising a little hell in one of the local bars. Damn police chased them down the street, and Alice had taken off her high heels to outrun them. Her bare feet kicking out behind her like a spooked jackrabbit, she'd outrun him, Hough, and his girlfriend, too. They'd lucked out when they spotted a moving streetcar, jumped on, and left the shouting cops far behind. God knows what would have happened if they'd been caught. They'd laughed about it on the drive all the way back to Port Hueneme. It's a wonder the police on that side of the border didn't stop them, they were so damn drunk.

With the thought of Alice's slim bare feet flashing through the dim light of that Mexican town and of him rubbing the soreness out of them the next day, he felt himself drifting off into sleep.

He came awake feeling the steep rise and fall of the hospital ship as it climbed what he guessed was a huge wave and then slid down the other side. *Must be a storm*, he thought. He heard sounds of men retching and thanked God he wasn't one to get seasick. *As much pain as I'm in, puking my insides out would probably kill me*, he thought.

"Medic," he yelled. "I need something for pain."

It seemed an age before a young man appeared and put Chester back into a drugged haze. Now he felt no pain for a while. It crept back to him again. They gave him another shot. The pain crept away. In and out of his pain and discomfort, he lost track of the days passing, though he was dimly aware when they pulled into a harbor and vaguely remembered the ambulance ride to the allied naval hospital in Brisbane. He was laid on a bed in a ward where he heard dozens of other wounded men calling out in pain, He wondered if some some were dying.

In one of his more lucid moments, a doctor leaned over Chester and said, "You need an operation on your left arm and leg or you might lose one of them, if not both. We have to do some surgery on your neck as well, or you might become paralyzed." *The son-of-a-bitch knows how to scare the shit out of me*, Chester thought; then he asked for another dose of pain killer.

Then—he wasn't clear how long afterwards—he felt himself lifted off his bed onto a gurney. "What in God's name is happening?" he asked.

"You're on the way to surgery. "You'll be like a new man when they finish with you."

It was like a slow-moving dream as they rolled him down a long hall and to the side of an operating table. "One, two, three," he heard someone chant and felt himself lifted from the cart and onto the table, where a bright overhead lamp blinded him. He didn't have time to complain before he felt the prick of a needle and pressure as the needle was taped into place. Tubing attached to the needle ran upwards to a clear bag of water, and he watched as a nurse injected something into the tubing. There was a babble of voices around him, but he couldn't make out what they were saying. His last hazy thought as he was turned onto his stomach was, "I hope to hell you all know what you're doing."

Awakening hours later, fear sliced through him like nothing he'd ever experienced before. Not even the bombs going off around him had frightened him as much as the fear flooding him now. It felt like

CHAPTER 36 • CHESTER

something was attached to his skull and he was being pulled toward the head of the bed. When he tried to move his arms or legs, they wouldn't budge. Something lay tight across his chest, stomach, and legs, holding him down. In a panic, he screamed, "Medic. Medic." He didn't recognize the croak that came from his throat as his own.

"Easy sailor, easy. You're going to be OK," a voice reassured.

Chester turned his eyes in the direction the voice came from, and the face of an angel came into view, an angel with a nurse's hat and uniform. "What in God's name?" he croaked. "I'm strapped down. I can't move."

"You're immobilized to keep you from moving. The straps are because we didn't want you flailing about when you woke up."

He felt sweat running down his face, but, when he tried to reach and wipe it away, his arm wouldn't move. "God damn, I hate being strapped down! And it feels like my head's being pulled off my shoulders"

"We'll take the straps off shortly. But you'll have to take things slowly. You had some really serious fractures of your neck bones and some serious shrapnel injuries to your arm and leg. The traction you feel is to keep you from moving your head and neck till they heal. The bones, muscles, and ligaments in your neck need time to heal. You won't be able to move your head in any direction for quite a while."

"Where in the hell am I, anyway?" Chester asked and remembered even as she told him.

"On the ward of a hospital. In Brisbane, Australia. You were brought here after you were wounded."

"Jesus. Give me something for pain. Quick. I feel like someone hammered nails into the top of my head." Out of the corner of his eye, he could see the nurse prepare a syringe, plunging the needle into the top of a bottle and begin drawing a liquid from it.

"Well, sir," she said, "they did just about that. Only they screwed metal screws into your skull rather than nails. It's to help keep your broken neck bones in place so they don't injure your spinal cord while they heal," she said as she thumped the air bubbles from the syringe before plunging it into the IV tube attached to his arm. "We'll be getting you out of the bed as soon as possible. But we have to wait till those broken bones in your neck heal some. It'll take a while till you can go into a regular neck brace. So, rest easy now."

His heart started racing, and fear was still contracting his stomach into a painful knot. "God-damn-it-to-hell, I can't just lie here like this much longer. My head was strapped down the whole time I was on that ship coming here. They said when I got here, I'd be put in a brace right away."

"Can't promise that now."

"What's your name, sweetheart?"

"Nurse Bennet."

"No. I mean your first name."

"*Nurse* or *Nurse Bennet* will do just fine."

"Okay, then. I'll just have to call you 'sweetheart.'"

"Like I said, call me *Nurse Bennet*. Not *sweetheart*."

He heard her from a long distance away. He had begun to relax into a creeping sense of well-being that stole over him as the drug she'd given him took him away, and he no longer hated the pieces of iron fastened to his skull. He ceased to care about anything. Even *sweetheart*.

Days passed as he moved from pain into a haze of drug-induced indifference, to a few moments of clarity between the two. On a morning when he was near the beginning of pain and his mind was still clear, his surgeon came in, looked at his wounds, and listened to his lungs. "Things are looking good," he said. "How's the pain?"

"It hurts."

The doctor chuckled. "Glad you have a sense of humor, sailor. It's going to help over the next few days. We're putting you into a neck brace so you can begin to move around some. We'll have the orderlies start getting you out of bed to sit in a chair and walk to the bathroom."

CHAPTER 36 • CHESTER

Chester's heart began to race. "If I could shake my head 'No,' Doc, I would. Standing up is going to hurt like a son-of-a-bitch. I'm sure this damn leg won't hold me. I'm afraid I may just topple over."

"You'll do fine. We've got a couple of strong orderlies who'll help make sure that won't happen."

"Well, at least I won't have to use that damn bedpan anymore." That was little comfort to him as his heart continued to hammer against his chest.

Next morning, Chester was wheeled into the operating room, where he lay sweating and more awake and aware than he wanted to be. When nurse *Sweetheart's* face came into view, he mustered a smile. "You going to dance with me when they get these bolts out of my skull?"

She smiled at him, and then her face was lost to him. When he awoke, *Sweetheart* was nowhere to be seen, but he was no longer stretched out, and nothing was attached to his skull. Instead, there was something fastened around his neck that held so tight he couldn't move his head up, down, or sideways. He panicked and started to call out, but as by magic, a nurse injected his pain meds into the tube leading into his vein.

When he awakened and called for the nurse, two muscled orderlies showed up and set him up in a bedside chair. "By God you two, this is the first time I've set in a chair since the day before my ass was nearly blown to high heaven." It felt as if his whole body was complaining, aching or hurting, but still he was thrilled to be out of a bed. As he sat longer though, the pain began to take away the thrill.

"Lord God Almighty!" Chester called out to the man in the next bed. His hands began shaking, and his stomach felt like he'd lose what little he'd eaten for lunch. "I swear to God, it's been four hours since they set me up in this chair."

"A quarter of an hour. That's all. Wait till they make you walk to the bathroom and back to bed. You'll have something to complain about then."

"Do you think I can live through that?"

"Most do."

When the fifteen minutes had passed, the orderlies appeared and helped him to his feet. The second he stood, a strong urge to piss gripped him so hard he cried out, "Get me to the latrine. Quick." With each step with his left leg, he felt stabbing pain that almost brought him to his knees, but with an orderly on each side supporting him, he was able to shuffle to the bathroom and then back to bed, though it again felt like he was walking with a hot iron shoved up his left leg from ankle to hip. As they lowered him into bed, he groaned. "This would be a lot more fun if you'd get that pretty young nurse of mine to help."

"You must not be hurting as much as you're letting on if you can think about pretty nurses."

"Go to hell."

The orderlies laughed as they left the room.

Easing back against the pillow with his eyes closed, he pictured the knot of golden hair tied behind his nurse's head and fantasized loosening it, watching long strands cascade down her back to below the waist.

"So how did it go?"

His eyes popped open to see a woman's eyes, the color of sparkling jade, looking down at him. Her small, heart-shaped face broke into a smile.

"Damn—you startled me. I think I was asleep."

"For the last three minutes, to be exact."

"Where were you when I really needed you?" he demanded. "I almost died sitting in that chair waiting for you. Then who showed up? A couple of gorillas with no pity. I thought I was going to die."

"I think you'll live. And I'm going to give you your pain meds now." She bent close to his arm ready to fill his veins with comfort.

"Christ, you smell good," he said as he caught a whiff of something sweet, like roses. The smell raised his spirits. Cleared away some of his pain even before she fed the drug into his arm. As she walked away, he twisted his body as much as he could and watched her disappear down

CHAPTER 36 ✦ CHESTER

the rows of men lying in their beds. *Damn,* he thought, *looking at a pretty woman is about as good as one of those shots.*

Some days later, as he began craving more pain medicine, he realized he was wanting it more because of the good feeling it gave him than for any pain he was in. He'd come to love the calm joy that stole over him when the drug hit home. *Damn,* he thought, *am I turning into an addict?* Another question nagged at him: *What will I become if I give in to this craving?*

Damn, he thought. *I better get off this stuff.*

Later that day, when the nurse came to check on him, he said, "I got something to tell you, sweetheart."

Her brow knotted, and her mouth firmed into a serious line. Then she said, "That's *Nurse Bennet*, sailor. Remember?"

He smiled at her and said, "Sorry, *Nurse Bennet*. But can I sometimes call you 'Honey'?"

She shook her head, much as he remembered his mother doing when he was a boy and she had completely given up on getting through to him. "You're hopeless, sir." She pushed a dose of his pain meds into the tubing to his IV.

As he felt the calm wash over him, he remembered he was going to tell her about his fear of becoming addicted. "*Nurse Bennet. Honey. Sweetheart.* I had a thought. I need to stop taking so much of this damn stuff you just gave me. I'm liking it as much as I do your pretty face. That's too damn much."

"I'm glad to hear that, Mr. Scarsdale. I'll let your doctor know."

As she turned and walked to her next patient, he called, "Remember? It's *Chester*. You should call me *Chester*. Or *Sweetheart* if you want."

She kept her back to him as she began fluffing her other patient's pillow.

Three days later, when she came to him after his head was almost clear of the drugs and his craving was less, he wiped the grimace of pain off his face and smiled at her. "When this war is over, sweetheart, and I get this choker off my shoulders, I'm going to come looking for you," he told her.

"Sorry, sailor, but see this ring on my finger? I've been wearing it ever since you landed on this ward. It means that even if I appreciated your interest, my husband wouldn't approve." She helped him to his feet, walked him toward the latrine, and let him open the door.

He paused before entering and said, "Can't blame me for trying."

"I don't. It's just my husband who might." She gave him a pat on the shoulder, a big smile, and a pretty view of her face before she guided him on in and pulled the door closed.

CHAPTER 37

Ruth

→› ✤ ‹←

Ruth heard the front doorbell ring and stood up from where she was sitting on the living-room couch, mending a hole in the toe of Ed's sock. Through the window in the front door, she spied her papa standing with his hat pushed back from his forehead, his brow furrowed, and his mouth set in a determined line. Mother stood behind him, almost hidden from view. Ruth felt her pulse quicken, the sight of them unannounced at the door making her stomach knot. *What are they doing here?* she wondered. Was it another tragedy they'd come to report? Since she'd come to live with the Williamses, her parents had stopped by but never without calling before showing up on the doorstep. She hoped nothing more had happened to them.

When she opened the door and saw Mother's face, pale and drawn and Papa with the lines of worry channeling across his high forehead, her heart sank. "What's happened, Papa? Are you all right, Mother?"

Papa held out an official-looking envelope, "This was forwarded to us here in town. It's from the war department, so we thought we should bring it over straight away."

Her heart jumped into her throat. She did not want to take the letter, dreading that it brought awful news about Chester—being hurt—or killed. Her head began to spin, and she reached for the door frame to steady herself.

"Let's all go inside and sit down," Papa said, taking Ruth by the arm and leading her to the living-room sofa; he laid the envelope on the coffee table in front of her. He and Mother, faces grim, sat in chairs across from her.

"Oh, God, Papa. I know it's bad news. Chester's hurt." She couldn't say, "Or dead." Her eyes filled with tears as she stared at the letter, wishing it would disappear.

Mother stood, came to sit beside Ruth, and put an arm around her shoulder. "I know you're scared and upset, Ruth, but you have to open it. I'm right here for you. Your papa is, too."

Ruth was not that much comforted by her mother's presence. In the past few weeks, she had come to rely on Joe's mother and right now preferred the comfort of Ethel's arms. Ethel had told stories to Ruth and Charlie about Chester when he was a boy and young man running around with their son. They had some good memories of him alongside their aggravation with the troubles he had brought to Ruth—and Alice Jenson. Ruth wanted them here.

But Ethel and Ed had not appeared. They were in their bedroom, still napping. Hating to wake them but needing their presence, Ruth called out, "Ethel. Ed. Please come to the living room. Call Charlie to come in, too."

CHAPTER 37 ✦ RUTH

The bedroom door opened, and Ruth could hear the Williamses entering the kitchen and Ed calling to Charlie in the backyard. He and Ethel then came to the door and stood just inside the living room, their caring faces more a comfort to Ruth than the presence of Mother and Papa. Ethel asked, "Is everything all right, Ruth?"

She could not hold back the tears then, and they spilled over and ran down her cheeks. She wiped at them and tried to compose her face as Charlie came in from the backyard. His eyes darted from her to his grandparents and back again. She knew from the widening of his eyes and downturn of his mouth that he knew something wasn't right. She held out her hand to him.

"What's wrong?" he demanded, though the quaver in his voice made him sound younger than his ten years.

"Your mama got a letter from the war department about your daddy," Papa said before Ruth could answer.

"Is Daddy all right?"

"Come sit by me, Charlie," Ruth invited, and patted the couch cushion beside her. "I'll open and read it to all of us, so we'll know."

Ruth reached and took hold of the envelope, dreadfully afraid opening it would unleash a lethal force not unlike the one that destroyed her folks' home. Its contents could destroy something of her. And Charlie. She pushed backward into the velvet-covered couch and tore the flap open, withdrew the folded letter but couldn't bring herself to unfold the page and let loose the storm. It was like a booby trap; open it, and the explosion would tear her apart. Damage Charlie. *If only Joe were here*, she thought, but he was out at the farm.

"Why don't you read the letter, Ruth," Ed encouraged. "You get letters like this regardless of how bad things are, just to let you know. He just may be ill or wounded."

Wordless, the others waited as she slowly unfolded the letter and with trembling voice began to read.

Dear Mrs. Scarsdale,

We are writing to let you know that your husband, Chester Scarsdale, was injured in battle and is presently in a surgical hospital in Australia, where he is recovering from wounds received in battle. In his current state, he is unable to write you, but, in all likelihood, he will make a full recovery. You might like to know that he will receive a Purple Heart and a Navy Corps Commendation medal for an earlier action where he risked his life to save a fellow Sea Bee and a Marine. He sends his love to everyone.

Sincerely yours,
Lieutenant George Brandon, U.S. Navy
June 25, 1944

"Thank the Lord he'll recover," said Ethel, and Ruth's mother followed with an "Amen."

Ruth looked at her Papa and then Ed; both kept a stoic look on their faces but said nothing. Ruth silently let tears run down her face as she clung to Charlie. The stillness in the room seemed to go on and on. Charlie stood, breaking the silence by asking, "Are you sure he'll be okay?"

Ed spoke up, saying, "Yes, Charlie. They don't say how he was hurt—or where. But he will be fine when he heals from his wounds."

"Will he be coming home when he's better? Will I get to see him right away?" Tears slid down Charlie's cheeks, and his mouth trembled.

Ruth took his hand and said, "Of course. As soon as he gets here."

"That he's hurt is bad news, Charlie, but he's in a safe place now, too. You can be thankful for that," Ethel said.

"They said Daddy's getting two medals." Charlie's face lightened, and a smile broke through. "He can tell us all about what happened when he comes home."

"Yes, he will, Charlie," Ruth wondered at Mother's and Papa's silence. Could it be that they had hoped Chester wouldn't come home? The awful

CHAPTER 37 ♦ RUTH

thought then struck her that, had he been killed, she would not have to face the prospect of telling him she was pregnant or deciding between him and Joe. She felt her face flushing red as a wave of guilt over the thought broke over her.

Ruth's papa asked, "What's wrong, Ruth?"

Hearing her papa's voice broke something in Ruth, and it felt as if her heart was tearing in two. She still loved Chester. And she loved Joe.

"Mama? Are you okay?" Tears sprang to Charlie's eyes again, and he grabbed Ruth's hand.

"Of course, she is," Ed said. "She's just relieved that your daddy's going to be okay. They'll take good care of him in that hospital. Now you go on back outside while we grown-ups talk."

Ruth nodded to Charlie, and he turned and headed out the door.

Though not asked, the Williamses followed Charlie out of the room and stole away to another part of the house, leaving Ruth with her parents but feeling very much alone. She so wished Mother and Papa would leave and that Joe would come for Sarah.

CHAPTER 38

Chester

⇢ ✤ ⇠

After a week of being off the drugs, Chester realized he wasn't thinking so much about wanting them. The craving was almost gone. The pain was almost gone as well, only flaring up to become almost unbearable when he made sudden moves, bumped into something, or woke up in the middle of the night thrashing about in a nightmare. The wounds didn't hurt as much. The itching from the hundred or more stitches that ran up and down his left arm and leg and on the back of his neck were not much worse than the mosquito bites he suffered in the jungle. He could live with that itching now that there were no more bugs around. Or Japs shooting at him. No more artillery shells or rifle bullets aimed at him. No more bombs dropping. No more new wounds to have sewn up. The itch that started up every time he saw Nurse Bennet could not be scratched. It was made worse when she did not show for two days in a row.

On the second day of her absence, after having an X-ray of his neck, his doctor came in holding an X-ray film.

"Good news. The bone is forming nicely around those steel rods and screws I put in to hold your neck in place."

Chester chuckled, "Doc, I've always had a lot of iron and steel in my backbones. Didn't think I'd ever need to have more screwed in."

The doctor laughed and said, "I like your attitude, sailor. You'll be okay."

"That's so, doc. Unless, when they send me back into the jungle, I don't duck fast enough when they start shooting at me again. Or bombing me."

"You won't be going back into the jungle, sailor. Your fighting days are over. You'll head out to a rehabilitation hospital in the States when you leave here, tomorrow. It's likely a desk job or a discharge after that." Chester felt lightheaded, and his face flushed hot. A deep roar began in his ears and tears sprang to his eyes, though he did his best to hold them in. The idea he wouldn't have to face the mosquitos, dampness, jungle rot, bad food, and crazed Japs trying to kill him him was dizzying.

"You okay?" his doctor asked, a frown creasing his brow.

"Yeah, Doc. It just hit me hard what you said. In a good way. But I wasn't expecting that kind of news."

"Would like to have told you sooner. Get you used to the idea before we ship you back home. But truth is, it was only decided yesterday. You're doing pretty well, and we've got a whole boatload of new casualties coming in practically every day. We're swamped. Need your bed." He turned without another word and walked to the next man down the row of beds and delivered a different message. "You gotta stay around a few more days, sailor."

When the doctor moved on again, the man turned to Chester and said, "You lucky bastard. Wish I were going home to the States with you."

"Hell. I do, too. But you'll get there. Just give it time." The man reminded Chester of Hough. He felt a twinge of sadness thinking of his buddy still out in the thick of it. *Better him than me, though*, Chester thought. He'd received a letter from Hough saying, *with you gone I have twice as much work to do. These new fellows I'm working with look well fed and tough, but they don't do half the work you did. I miss you, you cantankerous bastard. Thank God Polk has kept his ass out of a sling and is still with me.* Chester's thoughts turned to home. He realized he needed to write a letter to Ruth and Charlie. To Alice. He wasn't sure what to write; he wasn't in any mood to think about what he would find when he got back to the States—or how he would handle it. When he asked for it, a medic brought him a pencil and paper. He sat for a moment wondering if he should write Alice first—or Ruth and Charlie. With a sigh of frustration, he began to write:

Dear Charlie and Ruth,

You'd laugh if you saw me. I have a horse collar strapped around my neck. It's called a traction brace. It keeps me from moving my head. Wearing it, I can't injure my spinal cord while my broken neck heals so I guess I won't complain too much. I hate it more than I do the stitches in my arm and leg. My neck itches so much at times that if I could get to it, I'd scratch till I bleed. The doc says I'll be headed out of here to the States and won't be going back to the fighting. I'll let you know more when I get back to a rehab hospital somewhere in the U.S. I'm shipping out tomorrow, and it shouldn't be all that long till I get to the States.
Chester

Laying the finished letter aside, he took a second sheet and sat staring at it, not knowing what to write Alice. He hadn't let her know, like he had Ruth, that he wasn't sure what he'd do once he got home. She thought he

CHAPTER 38 ✦ CHESTER

was coming home to her. He reread the letter to Ruth and Charlie and decided to write one just like it to Alice. It wouldn't give anything away.

*

Ages seemed to pass, though it'd been only twenty-four hours after the doctor told him he was being sent back to the States, when in the hot afternoon, Nurse Bennet came in with his discharge orders. She helped him get his stuff together, smiled, and said, "Good luck, sailor."

"Gonna miss me, Nurse Bennet? I'm sure gonna miss you."

"You really are a flirt, Mr. Scarsdale. Anybody ever tell you that?"

"It's what I live for."

She gave him a smile, and it was wider and more beautiful than any she'd ever lavished on him before. "Have a safe voyage home, Chester." She left him sitting on the side of his bed where he stayed until a burly aide came in and helped him into a wheelchair, wheeled him into the midday heat, and loaded him into an ambulance. "You're not as pretty as my nurse," Chester quipped.

"Pretty enough to get you on board for home, though, sailor," the man said. "Isn't that pretty enough?"

"Damn right."

On the hospital ship, he was put in a special bed that had been improvised to keep him from rolling off onto the floor as the ship rocked from side to side. He refused pain medication but accepted something to help him sleep at night. As he drifted in and out of the drug-enhanced sleep, or was pulled violently from a dream or nightmare, thoughts of the mess he was going home to boiled in his mind. He tried to calm himself by picturing Nurse Bennet, but that didn't help after the first days at sea, as her image faded. He wished at times that he'd healed well enough to get back to his unit and join Hough and not have to face Ruth and Alice. Images of Charlie, or of Bethany in Alice's arms, swam in and out of his consciousness, and he couldn't picture how he would tell Charlie about leaving him, or how he could let Bethany grow up without a father. Be a bastard child. As memories of Nurse Bennet faded away, he replaced them with pleasant recollections of Alice lying with him back in Port Hueneme. Back then, her soft skin and gentle touch smoothed away his fears about going to war. Now memory of her touch soothed his fears of returning to the home front.

Irrational fear crept in during some long nights as he imagined Japanese submarines lurking in the dark water, ready to launch a torpedo. Even ships with a Red Cross painted on them were not spared.

His leg wound opened a few days into the crossing and began to drain. The onboard doctor said, "You're lucky it's not infected, but you'll need some minor surgery to remove a small piece or two of shrapnel the other doctors missed finding." Chester hated the idea of being cut on again. At least the brace on his shoulders wasn't causing his back and shoulders to ache quite as much.

A storm hit four days into the crossing, and he had to stay in bed except to go to the latrine because the pitching of the boat unbalanced him. If he fell, he was told, he could fracture the bones in his neck again. Maybe become paralyzed. He was thankful for the two strong orderlies who helped him.

It seemed that his ship would never steam into harbor when, finally, the ship's intercom announced they were in safe American waters and that it would be American soil they'd soon be stepping onto. The boat pulled into port after what seemed a lifetime, and an orderly wheeled him down the gangplank onto solid ground. He wanted to kneel down and kiss the ground. Couldn't, though. His neck, arm, and leg wouldn't allow him to get back up again if he did. Relief swept over him like a cool Oklahoma spring breeze. The warm coastal breeze that bathed them as he was wheeled to transport was so unlike the intolerable heated air he'd slogged through in the tropics. It felt and smelled wonderful.

CHAPTER 38 • CHESTER

There was no one on this shore shooting at him, bombing him, strafing the very ground he stood on. He took a great breath and let it out slowly only to find that he let some of the good feelings escape with it. A different war zone waited for him back in Hobart, and he had no idea how he could withstand the assault that was coming. *If I could get rid of this brace*, he thought, *I'd try to get on the next boat to the Pacific.*

On the ride to the onshore hospital, his leg began to ache, and his mood soured. On arrival, he cursed at an orderly who told him he had to wait for a doctor to write the orders for admittance. He wanted to curse the doctor, who told him, "You'll have to spend a few days here while we get some more shrapnel out of that leg." Then he almost fainted when the doctor added, "Says here you'll then be transferred to the William C. Bordon General Hospital in Chickasha, Oklahoma."

I'm going to Oklahoma, he thought. *I survived those godforsaken battlefields overseas. I hope to high heaven I survive the one that's waiting for me back here on the home front.*

CHAPTER 39

Ruth

⇢ ✾ ⇠

Ruth hadn't told Joe she was pregnant. There had been no one but Joan she felt comfortable enough with to pour out her fears. Constantly on her mind was the question, *What am I to do? What am I to do?* That thought nagged at her every day, seven days a week. It faded to a whisper only when she was in Joe's arms.

The doorbell rang, startling Ruth out of her reveries. She laid down the potato she was peeling and dropped the knife into the sink. At the front door, she saw the postman walking away, and, as she stepped onto the porch, he turned and gave her a salute. In the covered mailbox was a thin letter from Chester addressed to both her and Charlie. It had been days since the letter arrived letting her know he was on his way home and this letter most likely would let her know when he'd arrive. Her hands

CHAPTER 39 • RUTH

trembled as she held it, her heart pounded against the inside of her chest so rapidly, she was afraid it would burst out and run away.

She walked to the couch, sat down and thought of Charlie who was in his room building something with his erector set. She was tempted to read the letter without him but then relented and called out, "Come on into the living room, Charlie. It's a letter from your daddy." Charlie came running and stood jumping from one foot to the other, shouting, "What does he say. What does he say?"

"Hold your horses, young man. Give me time to open it." *I wish you weren't here while I open it*, she thought. *I hope it doesn't make me cry.* She took a deep breath, and sliding her fingernail under the flap, slowly forced the envelope open, and read;

> *Guess what? I'll be seeing you all soon. They're sending me to the William C. Bordon General Hospital rehab center in Chickasha, not all that far from Hobart. I'm not all that sure when I'll get there. They got to cut a few more pieces of shrapnel out of my leg before I leave here. Look forward to seeing you. Chester*
>
> *P.S. It'll be a while before I can wrestle you, Charlie. I'm so skinny I couldn't wrestle a fence post.*

In the days that followed, Ruth's thoughts and feelings were in a tangle as she spiraled between excitement that she would see Chester and the sensation that she was at the bottom of a deep hole, out of which she could not climb to safety. She was short with Charlie. The embraces of Joe sometimes left her confused and unhappy. Joan, Ethel, and Ed were the only ones she felt some sanity being around. Joan would sit with her and let her weep and worry. The Williams would sit quietly at the kitchen table with Ruth, not ask how she felt, not give her advice, or not bring to the table anything having to do with Joe. They most likely knew about her and Joe, but they kept their counsel.

On Sunday evening, several days after receiving the letter, she sat relaxed with the two of them as they lingered after dinner, sipping their iced tea out of glasses decorated with blue violets. Charlie had gone off into the living room to read a comic. It was a rare moment of peace for her. The moment was shattered by the shrill ring of the phone.

"I'll get it, Ruth. Be back in a minute," Ed said as he stood, but Charlie yelled, "I'll get it."

The ringing stopped, and her heart almost came to a standstill as well when Charlie yelled, "There's someone who says they're from the hospital wants to talk to you, Mama."

Her heart then ran wild in her chest as she rushed to the phone and breathed a tense, "Hello." A tired-sounding male voice identified himself as from the rehab hospital in Chickasha and then said, "Mrs. Scarsdale, your husband, Chester, was just admitted this evening, and he asked me to call and let you know he's here."

"I'll come right away."

"No. It's too late today. We've got to get him settled. And he said I should tell you to wait until day after tomorrow before you come. They will be taking the neck brace off sometime tomorrow, and he'd just as soon nobody sees him till it's off. He hopes you'll understand." Charlie tugged at her arm as soon as she hung up. "Was he talking about Daddy? Can we go see daddy? Can we go? Can we leave right now?"

She scowled at him and motioned him to sit down. "Can I have a minute to think, Charlie?"

"When can we go, Mama?"

"I don't know for sure. He doesn't want us to come tomorrow because he doesn't want us to see him in the neck brace. They're taking it off tomorrow." Charlie bounced on the divan, his excitement spilling out of him. "I can't wait. I can't wait."

"Take your comic book to your room now, Charlie. I need to talk with Ed and Ethel." Charlie scrunched up his nose in aggravation but grabbed

CHAPTER 39 • RUTH

his comic and slammed out the kitchen door. The two Williamses then stepped on into the room from the doorway, where they had been standing. Ethel sat down on the couch beside Ruth and Ed in a chair across the coffee table from her. She could see concern in their eyes. They sat quietly with her, not intruding into her anxious thoughts.

Her mind whirled, and she became breathless. Had she not been sitting down, she might have fallen into a faint. This was too abrupt for her, Too soon. Too . . . ? She couldn't wrap her mind around the fact he was already here. She wasn't ready to see him yet, wasn't exactly sure what she wanted to say to him, how she was going to be able to tell him she was pregnant.

What was Chester going to say when he found that out? Would it make it easier for him, leaving it open to go to Alice, or would he decide regardless of whose baby she carried, he wanted to stay with Charlie and her? She wasn't very far along. She could get rid of the baby before he knew about it. Could she do that? God help her, she didn't have any answers.

She wanted to drive there that very night, not wait till the day after tomorrow to go, whether he had the brace on or not, whether he wanted her to come or not. But she didn't want to drive there and have to drive back after dark. Not in the state of mind she was in. Not if she was torn apart by anything that might happen between her and Chester. But she was not going to wait until day after tomorrow.

Ed and Ethel stood up, and Ruth tensed when the front door opened, and Joe and Sarah walked in. They were both smiling, but Joe's turned to a frown.

"Where's Charlie?" Sarah asked, her pretty face flushed with excitement. I found his pocketknife he thought he lost. It was in the barn."

"He's in his bedroom, Sarah."

She burst through the swinging door to the kitchen; a moment later, the bedroom door slammed shut.

Joe's mother gave him a hug, and then she and Ed went to sit at the kitchen table. Joe sat down by her and asked, "What's wrong, Ruth? You look like you just saw a ghost."

She wanted to burrow her face in his shoulder but held back. She almost feared Joe, feared that he could read the terrible thoughts roiling inside her. Her voice croaked when she said, "Chester's in Chickasha. Somebody over there called to let me know. I don't know what I'm going to do."

"You're going to go see him, of course. Get your things, and I'll drive you over right now."

Ruth almost blurted out that she wasn't a hundred percent sure she wanted him to go with her. Ever since she'd first made love to Joe, she had shied away from sharing her doubts about leaving Chester, even as she knew it wasn't right to keep them to herself. Joe deserved to know how torn she was. But she was frightened that, if she told him, he would turn his back on her. "Chester doesn't want me to come or bring Charlie till day after tomorrow, when he gets what he calls 'his choker' off. I don't want to wait, though. I will not, cannot."

"I'll drive you over whenever you want."

She took a deep breath. "Tomorrow morning. I need to go alone, Joe. I need you here when I get back, but I need to see him alone. And I need some time to myself before and after. The drive will help. I hate to ask, but is there any way I can borrow your pickup? I hate to ask the folks for their car."

"Of course. What are you going to do about Charlie?"

"He'll throw a fit if I tell him I'm going without him, and I can't deal with that right now. He'll throw less of one if I just go without telling him where."

"You drive Sarah, Charlie, and me out to the farm tonight. Charlie won't have a fit about you leaving him if he can spend tonight and the next day playing with Sarah."

"Won't he be suspicious about me coming along and leaving with your truck?"

CHAPTER 39 • RUTH

"You have to run some errands for your folks tomorrow, don't you? Can't do that without borrowing my truck. When you're finished seeing Chester, you can bring it back, and I'll drive you and Charlie back to town. Charlie will never suspect a thing."

Little was said when she left Charlie, Joe, and Sarah off at the farm. The headlights cut through the gloom of the night, illuminating the black ribbon of the road guiding her back to town. Tomorrow morning, the road she followed would take her to see Chester and to a decision she might have to make and live with for the rest of her life.

CHAPTER 40

Ida

⇢ ✾ ⇠

Sitting down to breakfast with Bob, Ida reached for a biscuit. Though not really all that hungry, she nibbled at it and then served herself a piece of bacon and a fried egg. She'd been startled last night when Ruth called and told her and Bob that Chester had arrived in Chickasha. Since then, she couldn't get Ruth and Chester out of her mind. Had Ruth started for Chickasha yet? What would go on with them when she arrived? So many questions whirling about in her head. She felt dizzy and then frightened that she might be having another spell with her heart. Between bites she asked, "What do you think Ruth's going to say to Chester today?"

Bob looked up from his biscuits and gravy, shook his head, chewed, and swallowed before he said, "No idea. I wouldn't want to be in her shoes

CHAPTER 40 • IDA

right now. Still married to that no-account Scarsdale and all involved with Joe."

"The Williamses are good people, Bob. They took Ruth to their heart. And Joe's their boy. They did a better job of raising him than the Scarsdales did Chester. Joe's turned into a solid man, you'll have to admit, even though you never liked him."

"I guess I'll give you that. I've come to realize that Joe's a different man now than when I knew him back in his twenties. It helped that he offered to let me borrow his tractor for a few days. That was big of him. As to what Ruth will do, I don't know. She's blind, deaf, and dumb when it comes to Chester. Always has been. If he says he'll give up Alice and her kid and come back to her, Ruth'll fall all over herself letting him do just that."

"I think you may be absolutely right. And it would be a crying shame, as far as I'm concerned."

Taking a last swallow of his coffee, Bob rose from the table and reached for his hat. "I'll be out at the farm for a while today. I need to keep cleaning up the mess that tornado left for me. There's a good crop of cotton flowering out there that the tornado didn't touch, but there are weeds in it that'll need choppin' soon. We make a good crop this year and next, it'll put my mind at ease. And I'm thinking about finding us another place in the country to move to. I can't abide living here in town."

That was news to Ida. Now that she'd settled into the house here in town, she was growing to like it. "Might be best if we stayed right here, Bob. The place is growing on me. It was getting hard on me—all that work out there on the farm. I manage better living here. I can walk over to Joan's from here. If I need something from the store, it doesn't take driving ten miles to get it"

Bob grunted and said, "You might be right. But I'm still going to see if I can rent another 160 acres. I don't have those animals to look after anymore. I'll need to buy a tractor for myself, and, when I do, I can farm more land. But I hate givin' up usin' horses. And I miss not having all that fresh milk and butter."

She'd seen tears in his eyes when that Jersey and those two old horses were loaded and carted away. He was probably more torn up about that than he'd be if she up and left him. "Everybody in this county thinks you've been a fool using those horses to farm with as long as you did. Nobody's without a tractor these days. And you have Joe's tractor to practice getting used to driving one."

Bob nodded and left by the front door just as a freight train rolled by on the tracks a block away. The floor shook. Ida rose and began to wash the dishes and put away the leftovers. There was a half-sewn quilt she needed to get to, and Joan had asked her to make some summer dresses for Elizabeth and Bertha. She hoped Ruth didn't give in to whatever it was Chester asked of her. He'd want it all, both Alice and her baby and Ruth and Charlie. Her Ruth had put up with just about anything to stay with that man—would even forgive him for sleeping with her mother. But Ruth wasn't likely to ever be all that forgiving of her if she ever found out for sure what she suspected. And she wouldn't put it past Chester to tell Ruth just to hurt her if she decided to have no more to do with him.

A knock at the front door interrupted her thoughts. Annoyance tightened her face into a frown; she wasn't in the mood for company right now. Whoever it was would want to talk about Ruth and Chester, and she wasn't in the mood for I-wonder-what's-happening-over-there-in-Chickasha. She called out, "Come in," too harshly; she thought and hoped the person on the other side of her front door didn't hear it.

Joan and her two girls came trouping in and joined her in the kitchen. She hadn't been expecting them but it was a pleasant surprise. The girls were both wearing the yellow summer dresses Ida had sewn for them after moving into town, and they looked like two energetic bursts of sunshine. They took one look at the biscuits and lukewarm gravy, and their faces lit up.

CHAPTER 40 • IDA

"Can I have some biscuits and gravy, Grandmother?" Bertha asked, her wide brown eyes pleading.

"Me, too, Grandmother," Elizabeth said and picked up a crumb from out of the bowl and stuck it in her mouth.

"You two already had your breakfast," Joan said, and both girls' mouth turned down in a pout.

"Why don't you let them each have half a biscuit and what gravy's left. They're both skinny as a rail." Joan was the only one of her three girls who hadn't put on an extra twenty or thirty pounds since getting married. She and Bob had been overweight since their thirties. Joan didn't make trouble about any of them being overweight but was always eating like a bird to keep her own weight down.

"Okay, but I want both of you to go out in the backyard and play when you're done eating. I need to talk to your grandmother."

When both girls were out of earshot ten minutes later, Ida cocked her head, arched her eye, and asked, "So what is it, Joan?"

"Ruth is going to kill me for telling you, but I think you should know something that's going on with her. But you have to promise not to tell Papa."

"Bob and I already have too many secrets between us, Joan. Now you want there to be another?"

Joan stared at the floor and shook her head. "I should have kept my mouth shut, Mother. Just pretend I didn't say anything."

"No, you don't," Ida said. "You've already let the cat half out of the bag. Can't keep it in now." Ida used the iron-hard tone of voice she had when the girls were growing up. And like it mostly had done all their young lives, it would make Joan think twice before denying her.

With a low whispery tone that Ida couldn't quite hear or understand, Joan said something but the only word loud enough to hear was, "Ruth."

"Speak up now. I didn't hear a word you said but 'Ruth.' What about Ruth?" Color came to Joan's cheeks, and she took a big breath. "Little pitchers have big ears, Mother. I don't want to speak up." She took another big breath and then her whispers come loud enough for Ida to hear. "Ruth's in a family way. There's a lot more she's having to contend with today than just visiting Chester and finding out what he's going to do."

"Lord, have mercy." Blood rushed to Ida's face, and her heart speeded up. "I had no idea. But the way she's been carrying on with Joe, I'm not surprised. Did she tell you what she's goin' to do?"

"She has to see Chester before making up her mind what to do. I told her she ought to leave him and be with Joe. But she's so mixed up about the whole situation, she doesn't really know her own mind."

Ida remembered when she was scared to death she might be pregnant by Chester. She would have gone to that old woman for an abortion had she been pregnant. But the thought of her daughter putting herself in the hands of someone like that just to stay with Chester made her heartsick. "I hope you and Pearl can stand by her through this," she said. "Ruth is more than helpful to her Papa and me, but she keeps her distance when around us."

"You know why that is, Mother? I've noticed and brought it up to her, but she just clams up. What happened between you-all?"

Ida wanted to lay it all off on Bob. Tell Joan it was because he had been so hard on the boy and was talking down Chester all the time in the boy's presence. And if Joan pushed, that's what she would do. "I really don't know."

"What's really on my mind, Mother, is what we can do to help Ruth make the decision that's best for her. Or try to. She belongs with Joe. Problem is she's always been crazy about Chester no matter how bad he treats her."

The girls came running in from the backyard talking excitedly about a stray tomcat they saw in the alley. "It jumped the fence and let us pet him," Bertha said. "Can we take him home, Mama? Can we? Please. Please," Elizabeth pleaded.

CHAPTER 40 • IDA

They were a cute pair, and she loved them dearly. The excitement made their eyes sparkle. Girls always found a way to her heart, but these two were special. They were her granddaughters. Pearl's boys had been her first grandchildren and had been cute, but she'd always kept her distance and resisted getting close to either of them. Heaven help her, she'd certainly never admit that to anyone but herself.

Joan said, "No. That cat probably belongs to somebody. And it's time for us to leave."

It was sad to see the brightness in their eyes dim and fill with tears.

"Come here, girls, and give your old grandmother a hug. I can almost promise that cat of the Murphys next door will be here next time you visit." They came to her, and with her handkerchief, she wiped the tears from Bertha's cheeks and would have from Elizabeth's if the child hadn't already used the back of her hand. She saw them all to the door and stood there waving until they turned the corner, the two girls throwing her a kiss just before they disappeared. The ache she usually carried in her heart had begun melting away with their visit, and it melted more as she caught their kisses and brought them to her lips.

As she turned from the door, she glanced at a picture of Winston. Pearl had given it to Ida after the tornado. It was a copy of Winston's senior graduation picture. She crossed the small room, took it from the shelf, and gazed at it. Not long after the tornado hit, she'd received a letter from Winston telling her he was being transferred back to the States. It would be hard to put into words the relief she felt on reading that letter. It took away some of the misery and heartache she felt over the loss of her home to the tornado.

Pearl had also given Ida a snapshot of Brian sitting astraddle the home place's coal-oil barrel. It had pained her to see him in the tiny picture rather than in the large, tinted one on the living-room wall. In the time after the tornado, when she had no picture of him at all, she'd come to realize it was something of a relief not to be reminded of his passing as she had in her destroyed home every time she'd walked into her living room. As soon as Pearl handed it to her, Ida knew she would put it away in a drawer with the few keepsakes that had survived the storm. Something to sometimes take out and remember and grieve. But she saw her living son's picture every day, and it helped keep unhappiness at bay. Even made her smile.

She placed Winston's picture back on the shelf, and her thoughts turned again to Ruth. *If only Ruth would come to her senses and choose to live with Joe and have his baby, she could in time patch up things with her oldest daughter. Maybe if she had this child, it would be a girl. That would please Ruth and would certainly please me,* she thought. *But God knows, things do not always pan out the way I want.* She went to her rocking chair, took up her sewing needle, and began to stitch, waiting as patiently as she could to find out from Ruth what course her life would take in the weeks, months, and years ahead. *Please God, let her choose happiness over misplaced love.*

CHAPTER 41

Bob

⇉ ✽ ⇇

As Bob drove out of town, he couldn't take his mind off Ruth. Off Chester. She had to be well on her way to Chickasha by now; probably lit out before sunup. There was no doubt in his and Ida's mind that she would be better off divorcing Chester and marrying Joe. He'd wanted to tell her that but always tightened his lips before he blurted out the idea. Couldn't say too much to Ruth these days without her getting her back up. Resenting almost everything he said, though she didn't say anything much back to him. But he could see the resentment in those big old brown eyes of hers. And the pinched curve of her mouth.

As he turned off onto the dirt at the crossroads where Babbs School sat, his thoughts turned to the tornado. He shook his head and frowned. The blasted thing sent his house and outbuildings scattering all across his neighbor's thirty-acre pasture. Funny thing though, it left this car setting where it was, leaving only a few dents and scratches on one side where it was hit by God knows what the funnel threw at it. First time he started it up, it ran just fine.

He turned into the driveway and the same, strange feeling washed over him that he felt each time he visited, like he was in a bad dream and, if he could just wake up and blink his eyes, the house and all the outbuildings would still be standing there. As he rolled to a stop, where, for over thirty years, he'd parked in front of his now-missing home, he blinked. Didn't help. The house was still gone. *Don't be a fool*, he thought. *You know this isn't a dream. Still, it is strange.*

Talk about strange, he had a hard time believing that he and Ida were getting along a little better since the tornado. They'd pulled together like a good team of horses to get over the worst of the loss and settle into their place in town. Wasn't easy; they both were shell-shocked at first. Didn't know what to do. Of course, things wouldn't have been as smooth if all three girls hadn't pitched in. Been a lot of help to them. Ruth and Joan both living in town near them had helped out a lot. Pearl came by every time Bill and she drove to town. His sons-in-law were a help, too. Bill had taken care of Bob's stock till they sold, and George worked to get him and Ida settled there in town. Pearl's two boys and Charlie worked like Turks to help salvage what little could be found lying in the pasture. It was like going on a treasure hunt for them as they trudged through the pasture picking up any little thing that looked salvageable. Even little Elizabeth and Bertha came out a couple of times and tried to give a hand. Joe Williams and Sarah had come to help, and Joe's tractor was a Godsend.

Bringing casseroles, platters of good, cured ham, cakes and pies, ladies from the church where Joan, George, and the girls attended services made sure there was something to eat during those first few days after he and Ida moved into town. The minister, though, was a pain in the kiester, going on about God's will and being thankful the Lord had spared them. Like

CHAPTER 41 ♦ BOB

Ida, he would have been a lot more thankful if the Lord had taken that funnel back up into the clouds sooner than He did. Bob never thought much about whether there was a God or not; he lived a fairly moral life, at least he had over the past twenty years, and he figured if there was a heaven, he'd likely be there. Or nearby, anyway, if the Catholics were right and there was a purgatory. He doubted, though, that there would be many Nazis or Japs in heaven. No fascist Italians. They were killing and maiming too many of the fine young men of this and other allied countries. And some like Chester, whose goodness he had his doubts about, might squeeze their way in if the Good Lord chose to give them credit for helping fight this war. Getting wounded. Getting killed.

He had come to like Joe Williams. He had to admit that Joe was reliable. Steady. A man that would be a better influence on Charlie than Chester would ever be.

He let his eyes travel over the wreckage that had not yet been cleared away. He'd have to make a pretty big fire to get rid of all that splintered wood and then make a lot of trips to the dump to rid the place of what he couldn't burn. In time he'd turn this half acre of farmyard into tillable land. There was no way he could afford to rebuild. Made him wish he hadn't sent that insurance man on his way when he stopped by. As he walked over to the fence out beyond where his house once stood, inch-and-a-half-long grasshoppers leaped away to avoid his feet. At the edge of the cotton patch, he stooped down and picked off a cotton flower and brought it to his nose, knowing full well there would be no odor. He always wondered how such a pretty flower could have no smell. Shouldn't be surprised; it was hard to find a flower that could survive in this part of the country and manage to have any smell. Ida's zinnias, the only thing she could ever get to grow, would be blooming soon in what had been their front yard. They had no scent, either. Pretty, though.

He heard hard clods of dried mud crunching under tires and, looking around, saw Bill Dennison's old green Ford truck pull into the drive and park. Bill stepped out and, coming up to Bob, drawled, "Tore the place all to hell, didn't it. I have to get used to the sight every time I drive by."

"Ain't that the truth? I can't get used to it. Want to think it's a nightmare, and I'll wake up and everything'll be in its rightful place."

"You expect that cotton flower to smell good?" Bill asked. "There's about as much chance of that as there is you'll drive in here and see everything still standing."

Bob let the flower drop to the ground, embarrassment coloring his cheeks even though he knew Bill was teasing. His eye caught the slight movement of a horny-toad lizard sitting in the shade of a goat-head sticker patch's leaves. "I darn well know that, Bill." His words came out a little harsher than he wanted. In the quiet that followed, he reached down, picked up the small toad, set it in the palm of his other hand and watched it swell up, look larger, a way to discourage something from eating it. *Don't have to worry about me*, Bob thought. *I wouldn't care to take a bite.*

"Those things can spit in your eye, Bob."

"I wasn't born yesterday, Bill. I'm not going to get it that near my eye." He stooped down and placed the lizard back in the sticker patch, and it retreated into the sparse shade of the thorny plant.

Bill took out his pipe and began filling it from a leather pouch he took from his pocket. "Ida called us last night and said Chester was at the rehab place in Chickasha. That he'd told Ruth to wait a day, but she was bound and determined to take off this morning."

"I suspect she's on her way right now." Bob made a face. "I offered to drive her, but she turned me down."

"Tell you the truth, Bob, I think Ruth's better off getting rid of Chester and makin' a life with Joe Williams. Nobody but can help seeing there's something good going on between the two of them." Bill struck a match against the striker on his matchbook and, putting it to the bowl of his pipe, sucked the flame into the tobacco, sending billowing clouds of smoke spiraling up into the cloudless sky.

CHAPTER 41 ✦ BOB

"I think so, too," Bob said, "but what happens, happens. Ruth's grown pretty strong-minded lately. She's not takin' advice from anybody these days, much less me."

"That's so." Bill held the pipe suspended from his teeth while he dug into his overall's pocket, came out with some folding money, and handed it to Bob. "Sold those two hogs of yours at an auction yesterday. Got a decent price, too."

No surprise there, Bob thought. *I took good care of them.* "I'll miss all that bacon and ham come winter. But there was no way I could raise them to butcher now, me livin' in town."

"Can't hardly believe those hogs had that barn blown right off them and didn't have as much as a scratch on their tough hides to show for it."

"It's a miracle none of my other stock suffered. Even old Hitler got the wash house blown off him and didn't get any scrapes. It's a miracle he wasn't picked up and blown a half mile away, like some things did."

"Glad you gave him to my boys."

"Couldn't have a farm dog in town. Your boys lookin' after him okay?"

"They've always loved that old hound. He's doing fine. We've had to come over here a couple of times and fetch him. Like the rest of us, he don't want to believe this all happened."

"Good to hear." Bob's throat tightened as he thought about his animals surviving and how much he'd felt relieved when they were all accounted for. Things wouldn't have been so hard on him if he could have kept his livestock. But then, even though the storm hadn't taken his animals, he'd still had to lose them. It was clear that while living in town he couldn't take proper care of livestock, so he sold them all. It hurt every time one was hauled away. The two horses, the milk cow, and a couple of the yearlings he'd bought earlier that spring had been down in the pasture and hadn't been so much as touched by the tornado. He felt even sadder at the thought that no one but the dog-food company had been interested in taking his two old workhorses. He wasn't ashamed of the tears he'd shed when the company truck loaded them and drove away. The old Jersey cow that his neighbor Tatum bought, he missed, too. There had been a comfort in leaning his head into Isabelle's flank and milking a full bucket of cream-rich milk from her. The rickety old hen house had been the only thing to survive, and the laying hens inside had walked, hopped, or flew outside when the storm passed as if nothing had happened around them. He gave them all to Pearl, who promised to keep him and Ida in eggs.

"How's that tractor you borrowed from Joe workin' out? You must have been the last farmer in Oklahoma to give up his horses."

Bob shrugged. "I prefer horses." He glanced over at the iron contraption sitting in the sun and soaking up its rays. "That tractor seat is so hot it'd fry an egg. And I have to sit on it when you leave."

Bill laughed and pulled his cap down further on his forehead. "I gotta get on, Bob. Anything I can do for you before I leave?"

Bob didn't want company right now, even though there were things Bill could help doing. "You go on home now. I got everything pretty much in hand right now."

He watched Bill as he got in his car and turned onto the road, a plume of dust kicking up behind him as he drove away. Bob then walked into the side yard, and cranked up and mounted the tractor. Sure enough, the seat was almost too hot to sit on. He had no choice but to sit on the thing with all the work needing done around the place. He wouldn't have the money to put down on one of his own until this and next year's cotton crop came in. He missed the smell of his horses, their sweat, the hay dust in their hair, and the thick odor of horse hooey. It was a lot more pleasant than the gol-darn smoke this four-wheeled beast poured out its smokestack. Overtaken with sadness, he sat for a few minutes on the hard metal seat, let the motor idle and his eyes wander over the trash-strewn yard, and thought, *I sure do miss the way this place looked just a few short weeks ago.*

CHAPTER 41 • BOB

Pushing in the clutch, he put the tractor into gear, wishing he had a pair of reins in his hand rather than a steering wheel. This metal monster didn't respond to, "Giddy up," so he let the clutch out and drove down to where the barn once stood. A single wall needed to be pulled down today; keep some neighbor's kids from coming over and fooling around enough to have it fall on them. He thought of Ruth again and wondered if she had reached Chickasha by now. Wondered how it would go when she walked in on Chester unannounced. Wondered if she had decided what she was going to do—give him walking papers or go back to him. He hoped she had enough horse-sense not to walk back into her stormy marriage to Chester Scarsdale.

CHAPTER 42

Chester

→→ ✸ ←←

Chester awakened the first morning he was in the William C. Bordon General Hospital to see the room flooded with warm, summer sunlight. With some effort, he swung his legs over the side of the bed and sat up. His right hand grasped the edge of the bed, and he swore. The damned neck brace was bent on choking him to death. He wanted to shake his head, shake out the cobwebs that had crisscrossed his brain during the night, encasing his scary thoughts and letting him sleep. The neck brace wouldn't permit that.

He sat there and thought back over the past two days. When he'd come out of that hospital back east, after mostly recovering from the surgery on his leg, he'd been wheeled onto a train with scores of other recovering men. Both nights, the rhythmic clicking of the rails and the rocking of

CHAPTER 42 ✦ CHESTER

the railcar had lulled him to sleep as he sped through the the darkened countryside. He'd awakened yesterday morning with a nightmare of being back on the island. Then he'd felt the tension in his stomach grow the closer the train came to Oklahoma City. The ambulance ride from there to Chickasha seemed to have taken hours.

His leg and arm had itched like a son-of-bitch from the time they loaded him on the train till he was finally wheeled onto the hospital ward and left setting by his bed in the wheelchair. He tried to get himself oriented, but couldn't seem to remember what the date was.

"What's the date today?" he'd asked an orderly helping a man with both arms in casts.

"Sunday, August 13, 1944," the man said. "And in case you haven't discovered that big clock down there on the wall, it's 6:30 p.m.—dinnertime."

"Are you trying to be a smartass, mister?"

"Maybe a little. It's been a long day. Sorry."

Chester had tried shrugging his shoulders, but they wouldn't shrug; the brace on his neck wouldn't let them. "Can you make a couple of calls for me?" Chester had asked the smartass, and when the orderly agreed, Chester told him first to call Alice, and then Ruth. "Just tell Alice to come tomorrow and make up some excuse to get Ruth to come the day after." The man raised an eyebrow and Chester grunted, "It's complicated. Don't ask."

After the orderly left to make the calls, Chester had wheeled himself over to a window and sat gazing out at a field of cotton that was in full bloom. The sun was low in the west and would soon be disappearing. *I wish to hell I could disappear for a while,* he'd thought. In the next two days, he had to face two women and come to a decision. *God knows, I don't know what to do.* A tear of frustration rolled down his cheeks. *Unmanly,* he'd thought. *That tear is unmanly. Damned if I didn't face those Goddamn Japs without crying. Why can't I be a man now?*

After dinner and talking for a while to the man in the bed next to him, he'd asked the nurse for a sleeping pill. The narcotic and his exhaustion let sleep steal quickly over him. He'd drifted off, fears of the home war suspended—if only for a brief night.

Now, it was Monday, August 14, 1944, and he didn't have to ask anyone to know that. Having slept soundly, the strong urge that had finally awakened him insisted that he not wait to take off to the latrine. He called to a nurse two beds down tending a man's bandaged arm, "Nurse, can you get someone to get me a wheelchair?"

"I'll be there in just a second," she said.

"That's about how long it'll take before I piss my pants," he replied.

She called out to an orderly who appeared through the far door, "Wheelchair, please," and then came over to Chester. "Let me help you stand." Chester grasped her hand and forearm and used them to pull himself to his feet. The sweet smell of her perfume almost overwhelmed the odor of the Pine-Sol-washed floors and the stale sweat under his neck brace.

She gave him a strained smile and squeezed his arm more tightly as the orderly came striding down the ward, maneuvered a wheelchair behind Chester, and took his other arm to help settle him into the seat.

Ten minutes later, as he was wheeled out of the bathroom, and pushed toward his bed, he saw Alice sitting in his bedside chair. She fixed her eyes on him briefly, but there was no hint of recognition, and she looked away. Then her gaze flicked back to him, and her eyes widened.

"Chester," she cried, so loud that several of the men in the other beds turned to stare. She leapt to her feet, looked wildly from the orderly back to Chester. "Chester," she cried again, as if he had not heard her the first time.

When the orderly wheeled him to where she was standing by his bed, she grabbed one of his hands and brought it to her lips. "Oh, Chester. I'm so sorry."

CHAPTER 42 ♦ CHESTER

"I'm a sight, aren't I?" He laughed one of his deep-throated, smoker's laughs, and then coughed. "I'd love to get a hug, but it'd feel like you were hugging one of those state fair mechanical clowns."

"My poor baby. You look like you haven't eaten for months." She kissed his hand again.

"We didn't eat too well out there in the jungle, and then I went and got myself almost blown to kingdom come. Kind of took my appetite away."

Alice broke into tears, and buried her face in her hands.

"Hey, don't cry. I made it home. Right this minute, I feel like I'm about the luckiest bastard alive."

Alice took a deep breath and wiped at her tears with the back of her hand. "I know you wrote me that when I saw you, I'd probably be shocked. Shouldn't be surprised by the way you look. But I guess I just couldn't believe you'd. . . . " She paused.

"That I'd look like I was half dead?" He shook his head. "Well, when I look in the mirror, I have a hard time believing that the corpse looking back really is me." He coughed up some phlegm and spit in a coffee can sitting at his feet. "Damned if I didn't catch a touch of pneumonia before I got here, but I'm just about over that, too."

The orderly broke in and said, "We'll need this wheelchair, sir. Let me help you sit down and then y'all can talk." He took Chester's hands from Alice and, pulling him to his feet, lowered his butt onto the chair. Chester screwed his face up in pain as he bent his injured leg. "God damn it and go to hell but that hurts."

Alice burst into tears again.

The orderly dragged a chair over from another bed. "You can sit here, ma'am." He then pulled a curtain around them. "This'll give you a little privacy." Chester reached and took Alice's hand. "I said don't cry, now. I'm going to be just fine. They'll be taking off this goddamn brace for good soon. It's been settin' on my shoulders and around my neck for what seems a lifetime. When I get the damn thing off, then

I can give you a proper hug. Get one, too." He patted her hand and then stroked it.

He was glad to see Alice's sobs turn into sniffles and then stop. She pulled a handkerchief from her purse and wiped at her eyes. They sat there in silence then. He didn't know what to say and waited for her. But she sat looking at him as if she couldn't quite be sure he was really there. He wondered now why he had arranged to see her first. He'd thought it would be easier for him to make up his mind about which woman he would end up with if he saw her first. Most of the times he'd dwelled on it, Alice seemed to be the one he wanted to live with. Now, with her pretty face reddened, her eyes watery with tears, and the death grip she had on his hand, he felt overwhelmed with doubt. It didn't help him choose what he wanted when she finally spoke.

"I missed you so much, Chester. It's been hard without you. I need you. Bethany needs you. I was afraid she'd have to grow up without a daddy."

Chester felt a lump growing in his chest closing off his breath, killing his words. He thought of Charlie and how he might have to finish growing up without a daddy. He wanted to shake the thought out of his head but knew it wouldn't budge. *Still*, he thought, *right now I should comfort Alice, tell her not to worry. That I'll be with her and Bethany.* But the words stuck deep in his chest. Ruth and Charlie were coming tomorrow, and he had to see them. See what he felt about her. Then maybe he could tell Alice what she wanted to hear. Or not. Desperate for something to say, he blurted out a question, "Where is that baby girl of ours?"

Alice's face lit up. "She's downstairs in the cafeteria with Sister. Mildred drove me over. She's been such a help to me and Bethany."

"Do I get to see her?" He did not want to see her yet, he realized. Somehow until now the idea he had a baby girl had been just that. An idea. Not altogether real. Seeing her was going to make everything so much more real. The thought soured his stomach. He and Alice could no longer have the carefree time together they'd had when he was at Port Hueneme in California. Just the two of them.

"They said I couldn't bring her up here."

"I guess they have to remove my choker first. Then I can come downstairs to see her."

She stood, and her eyes brightened. "You can look out the window. I'll run downstairs and take her outside." She turned to go but was stopped by a call from outside the curtain.

"Scarsdale. Your breakfast is here."

He was relieved to have a few minutes' reprieve. He'd feel more like seeing Bethany on a full stomach. "Bring it in. I'm starving to death. You had breakfast yet, Alice?"

"We stopped on the way here." She smiled at him and sat back down.

The curtain was drawn back, and the orderly set a tray across Chester's lap. The fried eggs, biscuit, and bacon made his mouth water. "Let me finish this, and then you can let me see her."

As he began to eat, Alice sat down and squirmed in her seat, couldn't seem to sit still. Twice she opened her mouth as if she were going to say something but closed it. He saw her eyes begin to tear again.

He paused with his fork raised from the plate and asked, "You want to say something, Alice?"

"Have you told Ruth yet about us? That you're going to ask for a divorce?"

He let the fork full of eggs drop back onto the plate. "I told her to come over tomorrow so I could tell her." But he wasn't sure what he would tell her.

"I wish you'd already told her." She cast her eyes down, and her brow wrinkled.

"Don't worry about it, Alice. I'll tell her. And I'll need to have a talk with Charlie as soon as I'm up and around. Tell him. I wish I didn't have to do that. It's going to hurt him something awful."

"I know. I feel sorry for Charlie. But I'll try to be a good step-mother for him."

They sat silently as Chester finished eating. He wished she hadn't brought up Ruth. Or he hadn't thought of Charlie. Particularly about leaving Charlie.

Alice stood, smiled, and kissed him on his forehead. "I'm going to go down and find a place to nurse Bethany. Give me twenty minutes, and then have the orderly take you to those windows over there, where you can look down and see her." She squeezed his hand and walked away. At the doorway, she turned and blew him a kiss.

"Good Lord," he thought. That's a damn pretty woman."

CHAPTER 43

Ruth

⇢ ✽ ⇠

*I*t seemed to take her hours to reach the north side of Chickasha and turn onto Dan Allan Drive, though she figured a wristwatch would tell her something different. Thing was, she didn't own one. As she reached South Twenty-Second Street and turned to drive the few short blocks to the hospital parking lot, she grew lightheaded. She couldn't seem to get her breath as she pulled the car to a halt in the hospital parking space. The mild heat that had built during the morning now seemed unbearable. Her mouth was torturously dry. Feeling faint, she leaned back, scooted down, and rested her head on the seatback.

She had awakened that morning to find a large hollow place inside her that was emptier than one of Papa's water tanks after a summer's drought. She'd have thought a hollow place wouldn't be heavy, but it was. It weighed her down. Kept her lying in the bed longer than she intended. Finally rising, the extra weight slowed her down. She washed her face, combed her hair and put on makeup. Dressed in one of the new dresses she'd sewn and put on her new shoes. An overwhelming anxiety and dread made these simple acts drag on and on. She would have left without saying anything to the Williamses, but when she emerged from her room, Ethel confronted her.

"You get yourself in the kitchen right this minute, young woman. You'll not take this on without something in your stomach. I baked some biscuits and made eggs and bacon."

At the table, Ruth ate only a few bites before tears sprang to her eyes. She put down the fork and buried her face in her hands. "I just can't eat any more . . ." She couldn't go on.

Ethel patted her on the back. "That's all right. Things are going to work out for you, one way or the other. And you're welcome here whatever goes on in your life. Charlie, too."

Papa and Joe had both wanted to come with her. Charlie would have thrown a fit if he had known that she was going without him. She would bring Charlie to see his daddy another time, but this first time, she had to face Chester alone. Joe didn't want to have her face Chester without his support. But she had to do this herself, though she did not yet know what "this" was. Now she sat taking deep, labored breaths; she wasn't sure she could do it alone.

"Are you all right?"

Startled, Ruth opened her eyes to see a woman in the white uniform of a nurse standing by her open window.

Ruth shook her head but said, "I'll be all right. I'm just a little nervous. I'll be fine in a moment."

The nurse put her hand on Ruth's shoulder and asked, "Are you sure?"

Ruth took a deep breath. "I'm here to see my husband for the first time since he was wounded. I think I was just overcome for a minute." Her

CHAPTER 43 • RUTH

heart slowed, and her head cleared as the nurse kept her small, manicured hand resting on Ruth's shoulder.

"Let me walk you inside, where it's cooler. We can find a doctor if you need one."

Ruth climbed out of the truck and stood holding onto the door, letting the morning air caress her, hoping it would carry away some of the huge knot of anxiety sitting in her stomach alongside the baby. She wondered if the baby felt crowded by the company it shared. She wanted to climb back in the truck, try and relax before going in to see Chester, but knew she couldn't relax no matter how much she poked along.

The nurse gave Ruth a gentle pat on the back and, gripping her arm, slowly walked with her to the front door and into the cool lobby of the hospital. The thick odor of antiseptic, fouled wounds, and hospital food coming from the cafeteria hit her, and she had to swallow to keep her gorge down. An oak chair, inviting and well-used, groaned as she settled onto its hard, shiny seat.

"Sit here, and I'll go fetch you a glass of water."

As the nurse walked away, Ruth leaned forward and put her face in her hands for a moment, then sat up and looked at the large wall clock across the lobby from her. It told her that it had taken her almost three hours to make the journey. She'd started driving at near five o'clock. As the sun came up, she saw cotton fields in full bloom lining the blacktopped Highway 9. As Joe's pickup rolled along at thirty miles an hour, warm morning air flowed in through the open windows and washed across her face and neck, mussing her carefully combed hair. The seventy-five miles to Chickasha loomed in her mind as being halfway across the country, further than the earlier trip she'd made from Weatherford to her folks' place. It wasn't; she knew that. Knowing didn't dispel the feeling.

At the outskirts of Gotebo, she slowed to twenty as she drove through. She could not afford a ticket from the local sheriff. Passing through

Mountain View, she thought of Chester's grandparents, who had lived near there before they passed away. He still had an uncle and aunt living on farms outside of town. It had been over three years since she and Chester visited them, and, as she passed the turnoffs to their farm, she felt a pang of sorrow that she might never see them again. Then she thought, *You don't have any idea about whether you'll see them again.*

Speeding up to thirty miles an hour, she reached Carnegie and Fort Cobb, each time slowing, but with hardly a glance at the businesses she passed or the people on the streets. Her mind was in a whirl as she drove nearer and nearer to the hospital where Chester lay, not expecting her. The miles of blacktop looming on before her had looked endless.

She'd stopped at the Chance Café in Anadarko and sat a few minutes with a cup of coffee; then she made a trip to the bathroom. It was killing time, sitting over her coffee and then fussing with her makeup in the bathroom. And now her makeup was a mess. She sat dreading the next few minutes. Or hours.

Looking around the lobby, she saw a score or more young men in their late teens and early twenties sitting near her, or making their way through the lobby, or coming in and out of the cafeteria. Most wore casts or had bandaged heads; some were minus a leg and walking with crutches. One had a cast on his leg and a cane that his single good arm helped steady him with. Two sitting in wheelchairs had no legs at all. They, like Chester, were all here to recuperate from wounds suffered in the awful wars going on in the South Pacific, Europe, and the Far East. It frightened her to think that Chester might be in the same or worse shape than some of these men. With a broken neck, would he ever be able to walk again as well as he once did? He hadn't said; made light of his injuries when he wrote her about them. Now she would see for herself; she wasn't sure she really wanted to.

The nurse returned with a glass of ice water and stood by while Ruth drained it. "Are you going to be all right now?" she asked.

CHAPTER 43 ✦ RUTH

"I'm okay now," Ruth said. She felt terrible. "Thank you for helping me into the building and for the water. I don't know what I'd have done if you hadn't."

"I'm just glad I could help," the nurse said and and then walked away.

Ruth watched as the nurse made her way to the door, pausing to pat the arm of the young legless man before pushing through the door and walking out into the sunlight. *For a nickel I just might follow her,* Ruth thought, but then steeled herself and rose to go the front desk and ask for the bathroom and the ward where Chester was.

As she rose, she saw a familiar face, and her heart sank. She lowered herself back into the chair and stared.

Mildred Jenson was standing in the door of the cafeteria holding a squirming baby who was crying her heart out. Coming down the hall was a young woman, her pretty face and curvy body turning the heads of several of the young men she passed by before reaching for the child. Having seen her only a few times before, Ruth had forgotten how young and pretty Alice Jenson really was. A hot wave of hate and jealousy rose in Ruth's chest, and she stood to confront Alice. Scream at her. Pull her hair. Demand she stay away from Chester.

But she couldn't do that to any woman with a baby in her arms. The child quieted as soon as Alice took it from Mildred; the two women then walked to the front desk and spoke to someone there before they walked off down a nearby hallway. *Thank goodness they didn't see me,* she thought. *No telling what would have happened if they had.*

Her heart sank as it dawned on her that Alice would not be here if Chester had not invited her first. *He told me not to come until tomorrow so we wouldn't see each other,* she thought. Calming her rage with Alice, Ruth turned it on Chester. *How could he?* she thought. She stood, walked quickly to the desk, and choked out the question, "Can you give me the ward number where I can find Chester Scarsdale?"

The clerk's gaze followed her finger as she moved it down a long list of names written in longhand on a well-thumbed page of paper. When her finger paused, she wrote a number on a slip of paper and handed it to Ruth, pointed her finger, and said, "Go down the hall there to the stairs and to the second floor. It's down the hall on your left. You'll have no trouble finding it."

"The two women who were just here talking to you. Do you know where they were going?"

"Do you know them?"

"They're from Roosevelt, I think. I see them in Hobart sometimes. That's where I live."

The woman hesitated a moment and then said, "They wanted a quiet place for the mother to nurse the baby. I sent them to an empty office."

"Can you tell me where the public toilet is?"

The woman pointed to a sign down the hall and then turned her eyes to a couple who had walked up beside Ruth.

"Thank you." Ruth hurried to the door and, going inside, she washed and dried her face. Straightening her shoulders, she pushed through the door and marched down the hall, hoping she did not pass an open office door and have Alice or Mildred see her. She ran up the stairs but slowed down as she approached the door to the ward. If Alice intended to return, Ruth wanted to be with Chester. Unable to keep the spite out of her thoughts, she whispered to herself, "Let Alice walk in on me and Chester. See what it feels like."

CHAPTER 44

Ruth

⇢ ✤ ⇠

Ruth paused at the door to the ward wishing that her heart would stop beating like the wings of a frightened scissortail. She thought of Charlie back on the farm with Joe and Sarah, and she remembered that Charlie's favorite animal in the *Dr. Dolittle* books was the pushmi-pullyu It was a cross between a gazelle and unicorn and had two heads, one on each end of its body. She thought of herself right now as one of those creatures, being pulled one way and pushed the other. She had two minds housed in her head, one drawing her toward Chester and the other drawing her toward Joe. The two halves were about to tear her head in two, and, on the walk up the stairs, she'd developed a splitting headache to prove it.

As she stood there, she saw more of the walking wounded, many of the less-lucky ones swathed in bandages and casts. She pushed in through the door, and saw a long room with rows of beds along the two walls.

She paused a moment and looked for Chester. Running her hand through her hair, smoothing it, she tried not to think of Chester as one of these wounded men.. Then she started walking down the ward looking right and left, wondering which of these beds was Chester's. Men in hard-backed chairs sat next to their beds—others lay attached to pulleys, weighted at one end and fastened to limbs on the other. Their eyes followed her as she walked past. Her heart sped up as she scanned the men but did not see Chester.

When she was halfway down the ward, a gaunt figure with a metal brace on his neck raised his hand and motioned to her.

She almost fainted when she recognized the man with huge blue eyes and skeletal face was someone she'd never have recognized on the street. Chester.

He frowned as she approached. "Hello there, Ruth. You weren't supposed to come till tomorrow." He sat by his bed next to a small enamel-topped table with a glass and a pitcher of water sitting on it. He turned to reach for the glass, raised it to his mouth and drank. He moved like a mechanical man, his whole upper body, neck, and chest turning as one.

The sting of his greeting pierced her, and Ruth didn't know what to say. Or do. She stopped two feet away from him and began to cry.

He pointed to an empty chair sitting next to him. "Come on and sit down." Chester said nothing about her tears. Didn't offer to kiss her or give her a hug. She hadn't volunteered to give one, either. "Are you in any pain, Chester?"

"Well, yes. I'm sittin' on a whole pile of it. But this isn't anything like it was even a week ago. And even though these weak little bastards they're giving me for pain are nothing compared to what they first gave me, they help some. Otherwise I'd be really complaining."

CHAPTER 44 ✦ RUTH

They were beating around the bush, Ruth knew. But she didn't know how to bring up seeing Alice. *And Chester must be burning up with the fear I will*, she thought. "You look like you haven't eaten for a month. Are they feeding you okay in here, Chester?"

Chester grunted and said, "Five times a day. Not home cooking, though. All those months I spent in some backwater islands, there were lots of times I had damn little to eat. There was one time when I was thinking my shoe leather looked appetizing. Back then I'd have thought what they serve up here was a feast. So, yeah, they're feeding me fine."

"From the letters you wrote, Charlie and I had no idea what you were going through."

"They didn't want us writing anything like that. Might give the Japs the idea they were winning. I want to tell you, those letters from you and Charlie got me through the day a few times." Chester's eyes kept looking past her, and she knew he was looking for Alice to come walking in the door.

"We worried about you, not knowing for sure you weren't in the thick of things. Might get killed."

"I was that." Chester's eyes seemed to lose focus, and he stared at the floor, not speaking for a long minute. Then he glanced at the door again.

"When you wrote me about Alice. About maybe not coming home to Charlie and me. It hurt worse than you can imagine."

Chester remained silent, and his gaze shifted to the floor again. He had a faraway look she'd seen so many times in the past when he was stressed. He'd once told her that he just tried to not think—get away from all his troubles. When his eyes rested on her again, he was frowning, screwing his face up into a pouty, hurt look. "Hell, Ruth. What was I supposed to do? Lie to you? Not tell you about Alice? You think I wasn't going through a lot of hell, too? And it wasn't just coming from the Japs. I didn't know what the hell to do about Alice. Or you and Charlie. Do you think you were the only one hurting?"

As Chester spoke, Ruth felt a bubble of heartache and anger beginning to swell inside her, and only knowing what Chester had gone through kept her from letting it escape. Then the bubble burst, and she blurted out, "I saw Alice downstairs going into the cafeteria."

"Hell, I told you not to come till tomorrow."

"You did do that. And now I know why."

CHAPTER 45

Ruth

⇾ ✽ ⇽

Over a year had passed since the day she'd visited Chester on his return from the war. Sitting here now on Joe's and her front porch, looking out over the land, she watched as a gust of wind washed over the cotton. The solid green leaves swaying together looked a little like ripples dancing across Joe's pond when touched by a sharp burst of summer breezes. In the last ten days, she'd watched all the cotton flowers in the field turn from white to pink, and now, overnight, they had turned blood-red, a color that would last only one day. By this time tomorrow, they would have all dropped to the ground. Over the next few weeks, the cotton bolls those flowers had generated would ripen and burst open, turning the fields into a sea of pure white. The image reminded her of the flowering romance with Joe. They'd made love and the little beings their love had generated inside her were precious. The second one, now growing, and who, one day, like her first, little Esther, would burst forth destined, she hoped, to live in a world where no terrible war was going on.

It had been two weeks since Germany had unconditionally surrendered. She hoped and prayed it would not be long until Japan surrendered as well. Her brother Winston had survived the war so far without being hurt and, God willing, would be back in Hobart before long. Ruth was eager to see her brother again. Mother was on pins and needles waiting for him. She wondered if the war had changed him. She'd read that it changed many of the men—and not for the better. Chester? It would have taken more than a war and getting all those injuries to change him. He was the same old Chester. She hadn't needed to be in the middle of the fighting to have the war change her, change her life. It had changed her, though. For sure. She felt a twinge of guilt thinking that the war had changed her life for the better when so many others suffered so. Had it not been for the war, she would never have found the happiness she felt now.

Looking at the cotton, her thoughts turned to all the times in the past she had labored in the fields. She would never, ever again chop cotton or pull bolls; she was a farm wife who kept the house and took care of her growing family. She had a loving man to do that heavy work. Or see to it that it got done. She had read about women in some country, maybe it was China, who went right on working at what they were doing until they went into labor. They'd just squat to have their babies, wrap them up, put them on their backs and keep right on working. That didn't sound possible to her. She'd spent a week and a half in bed getting her strength back after having Esther. Healing. Letting someone care for her while she nursed the beautiful little girl who was napping beside her on a blanket. Her reveries were broken by a cry from inside the house.

"Mama. Sarah took the last cookie, and she won't give me a bite."

Ruth smiled. The two of them were more like brother and sister now than good friends, though they were still that, thank goodness. It had made the transition to living full time with Joe a lot faster and easier than she'd imagined it would be. "If I remember right, Charlie, Esther had one, and you had three of the last four while Sarah was down at the barn helping Joe. Don't be a pig."

"I'll give him a bite, mama," Sarah said.

"Don't you dare. He's had more'n his share already." She wished some of Sarah's generosity would sooner or later wear off on Charlie.

There was silence then, Charlie probably sulking. He was a bit like Chester that way, expecting things to go his way too much of the time. Thank goodness she'd finally come to fully realize how selfish Chester was, how hard it had been to live with him all those years. It had taken that trip to the rehab hospital to make that all too clear—finally—and at last. She could remember that day like it was yesterday.

When she'd said, "I saw Alice downstairs," Chester became impossible.

"So what?" he growled. "She brought the baby for me to see."

"Does that mean you've made up your mind?"

"I'd really decided to come home to you and Charlie until I heard from Alice about you and Joe."

Aware of the other men on the ward, Ruth lowered her voice. "You didn't write me anything about that."

"How could I write? I didn't know about you and Joe till the goddamn Japs had practically killed me. I only learned about it from Alice while I was in the hospital overseas. Before that, I'd decided that the thing with Alice was a mistake."

Ruth's face had grown warm. "And what was I to do? Sit around till you made up your mind?" She spat back in a strained whisper.

Chester swelled up with indignation and spat back, "I don't know what you could have done, but I can think of a lot of things instead of two-timing me with Joe. Hell, the two of us were best friends back years ago. How in hell could you take up with a friend of mine while I was overseas crawling through the goddamn jungle, starving half to death, getting shot at, and almost getting my ass blown up?" He looked past Ruth and called, "Nurse, get me a wheelchair. I need to go outside and smoke."

The nurse, at the other end of the ward, tending to someone's wounds called back, "I'll get it as soon as I can."

Ruth, seeing the wheelchair sitting two beds down and not being used, brought it and helped Chester stand and lower into it. She rolled it out onto a shallow porch that ran along one side of the ward and parked it far away from the other men smoking there.

Once on the porch and sitting in a wheelchair, Chester's hands shook so hard he had trouble getting a cigarette out of the package, but she couldn't bring herself to volunteer doing anything else for him. When he finally managed to light up, he took a deep drag, let out an explosive cloud of smoke and then took several more before he spoke again.

"Tell you the truth, I still don't know what to do. It's tearing me apart. You and Alice both here. It's just not clear what I want to do."

She looked at him with eyes that seemed to have had a veil dropped from them and now lay at her feet. He was a good-time-now, damn-the-future sort of man. Fun at times. Personable at times. Lovable at times. And she did love him. But in light of what she had with Joe, she was seeing clearly that his childish, self-centered existence was something she couldn't—wouldn't—live with any more. He hadn't matured like Joe, never left his adolescent flightiness behind. Chester was and always would be the spoiled brat his mother allowed him to be. A man so impulsive he'd probably even seduced her own mother. She did love him. But she didn't respect him like she did Joe. And she loved Joe. And she had hoped that the love, respect, and affection for Joe that had blessed their time together so far would grow into a far deeper, abiding love. God help her, it had happened. And now, as she sat on her and Joe's front porch, she knew it would last.

That day a year ago, standing on the balcony off the hospital ward, she'd said, "Well, Chester, it's become clear to me. It's over between us.

CHAPTER 45 • RUTH

You and Alice, I hope, will have a long, loving, and peaceful life together." She'd turned and walked away, not looking back, leaving Chester speechless. Left him to Alice and their new baby.

After crying half the way back to the Williamses' home, she came more and more to believe that leaving Chester, even though she still loved him, was best for her. Now, sitting here on this porch, she was happier than at any time in her adult life.

In a few minutes, Joe would come up from the barn. Pearl and Joan were probably both on their way, bringing a green-bean casserole and a salad. The Good Lord only knew that those two strapping boys of Pearl's could eat twice what anybody else would. Joan's two ate like sparrows, so there should be enough food for everybody.

Papa and Mother would soon be arriving for dinner as well, bringing with them Ed and Ethel Williams, Mother's famous deviled eggs, and Ethel's prize-winning banana and vanilla wafer pudding. Ruth had a large mess of black-eyed peas cooking. The cornbread batter was mixed and ready for the oven. Her papa loved black-eyed peas more than anything, and Ed couldn't stop praising her cornbread. She loved Joe's parents, and they treated her like their own daughter. Ruth thought sometimes that Ethel loved Charlie as much or more than Sarah. Ed didn't let Charlie win at checkers anymore; these days, he had a hard time beating that new grandson of his.

Papa was working so hard now to farm two pieces of land with that new tractor of his. He wouldn't admit it, but Ruth believed he loved that tractor almost as much as he had Old Tony and Big Jewel. Working as hard as he was, he deserved a good mess of his favorite food. He'd become so much nicer and happier over the past year.

Mother had fallen in love with Esther, and, when she came to visit, couldn't keep her hands off the child. And Esther loved her grandmother dearly. Losing their farmhouse had been awful for them at first, but Papa's fields of cotton would always be there to keep him occupied. And he liked living so near the domino parlor now that he could walk there every day if he wanted. Mother hadn't believed she'd get over losing her pictures and treasured knickknacks. "I have lost all my precious memories," she'd said. But she didn't have to work so hard now, and she had Joan and her other two granddaughters close by. And Mother had grown so fond of living in town, she'd never go back to a farm to live.

Ruth, on the other hand, had decided to let go of some of her not-so-precious memories; let forgiveness of her mother wash bad memories away. Let her love for Joe push back down any longings for Chester that surfaced.

Right after her visit with Chester, her heart in her throat, Ruth'd driven Joe's truck back to the farm. The kids were happy to see her but soon ran off somewhere to play or explore, and left her alone with Joe. She became shy and a little frightened about what she wanted to say to him, so they sat silent for what seemed an age.

Joe waited for her to say something first. Didn't rush her. Was patient.

She'd never tell Joe she had been unsure of what she wanted right up until the very moment she was with Chester. But she had to tell him about the baby. About wanting to spend the rest of her life with him. "I don't know where to start, Joe."

"Just tell me about what happened."

"It was awful seeing him. He looked like a skeleton. And he was wearing this awful neck brace."

"That must have been hard. This war damaged a lot of men."

"I'm not sure it changed Chester all that much, but I didn't stay around long enough to find out."

"How come?"

"I walked out on him."

"What happened to make you do that?"

"Alice was there at the hospital. With the baby. I saw her before I went up to where Chester was. When I said I'd seen her and realized why he'd put me off seeing him for a day, he got mad."

CHAPTER 45 • RUTH

"And?"

"He threw a tantrum and started saying mean things to hurt me."

Joe reached out and took Ruth's hands in his. "I'm so sorry you had to go through that."

"No. I'm glad. I had my eyes opened. Accepted, for the first time, what kind of man he is. Not the man you are by a long shot. But Joe, I know one hundred percent now that I want nothing more than to be with you." Tears had come to Ruth's eyes and coursed down her cheeks. "I know you've said the same thing, but I'm scared. Will you really want to marry me if I divorce Chester?"

"I want nothing more than to marry you Ruth. I've said that all along."

Ruth knew she had to tell him she was pregnant and was afraid of what he would say when she did. But now was the time. She couldn't put it off. "I have to confess something to you."

Joe's eye grew large, his mouth turned quizzical, and his forehead tightened into deep ridges. She blinked away more tears and took a deep breath before she said, "I'm pregnant with your baby, Joe."

He smiled that wide smile of his, grabbed her in a bear hug, and held her close. "That makes me so damned happy I can't tell you." Then he relaxed his hold on her and said, "I need to be more careful with you now, don't I?"

She laughed. "Not all that careful."

"I guess you can't say, 'Maybe,' to me anymore, when I say we need to get married."

"I don't remember ever saying that."

"You didn't have to. I knew you were sitting on a fence till you saw Chester again. But I was willing to wait."

Relief swept over her, and had she not been in his arms, she might have swooned. It was a memory she would always carry with her.

And now, sitting on their front porch, looking out over their cotton field, feeling the happiness that memory brought, and knowing she would always be with him, she felt giddy. It only lasted a moment, though, because she saw a car approaching with Chester at the wheel and his nearly two-year-old girl sitting on Alice's lap peering out over the dashboard.

She called out, "Charlie, your daddy's here." Chester had been back in the States for over a year, and Charlie seldom saw him now that Chester and Alice had moved to Tulsa. Seldom was too often for her. Charlie talked less and less about missing Chester. He would have once pitched a fit if he saw who was with his daddy. Mildred and Corky Alred were sitting in the back seat. He wouldn't do that now. He'd grown up a little over the past year.

Charlie opened the screen door halfway and peered out, his face turning dark as he saw the car turning in. "They brought Corky and his mother with them. We don't fight any more, but I don't like Corky all that much. And his mother really doesn't like me. Tell daddy I don't want them along."

"I'll do no such thing. Now, go get your shoes on."

"I want to see daddy. Not all those other people. Not Corky, for sure." He ducked back into the house.

Sarah came out onto the porch and sat down on the blanket beside Esther. "I wish he didn't have to go, mama. Who am I going to play with while he's gone?"

"You can play with Esther."

"She's asleep."

"Not for long with all this racket."

Chester exited the car and limped up to the porch. His leg wounds were healed, but he'd probably limp for the rest of his life. "Hi, Ruth, Sarah. Charlie ready?" He raised his nose and breathed in.

"Getting his shoes on," Sarah said.

"Something sure smells good, Ruth."

"Black-eyed peas," She said and then lowered her voice. "Charlie doesn't get along with Corky all that much, and he thinks Mildred doesn't like him."

CHAPTER 45 ✦ RUTH

Chester's face clouded over, and his eyes narrowed. "It's nonsense that Mildred doesn't like Charlie. And, when they're with me, Corky and Charlie seem to get along just fine."

Ruth took a deep breath. Chester didn't see what he didn't want to see. He was being Chester, and though she didn't like how he acted, Charlie loved his daddy, and she wouldn't get in the way of that. And that was all right with her. Particularly since she didn't often have to surrender him to Chester. "I hope you all have a good time today, Chester."

"We will," Chester said. "We're meeting a buddy of mine from the war. Got wounded three months back and got sent home. A man by the name of Hough. I might not be here if he hadn't pulled me out of the shelling and got me to a medic. Him, his wife, and his five kids will be there. Charlie will like Hough's middle boy."

Charlie came barreling out the door and gave his dad a big hug around the waist and then shouted, "I'm really glad we're going to the forest preserve. Think we'll see some deer and buffalo? Can I ride in the front seat with you?" Any resistance to going seemed to have disappeared. More than likely, he was putting on a show for Chester. Trying to make the best of it.

Alice peeled out of the car and, giving a half wave to Sarah and Ruth, climbed in the back seat with her sister and nephew. Ruth's estimate of her went up a notch seeing she was paying attention to what she figured Charlie would like. She waved back and smiled at her. Corky had a curious look on his face, and Ruth was glad not to see the scowl he used to always carry around. His mother, though, kept her eyes fixed on something straight ahead. It would be a tense drive to the park, Ruth thought. Hough's family would lessen that tension. She hoped.

Chester walked to the car with an arm around Charlie's shoulders. Ruth knew, though it was hard to accept, that, in many ways, they were two peas in a pod. Same blue eyes. Same quick temper. Same charm. Same walk. But Charlie had qualities that Chester never had nor would ever develop. He took other people's feelings into consideration. Wasn't so set on having his way no matter what it cost those around him. Though Chester's influence on Charlie was strong, her boy was coming under the steady, honest influence of Joe's stable, loving ways. Joe let Charlie help him with the chores and odd jobs around the farm, digging post holes, stringing barbed wire, feeding the livestock, gathering the eggs with Sarah, learning that good, hard work was important.

"Goodbye, Sarah. Goodbye, Mama. Tell Joe I said goodbye." Charlie leaned out the car window and waved once to her and Sarah, and then was lost in a cloud of dust as Chester's car headed south for the mountains of the forest preserve.

Though she hated to admit it, she could never love Joe as passionately as she had loved Chester when they were young. In some small corner of her heart, she still felt love for Chester. Always would. But it didn't get in the way of loving Joe. Not one whit.

She heard the barn door open and close and saw Joe walk toward her, slow and easy, smelling of hard work's sweat. All thoughts of Chester disappeared. Joe was so solid and dependable. And she loved him so very much. It was a different kind of love than she'd felt for Chester. That was it, not that she'd loved Chester more. It was just a first love. A young love. But love of someone whose return love was so undependable. Joe's love, she believed, would forever be dependable. Unlike Chester, Joe was home every night enjoying her. And their growing family.

He stopped at the edge of the field and from one of the cotton plants broke off a branch that had several blood-red cotton flowers attached to it.

Ruth smiled up at Joe as he stepped onto the porch, reached down, ruffled Sarah's hair, pushed a lock of hair from Esther's closed eyes, and kissed the top of Ruth's head. He fumbled to attach the branch of flowers into her hair. She reached up and held the branch in place as the three of them gazed off across the growing field of plants swaying in the wind, all bearing flowers that promised a thick strand of white cotton come November. Cotton plants put down roots deep into the soil for water and to hold the heavy weight of their cotton. She was putting down roots here as well, deep and solid.

She patted Sarah on the back, looked down at Esther, smiled, and then took one of Joe's work-roughened hands, smelling of hay, sweat, and barnyard grit, and brought it to her lips.

Acknowledgments

I flew to Tempe, Arizona on March 3, 2020, intending to stay two weeks. During those two weeks the danger and spread of the Covid 19 virus convinced me to stay out of airplanes so I sequestered myself in Tempe for the next four months. I was marooned on an island of calm surrounded by deadly disease. Fortunately, I was marooned with two very wonderful people, my niece and nephew, Carol and Larry Barkan. Isolated from most of the customary world activities that usually kept me busy, I had to find something to do when not keeping company with my host and hostess or while taking walks in the beautiful, early spring weather. I had brought with me a computer on which I had stored the false starts I'd made over the previous twenty years in my efforts to finish drafting a novel. I resurrected three of them, *The Cotton Flower*, *A Bird in Flight*, and *Leaving Texas*.

The safety measures that we all needed to take during the pandemic allowed me a great deal of time to devote to writing. On reading *The Cotton Flower*, which I'd written from a child's point of view, I decided to rewrite it from the viewpoint of four adults and a child. On finishing the new draft my niece, nephew or I, which one I have no memory of, expressed the idea that I read it aloud. So began a routine of an afternoon reading hour to precede our daily card game. Before I read a chapter aloud, I reread it and made corrections, then after I read it aloud to Larry and Carol and discussed with them their comments, I rewrote the chapter again. I have a great deal of respect and affection for Larry and Carol and appreciation for their careful listening, sage advice and encouraging comments that helped me capture more fully the story I wanted to tell. To them I give heartfelt thanks.

I also want to thank Thomas Connors who carefully edited the fourth draft of *The Cotton Flower* and asked the question, "You really like the passive voice, don't you?" You can guess what I attempted to do then, and if not, I'll tell you. When writing the fifth draft, I spent a lot of time going through the manuscript looking for the passive voice and changing it to active.

Special thanks goes to Elizabeth Turek. In July of 2020, after driving eighteen hundred miles from Arizona to Evanston to avoid the airways, I was walking down Central Street in Evanston and noticed a ballet school. While in Arizona I had also begun rewriting *A Bird in Flight*, a novel about a ballet dancer and it occurred to me that a ballet consultant could be helpful. I called the school and the person on the phone told me that they had the perfect person to help me, one that was a ballet teacher and had a degree in literature. Elizabeth was willing to give me her competent help with my efforts to understand and learn about the world of ballet and was such an excellent editor that I had her edit my fifth draft of this novel which I'd finished.

I'm also deeply grateful for the help of Nicole Gifford, my talented ballroom and Argentine tango instructor who asked one day if she could read the novel. It was now, I hoped, a finished final draft. I had no idea until that point that Nicole had been an English major in college and so read the draft with a practiced eye. It sorely needed another read-through. She polished this draft, making corrections and observations that were invaluable. Thank you, Nicole.

Seventy-five years ago, at age fourteen, I had my first date, and it was with a young Hobart, Oklahoma girl, Barbara Baumbell. In my memoir *Moving On* I wrote about that first encounter and a few months after its publication she called me to say she had read the book. This was the first time we'd spoken in fifty-three years. We reconnected then and though she lives in Tulsa, and I live in Chicago, we keep in touch. Over the past nine years, she has been a faithful reader of all my writing, and I want to thank her for her interest, encouragement and support.

To my relatives and the community of people living in and around Hobart, Oklahoma, I want to thank you for the experiences you provided me as a young boy and adolescent: attending a country school; hoeing cotton and pulling bolls; hearing tales of the Indian Territories and the early years of Hobart; learning about Frank Nash, the gangster; learning how to play dominoes, butcher hogs, share the fears engendered by WWII; and much more.

I would also like to thank those at 1106 Design for their help and guidance in publishing this novel.

About the Author

Cliff Wilkerson is a retired child, adolescent, and adult psychiatrist and psychoanalyst who now spends much of his time with his two sons and their wives, his nieces and nephews, grandnieces and grandnephews, brothers and sisters, and a myriad of friends and colleagues. He has published four previous books, *Beautiful Brown Eyes*, *Moving On*, *Still Moving On*, and *Siri Doesn't Tango*. He still teaches, reads, writes, travels, and goes ballroom or Argentine Tango dancing. He now lives in Evanston, Illinois where, alone or with friends, he takes long walks through its beautiful neighborhoods, historic town center, rose garden and other city parks, and along its lakefront.